TERROR NEVER SLEEPS

A Jack Gunn Thriller

Richard Blomberg

ISBN 13: 978-1-59298-895-2

Library of Congress Catalog Number: 2014922492

Printed in the United States of America

First Printing: 2015

18 17 16 15 14   5 4 3 2 1

Cover and interior design by Laura Drew
Cover photography © shutterstock

Beaver's Pond Press
7108 Ohms Lane
Edina, MN 55439–2129
952-829-8818

To order, visit www.RichardBlomberg.com
or call 1-800-901-3480. Reseller discounts available.

To all US Special Forces warriors, their spouses, and their children, with a blessing that I have prayed over our own children since they were babies:

May the Lord bless you and keep you.
May his face shine upon you and be gracious unto you.
May he lift his countenance upon you,
and bring you peace,
and keep you safe.

See glossary on page 336

Chapter 1

Dawley Corners, VA

"I'm scared, Mommy." Barett sat back up in bed, clutching his dinosaur pillow under one arm and his frayed security blanket under the other.

"Don't cry, honey. Daddy will be home tomorrow." Nina brushed her son's tears aside with her fingers, cupped his tender face in her hands, and gave him a kiss on the forehead. She inhaled the scent of baby shampoo from his tangled wet hair and snuggled him to her chest. Barett's Mickey Mouse night-light cast a buttery glow across the carpet. A constellation of fluorescent stars and planets were already glued to the ceiling of his brand-new bedroom and floating like luminous jellyfish in the dark above.

"But what if the bad guys kill Daddy?" Barett chewed on the fringe of his blanket.

"Nobody's going to kill Daddy," Nina quickly answered for the umpteenth time as she stroked his black hair. Barett nodded, locked on Nina's eyes. She closed the bedtime storybook and put it back on the nightstand.

Barett's lower lip quivered. "What if you die, Mommy? I heard you and Daddy talking." He started crying again.

Nina gasped. "You don't need to worry anymore, sweetie. Mommy's cancer is all gone." She crossed her hands across her chest and threw them up into the air. "Poof! And Daddy is a brave Sioux, just like you." She poked Barett in the chest. "If the president of the United States trusts Daddy to protect his country, I don't think we need to worry."

Sorrow instantly overwhelmed Nina, sad that Barett's last thoughts before falling asleep were to fear for his mommy's and daddy's lives—even though Nina frequently cried herself to sleep with those same fears. Barett, Nina's angel throughout her chemotherapy, reached up and brushed her tears away with his baby-soft fingers as he had done so many times before.

If Jack was Nina's soul mate, Barett was her heart mate. Nina's first pregnancy ended horribly with a devastating and unexpected miscarrage. Her second ended the same way. So after nine months of living on the jittery edge of sanity, wondering what would go wrong the third time around, Barett was her gift from God who miraculously joined the world on Nina's twenty-sixth birthday. She loved her *little bear* more than anything. She loved Barett more than Jack.

Trying to stay strong and keep up a good front for Barett while Jack was away, Nina snatched the dreamcatcher hanging from a tack in the wall above Barett's pillow and fanned his face with its eagle feathers as if she were trying to start a fire.

"Remember, Uncle Travis had a very special medicine man make this to protect you from bad dreams." She tickled his chest until he giggled.

"He's funny."

"Now go to sleep, honey. Daddy will be home tomorrow." She leaned over and gave him one last kiss.

Nina left his door half open, just how Barett liked, and went downstairs to lock up for the night. Everything in their condominium smelled fresh and new. The paint on the walls, the polish on the floors, and the carpet on the stairs. It was their first home and their first mortgage. Nina smiled, thinking of her husband, Jack, and how he had gone over the top to buy the most expensive door and window locks.

Being a Navy SEAL and the head of the Counterterrorism Task Force (CTF) made it nearly impossible for Jack Gunn to trust anyone. The only people he trusted were the other SEALs on his Ghost Team and Native Americans, like Nina and him.

"I'm not going to be a prisoner in my own home, Jack. Spend all the money on locks and guns and whatever else you think we need, but take a look around. We're not living in Afghanistan." Nina had opened the blind so Jack could look out and see their front yard of new sod, their one-inch elm sapling held vertical by three posts and gardening wire, and the empty lots across the street staked out for new construction. No one else had even moved into their building yet. They had first pick in the new ocean-view community in Dawley Corners, south of Virginia Beach.

"This is what I've always wanted, Jack," Nina had told him. "I know it's not Montana, but there's no place I'd rather be."

"The perimeter is secure," she could almost hear Jack saying.

Her smile vanished as she pulled back a corner of the curtain and watched a windowless panel van slowly cruise past their condo. It was the type of hammer-and-nail-laden van construction crews drove through their neighborhood on a daily basis, but not after dark at nine thirty on a Saturday night.

There was something about the van that sent a shiver up her spine as it crawled around the cul-de-sac and came back. She let the sheer curtain fall back into place and watched the headlights. They stopped at the end of Nina's driveway. With a growl of the engine, smoke puffed from the tail pipe into the chilled air. Now hiding behind the front door, she began to hyperventilate as she fought off the suffocating feeling of panic.

Nina felt guilty for cowering like a scared little girl. She knew if Jack were home, he would have put one of his patented *kill* looks on his face, stomped out the front door, and challenged the guys in the truck. He did stuff like that all the time. Most of the time, the other guys took off before he got close enough to do any harm; he looked that intimidating. Far from being politically correct, Jack was the man who backed down to nobody. Who feared nobody. Who suspected everybody.

Nina swallowed hard, checked the lock, and glanced up the stairs to make sure Barett was still in bed. Fingers trembling, she fumbled to get her cell phone out of her pocket to call Jack, but dropped it. Pieces of plastic and glass blasted in every direction, like a grenade exploding in the dark, when it hit the porcelain tile.

"Oh my God!" she gasped. That was her only phone. The van still rumbled in the street, not moving. She made out the silhouette of a stocking-capped, bearded man in the passenger seat. Her brain swelled like an expanding water balloon between her ears.

"Think, dammit. Think." She heard Jack's words reverberating in her head.

It was late Saturday night, her phone was trashed, their home Internet was not scheduled to be activated until Monday, which had not been a big deal because her smartphone functioned as a mobile hot spot for her laptop. All that had changed the instant her phone crashed.

Her feet felt as if they were stuck in cement, nailing her to the floor behind the door.

"The gun. I've got to get the gun."

She looked through the curtain at the van one last time, then stumbled up the stairs, went into their bedroom closet, and turned on the light. The gun safe still had the manufacturer's stickers on the anodized steel door.

She dialed three numbers stuck in her head. Nothing. She tried again. Nothing. The combination to the safe lay splayed across the entryway floor downstairs in a worthless cell phone microchip.

A noise outside spooked her. Her fingers trembled on the dial.

She tried the lock one last time and prayed. "Hallelujah!" The door opened. She grabbed the loaded shotgun. Jack always said it was the best gun for home protection. Point the scatter-gun in the general direction of your target and pull the trigger. It would blow a hole in the door the size of a basketball.

Nina had pulled the trigger on a shotgun once before. She blasted tin cans and beer bottles with her brothers back at the reservation garbage dump in Montana when she was a kid. The gun kicked like a mule and knocked her on her butt. It seemed funny at the time.

She flipped the safety off, racked a shell into the chamber, turned off the light, and tiptoed back out of the closet. The gun went first, with Nina's slippery finger on the trigger. Her eyes dilated to adjust back to the dark.

The condo was too new. Nothing looked familiar. Every shadow, every noise made her jump. The furnace kicked in. The bedroom curtain fluttered over the heat duct. She heard a noise in the hallway. Nina opened the door with the gun barrel.

"Mommy."

"Barett. Oh my God. I almost . . ." She covered her mouth, overcome by a sudden wave of nausea. Nina swallowed hard to push the bile back down as she propped the gun up against the wall behind the door, out of Barett's sight. She grabbed Barett, hugged him hard, and carried him back to his room. "Stay in bed, honey. Mommy will be right back."

Nina snatched the gun with her shaking, sweaty hands and quickly crept back down the carpeted stairs, trying her best to keep quiet.

The front door was still locked. The van was gone. She held the shotgun against her chest and fixed her eyes on the doorknob, dreading movement of any kind. Her heart raced as she waited in the dark.

The wind blew. The furnace kicked off. The doorknob did nothing.

She turned on the entryway light and scraped together all the pieces of her phone.

I can't call the police. The phone lines are down till Monday. I can't call or text Jack. He'll be pissed. It was probably nothing. No need to get all worked up. Just go to bed. Get a new cell phone in the morning before Jack gets home. And put that stupid gun away before you shoot someone.

Chapter 2

Nablus, Palestine

Jack Gunn pulled down the black-and-white, Arafat-style *kaffiyeh* wrapped around his head over the brim of his cornice-like eyebrows. He checked himself in a cracked mirror hanging above the rusty trough. He looked like one of them.

Ammonia from decades of men urinating against the same brown-stained concrete wall reeked from every pore of the dingy room. His eyes watered in the murky light as he peed. Black beard, dark skin, a crooked nose, a smattering of small scars. Good enough to pass for a Palestinian or Afghan—or better yet, the Native American he was. It would have been easier to blend in, though, if he were not the size of a six-paneled door. He pulled the tail of the checkerboard kaffiyeh snug around his neck and made sure the other corner hung over his shoulder, while he gathered his thoughts.

Jack's first trip away from home, from Nina and Barett, in over a year, and his nervous stomach was doing triple Lutzes from drinking too many cups of coffee. He had been anxious to get back in the field again and out from behind his desk, but as soon as his jet left Virginia, the home strings started pulling hard.

Nina and Barett had grown used to Daddy being gone for long stretches of time when he was the head of Ghost Team. Nina had learned how to live with an absentee husband. When Jack was promoted to head of the CTF a year earlier, one of the biggest benefits was being able to stay home, to be there to support Nina through her final rounds of chemotherapy for breast cancer, to help coach Barett's little league team, and to become a part of their everyday lives again.

Jack had been able to delegate and monitor every Ghost Team mission over the past year from behind his desk. But when Rami Salwa and Abdul Ochoka requested a face-to-face meeting to negotiate the return of eleven lost dirty bombs, there was no escape. Jack had to go. SecDef ordered it. The United States needed those bombs secured and off the market before some wacko got hold of them.

He rejoined the room full of bickering Hamas freedom fighters. Were he not used to it, his eyes would have kept tearing up. Not from the urine ammonia, but from the overpowering scent of rosewater, which the fighters must have bathed in to get cleaned up for the spicy, middle-of-the-night feast they had just finished.

Scrappy, dirty men dressed in camouflage and bandoliers of ammunition draped across their chests yelled and cursed and got in each other's faces. Some wore hats, others a variety of colored kaffiyehs, but all displayed the kelly-green Hamas headband, front and center.

For a big man, Jack moved fluidly, naturally. The Sioux Indian genes forming the backbone of his DNA, combined with years of training as a Navy SEAL, instilled in him the gift of stealth. He was a silent killer, with catlike instincts inherited from his great-great-

great-grandfather Sitting Bull and honed by his late Grandpa Joe.

Eyes right. Eyes left. He was constantly checking faces, postures, imprinting everyone in the room. He had been assured by Aaron Bach, his Mossad partner, that the location was as secure as any could be in the heart of the Hamas-controlled district in Nablus, Palestine.

"Nothing good happened after dark" was never more true than in Nablus. Middle of the night was Hamas time. Their sentries heard everything, especially Israeli security vehicles attempting to sneak up the main road out of the Jordan River valley to the West Bank city. Jesus himself had walked its streets. Crusaders had battled for its strategic high ground. Palestinians called it home. Tonight, its streets were quiet.

"Are they arguing about who gets to kill us or how they're going to do it?" Jack said sarcastically to Aaron, as he sat down next to him at the negotiating table.

"No. They want to know when," said Aaron, looking back over his shoulder.

"I'm a little rusty after sitting behind a desk for the last year," Jack said in a low growl to Aaron as he gave a disdainful look at the *hajis* crowding all around him. "What do you say, you take your side of the room and I take mine. Let's waste these fuckers and do everybody a favor."

"Take it easy, chief. You'll get your chance, but we have a little business to attend to first. Remember?" said Aaron matter-of-factly.

Across from them sat Rami Salwa, dressed in a black *dishdash*a topped with a black kaffiyeh, his chest adorned with a golden pin of obvious significance. Salwa looked taller, broader, and more arrogant than the rest. He stroked his jet-black beard as a couple of men pleaded in Arabic, using grandiose hand gestures. Their facial fluctuations showed frustration with what appeared to be opposing points of view.

Salwa held up a hand, swiveled toward Jack and Aaron, and the room fell silent.

"Abdul Ochoka will not make the same mistakes as Mullah Mohammed Abdul made in Pakistan. You won't be so lucky this time, Mr. Gunn," Rami Salwa proclaimed in perfect English, mocking Jack with a snarl. "Now that we've found what you stole, you Americans don't stand a chance."

The previous year, Jack had thwarted a terrorist plot by tracking down and killing their leader, Mullah Mohammed Abdul before he activated a plan to detonate eleven dirty bombs in eleven American cities. Mohammed had been the only person alive who knew the whereabouts of those bombs, or so Jack thought. The terrorists had been searching for their lost bombs ever since so they could pick up where Mohammed left off.

Across the table, Salwa rested his hand on Jack's confiscated handgun. He spun the gun on the table, like a form of Russian roulette. It stopped spinning and pointed at Jack. Salwa said something in Arabic, and the whole room erupted in cheers. Chairs grated against the stone floor. Boots scuffled. Men stood. Jack heard rounds being chambered.

It felt as though an entire nest of spiders were clawing at the back of his neck—an inherited sixth sense that warned him when guns were pointed at him and he was about to die.

Salwa smiled as he picked up Jack's gun. He turned the Sig Sauer P226 over in his hand, as though he were carefully admiring a fine work of art.

"It is embarrassing, don't you think? That Americans would be carrying German guns." He flicked the safety on and off. He ejected a nine-millimeter round into his hand, held it up to the light, and then reloaded it. Everyone froze. No one spoke.

Jack didn't flinch. His emotionless face seemed cast in stone. He had not risen to the top of the most elite group of terrorist fighters in the world by caving into bullies like Salwa. "I don't give a shit about what an idiot like you thinks. No wonder you're nothing more than a courier." Jack looked sideways at Aaron, then back at Salwa, ignoring everyone else in the room and their itchy trigger fingers.

Salwa clenched his teeth. His nose flared slightly. He white-knuckled Jack's handgun.

"I don't have time for child's games," said Jack. "I didn't come all this way to talk with some low-level jerk-off. I was told I'd be dealing with Ochoka himself."

"It's obvious you don't know what you're talking about or to whom you're talking," said Salwa. He pointed his gun at Aaron. "You asked me for a favor. Even if I could get in trouble for meeting with an old Mossad friend, I granted your request. I didn't owe you anything, but I said okay. And then you bring this asshole into my house, who disrespects me in front of my men. Why should we not take this infidel out back and split him open right now?"

A loud boom shook dust from the ceiling beams. The men fidgeted. All of them, including Aaron and Jack, knew only the big Israeli guns and missiles made the earth rumble like that.

Aaron sat up, elbows on the knotty tabletop. His white long-sleeved shirt was stretched tightly over his broad shoulders and bulging biceps without a wrinkle. His cheeks were more filled out than when Jack last trained with his team, years earlier. A touch of gray brushed the temples of his regulation crew cut, but he still looked as if he could give Jack a run for his money.

"You specifically said you had information from the Saharon branch of Al-Qaeda for the head of the CTF—and only him. I stuck my neck out to get Mr. Gunn over here from the States. Now, do you have something or not?"

"Well, that depends." Salwa raised his eyebrows. "I know the fairy tale of your Mr. Gunn and how he lost his nukes. I know how desperate this Navy SEAL commander is to find those suitcases." He waved the gun in front of Jack's nose.

Jack stared straight down the gun barrel. "What do you want, jerkwad? Money? Weapons? Power? Asylum?"

"Asylum! You insult me," sneered Salwa. "Why would I want to leave here?" he asked, waving Jack's gun around again. "You're the one needing asylum. I don't give a shit who you are or what you've done. You're in my house now. My house. My rules. You have one last chance. What's your offer?"

Jack felt Salwa's men pressing in, ready to carry out his orders. In one swift move, Jack grabbed Salwa's gun hand and twisted his wrist around so the gun was under Salwa's chin, the barrel pointed at his brain. Salwa winced. Jack had his finger on the trigger. His face was close enough to smell Salwa's lunch.

No less than a half dozen gun barrels pressed into Jack's skull and neck.

His cell phone vibrated in his pocket. Nina and Barett popped up in his consciousness for a split second before he switched that thought back off.

He and Aaron were on their own. They might manage to kill a few, but they would be dead, sure enough. Jack and Aaron made eye contact. Aaron nodded, and Jack released Salwa's wrist but kept the gun.

The atmosphere sizzled with electricity, like the pause before a lightning strike.

Jack ejected the magazine and tossed both on the table.

Salwa quickly straightened up, seized the gun, shoved the magazine back in, chambered a round, and jammed it into Jack's forehead. Someone restrained Jack's arms from behind. With his other hand, Salwa pulled a cell phone from his pocket. He thrust its screen inches from Jack's face.

"Now if you're done playing games, you can see I've got the nukes you seek. If you want them—if you want to see your wife and son again—you've got an important decision to make. What's your offer? You've got ten seconds."

Jack was used to risking everything, including his own life, to accomplish his mission, but the nerve of Salwa to bring Nina and Barett into the conversation darkened his mood even more than it already was. It was one thing to be enemies on the battlefield, but when Salwa threatened his family back home in Virginia, Jack would have just as soon killed him on the spot and taken his chances.

Jack looked Salwa square in the face and said through clenched teeth, "Rolf El-Hashem will be released from prison immediately and returned. In addition, fifty-five million dollars will be transferred to the bank of your choosing as humanitarian aid to the Palestinian people. Five million per suitcase."

"You Americans can do and say what you want when you're in America. But don't think you're going to sit here, you pig-headed son of a bitch, and tell me how it's going to be done here in my town. You don't fucking tell me anything. You understand?"

Jack said nothing.

"Americans don't fucking know anything about what goes on over here. You want peace. You want oil. You want, want, want. But all you've really got to bargain with is money," Salwa said.

"Your money is a fucking joke."

Jack said nothing and made himself look bored.

"Five million is a joke. Plus, what about the twelve security council men you killed? What about their families? What about an entire nation without leadership? Ten million per suitcase. Take it or leave it," said Salwa.

Salwa took a step back, stuck Jack's gun under his dishdasha, and paused. They heard another rumble in the distance. Someone's walkie-talkie rattled off some garbled gibberish. The men looked at Salwa.

"Ten million it is," said Jack, out of bargaining chips.

"When Rolf El-Hashem is safe, I'll let you know where to wire the money," said Salwa.

"Not until I get my cases," said Jack.

"Oh, you'll get your cases, Mr. Gunn. After I get half my money," said Salwa. "Oh, and by the way, I hope your family is okay."

"What'd you say?" Jack said. "Hey!" he yelled. "What'd you fucking say?"

But Salwa was already walking out, smiling, cell phone to his ear. He shouted a command. His men followed.

Jack pounded the table. "Son of a bitch has us by the balls, and he knows it."

Jack speed-dialed Nina, his heart was racing. It was her first time alone in their new home, and Jack knew she was worried with him being out on a mission and away from home for the first time in year. He squeezed the phone as if it were Salwa's scrawny neck.

"Dammit, Nina. Pick up the phone," Jack said. Four thirty Sunday morning. Seven hours of time change, so it was nine thirty at night in Virginia. Not answering, not e-mailing, not texting. "What the hell is going on?" He crunched on another antacid and swallowed. "I should've killed that piece of shit El-Hashem when I had the chance."

"Where's he fit in?" asked Aaron, as he quickly walked to the door and poked his head out several times to check the street.

"He was a plastic surgeon who worked for the Taliban. One of the infamous El-Hashems who almost got away with a bunch of dirty bombs. I should have followed my gut instinct and killed him when I had the chance, but we kept him alive for intel. We thought he might tell us where the bombs were, but he didn't know shit. Now that they already have the bombs, guess he can't hurt us anymore."

"Think they really have them?" asked Aaron.

"Like I said, he's got us by the cojones." Jack stood next to Aaron, ready to bolt, hoping an Israeli patrol did not mistake him for a giant terrorist. "I don't much like your Salwa friend either. Hope you don't mind when I kill him."

"He can't talk if he's dead. My boss needs him alive." Aaron handed Jack his backup handgun. "Were you able to bluebug his phone?"

"We'll know soon enough," said Jack. "Let's get the hell outta here."

They took off running into the night.

CHAPTER 3

Virginia Beach, VA

"Travis, wake up." Jaz shook Travis's shoulder and held firmly to his arm in case he took a swing. "Travis, it's okay."

"What the . . . oh, thank God," said Travis, exhausted but relieved to awaken from his recurring dream. He moaned, rubbing his chronically aching left thigh. He smelled like the eucalyptus aloe cream his pain doctors prescribed. The back of his T-shirt was drenched in sweat as he lay facing away from Jaz. His heart pounded in his ears. The sheets and duvet were long since kicked off his side of the bed after his high-flying nightmare.

Jaz rested her hand on the middle of his back. "You're freezing. Go put a dry shirt on, sweetheart."

"Three o'clock. Great," said Travis. "I might as well get up."

"The helicopter one again?" asked Jaz.

"How'd you guess?"

A year earlier, Travis was duped by one of his medical school buddies, Rolf El-Hashem, to accompany him on a medical mission trip into Pakistan. As it turned out, Travis was taken prisoner by El-Hashem and his Taliban thugs. They made a torture video of

Travis and were preparing for his public beheading when Jack and his SEAL team pulled off a prisoner exchange.

Jack had previously captured Rolf El-Hashem's father after he orchestrated an IED attack on a CIA convoy. So Jack set up an exchange: Rolf's father for Jack's only brother, Travis. But there was one tiny hitch. Before releasing Rolf's father, Jack had a tiny tracking device inserted inside his belly, which ultimately lead Jack and his Ghost Team to Chitral, Pakistan, for a showdown.

After his rescue, Travis had flown along with Jack on that mission into Pakistan, which is where Travis narrowly escaped death when the Taliban fired an RPG into the helicopter where Travis and the pilots waited.

"There's nothing you could have done to save those pilots, Travis. If you had hesitated for even a second, you'd have died too," said Jaz. "You know that, right?"

Jaz worked as an analyst for the CIA. A year earlier, she had been the liaison between her employer and Jack's Ghost Team. She had been stationed in Bagram, Afghanistan, directing and assisting Jack in tracking down Rolf's CIA-murdering father and helping oversee Travis's rescue. Throughout Travis's ordeal—being a tortured hostage and a victim of severe spinal cord injuries from the helicopter explosion—Jaz watched from behind the scenes as this incredibly brave and resolute man endured unbelievable hardship yet still prevailed. Travis was the man she had been waiting her whole life for. Travis was the man she married.

Travis let out a big sigh. "I know I did the right thing, but it doesn't make it any easier. They said it would get better with time, but it's been a year." He turned on his bedside lamp.

"It might be hard for you to see, but from where I sit, I think you're doing great."

"They got me taking pills for anxiety, pills for depression, pills for sleep, pills for pain. I mean, seriously. Pills and booze—that's what got me into trouble in the first place. That and that fucking prick Rolf."

Now Travis was definitely not going back to sleep.

"Son of a bitch. How could I have been so stupid?"

Jaz cleared her voice. "Language, remember? We've got tender ears here now." Jaz rubbed her seven-months'-pregnant belly.

"Oh shit. I mean, oh crap." Travis snapped out of his quagmire, leaned over, and kissed her stomach. "Sorry, little one." Then he lay on his side, facing Jaz, and gave her a kiss too. "I don't know what I would do without you, Mrs. Gunn."

"I love you too, Mr. Gunn."

"Really? You really love me, huh?" He tickled her side.

"I love you a lot more when it's not the middle of the night. Baby needs her sleep."

"Her? It's a girl? I thought it was a boy," said Travis excitedly.

"Well, now I think it's a girl. I've been getting a lot of indigestion, my belly button is swollen, and she kicks hard right under my ribs."

"What'd the ultrasound say?" asked Travis. "Oh, that's right. We'd rather trust old wives' tales than modern science."

"I don't want to know. It's part of the fun."

"Jack advised me that in situations like this, the best thing for me to say is, 'yes, dear.' And I always do what my brother says."

"Nina's trained him well," said Jaz, yawning. "Lie down. Maybe you'll fall asleep."

"You know, you might be the hottest-looking pregnant woman I've ever seen."

"Go to sleep," pleaded Jaz as she gave his giant head a push down toward his pillow.

"I've been thinking," said Travis.

"Oh really? Can't it wait till morning?" Jaz pleaded with a sleepy smile and another yawn.

"What would you say if I wanted to get back into doing anesthesia? The State of Virginia approved my license, and the VA Hospital in Norfolk has offered me a part-time position," said Travis. "I think it would help if I had something to do besides go to therapy and take pills."

Years earlier, when Travis struggled with many psychological issues relating to him and Jack growing up as orphans on the reservation in Montana, Travis lost his license to practice medicine after repeatedly failing rehabilitation from drugs and alcohol. Losing his license had been the key to him moving to Dubai to practice anesthesia at his friend's surgery center, the world-renowned plastic surgeon Rolf El-Hashem. Dubai was also a place where he continued drowning his sorrows in alcohol and drugs, which ultimately led to him falling into the hands of Rolf's Taliban thugs. For the first time in years, as clean as he could be while still taking pain medicines for his back, Travis had his license to practice medicine again.

"So you already have a job? When did this happen? I thought we said we'd discuss it with your doctors and make this sort of decision together, Travis."

"No, no, don't worry. It's not like that. I ran into one of the guys from the anesthesia group when I was at the hospital for therapy. He said they could always use someone like me. We'd still run it past my doctors, and then you and me would decide together. Absolutely."

"Well, it sounds like you've already made up your mind." Her smile was gone. "It's more important to me that you get yourself healthy first. Our daughter needs her daddy."

Travis swallowed hard, not wanting to upset Jaz any more than he already had. "I just thought it would help with the bills. What with you taking maternity leave from the CIA and us moving into the townhouse next door to Jack and Nina next month, well . . ." He rolled over on his back and stared at the ceiling fan blades, counting the revolutions, like counting his blessings.

He was blessed for Jaz dropping into his life like an angel. For the baby that he never dreamed of having. For the nurses and therapists who had pushed him relentlessly to learn to walk without a cane after getting blown from the helicopter. For his brother, Jack, for rescuing him from Rolf and his crazy band of Taliban lunatics.

Travis then wondered how much the "promise"—as Jaz and he called it—played into all the good things that had happened to him since the helicopter explosion. As he had catapulted through the air and crashed back to earth some sixty feet away, he made a promise to God, the white man's god. The god he never spoke with. He promised he would try to be a better person, a better Christian, if God pulled him through alive.

God kept his promise. Travis struggled with his, but with Jaz's devout faith and the baby coming, he was starting to see the bigger picture.

Jaz rolled over toward Travis and looked past him at their wedding picture on his bedside table. She in an ankle-length white empire chiffon wedding gown and crystal sandals; he in sand-colored pants, a white linen shirt, bare feet, and a white cane. They were on the beach at the Ritz-Carlton in the Cayman Islands, with some of the clearest blue water in the world as a backdrop.

Travis, Jaz, Nina, Jack, and Barett all huddled for a family photo as the sun set over the Caribbean.

"You're a good man, Travis Gunn," she said as she rose up on her elbow and kissed him. "Now stop worrying. When the time comes, we'll talk. Right now, I need my sleep. I have a big meeting with the director in a couple hours."

Travis breathed out a big sigh and kissed her shoulder as she wiggled around to find that sweet spot on her side of the bed, propping a pillow under her belly.

Right before Jaz slipped back to sleep, she said, "Remind me to call Nina tomorrow to see how she's doing with Jack out of town."

"Okay, honey. Go to sleep." Travis lay back in bed, trying to decide for the next three hours if he should get up or not.

Chapter 4

Dawley Corners, VA

Nina sat up in bed, startled awake by a knife-grinding-on-stone sound. Fear clutched her throat as she strained to hear. It was dead quiet except for the furnace. She glanced around the unfamiliar surroundings of her new bedroom, which reminded her more of a fancy hotel room than her own. The digital clock read 2:30. Her hand recoiled when she touched the cold steel of the shotgun under the covers on Jack's side of the bed. Her brain had taken its own sweet time falling asleep, processing every nerve-racking event from the day past, and the day to come.

What was I thinking? That those men in the van were going to break in or something? That I was going to shoot somebody with that damn gun? I must be losing it.

She scribbled on her internal to-do list in big letters: *get new phone.*

Cold beads of sweat trickled down the sides of Nina's face. She released a deep sigh and rubbed her eyes, relieved her recurring nightmare was only a dream. Between worrying if she was going to die from cancer or if Jack was going to die trying to be a hero, or both, she never got six solid hours of sleep. She worked hard to keep up a good front, but she was always exhausted, always worried, always alone.

As she lay back down on her pillow, she heard the knife-grinding sound from her nightmare again. The hairs on the back of her neck prickled. She caught her breath and did not move.

"Barett? Is that you, honey?"

No answer.

"Barett?" she said louder.

No answer.

The sound came again, but louder. Closer. Nina felt a chilling draft, heard a whisper, and froze. Something inside her screamed, "MOVE!"

But instead, she froze when she heard Barett cry out, followed by silence. It was a crowded silence. A deafening silence. The furnace kicked on. The curtains billowed over the floor vent.

Paralyzed in a surreal trance, unable to do anything but hold her breath, she listened. Was she awake? Was she asleep?

Her bedroom doorknob turned. The door moved in an inch, then stopped.

She had her answer.

Her stomach crawled as if she had swallowed a bowl of worms. Every jittery neuron in her body was firing.

"Barett?" she asked. "Barett," she pleaded.

The door inched slowly open. A head shadow appeared near the top of the doorframe, far too high to be Barett's.

She said "Jack?" at the same time as she shined her flashlight, which was clipped to the underside of her shotgun barrel, at the intruder's head. The shotgun she had slept with.

A man shoved the door all the way open, its knob punching a hole in their new sheetrock wall, and pointed a gun at Nina.

Nina pulled the trigger.

The dark room exploded with flash and lead. The blast knocked Nina back into the headboard. The bearded man was blown backward. His chest ripped open. His machine gun fired several rounds into the ceiling as he went down. Blood splattered everywhere. Smoke filled the room. She heard men yelling and found herself screaming while fumbling with the pump-action shotgun. She managed to rack another twelve-gauge shell into the chamber, but before she could fire again, a man jumped on top of her, pinning her arms and legs, while someone else started beating her face with his fists.

The last thing Nina remembered hearing was Barett's blood-curdling screams before the attackers knocked her out.

Nina faded in and out of consciousness, like waking from a nightmare, then picking it up right where she left off as soon as she fell back asleep. With one exception. Her nightmare was really happening. It wasn't a dream. Everything was reversed. She passed out to escape her living, breathing horror film poised to haunt her each time she woke and opened her eyes again.

She lapsed from one hallucinogenic scene to the next, like a Halloween house of terror. A man screaming in agony. Shower of blood. Glass breaking. Duct tape over her mouth. Wide-eyed Barett in the arms of a masked man. Duct tape around his head, over his mouth. Struggling to scream. To breathe. Another fist pounding her face. Lost in the fog.

Cold. Freezing cold. The smell of gasoline. A different language. Guttural, growling laughter. A needle plunged into her arm. Silence.

Chapter 5

Dawley Corners, VA

"I'm sorry, Mr. Gunn. I'm going to need you to stay downstairs until we've examined all the evidence," Detective Ron Porter said to Jack as considerately as possible. Porter was on loan from the Virginia Beach Police Department, seeing as the little beach community of Dawley Corners had never had a kidnapping or murder or anything of the sort before. "Let's go downstairs, where we can talk."

Porter had black bags under his eyes and a rumpled navy blazer that had not spent time at a dry cleaner in months. With a latex-gloved hand, the homicide detective lifted Jack's elbow to coax him up, but Jack was dead weight. A 230-pound boulder. He didn't budge from where he sat on the side of their bed, not in the slightest. Weary from an all-night mission in Palestine negotiating with Rami Salwa, followed by an eight-hour early-morning transatlantic flight and a quick drive home from the base to surprise Nina and Barett, only to find the front door lock splintered, his house destroyed, and his family missing, Jack was in shock. About the only thing he managed to do was call 911. That had happened two hours ago.

Jack had cried—really cried—rarely in his life. Grandpa Joe and the Zuya—a secret sect of Sioux elders who passed on to Jack the ways of their great ones, such as Sitting Bull, Crazy Horse, and Red Cloud—raised Jack to be strong. To use the wisdom and skills of generations gone by to defend the defenseless and stand up to the bullies of the world. Jack believed in their traditions and always tried to make the Zuya proud. Crying, he thought, might be a sign of weakness.

But the first time he witnessed a four-year-old Afghan boy get vaporized from stepping on an IED buried in their village marketplace, he lost it. After Jack rescued his younger brother, Travis, from a bunch of Taliban savages hell-bent on butchering him with machetes, Jack choked up, but did not cry. He didn't cry when he watched his alcoholic father burn in a car fire, but he cried his eyes out watching his mother go.

He never mourned and definitely did not cry for the lives of the hundreds of terrorists he and his Ghost Team had killed over the years. He stayed strong for Nina during her diagnosis, surgery, and chemotherapy. Even when his best friends and teammates died fighting and he escorted their bodies home to their loved ones, he didn't break. He was one tough son of a bitch.

But as he sat on the side of their bed, Nina's blood-soaked side, holding Barett's stuffed hippopotamus, staring at the blood splatter and foot-wide blast hole in the far wall, Jack lost it big time.

He buried his weary face in his hands, his chest heaving and sobbing. He didn't feel like the most feared SEAL in the world or the president of the United States' go-to guy. He didn't feel like the great Sioux warrior his Grandpa Joe had trained him to be or the head of the Counterterrorism Task Force.

He felt defeated. Totally and completely drained. Guilty for not being there to protect Nina and Barett. Guilty for leaving them home alone. Guilty for not calling Dewey Hamilton—Jack's second-in-command, who was in Virginia—to check in on Nina while he was in Israel. Guilty. Guilty. Guilty. Was he too proud to ask for help? Was he afraid of looking like the CTF director who did not have everything under control? How stupid could he be?

Forensic techs worked around Jack and dusted for prints, searched for hair, collected blood and tissue. Crime lab photographers captured the moment from all viewpoints: Nina's, Barett's, the intruders'. Empty shell casings. Angles of fire. Spent lead pried from the walls and ceiling. Shotgun pellets. Mushroomed .38-caliber hollow points. Tagged and bagged. They worked with precision. Little talking. Lots of action. Well coached. Just like a SEAL team, Jack thought.

"So you have a shotgun. Any other guns, Mr. Gunn?" Detective Porter asked.

"Just the one." Jack felt the blood drain from his face.

Detective Porter pumped his open palms at the floor several times to quiet everyone in the room. He held his voice recorder close to Jack's mouth. "Go ahead, sir."

"We kept it in the closet safe."

"Wife pretty good with it?"

"Good enough, I guess," said Jack.

"Pump, not semi-auto," said Porter. "Too bad. Could've got off a few more shots."

Jack said nothing. He smelled blood and gunpowder still. He imagined Nina sitting where he sat and how afraid she must have been. Her seeing the intruder. Her having to decide to pull the trigger. Then what? Only one shotgun hole. No bodies.

The answer was finger-painted in big bloody letters on the wall above the hole. It read, *BADAL* with a giant red *X* next to it.

"I know this is very hard for you, sir. I can't imagine losing my wife and son." Detective Porter's voice trailed off to a whisper. "Any idea what *badal* means?"

"A year ago, I declared a badal on the El-Hashem family for abducting my brother, Travis, in Pakistan. I'm sure you've heard of them. They're all over the BBC."

Porter shook his head.

"The El-Hashems are a famous Saudi family, rich beyond imagination, who singlehandedly finance all Taliban terrorists," Jack said.

"I don't get BBC," said Porter with a shrug.

"A badal is a blood feud that can go on for generations if you don't kill them all. It's a Pashtun Taliban thing my brother and I got caught up in."

"And?" Porter held the recorder right under Jack's mouth. "Did you?"

"Did I what?"

"Did you get them all?"

"All but one." Jack squeezed his eyes tight. A leftover tear trickled down his cheek. "I—*we*—set him free earlier today."

"So this was no accident? These men, whoever they were, knew exactly who your wife and son were and where you lived? They probably knew where you were too."

"I guess." Jack slouched. Guilty.

"Late Saturday night. New neighborhood. You out of town. Probably four to six, I figure. A nondescript vehicle big enough to hold them all." Detective Porter looked around. "Anything missing or out of place?"

"Hard to say. We just moved in."

"So, we got a van full of men, possibly Pakistanis if they're part of this badal thing, who attacked your family when you were in Israel, and now they have a twelve- to eighteen-hour head start." Porter looked at Jack, shaking his head. "We've got some work to do."

A clock ticked away the seconds. Porter scribbled something in a small notebook.

"Sorry to have to ask, but do you know your wife's and son's blood types?"

Jack put his hand on Nina's pillow and closed his eyes. He had heard Porter's question, but the thought that all the blood he saw splattered around the room might be Nina's and Barett's was too much to handle, even for him. Tears ran down his bearded cheeks. He floated away into his own world, like Grandpa Joe and Grandma Bear Nose had taught him to do after his parents died, to connect with their spirits. For what seemed like days but was merely seconds, Jack searched the vast blue and white clouds of Wakan Tanka's spirit world, until he saw them across a great divide.

"Baretty. Nina," Jack whispered.

He felt their pain in a gaping hole in his chest where his heart felt as if it had been ripped out. He saw them crying a mournful cry as they slumped on their knees, their heads hung low. Sage smoke filled the space between them and him, like a veil. Were they alive? Were they dead?

"I'm sorry, Mr. Gunn, but I have to ask. Do you know their blood types?" Detective Porter asked again.

"They're alive, detective," said Jack. "My wife and son are alive."

"I certainly hope so, sir. The first forty-eight hours are critical, as you know. We're going to need some luck, but we have a lot of resources we can use," said Porter.

Suddenly, Jack's thoughts changed, and all he could think of was his baby brother.

A year earlier, Travis had stood next to Jack on the bridge between Afghanistan and Pakistan after the prisoner exchange with Rolf El-Hashem—Rolf's father for Travis. After suffering imprisonment, beatings, concussions, and worse, after Rolf El-Hashem put him through a living hell, Travis also declared a badal on the El-Hashem family. Once Jack rescued Travis and after the helicopter explosion, Travis needed multiple surgeries to remove shrapnel from his back and decompress his spinal cord. He walked with a permanent limp. He received PTSD therapy daily. But Jack knew that if the terrorists had tracked down Nina and Barett, they could also track down Travis, and if they got ahold of Travis again, his little brother was a goner.

Detective Porter's cell phone rang, and he stepped out to the hallway. When he came back, he stood straighter and seemed rushed or energized all of a sudden.

"A fisherman called in a drowning victim they found down by Suffolk Plaza. No word yet if it's male, female, or a child. Pretty messed up, though." Porter looked Jack in the eye. "They're texting me the photo."

Jack looked dazed. He wanted to call Travis. He rubbed his burning eyes.

Porter's smartphone chirped. He opened the message and studied the photo without changing his expression. "Take a look."

Jack had seen thousands of SEAL and CTF confirmation videos of dead bad guys. Hell, he had contributed a few hundred videos of his own to the highly classified CTF library, thanks to the helmet cam he wore into battle. The videos were reviewed during mission debriefing to verify who had been killed and who had done the killing.

The point being, Jack was used to death. The dead guy on Porter's phone was indistinguishable from any one of Salwa's men Jack had faced the previous night in Palestine. But picturing *that* man attacking Nina and Barett in his bedroom sent a lightning bolt of dread down Jack's spine. He looked at the blast hole in the door and the blood splatters everywhere. His jaw dropped open. Everything was spinning in his head. He struggled to keep his emotions in check. He said nothing.

"Our first lead," said Detective Porter, resting a hand on Jack's shoulder. "A shotgun blast to the chest. He looks Middle Eastern. We'll get him to the morgue and start pulling traffic video. Here's my card. Call me any time. I'll be in touch."

All Jack could think of was that he had just released Rolf El-Hashem from prison, paid Rami Salwa 110 million dollars, and now Nina and Barett were missing, presumably in a horrible situation. His world was unraveling. It couldn't get any worse.

"Mr. Gunn," said Porter and waited. "*Gunn.*"

Jack jerked, startled from his trance, looking drunk and haggard. He stared at Porter.

"Someone's here," said Porter.

"Jack. Bro. I'm really sorry about Nina and Barett." Dewey stopped abruptly inside the door. He went quiet as he looked around the bedroom, scowling as he studied the blasted door and bloody message.

Dewey had also been at the bridge exchange with Rolf El-Hashem, at the helicopter explosion in Chitral, and at the freighter takedown in the Arabian Sea, when he and Jack sent Mullah Mohammed Abdul to the bottom of the ocean with a hatchet stuck in his chest. The same freighter where Jack and he decided to let Rolf El-Hashem live instead of put a bullet in his head, as he deserved. He had heard Jack and Travis declare the badal. He was seeing for the first time what that decision had meant to Jack's family. It was every soldier's worst nightmare that enemies would go after families instead of each other.

Dewey turned back toward Jack, locked eyes with Detective Porter for a second, who nodded back, and then said to Jack, "Hey, man, we gotta go. As bad as this is—and I agree it looks pretty fucking bad—we need to get back to the base and see what we can do to help find them."

"You go, Dewey. I'm done."

"No can do, brother. You and I have gotten through some pretty tough spots over the years." Dewey looked long and hard at the bloody sheets and pillow Jack was holding. "Nothing like this, though. But the only way we've ever managed to get through all the bullshit was to do it together. You had my back, and I had yours. That's the only way we've ever done it, and that's the only way we're gonna get through this. So, are you with me?"

Jack sat up a little straighter. "Yeah, I'm with you, Dewey."

At six-foot-four and 240 pounds, Dewey was an inch taller, ten pounds heavier, and a year younger than Jack. A couple of handsome, invincible men with one slight difference: Dewey had a head of hair and Jack shaved his. Other than that, they both had scruffy, steel-wool beards—Dewey's blond and Jack's black. They each had a smattering of battle scars, which had been at the root of countless beer-drinking challenges, trying to out-macho one another with their stories of cheating death and killing bad guys. They both sported tattoos. Their noses had been broken at one time or another, and their chests were as thick as they were wide. A pretty imposing twosome when they were all geared up.

"What was that? Did you fucking say something?" Dewey said loudly, like a boot camp drill instructor. He wiped tears from his bloodshot eyes.

Jack swiped his eyes too. "All right. All right. You big dopey pain in the ass. Let's get back down to headquarters and go to work. But first, I gotta find Travis."

"I already did. He's fine."

A small weight removed from his shoulders, Jack nodded. It was a "roger that" nod that meant, "I know what you're thinking, and I'm with you." He wiped his eyes again and took one last look around. The blood-scrawled *BADAL* and shotgun hole in the wall would be etched in his memory forever. He set his jaw, shoved Dewey out of the bedroom door in front of him, and never looked back.

"It's time to go do what we do. Hunt, track, and kill these fuckers," growled Jack.

"Roger that," said Dewey.

Chapter 6

Atlantic Ocean

Nina was startled awake by an explosion and instinctively curled up in the fetal position, tucking her head to her chest and clenching her teeth, waiting for the next kick, punch, whipping, or worse. Her capturers seemed real efficient at inflicting pain. They didn't waste any time making small talk or giving Nina a choice. They just came in, turned on the light, whaled away on her, turned the light off, and moved on.

She again heard the noise that must have awakened her. It was a loud slam, heavy metal on metal, followed by a ratcheting sound, like a car jack being levered up.

What happened next drove her nearly insane.

An explosion on the other side of the wall knocked her out of her bed. It was like being trapped in a metal barrel with someone pounding on the outside with a sledgehammer, over and over and over. She heard men laughing and a weak, tiny whimpering.

"Barett! Oh my God!"

She pulled with all her might at her wrists, which were zip-tied behind her back, but to no avail. She lunged off the bed, log-rolled across the floor, and stomped on the wall with her bare feet.

"BARETT! BARETT!" she screamed.

Then it happened again and again. Ten shots. Fifteen shots. Boom. Boom. She screamed hysterically, hyperventilating until she passed out.

Deciding to have a bilateral mastectomy had been an easy decision for Nina. Once she accepted the fact she had breast cancer, every ounce of her being focused on beating it. The right breast had cancer. She said take them both. She wasn't going to give cancer a second chance to come back on the other side. Once was enough.

Chemotherapy, on the other hand, was a whole different story. Chemotherapy killed all cells, both cancerous and healthy, but killed the cancer cells a little faster. At the time, Nina realized that if she was lucky, she would not die. She just *wished* she were dead while she suffered the nausea, vomiting, weight loss, hair loss, pain, and infections. And the day after Nina had started feeling alive again—once she recovered from a dose of cyclophosphamide and doxorubicin—it was time for another round. On top of that, Jack was gone most of the time, chasing bad guys halfway around the world and leaving her to fend for herself and Barett.

Barett became her sweet angel. He never complained and always helped. He'd lie in Nina's bed for hours while she struggled to keep her stomach down. He'd tickle her arms, get cold washcloths, rub her neck. Barett became her reason to breathe from one minute to the next. One day to the next.

Either way, Nina wasn't the type who gave up or laid around feeling sorry for herself. She came from the same cut of Sioux cloth as Jack. Maybe not a relative of Sitting Bull, like Jack and Travis, but her Indian surname was Kills-A-Crow.

Nina's family earned their name and honor at Little Bighorn

by killing the Crow Indians working as scouts for General Custer. Although the white man ultimately prevailed and, in the end, corralled the Sioux Indians onto reservations, the Kills-A-Crows had survived. Nina grew up knowing hardship and poverty, but learned to be proud of who she was and what her people stood for.

She bounced back to good health once they stopped pumping her full of poison. Her gaunt cheeks filled in, and her flowing black hair grew back. She had recently met with a plastic surgeon and was scheduled to begin reconstruction. Her marathoner's energy seemed endless, and she got back to distance running again. At five-foot-seven, long and lean, running was something she had always been good at. Jack slept at home every night, following his promotion to head of the CTF. Barett started enjoying the carefree life of a seven-year-old boy again. For the last year, they acted like the family Nina had always dreamed of. Nina's smile was back.

Her door banged opened, again. The round fluorescent light went on. Her panic returned as she came out of her unconscious nightmare the way she had gone in—screaming.

A bearded man in a long-sleeved dishdasha jammed a sizzling gun barrel into her temple. She felt the burn, smelled the singed hair. Someone else kicked her already broken ribs.

"That's for shooting my little brother, bitch."

She tried to roll away, but Hassan El-Hashem, the gunman, kept her pinned in place. He laughed through cigarette-stained teeth and crouched close enough that his beard brushed her face.

"Too bad he didn't make it. He would have enjoyed screwing your brains out," said Hassan.

Nina guessed his brother was the man she had blasted with the shotgun in the condo.

The four other similarly dressed men who had filed into the compartment behind Hassan stayed out of his way and backed against the wall. It was clear to see Hassan was crazy, the way he twitched and drooled like a troll whenever he got worked up.

Hassan had a tick or twitch in his neck, always torqueing to the left. It looked as if it hurt, the way it jerked his head to the side so hard. The more excited or upset he got, the more it twitched. Maybe he had Tourette syndrome. Maybe he was just crazy. Maybe both.

"That little boy of yours is a fighter, just like his daddy," he said.

Nina's eyes filled with rage. She stopped breathing. The gun barrel pressed hard into the soft spot of her temple. The floor shuddered and vibrated, as if someone were using an industrial-sized jackhammer nearby, shaking the very core of the room.

"But you don't need to worry. We took care of that."

"What did you do? Where's my son?" Nina said through clenched teeth and a jaw that felt broken.

"Shut your mouth," Hassan hissed as he pulled up Nina's blood-crusted nightgown, jammed down hard on her belly with his other hand, and then slid his twiddling fingers down her panties.

"Don't worry, Nina. That's it, isn't it? Nina?" He pulled his hand out, smelled it, and then grabbed his own bulging crotch. "We're just having a little fun."

"No!" She thrashed and flopped like a floundering fish about to be filleted.

Hassan put all his weight on the gun, leaning forward and mashing her head to the floor.

She didn't care. She screamed, "Where's my son? I want my son!"

"Soon enough, Mrs. Gunn. Soon enough," he said.

She stopped screaming, caught off guard by her tormentor's intimate knowledge of who she was.

"That's right. I know who you are. But don't worry. This isn't about you. Or at least it wasn't till you pulled that fucking trigger."

The room leaned slightly to one side and then the other. Then they rolled to the other side again.

"Just relax and enjoy your accommodations. It's going to be a long trip."

"Where's my—"

Hassan clamped his hand over Nina's mouth and signaled one of his men, who came over and handed Hassan a rag. Hassan shoved the filthy gag in her mouth while his assistant tied the ends into a knot behind her neck.

"In our culture, women are to be seen and not heard."

"F— y—" she struggled to scream through her gag.

Hassan's partner backhanded her with his ringed hand.

"I can keep this up all day long if that's what you're into, Mrs. Gunn."

Nina gave Hassan one of Jack's patented death stares. It did not seem to have the same effect. His partner gave her another slap.

"You want to kill me?" he sneered through rotting, broken teeth. "Here's a deal for you. Help me kill your husband, and I'll give you back your son. Actually, it's kill your husband *and* that brother of his for declaring a badal on us. A blood feud on us! Seriously, we invented badals." Hassan and his bloody-knuckled friend laughed. "Now you and your son will pay the price. And when your husband comes to rescue you—and he will—we'll kill him too. Because that's what happens when you pick a fight you can't win."

A lonesome, mournful ship's horn sounded. The vibrations through the floor picked up in pitch and intensity.

"Why you? Ask your husband when you see him in hell," said Hassan, smiling as he stood to go. "Feel that?" Hassan bounced with bent knees as if he were testing his footing, and he pointed at the floor. "They'll never find us now. You take care, Mrs. Gunn. And don't you worry about your boy. I'll love him like he was one of my very own."

Chapter 7

Dam Neck Station, Little Creek, VA

"Dewey, I'm freaking out," said Jack as they barged into Ghost Team's headquarters. A couple of SEALs familiar to Jack and Dewey turned from their computer screens, nodded, and went right back to whatever they were doing. Jack swiped freezing-cold rain from his shaved head and stomped his feet. He looked at Dewey with tears in his burning eyes. His face contorted as he struggled to master his raging emotions.

"We'll do what we always do," said Dewey.

"They got my boy, Dewey. The bastards got Barett."

Dewey went speechless. He shed his waterlogged fleece jacket and headed for the coffee pot, wiping his eyes too.

"They got Nina," Jack whispered. He looked at Nina's bloodstains on his clothes and visualized her pulling the trigger. Jack could smell her blood. Images of their bedroom kept replaying in his head on a loop, over and over. He dropped into a chair, limp as a rag doll, when he imagined what they did to Barett.

Nobody said anything for the longest time. Jack was too numb to move.

Someone mumbled on a phone. A TV droned in the background. Rain pelted against the windowpanes.

The room was nothing fancy. Standard government-issue. The desks, chairs, sofas, even the coffeepots were Navy blue, gray, or black. Take your pick. Constructed from metal, plastic, vinyl, or wood, they were cheap but sturdy. Nobody expected anything else.

"Breaking news. Unidentified sources close to the investigation say the body found near Suffolk Plaza may be the first break in the murder-kidnapping that happened late last night in Dawley Corners, south of Virginia Beach. There's no word yet on the abductees, Nina and Barett Gunn."

Jack's and Dewey's heads popped up to look at the TV. They were showing pictures of Nina and Barett, pictures Jack had let Detective Porter take from their condo.

Hearing the news commentator say "murder-kidnapping" set a siren off in Jack's head. Every protective nerve and fiber in his body started firing a million times a second. It went against his nature and genetics to take flight. He was more of a fight-to-the-death type of man.

Like his brother, Travis, Jack had never been one for going to church or turning the other cheek. But he liked one story from the Old Testament. Jack revered Samson for taking on, and killing, a thousand Philistines with the jawbone of an ass. Jack was a Samson type of guy. Give him the jawbone of an ass, and get out of the way.

Jack didn't know if he should be sad, embarrassed, or mad as hell. He felt utterly exhausted. So emotionally wrung out and wired that he felt like curling up in the fetal position and crying.

The last time he had felt anything remotely close to how he felt now was the day Nina was diagnosed with breast cancer. It was as if an eighteen-wheeler had hit him in the chest and knocked the wind, the life, and the joy right out of him. He and Nina spun out of control in a whirlwind of hopelessness for days, before learning her lymph nodes had tested negative for cancer. It had been their first glimmer of hope.

He felt embarrassed because the head of the CTF—his organization, whose motto was Terror Never Sleeps—got played by the likes of Rami Salwa out of 110 million of American taxpayers' dollars and the release of his old archenemy, Rolf El-Hashem. Sure, he was getting the eleven dirty bombs that had gone missing since the day Jack and Dewey sent Mullah Mohammed Abdul to his watery grave, but Jack had a sneaking suspicion that somehow Salwa had orchestrated the whole Palestinian meeting to get him overseas so he could abduct Nina and Barett.

And if he had any energy left, he was mad at himself for not fulfilling his number one mission. A year ago, if someone had asked, Jack might have said his number one priority was to protect the homeland. A lot had happened in the last year. A lot had happened in the last twenty-four hours. His number one duty had become to protect his family. That no matter what happened he should protect the ones he loved. And in that, he was an unforgivable failure.

So when under attack, all Jack could do was fall back on his training, and his training said, "When under attack, move, move, move." Jack got up, jerked his head for Dewey to follow, and headed for their office.

"Are we in that prick's back door yet?" Jack asked tiredly, approaching Chief Hector Martinez, who was standing near the door leading to CTF's operation center and Jack's office.

The CTF operation center was in one of several nondescript three-story gray stucco buildings at the Dam Neck naval station.

Since Ghost Team and CTF worked hand in hand, the two offices were adjacent and connected to one another. The SEALs who were handpicked and trained to be part of Ghost Team were the boots on the ground for Jack's CTF missions.

A security door on one end of the operations center led to Jack's office. A thirty-foot-long bar-height desk ran down the middle of the CTF team room, with stools stationed every five feet on either side of the desk. Down the middle of the desk ran power strips; blue NIPRNET and red SIPRNET wires; and a host of monitors, computers, and phones positioned at each CTF workstation. The far wall, opposite from Jack's office, was covered with LED screens that constantly monitored various situations around the world. Opposite Ghost Team's room, a hallway led to a well-stocked kitchen, a locker room, a weight room, and several call rooms for sleep. Everything they needed to compete with the world's deadliest terrorists.

Hector Martinez, Ghost Team's new leader after Jack's promotion, said, "Jack. I . . . I . . . I'm sorry for your loss."

Hector Martinez was nothing like Jack. Six inches shorter, with a straight nose and a full head of hair, the mere sight of him *did not* make babies cry. He was the firstborn of young Mexican parents who had lived in Tijuana. When his mother went into labor, his father raced to get her across the border before she delivered. Even though they had no money or insurance and were illegal immigrants, they knew their baby would be deemed a US citizen as long as he was born on US soil.

Hector's parents eventually became citizens and rented a small two-room dump in Logan Heights, a bad part of San Diego sandwiched between the Navy fleet base and downtown. Mexican gangs ruled the barrio. Martinez had to fight to survive. He was quick with the blade and quick on his feet. That was where he earned his nickname, Flash. He feared nothing. He craved adrenaline. He remembered everything he had ever been taught in the SEALs. He fought like a pit bull and had no problem whatsoever killing bad guys. The teams were the only place for a guy like Hector Martinez to utilize his God-given talents without going to prison.

"Stow that bullshit, Martinez. I don't need your sympathy. I need answers," Jack growled as he and Dewey walked in front of him and into the CTF center.

The two SEALs working at the long desk turned back to their monitors.

"I just thought—" Martinez's head bowed and his shoulders stooped as if he were singlehandedly hauling a two-hundred-pound log through Coronado's wet sand on Hell Week. Martinez followed them through the door.

"Chief Martinez?" Jack said in the tone a father would use to get answers out of a rebellious child.

Martinez's flat-topped head looked up with an "I didn't do it" expression on his face.

"Is the NSA's bug working on Salwa's phone or not? Yes or no?" Jack's face felt hot, and his eyes ready to pop out of their sockets.

"They lost his signal before they were able to activate the Trojan horse."

"Well, get it back. Salwa's all we got."

"He's disappeared into a dead zone. But before he did, they were able to get a rough triangulation on his position somewhere in central Mali." Martinez followed Jack and Dewey into Jack's office.

"I'll check in with Porter and see if they've identified the dead guy," said Dewey as he flopped down into a chair.

"Roger that," Jack said, shaking his head and coming back to reality for a bit. He picked up an encrypted phone and dialed a number he knew by heart while he took a seat behind his desk and massaged the creases of his forehead with his other hand. Every thirty seconds or so, he punched another button then waited on-hold some more.

"We'd be screwed if I hadn't jacked that slippery fucker's phone in Nablus," Jack said to Dewey, who was fidgeting on the other side of Jack's desk. "We're up a creek if we lose him now."

"Some but not all of the blood was Nina's," Dewey said when he got off the phone with Porter. He spoke in an up tone, as if it were good news.

"They got my family, the money, and Rolf El-Hashem out of prison." Jack kicked the underside of the desk. He was still holding the phone, waiting on hold. "All for a bunch of freaking bombs."

"Don't worry, bro. We'll find 'em," said Dewey.

"Well, tell him to check his e-mail ASAP," Jack said into his phone and slammed it into its cradle. "Fuck." He finished typing a message on his computer and logged off.

He rifled through status reports on his various SEAL teams deployed around the world, scanning their plans for the night-to-come's raids. He kept shuffling until he had gone through the entire stack. "Chief. Where's that El-Hashem report?"

"Right there in front of you. I put it there myself."

"The hell you did," said Jack, shaking his head, scowling.

Martinez got up, walked to Jack's desk, pulled the FBI document out of the mess, and handed it to Jack. He looked at Jack and shook his head. "Maybe you should just let us handle this, and you get some sleep."

"Maybe you should just mind your own fucking business and gimme that." He grabbed the brief, read it, checked the clock, and did the math in his head. "Fuck."

"Rolf El-Hashem made it to Jakarta, Pakistan, about the same time you discovered Nina was missing," said Martinez. "He's gone. Not a trace."

"And the bombs?" asked Jack. "Please tell me Ghost Team took possession!"

"They did." Martinez said, a slight quiver in his voice.

"And?"

"The Semtex was real all right, but the uranium was gone."

"Over a hundred million dollars for fucking duds! You gotta be shitting me," Jack bellowed.

"Fifty-five million, boss. We only paid half up front, remember?"

"Well, halle-fucking-lujah. I'm sure SecDef will be overjoyed to learn we gave the terrorists only fifty-five million dollars *and* eleven suitcase nukes. That should play real well with the president."

"We were fucked from the get-go," said Dewey.

"Salwa knew my family was being attacked and still had the balls to rake Aaron and me over the coals. It seems to me he's been promoted."

"What'd he need Rolf El-Hashem for?" asked Martinez. "Something doesn't add up."

"Favor to the family? This badal nightmare Salwa mentioned?" said Dewey.

"Maybe. I don't know. Salwa asked for the meeting. His only chip was a bunch of dummy suitcases," said Jack. "How'd he know we'd bite?"

"There is one other possibility," Dewey said ominously. "But you're not going to like it."

A year earlier, Jack, Dewey, and their Ghost Team carried out a mission in the middle of the Arabian Sea in pursuit of three Taliban leaders attempting to carry out their grand jihad. Those three were Mullah Mohammed Abdul, the spiritual leader and head of the Taliban security council; Ahmed El-Hashem, Rolf's father who had carried out IED bombing of the CIA; and Rolf El-Hashem, the plastic surgeon who performed identity-changing face surgery on the security council, then came out of the closet as a jihadist and tortured Travis, Jack's only sibling, to within one machete chop of his neck. Mohammed's sleeper cells and other El-Hashems had smuggled uranium from a Pakistani centrifuge facility and stashed eleven suitcase bombs at critical locations in the United States, intending to detonate them and throw the free world into mass chaos.

The CIA caught a whiff of their plan, and Jack's team flew halfway around the world and parachuted into the sea, attack boats and all. When they caught up with the terrorists' ship, Rolf's father was already dead, and Mohammed, the master planner, had escaped in a small boat. Mohammed was attempting to make the coast of Yemen with the twelfth suitcase, leaving Rolf alone, pleading with Jack for his life. Rather than pull the trigger when he had Rolf's head pinned to the ship's deck with his pistol, Jack acquiesced and had Rolf transported to prison at Diego Garcia. He told Travis that Rolf was dead. His brother had enough to worry about just recovering from his broken back, concussions, and the living hell that tormented his brain.

In Jack's world, the badal feud between the El-Hashems and Gunns had been over. At least all of the El-Hashems he knew about were dead, except Rolf, and he was behind bars. Little did he know.

Martinez closed Jack's office door.

Jack said, "Go on."

"We've always believed Rolf El-Hashem was innocent. We knew he was a criminal and that his dad led an IED team successful in killing a bunch of our guys. And that he was one of the El-Hashems. But we didn't think he had any real value as a prisoner." Dewey looked at Martinez then Jack. "We may have been wrong."

"Go on." Jack shifted in his creaking chair. Another low rumble of thunder rattled outside.

"Suppose Mohammed did tell Rolf where the other eleven bombs where hidden, before you sent him to the bottom of the ocean," said Dewey.

"And they needed Rolf released from prison to find their beloved bombs. Fuck," said Jack as he caught on to what Dewey was thinking. "It wouldn't surprise me one bit if Salwa was an El-Hashem." Jack slammed his desk so hard with his sledgehammer fist that it jumped up off the floor in rebound. "Dammit, I should've killed that ugly bastard when I had the chance."

"Roger that," said Dewey.

One of the CTF staff poked his head in. "Jack. Someone's at the front gate. He says he's your brother."

Chapter 8

Atlantic Ocean

"All hands on deck. Boss's orders." The bloody-knuckled man kicked Nina in her spine with the toe of his boot. "Hassan has something to show you." With a flick of his wrist, he cut her zip-tied ankles free.

Nina winced. As beat up as she was, her tiny body looked more the size of a child's. Nina slurred her words, "Where are we? What day is it?" She rolled over onto her knees and then to her bare feet. She lost her balance temporarily as the ship rolled. Her poop bucket sloshed back and forth in the corner. She defiantly looked the man in the face as she shuffled in front of him and out of her prison door, for the first time in days.

"Don't you go and get any funny fucking ideas. You're in the middle of the ocean. We have your son." The man shoved Nina, who was still stooped over like a hunchback. "Look at me like that again, and I'll take it out on your boy."

"Can I use a bathroom? One with water?" Nina said, changing the subject, diverting her eyes to the floor.

"I thought you might ask. Here." He handed Nina a handful of wet paper towels.

"What am I supposed to do with these?"

"Use your imagination. You've got thirty seconds."

"Do you mind?" Nina said, waiting for him to turn around.

"Get scrubbing or not, I don't care. Fifteen seconds."

Nina quickly scrubbed the crusted blood and snot from her face, then stuck the wad down her panties and wiped. She held the towels back out to the man, who knocked them from her hand with his gun.

"Need another lesson, wise ass?" He punched her in the gut.

She doubled over and threw up, but managed to stay on her feet as the ship leaned.

"I've got all the time in the world."

"Three hundred pounds against a hundred," she said, wiping her mouth with her sleeve. "Brave man." She shuffled out in front of him, still wobbly and dizzy.

"You just wait, smartass. You'll get what's coming," the bloody-knuckled man said.

It would have been safer to stay inside, but not tonight. Hassan had said to bring the prisoner on deck, and Hassan El-Hashem was boss.

The bloody-knuckled man put a rope noose, a leash, around Nina's neck before they walked out onto the afterdeck behind the superstructure. It was sunset, and they were alone. As alone as one can be in the middle of the Atlantic on a terrorist freighter.

Washed by the cool ocean breeze, breathing fresh air for the first time in she could not remember how long, Nina was in heaven. She closed her eyes and pictured herself floating above the flat seas all the way back to Jack, wherever he was. Her spirit was calling out to him. Beckoning him. "Jack. Jack. Here we are, baby. Come and get us, Jack."

Her master jerked the leash, snapping Nina to her knees and back from the beyond. She still wore the same nightgown she had put on days earlier in their condo. It was impossible to pinpoint where she hurt most. Her ribs ached with every breath from being kicked too many times to count. Her head throbbed constantly from the beatings and drugs.

For the first time, she could relate to the concussions Jack and Travis suffered from being dangerously close to powerful explosions. She was having a hard time concentrating, and she was nauseated all the time. It was different than chemotherapy nausea. She thanked God for small favors.

But what hurt most was her heart. What was happening to her little baby created a pain so great, a wailing so deep, that she wanted to die. She couldn't imagine what those coldhearted bastards were doing to Barett—if he were still alive. It was beyond her comprehension. She was desperate to kill them all, get her poor baby back, and take him home.

From where she kneeled on deck, she watched as the same door she had exited banged open again. Nina held her breath. Out walked six dark-skinned, bearded men. All wore baggy trousers and white knee-length *kurtas*. Most wore a headdress or skullcap of some sort. A few sported the green Hamas headband. All carried weapons.

Finally, out walked her little angel, holding hands with a beaming Hassan El-Hashem. Barett moved like a zombie, dragging his toes with every step, bloody drool hanging from his chin, a blank stare on his baby-soft face. Hassan kept a tight grip, propping Barett up. He stopped six feet from Nina and flicked his cigarette in a long arch over the ship's edge, like a shooting star sparking across the night sky to its death.

Barett didn't seem to recognize Nina at first.

"Barett, honey. Barett. It's Mommy." Nina stretched out her bound hands and lunged for her little boy.

The bloody-knuckled man ripped the leash, yanking Nina back to the greasy, steel deck.

"Please. Barett. Please." She collapsed in a heaving, pleading sob.

"Oh, isn't that sweet," said Hassan. He laughed, coughed, then started laughing again—a maniacal, neck-twitching laugh as if he could not get a joke out of his head. The others started laughing too, but they sounded more nervous, keeping all eyes on Hassan, waiting for the signal.

Hassan backed away, closer to the rail, keeping Barett just out of Nina's reach. He lit up another cigarette and inhaled deeply.

"My friend here says you still think you can survive, Mrs. Gunn. After everything that's happened, and you think you and your precious little boy here will just hop on a plane and go home. That's funny, don't you think?"

Nina shook her head. She desperately reached for Barett with her zip-tied hands and begged, "Please! No! Please!"

"Why don't you ask my family how it feels to win, after your husband killed so many?" Drool flung from the corner of his mouth with each violent twitch of his neck. "Why don't you ask my brother Rolf what it feels like to win, after your husband put him in prison? Why don't you ask your boy what it feels like to win?"

Nina looked up at Hassan for the first time, shaking her head. She thought his red, bloodshot eyes made him look like the evil one she saw in her dreams.

"Go ahead. Ask him."

Nina looked at Barett.

He looked back at her, bleary eyed.

"Barett. Sweety, I'm sorry. Oh my God, I'm so sorry." She reached out to him, but her master jerked her back again.

"I'm not sure you really understand what's going on here, so let me make it crystal clear." Hassan waved an open hand to the other men on deck. No one moved. The freighter still rumbled forward, beating to the southeast at ten knots through calm seas. A plume of diesel smoke ambled along behind in the darkening sky.

"Travis Gunn, the doctor, was your brother-in-law, right?"

Nina didn't move, shocked by the question.

Hassan pulled Barett closer to him and wrapped his arm across Barett's chest. "Right?"

"Right, right," Nina blurted, focused on Barett.

"Good." Hassan's neck twitched. "And Jack Gunn, the Navy SEAL and head of the CTF, is your husband and Barett's daddy, right?"

Nina nodded again.

"What you may not know is that those two made a colossal mistake last year when they foolishly decided to declare war, something us Pakistanis have called a badal for centuries. Now the way a badal works is your family, the Gunns, and my family, the El-Hashems, kill the other family, top to bottom. Grandparents, wives." Hassan pointed at Nina. "And children." Hassan pointed at Barett. "We wipe out all living traces of the Gunn family. Dead."

Nothing seemed to get through Nina's fog until then. When Hassan pointed at Barett, Nina started to panic. "No. No. No," she pleaded. "I surrender. Please. Just take me. Let him go."

"Believe me when I say that I would be fine with that. But that's not what your husband wants, Mrs. Gunn. He and his good-for-nothing brother are the ones who declared a blood feud on us. He's the one who killed most of my family and security council. But what has *he* lost, I ask?"

Nina did not move. Tears streamed down her face as she stood stranded on the deck, surrounded by Hassan's gophers, wearing her noose. "Please," she whispered.

Hassan took Barett by the hand and walked toward the rail. Ten, twenty, thirty feet from Nina. The rest of the men followed, leaving only the bloody-knuckled man holding on to Nina.

Hassan mumbled something to the men and then to Barett.

Nina could not hear what he said.

The men stepped back, giving Hassan space.

What happened next happened in an instant—a slow-motion, surreal instant. Hassan took Barett by both hands and swung him around in a circle. Once around. Twice around. And on the third time around, Hassan let go, and Barett went flying over the rail. He disappeared into the dark, screaming, until they heard a splash forty feet below.

Nina screamed hysterically as she scrambled to her bare feet and tried to run to the rail. Only, she made it about ten feet before her leash snapped tight and knocked her to the deck again. Her knees and elbow were bleeding from being dragged across the nonskid, but she did not feel it. She wailed and cried and pleaded, but to no avail. The men laughed.

"Please let me go. I want to jump. I have to jump. You win."

"Maybe you'll be a little more cooperative," Hassan said. "I'm sorry. But I need you a little longer. Bait, you know."

"I don't want to live anymore. Please."

"I know it's hard, but try to understand."

Nina slumped to the deck, weeping.

Hassan glanced over the rail. The darkness and water all blended into one. He spotted a solitary light trailing them on the dark horizon. He took one last drag on his cigarette, flicked it, and headed back inside, followed by his entourage.

"Don't worry Mrs. Gunn. You'll join your son soon enough."

Chapter 9

CTF Headquarters, Little Creek, VA

"Dewey filled me in, but how'd they find your house?" asked Travis as he limped into Jack's CTF office and took a seat, leaning his cane on the desk. The year of rehab and marriage had worked wonders for Travis. Thirty pounds lighter and bulked up across the chest and shoulders, even with a limp, he moved fluidly. He ran his fingers through his shoulder-length wet hair and hooked it behind his ears. He smelled like bacon, having grabbed a bacon cheeseburger and fries on the drive over. He looked worried.

"Hell if I know," said Jack. "I was worried they got you and Jaz too."

"You can stop worrying about me," said Travis, draping his dripping jacket over the back of his chair.

"After what you went through in Pakistan, round two would've sucked," said Dewey.

"I was a damn idiot. Declaring badal on the El-Hashems was like declaring war on Satan," said Travis, shaking his head. "I'm really sorry, Jack."

"I was right there with you, remember? And I have the scars

to prove it," said Jack. "I can take care of myself. But what kind of cowards go after a man's family?"

"Now we know, brother." Travis sat down across the desk from Jack.

Dewey had changed into dry shorts and a Maui sweatshirt. He pulled up a chair. "Can I get you one of these?" he said, holding up a steaming Styrofoam cup of coffee.

Travis nodded. His eyes were bloodshot and his lips quivered as he said, "Thinking of what Nina and Barett are going through is . . ." His wrung his hands to hide the tremors. "I mean . . ."

Jack reached across and wrapped his paw over Travis's. "We're gonna find 'em, bro. Don't worry."

"I mean . . . I can't stop thinking about how Rolf, a guy I partied with through medical school and worked side by side with in Dubai—the things he did to me . . ."

"We're gonna find 'em," repeated Jack, more confidently than he felt. "We found you, didn't we?"

"At least *I* don't have to worry about Rolf anymore, thanks to you. But what he would have done to Nina and Barett would be . . ." Travis looked like a nervous wreck.

"Stop it, Travis." Jack and Dewey squirmed in their chairs and met each other's gazes. "There's something you need to know. Something we haven't told you," said Jack.

Travis leaned forward and gripped the edge of Jack's desk. The stress of being a tortured prisoner of Rolf El-Hashem's in Pakistan, of dealing with PTSD, of recovering from spine surgery, and of being in chronic pain, had taken its toll. His bedroom eyes, his smirky smile, his swagger were all gone. If it hadn't been for his angel wife, Jaz, he would have surely died. Besides reconnecting with Jack and Nina and Barett, Jaz was the best thing that had ever happened to him.

But now, he steadied himself for another broadside. Just like being back in Rolf's torture chamber, bent over a chair with his pants on the ground, or having the side of his head bashed in with a rifle butt. "What? What is it?"

"Last year, while you were recovering from spine surgery, remember how Dewey and I flew halfway around the world to kick Rolf's ass, kill their grand jihad, and end this badal thing?"

"Yeah, well, I was pretty drugged up after going through spine surgeries. Most of it I'm trying to forget." Travis held up open hands. "What?"

"We caught up with the three of them—Rolf, his dad, and Mullah Mohammed Abdul—on a freighter in the middle of the Arabian Sea and stopped them before they blew up a dozen suitcase nukes, just like we told you."

"And killed them," said Travis. "I know. You told me."

Jack paused, staring into Travis's eyes.

"And killed them—right, Jack? Dewey? That's what you said." The pitch in Travis's voice ratcheted up.

Thc TV droned out in the main room. SEALs came and went. A housefly buzzed around the fluorescent light above them. Jack straightened in his chair, rubbed his eyes, and exhaled a long, slow breath.

"Rolf's dad died before we got there from that infected tracking device Preacher stuck in his gut, and Mohammed drowned, with a little help from me burying a hatchet in his chest." Jack looked at Travis. "But . . . I didn't put a bullet in Rolf's skull when I had the chance. Instead, I stuck him in prison for safekeeping."

"What the fuck!" Travis let go of the desk and leaned back. He shook his head. "Why are you telling me this now? It's a joke, right?"

"I figured you'd suffered enough. Letting you believe Rolf was dead would let you move on," said Jack.

"Well, you figured wrong!" said Travis. "You had no right!"

"We've been trying to track down the other eleven bombs since then." Jack forced the conversation forward, not wanting to spend precious time dissecting his decision to let Rolf live. "We had killed everyone who knew where the bombs were. Or so we thought."

"Or so you thought. Talk English, Jack," said Travis. "Stop beating around the bush."

"We located the bombs, or at least some Al-Qaeda prick who said he had the bombs. I traded Rolf for the bombs—the day Nina and Barett disappeared." Jack let out another breath. "And as things turned out, the bombs were fakes."

"You know what that crazy fucker will do, right?" said Travis. "We gotta find Nina and Barett." Travis hyperventilated. His face turned pale, his eyes rolled back in his head, and he keeled over, out of his chair, onto the floor.

"What the hell?" Dewey, who was sitting next to him, grabbed Travis's collar before his head hit the floor.

Travis was out cold. He twitched a few times and foamed at the mouth.

Dewey felt his pulse at the wrist.

"Thirty-six. Vasovagal," was all he said.

Jack helped Dewey get Travis rolled onto his back, pulled his knees up, and waited for the seizures to stop and his heart to beat faster so he could regain consciousness.

A vasovagal reaction, which they all knew, was a way the body reacted to shock or pain or any one of a thousand other situations. The drop in blood pressure and heart rate was always unexpected and dramatic. Most people were injured falling or banging their head on something on the way to the floor. Seizures were one of the ways the brain reacted to low blood pressure, but in no way indicated Travis had epilepsy, even though he had a history of concussions from what he went through when he was a Taliban prisoner.

Ghost Team guys from the outer room were drawn by the commotion. When they heard the diagnosis and saw Jack and Dewey had things under control, they drifted away as Travis recovered.

"Call the medic, just in case," Jack called out to Martinez as he kept two fingers on Travis's wrist pulse, which had already started to speed up.

Jack's head was spinning. Telling Travis that Rolf was still alive was like cutting open an old belly wound and ripping out Travis's guts. He hated himself for what he knew this would do to Travis. He hated himself even more for what it was doing to Nina and Barett.

"Dewey. Who do we know in Mali?" Jack asked with a deep, exhaustive sigh.

"A group of special-ops guys we contracted to go against Boko Haram in Nigeria. They got results, but we may need to bring in some foreign brutality for this one. It's gonna get messy."

"The Mossad's got brass balls, and they may have more to gain than anyone if we can find the bombs," said Jack as he scrolled. "Or at least they may know somebody."

"They sure as shit know how to get it done," said Dewey. "Ever wonder why Iran can never get their nuclear program going? Why their scientists' cars keep blowing up at the most inopportune times?"

The medic arrived and took over Travis's care. Jack got off his knees and checked his e-mail.

Dewey kept talking. "Aaron told me how they have agents in Tehran that cruise up alongside the scientists' cars on motorcycles when traffic is heavy, stick a magnetic hockey-puck-type bomb to its side, ride around the corner, and detonate it with their cell phone. It's the damnedest thing."

Jack barely listened to Dewey's nervous babble. With Travis heading back in the right direction, he tried to focus on the computer screen. Aaron had logged on and left a message: **Sorry about your family. We're tracking Salwa. How can I help?**

"I'll call at 0700 Israel time. Get some sleep. You'll need it," typed Jack.

Travis sat up and after fifteen minutes crawled back up into his chair. Dewey handed him a bottle of orange juice. His color slowly returned, along with his pulse.

"You okay?" Jack asked, handing Travis a box of tissues.

Travis nodded, blowing his nose.

"I'm really sorry I had to tell you like this, bro. We meant to tell you sometime, but were waiting for the right moment."

Travis nodded again but did not seem to care. He looked foggy or hungover. He was shivering.

Jack phoned Detective Porter.

"His name was Ibrahim El-Hashem. Mean anything to ya?" Porter asked.

"It rings a bell." Jack winced, wringing his hands around the phone receiver.

"He flew in from Tel Aviv a couple days ago. The condo was clean. No prints. Lab's working the pillow for DNA. Maybe we'll get lucky."

Jack heard Porter lighting up and talking to someone else.

"Oh yeah, we also got the plates and a description of the vehicle. The FBI's got it posted up and down the East Coast. Don't worry. We'll bust their asses."

Porter broke off the conversation again.

Jack couldn't hear what they were saying, but he felt Porter's excitement.

"Anything else, detective?" asked Jack, getting testy.

"I don't know what to make of it, but we just got a call from the Coast Guard in Charleston. Chief there says they just received a distress call from a long-haul fishing trawler two hundred miles out. Trawler captain just fished a boy out of the ocean. He was unconscious but alive, floating in a life ring. Got caught in their net, or they never would've seen him in the dark. A Coast Guard helo is en route to airlift him back to the hospital in Charleston."

"Are you shitting me?"

Dewey and Travis perked up when they heard the change of tone in Jack's voice.

Dread flooded every cell in Jack's body. Dread mixed with hope. Something in his brain snapped. At that moment, nothing else mattered. He stopped hearing or caring about anything else except the slightest glimmer of hope that Barett was alive. It seemed that everyone he loved, he had lost. He was not going to lose Barett and Nina. Not without a fight.

"It's gotta be Barett," said Jack. He jumped to his feet. "Porter. We'll call you from the air."

"Hold your horses, Jack," said Porter. "At least wait till the Coast Guard sends a picture."

"Not on your life. We'll be in touch." Jack already knew. He slammed down the phone, and the three of them raced back out into the bone-chilling rain. Jack and Dewey led the way, with Travis quickly recovering from his fainting episode and limp-running as fast as he could to CTF's private hangar, where the flight crew fired up the turbines for a high-speed run to Charleston.

Chapter 10

Atlantic Ocean

Nina's beatings suddenly stopped. Her compartment lights, which had been kept off continuously, except for beatings, now stayed on continuously. Food came morning, noon, and night. They allowed her to use the bathroom instead of the bucket. Her broken ribs and back felt better. The bloody-knuckled man even treated her to a shower.

Being alive was never worse.

Days and nights were one rolling, depressing continuum, like the Atlantic Ocean her freighter-prison steamed across. Five-foot swells. Ten-foot swells. Twenty-foot swells. The six-hundred-foot rust bucket seemed destined for the bottom, like a plastic toy boat in a bathtub. Mother Nature would surely sink it to extract penance for what Hassan had done. The sins of one, the penance for all.

Nina's tear ducts dried up. It was too painful to go on living, but not yet her time to die. Her angel was gone. Jack never showed. The gods had forgotten her . . . again. Just like they had forgotten her during chemotherapy.

She slowly slipped below the surface as she lost her lifesaving kick, her ability to see clearly, to feel anything but despair. As she drowned, suffocating on guilt and shame, her thoughts grew dark and stormy.

Why did I insist on buying that condo? Why kill Barett and not me? Why not Jack?

Nina was trapped in a wicked vortex, circling the drain, around and around. She was a strong swimmer, but sooner or later, she would lose the battle and be sucked under for the last time. She was tired. Oh, so tired.

Her will to live, her fight to survive, her desire to see another sunrise, had come from watching her little boy grow up. She used to feel that way about Jack, but having a baby changed everything. Jack was her hero, but Barett was the love of her life. Ever since the first day she held his slippery, newborn body and caressed him to her bosom, Barett had a grip on her that only a mother could understand. She had made him. She had grown him. She had birthed him. When they cast him over the side rail like a bag of trash, instead of the most precious jewel in the world, Nina died with him.

For what seemed like days, she floated somewhere between this world and the next in a place resembling a house of doors, nothing but doors. She searched the house frantically, opening one door after another, looking for something she never found. In fact, she never knew what she was looking for. The lonely feeling of dread propelled her, drove her on to the next room, the next door, while an alarm clock ticked away the seconds. Her time was almost up.

In her darkest moment, when taking another breath seemed impossible, days after Hassan had thrown Barett overboard, Nina's father appeared to her in a vision. Dead for five years, his spirit had been silent to Nina, her father's spirit keeper. She loved and honored him and had hoped to learn from his spirit and their Great Spirit, Wakan Tanka, after his passing about the mysteries of life. But her father's spirit never showed . . . until now.

Nina had thought his spirit was gone forever, after all the suffering she had endured over the last year. She was shocked to see him but hardly recognized him. He did not appear as the sixty-five-year-old father she had lost, but the twenty-year-old warrior she never knew. His eyes burned with eternal fire. His long, silky, coal-black hair was crowned with the family headdress of eagle feathers and colorful beads. Red broken arrows were painted on his cheeks. He wore animal-skin leggings and a loincloth. Tucked in his belt were his tomahawk and skinning knife. In one hand he held a spear. In the other, a Winchester. He looked ready for war.

"Nina, child. Why do you weep?"

"Papa, oh Papa. I miss you so much."

"I miss you too, little one. You and Jack and Barett."

"I want to come be with you, Papa. I can't fight anymore," she said and started to weep.

"You, Nina, were born to fight. Burning inside you is the soul of a warrior. The same spirit that burned inside me, my grandfather, and all those before them, burns in you." He caressed her face in his strong, gentle palms and looked deep into her soul. "Your fight is just beginning."

"But I'm so tired, Papa."

"It is not your time."

"I can't go on. I have nothing to fight for. They killed my baby. My angel," said Nina.

"He is not here," her father said.

Nina looked puzzled. "You must be wrong. I saw it."

"It was not his time either."

Nina sat up and gasped. Color streamed back to her cheeks. "Barett is alive?"

"He is." Her father nodded. "Now . . . are you?"

Nina looked around her dingy cell, as if seeing everything for the first time. The parts of her bed and objects in the room that could be turned into weapons glowed fluorescent green. Thoughts popped up in her consciousness—information she had never been taught—like how to shoot an AK-47; how to grind a shiv from a toothbrush; or how to construct a pipe bomb out of moth balls, Comet, lighter fluid, and superglue.

"Now what?" asked Nina.

"The Jesuit priests used to say, do unto others as others have done unto you—or something like that." Her father smiled.

Nina did too.

Her father held her face in his hands, kissed her on the forehead, and said, "Do like the Kills-A-Crows before you. Be patient. Be smart. Be always alert. And kill, or be killed."

"What? But—"

He held up a hand to silence her. "You won't be alone," he said and then vanished.

Nina's smile morphed into a determined glare. The weapons in her room still glowed. Her brain catalogued mountains of new information. She picked up the fluorescent toothbrush and started honing it down to a point on a rusted section of the bed frame.

How? Where? She had watched Barett fly overboard. Impossible, except her father said it was true. She knew if she ever wanted to see her son and Jack again, she needed a plan. She needed a gun or knife. She needed to kill Hassan.

CHAPTER 11

Children's Hospital, Charleston, SC

"V-fib. He's in ventricular fibrillation," Katie, the ER nurse, said matter-of-factly.

"Continue CPR," said Dr. Robb, the trauma physician. "What's his temperature?"

"Twenty-five degrees. It's a long ways from thirty-seven degrees." She nodded at the two respiratory therapists doing CPR. One did chest compressions with the heels of her stacked hands over the middle of Barett's sternum. The other squeezed an Ambu bag every few seconds, propelling oxygen down the endotracheal tube to his waterlogged lungs.

"Get the perfusionist down here STAT. We need to warm this little tiger up fast," said Dr. Robb, scratching his head.

"Stop CPR," the AED's computerized voice ordered. "Analyzing."

Everyone stopped what they were doing but didn't look happy about it. No chest compressions were pushing blood through Barett's cold body. No oxygenated blood was going to his brain, and that's all that mattered at the moment. The longer his brain went without oxygen, the greater the chance he would end up brain dead. The one thing he had going in favor of his brain was his temperature. The colder he was, the less oxygen his brain needed. But being cold was also what caused his heart to stop. Warming him up was his only chance to get his heart going again. Warm him up? Keep him cold? Either way, Barett was screwed.

"Shocking," said the AED.

Barett's tiny body lurched off the gurney as electricity shot between two paddles and through his heart. Everyone waited and watched the EKG for a couple seconds.

"Shit. Continue CPR," said Dr. Robb. "Where's my fem-fem bypass, dammit?"

"On their way," said Nurse Katie. "How long before you call it, doctor? They started CPR on the helo when he stopped breathing. That's over an hour already."

"You know the drill, Kate. They're not dead until they're warm and dead," said Dr. Robb. "It's a full-court press. Get the Foley catheter and gastric tubes in. Let's go, people. Warm him up." Dr. Robb's orders were punctuated as if he were a field commander who detested his enemy. Pediatric trauma teams defended their patients like momma bears defended their cubs. Any monster that did that to a young boy deserved to have a bucket of nails shoved down his throat.

"Dr. Robb. I can't hold the boy's father off much longer," said Charlene, the ER registration woman from the doorway. "Can you talk to him?"

"Mother?"

"Didn't say."

"Send him back."

"He's pretty scary looking." Charlene grimaced as if she had bitten into a dill pickle. "Security's standing by. There's three of them. One's a doctor."

"Thanks for the warning, Char," said Dr. Robb without looking at her. He concentrated, dressed in a gown, gloves, and mask, on sticking a spaghetti-noodle-sized bypass needle into Barett's groin. Barett didn't move, except for jerking one hundred times a minute as the chest compressions continued. His skin was cold, like a corpse's from the morgue. His color was blue, like a corpse's from the morgue. His EKG was flat, like a corpse's from the morgue.

Twenty minutes later, back in the ER waiting room, Jack looked dazed after the surreal experience of seeing his baby being kept alive by a code blue team doing chest compressions and giving breaths through a breathing tube. He stumbled, and Travis grabbed him under his arm. Dewey got the other, and they guided him to a sofa.

Headline news played on the TV suspended from the wall. A young couple tried to quiet their screaming infant, throwing desperate glances at the receptionist.

Jack slumped as if he'd been gutted, heart and soul. Stunned. Not moving. Barely breathing. Tears streaked his face.

"This has gone way too far," Travis said to Dewey. "Kidnapping a man's family, shooting up his boy, that . . .that . . .can't happen. These people aren't human." Travis buried his face in his hands, now sobbing.

Jack could contain his sorrow no more once he heard Travis. He struggled, trying to keep it in, but his sadness boiled through cracks in his walls of steel in the form of gasps and moans. The sound of a broken man.

"Stay with Jack," Dewey said to Travis quietly. "I gotta make a few calls." Dewey disappeared through the sliding doors, wiping tears from his eyes and punching numbers on his cell phone. He first called his wife, Suzy, to give her the devastating news. Dewey and Suzy had been best friends with Jack and Nina since BUD/S. Then he called their NSA contact to set up scans for satellite phones in the shipping lanes near where Barett had been pulled from the Atlantic. Then he phoned Detective Porter for an update.

Jack found himself floating again, searching across the great divide for Nina and Barett again. A cloud of smoke wafted between him and her. The smoke was sometimes thick and sometimes thinned to the point where he could see all the way to the far side.

Finally, in a clear moment, he spotted Nina and Barett. He cried out to them. Nina turned toward him. She looked resolute and at peace, as if she had made up her mind about something. She extended an open hand to Jack, and that's when Jack noticed Barett walking slowly toward him, already halfway across the divide before the smoke swallowed them both up again.

"Nina." Jack sat up suddenly, knocking Travis's hand off his shoulder.

"Shit, Jack. You scared the hell out of me."

"It'd be just like her. Save Barett, but not herself," Jack mumbled somberly. "Nina."

"The Coast Guard will start searching come sunup," said Dewey, back in from the cold.

The crying baby with worried parents had gone into the ER. Another waiting couple slouched on a sofa, watching *Late Night*, struggling to keep their eyes open.

"Little chance they'll find her if they threw her overboard too," said Jack with a crackle in his voice. "But I don't think they did," he said, remembering his vision. "She's a fighter and she's smart. Now that we got Barett back . . . we can focus on saving Nina . . ." Jack ran out of words.

"Gimme your hand, Jack. You too, Dewey," said Travis. While Jack had spent time being mentored by the Zuya growing up, Travis had been mentored by their Sioux medicine men. He learned the old ways to heal with herbs and chants and prayers. While he had ignored those teachings when he ran off to Boston and got into medical school, Travis's healing spirit had reawakened over the last year.

Jack and Travis sat on the sofa, while Dewey sat next to them in a chair. "Holy Father and heavenly spirits," Travis began praying, more evidence of Jaz's positive influence in his life. The sound of the TV drifted away.

Jack sensed each breath, each beat of his heart, as if it were work. As if he needed to remember to breathe, or else he wouldn't. He closed his exhausted eyes, leaned forward, and held on tight.

Travis prayed, "We ask you to intercede for Barett, lying in the room next door, where some of your best doctors and nurses are working on him. Warm him with your sweet love. Breathe life into his tender lungs. Squeeze his heart with the strength of his elders. Please God, send him back to us."

Jack moaned. His hands shook. Tears ran down his cheeks. "Father, please give me back my little boy. Give me back my wife. You have the power. I'll do whatever you ask—just save my family."

A Sioux mantra quietly welled up from inside Travis and boiled over like a pain-filled groan from the soul of the earth. Jack joined in. Dewey too. Their vigil fell in sync, back and forth, between this world and the next, as Travis moaned a healing song he had learned from their medicine man when he and Jack lost their parents in the car fire.

The clock ticked.

The second hand moved.

The rain fell.

The Father decided.

Chapter 12

Atlantic Ocean

Nina tumbled on wave after lonely wave of emotional chaos. Imprisoned in her steel cell, with nothing to keep her company but her thoughts and occasional visits from the bloody-knuckled pig, she fought for her sanity in the midst of great sorrow.

She could barely imagine what Hassan and his army of perverts had done to her little boy. Bits of dreams—no, nightmares—slinked around in the shadows of her cell, nipping at her consciousness. The terrorists snatching Barett from his bed and silencing him the only way they knew how. Shooting him up with drugs to keep him quiet. She teetered, beyond all limits of what she could handle.

When Nina sunk to the point of sobbing loneliness, when the millstone around her neck weighed a thousand pounds, the vision of her father popped into her head. He reminded her, "Barett is not dead." And with that, she stepped back from the cliff's edge with the tiniest glimmer of a smile.

Nina recalled the first time she met Jack. Everyone on the reservation knew who Jack and Travis were. When the train struck and killed the boys' cousin when Nina was six, the same age as Travis, Jack stood up for Travis when everyone else wanted to blame him. When Jack alertly pulled Travis from their burning car before their parents burned to death, Jack's stock rose some more. It seemed that whatever Jack did, he could do no wrong.

Nina was a crack athlete herself, especially in track. As she started winning events at high school track meets, Jack took notice. She set state records. Jack set state records. They started dating when she was a sophomore, and the rest was history. Nina smiled thinking of what Jack would think of her blowing a hole through Hasan's brother. Not a mother-sending-her-son-off-to-his-first-day-of-school smile, but an I'm-glad-I-killed-one-of-the-sons-of-bitches-with-the-shotgun smile.

Nina got back to her task at hand, singlemindedly honing the end of her toothbrush into a dagger, praying for another opportunity to even the score.

The ship shifted and squealed like a five-hundred-pound sow, creaking and groaning at every crack of the captain's whip, plowing ahead through endless blue-foam swells. Nina's bed vibrated constantly from the diesel engines below deck, which cranked out a steady twelve knots.

Suddenly, she perceived a distinct change in the ship's vibrations. The pitch of the engine dropped. Her room rocked less.

Footsteps raced past her room. Muffled voices yelled. The hair on the back of Nina's neck stood up. Was she next? Part of her wished she were. But she had fought through cancer surgery and chemotherapy and won. She knew she was a fighter. Her mind calculated and plotted as if it were on self-control. Her hands stopped shaking.

She heard a familiar voice outside her door. One that sent

shivers up her spine. Were they landing? Her toothbrush glowed in her hand. So did a three-foot strand of wire she had stripped from the bedsprings. She sat on her bed. Hid the wire under her pillow and formed a fist around her toothbrush. The steel hatch to her compartment swung open and clanged against the wall.

A gangly boy, no more than ten or eleven with long, tangled black hair, hurried in with a bowl of rice. Plain and brown. No utensils. Just a bowl. He seemed scared and out of breath. He kept looking over his shoulder like a beaten dog. A man-shadow lingered outside the door, but made no move to follow the boy in.

His frantic brown eyes looked straight into Nina's as he handed her the bowl. He glanced back over his shoulder, then back at Nina. He put a finger to his lips, shaking his head. She nodded. He pointed at her stomach, then brought his cupped hands up as if he were cuddling a baby, then motioned as if he threw the baby away.

Nina gasped, then started to quietly weep.

But the boy, after checking the door again, shook his head vigorously and wiped one of her tears.

He made another throwing motion, just like the last, but this time pointed at the floor. Then he made a different throwing motion, pointing to the same spot on the floor. The boy made a swimming motion with both arms, then a motion of grabbing onto something. He smiled. He pointed at himself swimming, then himself cuddling the baby.

Nina gasped, then cupped the boy's face in her hands, smiled, and kissed his forehead, understanding what he could not say. He had thrown Barett a life ring.

The instant the man outside the door yelled, the boy dashed out the door like a spooked squirrel. And along with his smile, Nina's smile vanished.

She heard some commotion and caught a fleeting glimpse of the boy flying sideways across the hallway, against the far wall outside her open door.

The man yelled in a foreign language. The boy pleaded back in the same. She heard him cry and plead the same words over and over. The man stepped into the doorway, his back to Nina. He growled something else slowly, then kicked and swung at the boy several times. The boy's cry grew weaker and weaker.

"Hey!" Nina yelled.

The kicking stopped. The bloody-knuckled man stood erect and crooked his head.

"That's right. I'm talking to you, asshole," said Nina.

He turned around, half-smiling and half-licking his chops as he strode through the doorway into her cell like a king to his court. He held a two-foot-long section of pipe an inch in diameter. The kind of pipe a ship had miles of, carrying water, heat, fuel, and electrical conduit from stem to stern. Mast to bilge.

He tapped the side of his leg with it. Then her metal bed frame. Then the steel wall above her head. Each clang sent a convulsion of dread through her, which she fought to repress with every ounce of courage she could muster.

Her father whispered in her ear. The ways of the Sioux from days gone by came back to her. Nina was a gladiator. The protector of the innocent, from people like the monster standing in front of her, banging his pipe around like the king-shit warden of a boys' prison.

He said something Nina did not understand. He pointed the end of his pipe at the middle of her chest and pressed her down until she was pinned to the bed under his full weight.

That she understood. Still dressed in her filthy nightgown, she fought back, but he was too strong. He took the pipe off her chest and pounded it against the bed frame, next to her ear, while he held her down with his other hand. Nina jerked, thinking he wanted to split her skull. He wanted something else.

One of his hooligans stuck his head in the room from the hallway, smiled, and stepped back out.

The bloody-knuckled man forced her mouth wide open and put the pipe between her teeth. He kept one hand on the pipe, pressing down. With the other he pulled his pants down, then jerked her gown up to her neck. For a split second he looked confused. No breasts where breasts should have been.

That was all the time Nina needed.

She twisted the toothbrush around in her hand and lunged up with all her might. She broke his grasp on the pipe and stabbed the sharp end of the homemade shiv into his neck, all the way in to the bristles.

He froze, spasmed, and lost his grip completely.

She quickly pulled out and stabbed again and again. She felt something pop. When she pulled out, bright-red blood, carotid artery blood, pumped from his neck like a water hose.

His look of shock quickly glazed over as he slumped forward, collapsing onto her, gurgling.

Adrenaline surged through Nina as her fight-or-flight instincts kicked in. "Get off me, you fucking asshole." She rolled him off her, onto the floor, as his eight liters of blood hemorrhaged from his vile body onto her, the bed, and the floor.

Nina stabbed the toothbrush into his neck one last time, for good measure, and left it. She sat up and screamed a blood-curdling shriek.

By then, the hooligans had arrived.

She grabbed the pipe and started swinging.

They took a second to check their dead friend, then pounced on her, pinning her arms and legs to the rack. She kept screaming until the first punch hit home. They jerked the strand of wire from her hand and wrapped it around her neck.

Everything slowed down to microseconds for Nina. She saw each punch coming in slow motion.

Her father stood above the men beating her, smiling and telling her, "Well done."

Jack and Barett were smiling too. She heard drums and felt a warm peace like never before. The punches continued, but did not hurt. It was as though it were happening to someone else. She smiled.

The hooligans stopped hitting her. Hassan walked in. He injected another syringe-full of clear liquid into the bend of her arm.

The room glowed with blinding light.

Nina closed her eyes.

Two down.

Chapter 13

Children's Hospital, Charleston, SC

Jack and Travis both shared visions of Nina that were remarkably similar as they slouched on the pleather sofas in the pediatric ICU waiting room in Charleston.

Travis saw Nina across the great divide too. And because Travis had spent more time being trained by the Sioux medicine men growing up and going to sweat lodge ceremonies, reading the spirits was something he was good at. There was one thing they both agreed on with 100 percent certainty: Nina was alive.

The only other thing they knew for sure: Barett was alive too, at least for now.

Once Dr. Robb warmed Barett to thirty-seven degrees Celsius, his heart was successfully defibrillated to a normal rhythm, and they stopped CPR. They admitted Barett to the pediatric ICU on a ventilator with a 30 percent chance of survival. Not to fully recover as normal. Just to survive.

Near-drowning patients needed to be kept in a drug-induced coma to give the brain time to recover from the swelling, seizures, and hypoxic damage from not getting enough oxygen. The most important organ of the body needed time, lots of time. Barett had nothing but time. He was in a drug-induced coma.

There were protocols to follow that would take days to weeks. For now, the doctors and nurses needed time to work a miracle and save Barett's life.

Barett had time. Jack and Dewey were out of time. Ghost Team was geared up and ready to go find Nina, Rami Salwa, and Rolf El-Hashem.

"I'll stay, Jack," said Travis. "I've been talking to Jaz back home, and she agrees with me. I'll stay with Barett, and you and Dewey go."

"I can't leave," said Jack. He dropped his head, then looked back up at Travis. "I can't stay either. I'll never be able to live with myself if I don't try."

"I've been talking to the doctors, and from what I know from my years in anesthesia, medical school, and research, I really feel Barett is going to be okay," said Travis. "I'll stay here with him. The baby isn't due for two months, and I'm pretty close to home if anything happens, anyway. In fact, Jaz and Dewey's wife, Suzy, may drive down for the weekend. It's only seven hours." Travis grabbed Jack by the arm. "You need to go, Jack. Who's going to find my sister-in-law if you don't?"

They sat in the same waiting room chairs they had staked out days earlier when they first arrived. Each patient's family respected the other's space, keeping an eye on one another's belongings when their time to visit came. An instant bond of hope and despair formed. There was lots of coffee, praying, and tears. Thank goodness for WiFi, smartphones, and TV.

Jack did not feel like a Navy SEAL as he waited for hours on end. He was Barett's dad. Travis was Barett's uncle. Dewey was Barett's honorary uncle. Uncle T. Uncle Dewey.

"It's where I belong, Jack. I can't save Nina. You guys can." He tapped his leg with his cane. "I'm a lover not a fighter, anyway. Remember?" said Travis with a proud smile.

"You still believe that crap?" Jack said with a loving, brotherly smile. "After everything you've been through. You're a better man than I."

"You can't do anything here, except go crazy," said Travis. "Sign the power of attorney so I can make sure things get done right, then go catch those bastards that did that to Barett. You'll know what I know. I'll make sure of it."

"He's right, Jack," said Dewey. "Barett's in good hands. Besides, we can always fly you back here at an instant's notice."

"Barett's a miracle. To find him hundreds of miles out to sea, at night . . ." Jack choked up. Feelings of guilt and abandonment flooded back. He sat for minutes with his face buried in his hands. "I gotta go say good-bye."

It felt like a lose-lose situation to Jack. Just as it felt every time he left Nina and Barett at home to go on a mission overseas.

Travis rested a hand on Jack's shoulder. "Barett's already a miracle. He's gonna make it, bro."

"I want to know everything that's going on. I'll call every day, and you can call me anytime, night or day." Jack handed Travis a card. "Call that number, and they'll track me down."

Jack stood and grabbed Travis for a bear hug. He cleared his throat. "They say things happen in threes. Last year we found you. Barett is next door. Let's go find Nina."

Jack went back to the unit to see Barett one last time and to talk with his nurses and doctors.

Out of his pant pocket, he pulled a feather and placed it on Barett's pillow. It was a tiny white-and-gray feather Travis had pulled from his hospital pillow the year before and gave Jack as good luck. It did not look like anything important, but to Jack it meant everything.

Eagle feathers meant everything to a Native American warrior as a symbol of bravery. Barett had shown extreme bravery in ways unknown to anyone during his captivity and recovery. In Jack's mind, Barett deserved the feather more than anyone.

Jack also pulled out his cougar totem and placed it on Barett's pillow. He bowed his head and said a prayer while holding Barett's tiny hand, hoping that it would not be the last time he would see his little boy in this world.

After a few words with Barett's nurse, and one last hug for Travis, he and Dewey rolled out of the ICU waiting room.

Jack turned and gave a thumbs-up before hustling to catch up to Dewey, who was already walking down the hospital corridor toward their helicopter ride back to Virginia.

Travis was suddenly alone, surrounded by silence and the two empty chairs next to him. He checked the clock. It would be hours before Barett's next doctor update. The same families were in the waiting room as yesterday, plus one new teenage mom and her parents.

In the unsettling solitude of the ICU waiting room, Travis's old demons found traction and clawed their way to the surface of his consciousness. Visions of his cousin being struck and cut in half by a freight train, right in front of Travis, when they were first graders, had tormented him his entire life. Everyone in the tribe blamed Travis after rumors spread that horseplay was involved. Travis and Jack both saw their cousin trip and fall under the train.

Travis had tried to reach out and grab his hand, which is what the others probably interpreted as Travis shoving their cousin. Either way, Jack was labeled as the good Gunn, and Travis the bad one. He left Grandpa Joe's and Grandma Bear Nose's home as soon as he graduated from high school and never looked back.

After that, Travis devoted his life to punishing himself, even though he had become a doctor. Tormented by guilt, he sank into alcoholism, drug addiction, and womanizing, just like his dad. There was no escape. He could not control himself. He ended up forfeiting his medical license after failing rehabilitation twice. He got a second chance by moving to Dubai and working as an anesthesiologist at Dr. Rolf El-Hashem's world-famous plastic surgery center. Rolf had big connections and big plans. The whole time of their *friendship*, Travis was just another pawn in Rolf's worldwide game of jihad; he just did not know it.

Travis stopped beating himself up for all his past mistakes once Rolf's terrorists grabbed him in Pakistan. Instead of wishing he were dead, as he had been doing for so many years, all he wanted to do was make it through another day. Survive another round of torture. For some reason—one he was sure he would never know—he survived when so many others, far more worthy than him, had died.

The mental anguish he suffered as a Taliban prisoner left scars—no, gaping holes—in his ability to see things as they are, not as they were. He stayed permanently trapped in that terrorist cave, duct-taped to a chair, getting his head bashed in by Rolf El-Hashem's rifle butt, a victim of post-traumatic-stress disorder, paralyzed by fear.

Sure, Travis had made progress in his PTSD therapy and rehabilitation of his back, but he preferred to stay busy. Going back to work practicing anesthesia would help. Having a baby would definitely help. Anything was better than sifting through old memories, over and over.

Jaz had become his beacon of hope, arriving in his hospital room on a billowy cloud a year earlier, as fragrant and lovely as the cherry blossoms of spring. She helped him stop blaming himself for the death of his cousin. For the car accident that killed his drunk parents. For fleeing the reservation and abandoning Grandpa Joe and Grandma Bear Nose, Jack, and the Sioux way of life.

Every time Travis hit rock bottom, she was there to catch him, like his own personal safety net. Every time he passed a new milestone in his therapy, she was there too. They explored every nook and cranny in the rehab hospital, talking, laughing, and walking miles a day.

Jaz reminded Travis often that she respected him before she fell in love with him for something Travis had done, but failed to remember. As Ghost Team's CIA liaison, Jaz had witnessed Travis putting everything on the line, including his own life, in an incredible display of bravery when it mattered most. The CIA would never have been able to track down and wipe out the security council if it had not been for Travis. Swapping Travis for Rolf's father and the tracking chip inside him helped the CIA locate their intact security council before they dispersed to carry out their grand jihad. Without him, the grand jihad dirty bombs would have killed thousands of Americans and changed life as they knew it forever.

In Navy SEAL and CIA circles, he was a hero. In Jaz's circle, he was a hero. In Travis's circle, he was just holding on, taking it one day at a time.

Who knew? Maybe watching after Barett while Jack and Dewey went to find Nina would be good for him. Maybe hanging around the hospital would be a good influence. Help him figure out the next step in his life. Deep down, he had to admit he was tired of feeling like the victim. He wanted revenge too, just like Jack. He wanted to stop the bastards from killing more innocent people.

He had lost his cousin, his parents, and his grandparents. He never got to say "good-bye" or "I'm sorry." He did not want Jack to go through the same nightmare. Not without a fight.

Travis got up and went into ICU to camp out next to Barett's bed and start putting the pieces of his broken life back together.

Chapter 14

Ivory Coast, Africa

"Intel coming in from multiple NSA and Mossad sources point to Timbuktu, Mali. The NSA's Trojan horse started kicking out data, and we've been able to tap into Salwa's phone. Hassan El-Hashem is reportedly there, so it's a good bet Nina is there too, if she's alive. And from the phone intercepts coming out of Timbuktu to Pakistan, it sounds like she is alive." Jack looked around into the eyes of his best men. Nobody flinched. Nobody said a word.

The floor hatch closed, and the compartment started to flood with saltwater. It smelled like the inside of a seaweed-washing machine. Mack, Snake, Dozer, T-bone, and Dewey—Jack's team—all looked back at Jack through their swim goggles.

Mack got his name for obvious reasons. Even by SEAL standards, he had a menacing look, like a Mack truck in your rearview mirror. A big, black eighteen-wheeler riding your rear bumper, blowing his air horn and flipping you off. He had a knack for electronics and killing.

T-bone, Mack's swim buddy, had been a D-1 wrestler at Minnesota before joining the SEALs after 9/11. Educated and as focused as a pit bull, he got his tag after spinning out of control in his marina-blue 1966 Chevelle 396 SS and wrapping it around a hundred-year-old oak tree. The team never let him live it down. His specialties were explosives and killing.

Dozer could fall asleep anywhere, anytime. Born and raised in Alabama, he could shoot the dick off a fly at a thousand yards, or so it seemed. He was hard to rattle, but when he got riled up, look out. He killed efficiently and matter-of-factly.

Snake, Dozer's swim buddy, was tall and lanky, different from the rest. A great climber and sneaker, he did a lot of their recon and knife work. He was the silent-but-deadly type. Only one thing freaked him out: snakes.

Jack continued, "Obviously, no one can know we're carrying out a mission in Mali, hence the backdoor approach we're so fond of. We hit the beach tonight, link up with some local contractors we've used in the past, catch a bird, stay out of sight, and hit 'em hard tomorrow night. When we do catch up with these bastards, it ain't gonna be pretty."

The freezing cold water was up to the knees of their wetsuits and climbing.

"I don't give a shit about the rules of combat or the Geneva Convention or these bastards' constitutional rights or anything else, for that matter. We're the judge, jury, and executioner. Period. There's a price to be paid."

"We do what needs to be done, just like always," said Snake.

"I'm in," said Mack with a twinkle in his eye.

"Roger that," said Dozer. "You'd do the same for me."

"We all would," said T-bone. "Family is sacred. Nobody fucks with our families."

They put their rebreather mouthpieces in and inhaled as the compartment flooded to the ceiling. Bubbles wiggled free and zigzagged to the top of their LED-lit human aquarium. They gave Jack the thumbs-up and settled into their seats for the ride. It was a great time to think, like the meditation time of a long run. And if you asked any one of them what they were thinking of, it would not have been of the mission, it would have been of home. Home and family was what they were fighting for. Defend the defenseless and protect what was theirs.

Jack and his team had come aboard the submarine a day earlier after catching an eight-hour hop out of Little Creek, Virginia, to the nuclear-powered aircraft carrier the *USS George H. W. Bush*, making its way south along the west coast of Africa.

Jack had called Travis from the *Bush* and got encouraging news. After the doctors started weaning Barett's sedation, they found his EEG brain waves looked "very promising." There was a chance they would have Barett off the ventilator in a few days. If everything went according to plan, Jack assured Travis that he hoped to find Nina and be back home by then. He felt a huge weight lift off his shoulders.

A well-coordinated helicopter lift from a Navy Knighthawk got them from the *Bush* to the *USS Virginia*, which surfaced at night. Jack's team fast-roped down to the *Virginia*, which then dove back down to five hundred feet, the only place an attack sub captain was ever happy. Jack's team ate a pre-mission meal and caught some shut-eye while the sub silently crept to Ghost Team's launch point.

The transport module for the SDV—swimmer delivery vehicle—was harnessed to the top of the nuclear-powered attack submarine submerged fifty feet below the surface of the Gulf of

Guinea, in international waters ten miles off the shores of Pointe Wameno, Ivory Coast.

Crammed into the forty-foot-long steel transport module were two electric-powered SDVs, Jack and his team, dry bags stuffed with their war gear, a square package of shrink-wrapped hundred-dollar bills, and the SDV drivers. They would only need one SDV for the night's mission. Once everything and everyone was stowed and locked down, they killed the lights. The nine-foot-round rear hatch of the transport module opened to the vast darkness of the Atlantic Ocean. The *Virginia*'s launch team of divers guided the SDV free of the hull.

The propeller, more the size of a ski boat's than a submarine's, spun slowly enough to count the revolutions, at first. As the whir of the electric motor increased, like a dentist's drill going from a growling idle to a teeth-grinding whine, the propeller's RPMs increased to three thousand and pushed the SDV away from the safety of the *Virginia*. Leaving a tiny trail of bubbles and turbulence, Jack and his team of five marauders headed northwest toward the Horn of Africa.

Coming up to twenty feet below the surface and swells, there was little for Jack to do but breathe and think as they plowed ahead for an hour. As the sound of his breathing and heart fell into a rhythm, he started to get an ominous feeling he could not shake. It was as if he were walking through a house of mirrors with a different nightmare around every corner.

Around the first corner was Nina. A hand smothered her mouth and nose. Her eyes screamed for air. Her head thrashed back and forth. Jack tracked the knife blade across her throat back to the handle, the fingers, the arm. Finally, to the maniacally laughing face of Rolf, still dressed in his prisoner clothes. Rolf cursed Jack, then looked back to Nina as he stretched his knife all the way to her opposite shoulder and drew it across her windpipe, laughing all the time while Nina shrieked.

In the next mirror, Jack saw himself as a ten-year-old boy tugging with all his might on the door handle of a burning Chevy Impala whose shattered back window he had already crawled out of, pulling Travis along behind. Flames roared from the engine, the hood long gone. His dad slumped against the steering wheel, already cooking. His mom's clothes smoldered and then burst into flames. Her panicky eyes held his gaze. Her hand pried his off the door and shoved him back as she screamed, "Run, Jack, run." The car mushroomed into a fireball.

Jack turned away, only to see Travis writhing on the ground in pain, under a searing light. His mouth taped shut. His eyes taped open. Blood streamed down his face. His wrists and ankles were duct-taped together. Sweat and blood mixed with dirt smeared his face. A hatchet was buried in the dirt next to his head.

Jack saw a hand wrap around the handle and rock the hatchet up and down until it broke free. Dirt clumps showered Travis's head and eyes. A man in a dishdasha kneeled next to Travis, his back to Jack. He raised the hatchet high above his head. The man, whom Jack recognized as Rolf, momentarily glanced back at Jack over his shoulder, smiling. Then Rolf looked back to his business at hand, as if unconcerned that Jack watched.

The electric-motor whir dropped slightly in pitch, joggling Jack back to reality. The SDV angled toward the surface. Jack checked his watch and the display panel. They were right on schedule.

The SDV halted outside the surf break, a half mile off a remote stretch of the Ivory Coast beach. Side hatches slid back and locked open. Jack and the rest of his team unloaded their gear from the SDV and switched their waterproof weapons to hot as they treaded water, kicking their fins up and down.

Jack imagined Rolf sitting far away in some Pakistani compound, drinking piña coladas with his eleven suitcase nukes, and counting 55 million dollars. All thanks to Jack.

Go ahead, you prick. Relax. Drink up.

Jack side-kicked through the warm water, towing his dry bag behind. They all put fins on the sandy bottom at the same time, while constantly scanning the beach and trees with their NODs—night observation devices—looking for threats.

The two-foot surf lapped up on a lifeless strand of beach framed by palm trees and tall grasses. Hot breezes from the distant Sahara smelled of coffee or cocoa. A crescent moon approached the eastern horizon. Sagittarius the Archer held its position directly overhead, centered around Orion's Belt.

The Native American side of Jack revered Sagittarius. Seeing it brought back fond memories of hunting deer with a bow and arrow. Of feeling Grandpa Joe's massive hand over his, teaching him the correct grip and throwing motion of a spear. Of sitting around a powwow fire and listening to Grandpa Joe tell old family stories.

Jack had no time for Sagittarius tonight. Old stories either. He was writing a story. One he knew the ending of—at least the part where Rolf died a miserable but certain death. The other parts were still a little foggy.

He put Rolf out of his mind and focused on Nina. Ghost Team had a long way to go, and they were on their own, headed into very hostile territory. It was the kind of territory where if anything went wrong, the president of the United States would deny everything. It was the kind of territory where if anyone discovered

Jack and his team, they would simply die and wither away into the sands of the Sahara, never to be heard from again. The kind of territory Jack loved.

The ancients were stirring within Jack. He felt their drum beat in his heart. Instincts inherited from Sitting Bull came to life. Experiences from years of leading the SEALs played over and over in his head. Jack's team had memorized their mission plan. They were ready to go.

Back on dry ground, beneath a stand of palm trees, he stowed his gear. He stuck his throwing knife in the sheath on his belt. Put his nine-millimeter in its holster. Slipped his MOLLE vest on with its pockets stuffed with death toys. He chambered a round into his HK416 and slung the pack carrying the bundle of cash over his left shoulder.

Rolf would have to wait. Jack had more pressing needs at the moment. He had a wife to save and a whole bunch of assholes named El-Hashem and Salwa to kill.

CHAPTER 15

Ivory Coast, Africa

Ghost Team patrolled a couple of miles inland on foot through vast rubber tree plantations. Tall trees. No brush. Pitch black. Easy walking. It felt good to stretch their legs and warm up.

The fragrance reminded Jack of haying time in Montana. Cobalt-blue skies speckled with cotton-ball clouds. Fields of sweet clover running as far as the eye could see. As Jack stalked around rubber trees, he smiled at the thought that at that very moment some boy in Montana might be stretched out on his back in the middle of a green clover field, without a care in the world other than if the clouds looked like a horse or dragon.

He grabbed a protein bar from a leg pocket and shoveled it in along with some water through the sip tube Velcroed over his shoulder. At 230 pounds and carrying another fifty pounds, he burned through calories like a triathlete. He wolfed down two more bars.

Trucks approached from the northwest. Two sets of headlights bounced over roots and rocks, grinding back and forth between first and second gear. Ghost Team split up, three and three, on either side of the one-lane dirt road.

"Last chance," said Jack into his microphone. "Door's still open," meaning they could all jump back into the ocean, get in the submarine, and go home.

Jack heard five clicks in his ear bud. Everyone was all in. As the trucks drew up on Ghost Team's position and stopped, boots hit the ground. Men fanned out. The engines went silent. Everything went silent, except for the crickets, frogs, or whatever else slithered, crept, or flew through the Ivory Coast forest. The driver of the lead truck got out, lit up, and leaned against his heavily modified Toyota Land Cruiser.

Jack gave the team two clicks, followed by one. Simultaneously, all six SEALs jumped up onto the road.

"Drop your weapons," ordered Jack.

"Why, Jack Gunn—you old son of a bitch," said the smoker with a distinctly French accent.

"How ya doing, Vic," Jack said to the man he knew as Victor, a mercenary the CTF had contracted with in the past to take care of regional issues when it would have been impractical or impossible for Jack to send in a team. Victor was obviously ex-special forces. He hired skilled guns and got the job done no matter how messy. And all for a fair price.

"You got my money?" said Victor.

"Hi, Jack. How's it going?" Jack said mockingly.

Victor smiled. "Hi, Jack. How's it going? Ya got my money?"

"Good to see you too, old friend." Jack handed over a bundle from the money pack. "Fifty now. Fifty later. Just like we agreed."

Victor took the wad and bowed his head in thanks. "How much funny-money you got in there?"

"Let's get moving. Moon's rising," said Jack.

"Why don't you—"

"Let's go, Vic," Jack said, staring Victor into submission. "We've got a bird to catch."

"You're the boss."

Jack trusted Victor about as far as he could throw him. Mercenaries like Vic would kill anybody, for anybody, if the price was right. They would just as happily do Boko Haram's dirty work as Jack's.

They bounced and bobbed for a couple hours through the dark on plantation dirt roads, never seeing another vehicle. Rubber plantations had replaced cocoa plantations in many African nations, as rubber was easier to grow, took less work, and yielded more money.

Men to work the fields were hard to find, and poverty was as chronic as hunger. Children abandoned school to earn bread money for their families. Child trafficking from neighboring countries, like Burkina Faso and Mali, was lucrative. Thousands of children went missing every year, gone to work on the plantations.

Child slaves in the twenty-first century. It was a big problem. But it was not Jack's problem. Not unless the president ordered him to shut it down.

As they got farther inland, plantations gave way to rain forest, slowing the two-vehicle convoy down to a crawl as it maneuvered over tree roots, mud holes, streams, and of course, lizards.

Africa had lizards of all sizes and colors. And they all seemed to be mating in the middle of the road, frozen in place by the headlights. Jack's Ivorian driver steered right down the middle the best he could, no matter what lay in his path. It was a bumpy, crunchy, messy ride.

"Salwa's done all that? He got the money, the nukes, Rolf El-Hashem, and your wife?" Victor asked. There was no mistaking from the sarcastic tone in his voice what he thought of the world-renowned Jack Gunn, terrorist exterminator extraordinaire. Victor glanced at the other half of his money, securely resting on the floorboard in Jack's backpack, between his boots, under his gun. "I always took him for a low-ender," Victor said, back in his normal tone.

"He'll be a dead-ender when I'm finished," said Jack.

"Best guess, Salwa's holed up in Timbuktu. No visual confirmation yet, though," said Victor. "My old team's pulling out. Al-Qaeda's moving back in, just like before."

"What about the RAF or the Brits?"

"Brits are long gone, and the RAF couldn't fight their way out of a paper bag. Most are deserting. There's more money to be made smuggling food, gas, cigarettes, and cocaine, anyway."

"Good," Jack said more bluntly than intended.

"They're cutting off the hands of thieves, stoning adulterers, whipping women who won't cover their faces," said Victor.

Jack stared straight ahead.

"They're murdering Christians, for Christ's sake," Victor pleaded. "What's so fucking good about that?"

"No one will be watching over our shoulder. Kill whoever we need to. I'll get my scalps, one way or another." Jack thumbed his knife blade and slid it back into its sheath. "Somebody's going to pay."

"Roger that," said Victor.

They bounced along through the forest. The warm air smelled like rotting bark as they climbed away from the coast and plantations below. The moon hung at eleven o'clock.

"How much longer?"

"Another hour."

"Pull over. I need to take a piss," said Jack.

It seemed Jack wasn't the only one. The safari-style Land Cruisers stopped in the middle of the road. The roof tarp had been rolled back, uncovering the second row of seats, so two of Jack's men could stand as they drove, watching their flanks for threats with night scopes. Victor's men sat in the rear seats, dozing. Everyone piled out for a quick pit stop, then saddled up and moved out again.

"What the—" Snake yelled and collapsed into his seat, his rifle butt banging off Mack's shoulder sitting next to him.

The driver hit the brakes. T-bone stood up next to Mack, scanning for muzzle flashes. Jack swiveled around from the shotgun seat with his flashlight.

Snake grabbed his ankle and tore away at his pant leg, trying to get to skin. "Something fucking bit me."

That got everyone's attention. Flashlights turned on immediately. Their beams shined everywhere. Boots shuffled, clumping the floorboard like a Mexican hat dance.

"I got it," said one of Victor's men, holding up a three-foot-long snake, its green body wrapped around his arm, a hint of blue skin visible under its scales.

"What is it? What'll I do?" said Snake, fingering the fang marks on his ankle.

"Must have dropped in when we stopped," said Victor.

"One of yours, Snake," quipped Jack with a chuckle, the first one he had in he could not remember how long. It felt good, but was short lived.

"Fuck you, Jack."

"You could do what the Ivorians always do," said the driver.

"Yeah, what's that?" asked Snake.

"Everyone knows that snakes are obviously scared of worms. Cut a worm in half, and put the tail end on your bite. Let it wriggle until it falls off. After that, mash the head and tail sections into your bite. By killing the snake's most feared enemy, the snake's venom will have no power over you. You'll be fine in two or three days." The driver ended with a smile and continued down the road.

"That's the biggest bunch of horseshit I ever heard," said Snake. "Jack?"

"You heard the man."

"You're an asshole."

"Take it easy, Snake," said Jack. "It's just a tree snake. Non-venomous. Put some bacitracin and a Band-Aid on it. Your biggest problem is infection."

"Fucking snakes, lizards. I hate this place already."

"Quit your bitching. We just got here," said Jack. "You'll have a lot more reasons to hate it by the time we leave."

Even Victor's men agreed with that.

They rumbled on for another hour before veering off onto an overgrown road that resembled a forgotten jungle path. Branches scraped the sides and top of the jeeps as they plowed forward through the dense foliage.

Snake pulled the roof shut.

Another fifteen minutes, and they punched through the jungle to an opening. A large, ancient-looking helicopter waited for them in the predawn light, perched on a clear-cut rise surrounded by dense jungle. A half hour after that, they were airborne, heading due north, just above the treetops.

Next stop, Mali.

Chapter 16

Timbuktu, Mali

It's hard to disguise height and brawn and whiteness. Even if Jack wasn't white-white, he was a lot whiter than black. And the city of Timbuktu was as black as they came. Anyone white was from somewhere else. Anyone black had other things to worry about, now that the French and all the other white people had pulled out. They had abandoned ship. Took their talk of peace and hope and went home.

Traveling in two open Land Cruisers—like the ones they had left behind in the Ivory Coast jungle along with Victor, his men, and fifty thousand more dollars—was no longer an option for Jack and his mostly white Ghost Team. Mack and Dozer were fine; they fit right in riding shotgun with the Malian drivers Victor had recommended. Jack—along with pale faces Snake, T-bone, and Dewey—rode in the rear of their cargo trucks, hidden from view.

The seventy-year-old leaf springs of the WWII trucks rode as if there were no shock absorbing going on at all. It was pure metal on metal. Pure pain and cursing from the white guys in back every time they creamed another pothole.

Since night had set in and they had not seen another soul for an hour, the drivers pushed the green, rusty behemoths to their limits. Headlights were completely out of the question for their clandestine mission, so the drivers used night vision goggles, as did copilots Mack and Dozer. Mack and Dozer tried to spot upcoming obstacles, and the drivers tried to avoid them. But at that speed, if they managed to stay on the road, Jack was happy.

In the fourteenth century, Timbuktu was the center of commerce and Islamic culture. Seven hundred years later, Timbuktu was at the end of the road. The desolate and dangerous Sahara stretched for hundreds of miles to the north, east, and west.

The Saharan branch of Al-Qaeda had seized control of all Mali lands north of Timbuktu, following a military coup in 2007, and had instituted *sharia law.* The bad kind of law where if you did not do what they said to do, justice was swift and severe. They were in control. The land was too big and they were too slippery.

Rami Salwa led a splinter group called the Sharia Battalion. They ruthlessly punished the people of Timbuktu, sparing no man, woman, or child from their wrath. The same Rami Salwa that Jack was looking to kill, right after he got Nina back.

"Pull over," said Jack to the driver through a peephole from the back of the truck.

Timbuktu's compound walls rose from the midnight sand two miles ahead. A pair of headlights approached a mile off. Sand blew across the rocky road, blurring the final six inches above the ground like a moving cloud.

"Welcoming committee?" said Dewey.

"I doubt it," said Jack. "Whatever happens, keep it quiet." He heard five clicks in his ear. He powered up the satphone and placed a call to Martinez back at CTF control in Virginia.

"What about the *Bush*?" asked Jack.

"Headed up to the Mediterranean. Everyone's nervous with haji holding eleven nukes. You know he's not going to wait," Martinez said.

"Not even a couple choppers for evac?" asked Jack.

"They're long gone, and you're too far up river. Anything local?"

"We're just about to find out," said Jack, checking the approaching headlights again. "Any useful intel out of Timbuktu? Internet, satellites, anything?"

"No flyovers with everything heating up to the north," said Martinez. "All birds have been tasked to the Middle East. Haji shut down the Internet in Timbuktu. We're getting sporadic triangulations on Salwa's phone, though."

"And?"

"He's in northeast Timbuktu, all right, but we can't nail him any closer than that. Hard to crack Mali's phone net, and it appears you're having a sandstorm that's really screwing with reception," said Martinez.

"Not the only thing it's screwing with." Jack cleared sand from his ear.

"Very little chatter, but we believe Nina's with Salwa, Jack." Martinez sounded hopeful.

Jack paused a moment as a lump of fury swelled in his throat. "Anything else?"

"We believe the man who abducted Nina and Barett is Hassan El-Hashem."

A shiver ran up Jack's spine. A line of El-Hashem faces formed in his brain. "Location?"

"A compound in the northeast sector of Timbuktu. Probably the same one as Salwa."

"Anything else about Nina?"

"Nothing other than we believe she's alive from what the interpreters read between the lines of their two phone calls."

Brakes squealed alongside their truck as the southbound truck stopped to talk.

"We got company. Later."

"Roger that. Be careful, Jack," Martinez said and terminated the call.

Snake, T-bone, and Dewey flipped their safeties off. Snake pointed his weapon at the truck driver's head through the canvas—or at least his best guess of where the driver's skull was. Jack held his index finger up to his lips and pulled out his knife.

The driver from the other truck yelled something in what sounded like French. There were two guys in the front seat. Judging by the tone of his voice, the driver was in a hurry. Jack's Malian driver shouted a question back. The wind's howl swallowed their words before they left their lips.

Jack checked Mack, riding shotgun, through the peephole to the front cab of the truck. Mack was eyes on target, finger on trigger. Dewey and T-bone crouched by the tailgate flap, ready to jump from the back of the truck. Jack imagined Dozer, who was riding shotgun in their second truck convoying right behind Jack's, was getting ready for action the same as Mack. If they had their choice, they would dispose of their French friends quickly, but it probably was not going to go down quietly.

Jack snuck under the tarp and out the back of the truck, knife in hand. He dropped to the swirling sand and circled up the passenger side of his truck. Jack's goggles protected his eyes, and the bandana covered his nose and mouth. His spider was quiet. No guns were pointed in his direction.

He crept across the front of his truck, around the back of Frenchy's, and lifted their rear flap, which buffeted and popped in the hot wind like a snapping towel. Frenchy was running a load of weapons and ammo. No heat signals. There was still just the two of them.

Jack signaled Mack with a zero sign, then motioned he would move up to the passenger side. Mack interrupted the conversation between his driver and Frenchy with some choice English profanity yelled from one truck to the other. Their French-speaking friends started squirming around, reaching for their radio. They gunned their engine.

Jack jerked open the passenger door. "Not so fast, Pierre."

Jack reached in and nailed the man riding in the passenger seat with a hard right to his jaw, which seemed to knock him unconscious. Jack's silhouette filled the far window of Frenchy's truck as he stepped up on the running board. He grabbed the slumped-over man's collar, jerked him back, and held him up with his left elbow. With his right hand, Jack stretched his razor-sharp knife across the dazed passenger's neck.

"Kill the engine. Kill the lights," Jack said to the driver, threatening him with the tip of his knife and a growl that meant business in any language.

The obviously shaken driver did as he was told and put his hands up. Dewey jumped out of the back of the truck and ran to the front, where he jammed his gun barrel into the side of the driver's head.

"Where are you boys off to in the middle of the night? Don't you know the desert is a dangerous place to be?" asked Dewey.

They said nothing.

Jack's Malian driver repeated the question. Sand blew through the cab. They still said nothing.

Dewey punched the driver in the side of the head with the heel of his free hand. Jack dragged the wobbly passenger out of the truck and stood him up against the side of the open cab.

"I don't think you understand, you weaselly son of a bitch. You are going to die here if you don't start talking," said Jack as he sheathed his knife. "I don't think these boys are French at all. What do you think?"

"Nah. They're definitely not French. Too ugly," said Dewey with a laugh. "That's some nice shit you boys are carrying. Who're you running weapons for?"

Dewey's smile was gone. He pulled the driver out by his collar and dragged him around to the back of the truck. Sand had already drifted up against the truck tires. The lights of Timbuktu in the distance had disappeared, swallowed in the building fury of the storm.

Jack dragged his passenger around from the other side and shoved his face into the cargo hold.

"He asked you a question, jerkwad. Who are you working for?"

Jack shouldered his rifle and pressed the barrel against the base of the passenger's skull, pointing directly across his brain at his eye socket.

"You're working for Rami Salwa, right? Where is he? Where's Hassan El-Hashem?" Jack screamed.

The two men pleaded that they didn't know any of those people. That they didn't know anything. They were just driving the truck from point A to point B. They didn't know what was inside.

"Get on the ground," ordered Jack.

The two prisoners looked at each other, then did what they were told.

"You heard him. On your bellies, you stupid sons of bitches," yelled Dewey. "Hands behind your back. Cross your legs. Head to the side."

They turned their heads away from the wind. Dewey zip-tied their wrists and ankles.

"One last question," said Jack.

The prisoners struggled to breathe in the swirling sand, but said nothing.

Jack got down on his knees, between the two prisoners, a pistol in each hand and pressed into their necks. He leaned forward on the guns, his head inches from their ears. In a deep, controlled growl, he said, "Have you seen a white lady?"

They lifted and turned their heads to briefly look at each other, then started shaking their heads. Jack was no rookie. He knew thc signs. He had his answer.

"Where is she?"

They started pleading again. "I don't know anyth—"

Jack and his men knew each other and their situation without having to spell it out. They were all alone, deep into enemy territory with no room for errors or second-guessing. Even though the president of the United States of America had sanctioned their mission, no one had their backs and no one was coming to bail them out. If some low-level El-Hashem terrorists had the misfortune of stumbling into the middle of Jack Gunn's rescue mission in the middle of the Sahara, threatening the very lives of Jack and his team, plus Nina's, and if they were discovered . . .well, it was not

Jack's problem. Their time had come. Judge, jury, and executioner.

Jack pulled both triggers. The wind snuffed the bark of the guns.

"Fucking assholes." He stood. "Throw 'em in, and wire the bitch." Jack braced himself against the crosswind and looked toward Timbuktu. "Move out."

Chapter 17

Timbuktu, Mali

Jack and Dewey fought the blistering headwind, riding the electric motocross bikes Dozer had hauled up from Bamako in the back of their second truck. They angled across the desert to get outside the northern edge of Timbuktu. They were a full two miles from Snake and Dozer, positioned on the southern edge of the Saharan town; and a mile from Mack and T-bone, stationed near the main entrance to the city's center on the western edge, halfway in between.

On a perfectly still night, the loudest sound the prototype Zero MMX motorcycle made was a variable-pitch whine, like an ultra-quiet food blender changing gears. Missing was the unmistakable pop and howl of a two-stroke motorcycle engine winding up and down the RPM scale, like a Kawasaki motocross bike wringing it out. A three-foot antennae extended out of each SEAL's backpack, connected to an LED screen on the handlebars and wireless Bluetooth earbuds.

Matte-black finish. No intake or exhaust heat signals. Infrared lights. Stealth was its middle name. It made barely a whisper on a quiet night. In a violent West African *harmattan*, it was invisible.

Any exposed skin would have been shredded in Mother Nature's sand blizzard. Only crazy people went out in a harmattan. The abandoned streets looked like the lunar surface: gray, stony, and lifeless.

When they were all in position, Jack signaled, "Three. Two. One. Execute."

Frenchy's truck, which Mack and T-bone had parked in the city center with its two dead occupants, erupted like Mount Vesuvius. Flames and secondary explosions rocketed up and out. RPGs careened wildly in all directions, like a fire in a Chinese fireworks factory.

All six SEAL riders moved out into the deserted streets of the Al-Qaeda–controlled city, their ears trained to the cell phone calls they were intercepting. As they drove, they also watched the LED screens on their handlebars, which lit up in a sudden flurry of phone activity caused by the explosions, just as Jack predicted.

Al-Qaeda was like anyone else. No one wanted to go out in the storm, but everyone would want to know what exploded. Curiosity kills the cat. Their screens showed the locations of the phone callers they were eavesdropping on.

In complete and utter darkness, they rapidly patrolled the back streets of Timbuktu in grid-like fashion, systematically criss-crossing the one-by-two-mile city of mud compound walls and desert scrub. There were no streetlights or electricity except for the houses of those wealthy enough to own their own generators. There was no moon. Not tonight. Only sand. Lots and lots of skin-peeling sand.

Jack worked the northeast quadrant, known for its bigger, more opulent compounds and the signals Martinez had intercepted. The bigger the compound, the bigger the man. Like cars and boats and guns.

He rolled around the corner of a ten-foot-high compound wall to come face to face with two jeeps moving quickly toward his position. He planted his left boot, kicked out his right, and cranked the throttle. The bike hula-hooped around his leg, and he took off around the corner, the same way he had come.

Jack hunched low behind the handlebars. No lights. No sound. His face was inches from the LED screen when it started flashing. His earphones crackled from the bluebug installed on Salwa's phone. He strained to listen to the male voices, but reception was sketchy and Jack's Arabic rusty.

The jeep engines revved as they fishtailed around the corner, chasing Jack. Just before their headlights caught him, Jack banked left around another corner, then another in the opposite direction. He disappeared into the maze of alleys leading away from the target compound.

He picked up the conversation between the two jeeps on his scanner. They weren't sure if they had seen anything. They headed back to base.

Ghost Team quickly rendezvoused on Jack's position. Salwa's phone signal dropped off Jack's screen. No more chatter. No more leads. Just a weak signal for a few seconds along the south wall.

Mack gave T-bone a leg up to boost him over the compound wall. T-bone unlocked the gate, and they drove all six motorcycles into Salwa's compound and closed the gate again. Or more accurately, the wind slammed the gate shut. Mack stayed out of sight, near the gate, to cover them against counterattacks and recharge their bikes with their portable generator.

Nothing moved in the central courtyard but mini-tornadoes of Saharan sand whipped into a frenzy. No sentries. No dogs. No floodlights. The SEALs' electronic gadgets and technological gizmos, while great at getting them on target, had done all they could.

It was time for the SEALs to do what they were trained to do. Use the miserable conditions to their advantage, hit with intense violence, grab Nina, and if Jack had anything to say about it, kill everyone responsible, then slip away in the mayhem.

"It's go time, boys," said Jack as they huddled out of the wind. "This is as far down range as we've ever gone. Even if we kick ass, we've still got to evac three hundred miles just to catch a plane. I didn't come all this way to go home empty-handed. So, you boys see things going bad, get the hell out. I'll take out as many as I can."

"We ain't leaving you or anybody else behind, dipshit. We're SEALs," said Dewey.

"Dewey, I'm ordering you to get these boys home."

"Forget about it, Jack. Court-martial me when we get back—I don't really give a shit. We're family. Nina and Barett too," said Dewey. "You'd do the same for any one of us, so let's go get some while the getting's good, and stop fucking around."

Snake, Dozer, and T-bone nodded. They bumped fists in the middle of the huddle with Jack and Dewey. There was a brief lull in the storm. They took off toward the main building. NODs on, weapons hot.

Normally, Jack carried 120 rounds into battle. Too much ammo weighed him down, and the choppers would always drop more ammo if they got into a firefight. But there were no friendly choppers within a thousand miles. As big and hard and fit as Jack was, five hundred rounds clipped to his belt and stuffed into leg pockets were a load. But even with that extra weight, he moved with the fluidity of a cantering German shepherd. All business. Head steady. Sharp teeth. Vicious bite. Eyes locked on. A human heat-seeking missile.

His team would follow him wherever he led, like musketeers. All for one and one for all. But with that loyalty came great responsibility.

Each of his men had a wife and family. Jack knew all their faces and names. What grade they were in. What cartoons they watched. What their favorite fast foods were. Home was all guys talked about during the long stretches down range. When one of Jack's guys went down, and they had, it hit hardest back home.

Jack and all his guys lived with death. It was part of life. Part of their job defending the nation from terrorism. If they were afraid to die, they could not do their job as SEALs. They understood it. But explaining to a child that Daddy would not be coming home anymore was the hardest thing Jack had ever done. None of the glory and honor of having died defending their nation made one iota of a difference to a heartbroken child. They all knew it, but that also did not make one iota of a difference. They were doing what they were born to do, and that was the best and only answer they gave.

None of it would make a difference to Barett for what he had gone through. For that reason, Jack would carry a burden of guilt all the days of his life.

As they reached the main building, the team lined up along the wall of the main building, behind Jack. He tried the door. It was locked. He signaled T-bone, their explosives expert, with hand signs.

Jack peered across the courtyard with his NOD and saw nothing but swirling sand. If anyone discovered them, they were screwed.

Jack did a quick comms check with Mack.

"Clear," said Mack from his outpost near the compound gate.

Thirty seconds later, T-bone held up three fingers, then two, one, and zero. The pushing charge blew the door across the big house entryway in a thousand different pieces.

Jack didn't wait for the smoke to clear. He led the way with his rifle at his shoulder and his eye looking through the infrared scope. Right, left, center. He scanned rapidly and constantly as they moved. They fanned out, automatically dividing the room into five separate kill zones, just as they had during training. Boots scraped in the dark. They sidestepped toward the noise.

Jack tossed a couple of fragmentation grenades around the corner. "Frag out."

His men made sure they were out of direct line of fire from the hundreds of pieces of shrapnel. After the grenade exploded, they bolted through the smoke, guns blazing in all directions as enemy heat signals arrived and started shooting back.

A bearded man who was no more than twenty years old ran into the room from a hallway and headed straight at Jack. He squeezed a grenade in each hand, then released the pins as he kept running. Jack put a round between his eyes, rocking him backward, off his feet. But the grenades flew forward, rolling toward Ghost Team.

"Grenade!" yelled everyone on the team as they dove in the other direction, faces down.

The noise, the flash, the pain. Nothing anyone could train for.

Jack rolled onto his knees, head down, puking. The dizziness returned. He had forgotten how concussions felt. It had been a year since Rolf El-Hashem had tried to blow the Konar River bridge out from under Travis and Jack. The frequency and severity of Jack's concussions were a big reason why he took the job leading the CTF and got out of fieldwork. Too many concussions risked permanent brain injury.

The other four jumped up and returned fire, advancing. T-bone limped, doubled over, holding his gut with one hand and shooting with the other.

Their bullets started finding their marks. At least six bearded men in baggy trousers and white kurtas lay motionless, blood pools expanding on the floor around their heads, AK-47s at their sides.

"No time, brother. We gotta go." Dewey jerked Jack to his feet.

Dewey had been watching out for Jack, and vice versa, since they were baby SEALs celebrating their surviving Hell Week, the worst and best week of their lives. Dewey was big, tall, and had a shit-eating grin on his face more often than not. Unlike most Deweys, he was not a big, flabby cartoon duck but was as hard as steel.

When an obnoxious group of fraternity boys had started picking on the buzz-cut swabbie in a downtown bar, Dewey didn't back down. He was king of the world. He had just survived Hell Week and had slept a total of four hours in five days. Jack jumped in to help his teammate. It got ugly fast—for the drunks. It was the most fun Jack and Dewey had had in months.

The military police locked down the San Diego bar, but not before Jack and Dewey flew the coop and slipped next door to seal their bond over a bottle of Jack Daniel's and beers. They had been swim buddies, covering each other's backs, and best friends ever since.

Jack regained his bearing, though he suffered from a splitting headache and waves of nausea. Dewey, Dozer, and Snake led the assault, racking up bad guys. Jack and T-bone covered the rear as they limped through the compound, supporting one another and furiously lighting up anything that moved, in full automatic mode on their assault rifles.

Mack broke in on their earphones, telling them the storm was dying quickly and a small convoy of three vehicles had just left the far end of the main building, headed toward the compound's main gate and his position. They were led by the same two guard jeeps that had chased Jack earlier. Mack's scanner lit up with Salwa's number.

"Do what you can, Mack. Be there in five," said Jack.

Just then, a hellacious barrage of enemy gunfire erupted, pinning the team down where they were.

Jack associated the sound of a whip crack with an enemy bullet whizzing past their ears at supersonic speeds. Like Chuck Yeager breaking the sound barrier riding a bullet. The louder the crack, the closer the bullet.

The crack told Jack they were missing his head by at least a foot.

Jack lobbed more grenades and flashbangs, then returned fire and moved. Jack helped lift T-bone to his feet with his free hand while T-bone pressed a hand over his bleeding belly wound.

Dewey, Dozer, and Snake quickly dispatched Salwa's rearguard shooters with precise, two-shot bursts through the head and chest. Since receiving Mack's message that Salwa's convoy had left the compound, Jack ordered the team to finish up fast. The air was thick with smoke and dust and the smell of burnt gunpowder.

In the last room before reaching the garage, Snake discovered an old cot with four rope wrist/ankle restraints. A bearded man lay splayed across the bed, gutshot but still breathing.

Jack shook him by the collar. "Where is she? Where's my wife?"

he screamed over and over, slamming the man's head on the bed.

The man struggled, then held his head up. "So you did come, Mr. Gunn."

Jack stopped shaking. "Who the fuck are you? Where is she?"

"I knew you'd come. As long as I had her, I knew you'd come."

"It was you?"

"Badal, Mr. Gunn. Compliments of the El-Hashems." He smiled a blue-lipped smile. Blood welled up from the corners of his mouth as his head twitched and twitched.

"You were in my home?" He slammed Hassan El-Hashem's head down. "You did that to my boy?" Another slam. "You tortured my wife?" Jack ripped out his throwing knife.

"That boy of yours was a fine one. Just a chip off the old block, as you say."

"Not *was*, asshole. *Is*. He's doing fine. A lot better off than you're going to be."

Hassan El-Hashem looked puzzled.

"That's right, you fucking scumbag," yelled Jack. "Where'd they take my wife? Where'd they go?"

Hassan got tight-lipped again. Set his chin.

Dewey gave Jack the swirling finger. "Let's go."

"Time for a little payback, you son of a bitch." Jack stuck his pistol in Hassan's mouth. "Choke on that, motherfucker." He pulled the trigger, blowing Hassan's brains through the mattress. "No virgins where you're going, asshole," said Jack as he climbed off Hassan's lifeless body.

Judge, jury, and executioner.

After some quick recon, Jack found a woman's bloody nightgown under the bed, against the wall. Jack grabbed it, knowing it was Nina's, stuck it in his pocket, and shot Hassan in the chest.

"Fucking asshole." A foul-smelling bucket sat in the corner. A cat-o'-nine-tails too. Jack picked it up for a closer look. The whip's nine blood-crusted leather tips were stiff and worn.

He was neither dizzy nor nauseated anymore. He led the team on a dead sprint out the garage door and back across the compound, buddy-carrying T-bone as they went. Mack had their bikes charged up and ready to go.

Salwa's signal had faded into the Sahara. Timbuktu stirred restlessly, awakened by the explosion, firefight, and the weakening storm. Random gunfire punctuated the edgy night.

Jack jammed a fresh magazine into his rifle and jumped on his bike, ready to charge after Salwa's caravan. But Mack stopped Jack in his tracks when T-bone collapsed to the ground in agony.

Salwa had a head start, but Mack had kept him on an electronic leash. A leash Jack wanted to turn into a noose. But first things first. T-bone was down.

Chapter 18

Children's Hospital, Charleston, SC

"Today's the day. Keep your fingers crossed," said Travis.

"I don't know if I'm ready. What if he doesn't wake up?" whispered Jaz.

"He's gonna wake up," said Travis. "Remember, Jack doesn't want Barett to know anything about what's going on with Nina." He spoke to Jaz and Suzy, Dewey's wife, as they scrubbed their hands with sanitizing foam. "Depending on how this goes, of course," he murmured, afraid to say out loud what everyone was thinking.

"Let's pray," said Jaz.

When the going got tough, Jaz really shined. At seven-plus-months pregnant, she did not look like a force to contend with. But whether she was working in some CIA craphole overseas or in a cushy office in the States, she constantly evaluated and assessed the situation. She was a lot like Jack in that she could not turn herself off and on. She was always on duty.

Travis did not know if she was that way because she grew up in the projects of Oakland with her single-parent mom and seven younger siblings. Maybe it was because she did nothing but study on her way to a 4.0 and a degree in Middle Eastern studies from Berkeley. Maybe it was because her biggest fear in life was failing and letting her family down. Whatever it was, Travis knew he was one lucky man.

Jaz seemed so comfortable with her faith. So bold and confident. Travis desperately wanted that same feeling, especially now as Barett's life hung in the balance.

"Heavenly Father," began Jaz as the three of them gathered in a tight circle with their arms wrapped around each other's shoulders or waists. Heads bowed—something else they had gotten used to doing when Jaz prayed.

"Heavenly Father, we know you love Barett even more than we do. He's endured more than any one person, much less any boy, should have to go through. He's fighting for his life, Lord. We're asking you . . ." Jaz squeezed the group and raised her voice. "We're begging you to send Nina and Jack's little boy back. Give him back to us, Lord. Heal his brain. Heal his lungs. Send him back, Lord. We love you, Lord. In Jesus's name, we pray."

"Amen," they all said and held their huddle for a second longer before taking their seats.

"Thank you, Jaz," whispered Suzy.

"Dr. and Mrs. Gunn," a nurse called from the doorway, bringing them back down to earth.

"Hey, Caroline," said Travis. "What are you doing here? I thought you were off today."

"Hi, Dr. Gunn. I heard they were taking our little man off the ventilator. I just wanted to be here," she said.

"Caroline, this is my wife, Jaz, and our good friend Suzy," said Travis.

"It's nice to meet you both. How was the drive?" asked Caroline.

"Not bad at all. We talked the whole way," said Jaz.

"Seems like ages since I had a conversation with anyone above the third-grade level," said Suzy. "I loved it."

"If you don't mind my asking, when are you due?" Caroline sweetly asked Jaz.

"I'm thirty-four weeks," said Jaz, rubbing her belly.

"Do you know what it is?" Caroline asked.

"It's a surprise," said Travis. "We've got a pool going on sex and birth weight. You can get in for a buck."

A nursing assistant came up and whispered something in Caroline's ear. "It's time. Follow me, please."

Jaz, Travis, and Suzy followed her to Barett's bedside. Feeding off Caroline's nonverbal signals, Travis felt lighter—until they walked in and saw Barett.

They already had the breathing tube out and the ventilator removed from Barett's room. The alarms were silent. The room was quiet enough to hear his tiny little breaths from under the oxygen mask. His eyes were closed.

Jaz went up one side of the bed, Travis the other. Suzy stayed at the foot, out of the way. They each took a tiny hand in theirs and watched him breathe, mist forming inside the mask each time he exhaled. Jaz smiled. Travis was an old softy, so he welled up immediately.

Travis called his name softly, "Barett. Barett. Open your eyes. It's Uncle T."

Nothing happened.

Travis leaned over and repeated his plea into Barett's ear. He hardly got the words out before cracking under the pressure.

Even with all his medical training and everything else he had survived, his nerves were shot. Everything was on the line for Barett. His whole life hinged on the next few minutes, or so it seemed to Travis.

Still nothing.

Jaz stood on her tiptoes and leaned over the bedrail so her face was inches above Barett's. "Barett. Honey. Open your eyes, Barett."

Nothing.

"Barett, honey. Open your eyes. It's Auntie Jaz."

There was a flicker in his eyelids, as if they were struggling against glue to open. His hand twitched.

Jaz gasped and said, "Barett, sweetie. Open your eyes."

Barett's eyes cracked open halfway. In a weak voice, he said, "Hi, Auntie Jaz. I heard you calling."

And with that, the celebration began. Euphoria welled up out of Jaz, Travis, and Suzy. If the energy of hugs and kisses and thanksgivings could have been harnessed, they could have powered the universe. The entire ICU staff joined in as well. They knew well enough to celebrate the triumphs and mourn the losses. Working in a pediatric intensive care unit, there were plenty of both to go around.

Travis pulled out the card Jack had given him and placed the call. Two hours later, after Barett had fallen back to sleep, Jack was on the line.

"It couldn't have gone better, bro," said Travis. "He knew who we were the instant he opened his eyes."

"I can barely hear you, Travis. You'll have to speak up," said Jack into his satphone as he stood next to his motorcycle, still breathless from bugging out of Timbuktu and racing into the Sahara before they stopped to regroup and tend to T-bone's wounds.

"So Barett's really okay?"

"He looks great. He stayed awake for about fifteen minutes before he fell back to sleep. They say he'll do this for a couple days as he continues to recover. He's been through a lot, but he's a fighter just like his daddy," said Travis. Jaz had her ear up to the phone too.

Jack teared up, as his fears of losing Barett boiled over. "What did he say? Did he ask about us?"

"They don't want him tiring himself out, but no, he didn't ask. I did like you said and didn't bring anything up."

"Good, Travis—you guys are doing great," Jack said, turning away from the other guys, who were attending to T-bone and his belly wound. "I can't tell you how much it hurts to not be there. I . . . I . . ."

"We know, Jack. You don't have to say anything. We know," said Travis.

"We love you, Jack," Jaz said, leaning over Travis's shoulder.

"I love you too," said Jack.

"So, how's it going? Did you find Nina yet?" asked Travis.

"We're close," said Jack. "Hopefully in the next twenty-four hours." He spun around to check his tracking screen on his handlebars.

"You sound a long way away, but I know better than to ask where. Too many ears listening, right?"

"You guessed it," said Jack. "Hey, we gotta go, but I can't tell you how great this news is. We should be back in two to three days. Call me if anything changes. I love you guys."

"We love you too, Jack. We can't wait to see you and Nina."

The line went dead.

Jack stared at the phone for a second before sticking it back in his pack. He wiped gritty tears from his eyes. A fire started to smolder in his gut as he no longer had to worry about Barett and could focus all his energy on catching up to the bastards who had Nina. He set his jaw, his eyes, and his scowl and slowly morphed into one of the nastiest death stares ever seen.

When the guys noticed, they all went stone quiet in the early-morning light and stopped what they were doing.

"Thirty minutes to sunup. You better get going," said Jack as they loaded the second motorcycle into the back of one of their WWII cargo trucks the Malian drivers had driven them up in earlier that night, when they attacked Timbuktu.

T-bone, stretched out on the makeshift cot, was already starting to doze from the morphine. A bloody compression dressing was taped over his penetrating belly wound. A liter bag of saline dripped into the big vein in his elbow, along with a gram of antibiotics.

"Roger that," said Mack, T-bone's swim buddy.

"SecDef wants us to press on and shut these guys down before the trail goes cold," said Jack. "We'll hook back up at home."

He jumped up inside the back of the truck and squatted next to T-bone. "Hang in there, bro," he said, resting a hand on T-bone's forehead.

T-bone cracked open his droopy eyes and gave Jack a weak smile.

Jack jumped back down and pulled Mack aside. "Keep an eye on these bastards."

"Roger that, Jack. I got this," said Mack. "Good hunting."

The Malian drivers started the truck while Mack jumped in and leaned out the passenger window to give Jack a brother's handshake. "Go kick some haji ass for me, and we'll see you back home at Boneshaker's."

"Once you make Bamako and link up with HQ, tell 'em to be on their toes. A shitstorm is coming," said Jack.

"Roger that." As the truck sped down the road to the south, blowing sand quickly swallowed the boxy shadow and Mack's outstretched arm with a thumbs-up. The second truck followed.

Dewey, Snake, Dozer, and Jack sat astride their dirt bikes in the swirling storm, surrounded by a million square miles of desert. Covered head to foot in black; their NODs flipped down in front of their goggles; rifles strapped across their chests; backpacks bulging with breachers, frags, therms, food, and water; and Kevlar saddlebags carrying launchers and ammo; they looked more like ninja warriors than SEALs.

They turned their bikes to the northeast and switched on their tracking systems. All screens showed the same thing. A red blip—thanks to Mack sticking a magnetic tracker to the side of Salwa's truck—moved off to the east-southeast, on the other side of the Niger River, headed for Gao and Al-Qaeda's mountain caves. Hundreds of miles inside Al-Qaeda–controlled territory, Gao was just as bad, maybe even worse, than Afghanistan's caves, where Jack and Dewey had started the fight after 9/11. They were hundreds of miles from friendly forces. Hundreds of miles from air support. It was a piece of cake to defend, and a nightmare to attack.

They flipped on their infrared headlights and taillights, invisible to the naked eye. It was still dark out, but to the four warriors lucky enough to be wearing the new quad-tube NODs, they saw everything in front of their motorcycles as though it were daytime, only colored in Martian green. The taillights stood out like green stop signs. Most importantly, they saw well enough to race motorcycles across the dark desert at top speed without worrying about being seen or heard.

They made a wide circle around Temara, a river town halfway to Gao, as night turned to day. They changed back to their desert camouflage clothes, but the black bikes still stood out in broad daylight against the sand.

The harmattan had left a messy trail of debris and drifts where none had existed twenty-four hours earlier. Local men dug one another out of their homes. Women butchered dead livestock. Children carried jugs to the wells and back.

Five miles past Temara, as the team stuck to the high terraces above the winding Niger River, rear-guard Dewey broke in, "We've got company."

They stopped and heard what sounded like a swarm of bumblebees behind them, buzzing and zipping in and out of the hive. Jack listened hard, turned his binoculars back to the west, and waited.

Nothing moved for a minute, but then he spotted them. Black specks crossed the top of a dune and disappeared below Jack's line of sight, coming toward them. He counted one, two, three . . . eight bees on motorcycles, following their trail in the freshly laid sand.

"We must have picked them up at the last town. Gotta keep moving," said Jack.

"Uh, Jack—we have a small problem. We're down to ten percent on our batteries. We run outta juice with haji hot on our ass, and we're screwed," said Dozer, the quiet bull.

"Fucking bikes," said Jack, cursing his motorcycle. He studied their pursuers for another minute through the binoculars.

"Let's find some coverup by those rocks and get that fucking generator cooking." Jack motioned over his shoulder at an outcropping. He did the math in his head as they rode. Four bikes.

Each one specially designed to take a full charge in one minute. Two minutes to get the generator cranking. He needed to take a piss, anyway.

"It's gonna be tight," he said as Dozer started the high-tech gas generator.

"Snake, Dewey—launch the bird. Slow them bastards down," ordered Jack.

Dewey pulled a package from his saddlebag. Snake grabbed the two-foot-long launch tube and the electronic launch gear. Dewey powered up the handheld flight-and-weapon-control module. A minute later, Snake punched the launch button. The miniature plane with folded-back wings pogo-jumped out of the tube and into the air. At the peak of its jump, the backpack drone's front and rear wings sprung out and locked in place. The electric propeller immediately kicked in, and off she buzzed, carrying the explosive punch of three grenades.

"Bird in the air," said Dewey.

Dewey took control, his eyes buried inside a plastic tube shielding an electronic screen showing live video from the nose cone of the UAV. His right hand maneuvered a toggle, and the remote-controlled plane leveled off, going sixty miles an hour.

From two hundred feet up, the motorcyclists came into plain view within a minute. Dewey targeted the lead rider and drove the plane right down his throat.

They heard the explosion before they saw the black smoke. A couple minutes later, as they buttoned up the generator, everyone's ride fully charged, Jack spotted the remaining bikers bugging out, heading home. "Have a nice day, boys."

Jack checked Salwa's convoy blip on his handlebar screen. They were still moving, a little over halfway to Gao.

"They're not as far as I thought, but we gotta cut the corner if we want to catch them before they hit the caves." He traced a different route on his map for the others to follow.

"Cross the river? On these?" said Dewey. "You know electricity and water don't exactly mix."

"Don't be such a pansy ass. You could use a jolt," said Jack.

"I'll give you a jolt, you fucking jarhead," said Dewey with an ornery smile.

Jack fired up the satphone to check in with Martinez back in Virginia before they moved out. Not long after he started talking, his shoulders slumped. Energy drained from his face. His eyes glazed over.

"When?"

He listened, staring at the ground for another minute before saying "Roger" and hanging up.

Jack looked back to the west. The smoke was gone. He looked at Dewey, Snake, and Dozer.

"They didn't make it. Mack and T-bone were ambushed by their own drivers and dumped in the middle of town." Jack wiped his face with his glove. "They're making a big deal about it on the Internet."

"Fucking Victor set us up," said Dewey.

"Al-Qaeda's into everything. Everybody's turning," said Jack. "I don't know about Victor, but his drivers for sure."

"They sending a team in to get them?" asked Dozer.

"Big State Department clusterfuck, as usual," said Jack. "We can't worry about that right now. We can't let these bastards get away with this."

Their mood changed from being four exhausted overnight road trippers to four human switchblades searching for their next target.

"Move out." Jack pointed a finger toward the river and took off. The other three followed. No wavering. No looking over their shoulders. They just locked on the tail of the bike in front of them.

Jack could not get it out of his head. Two more friends to bury. Two more wives to face. Five more kids without dads. How many did that make?

Jack was harder on himself than anyone else. Even though he realized he had nothing to do with the fact that the terrorists had acted alone when they stalked his house and kidnapped his family, he still felt responsible. And now, T-bone and Mack were dead. His friends who gave their lives for Nina and Barett.

None of the guys would have blamed Jack for anything that had happened or for T-bone and Mack getting killed. They put their lives on the line every day for each other. But that did not matter to Jack. He should have been the one to take the bullet, not T-bone and Mack.

Jack knew he would die in the line of battle. It was his destiny as a warrior and descendant of Sitting Bull. He did not fear death for himself, but he did for his teammates—and for Nina.

As Jack rode on, the faces of Mack and T-bone were replaced by Nina's in some sort of sorrowful, smoky mirage where she was crying. Jack's eyes narrowed. He hunched over the handlebars of his motorcycle and punched it. Dewey, Snake, and Dozer did the same. They jumped dunes, skirted rocks, and singlemindedly zeroed in on the Niger River.

Chapter 19

Gao, Mali

Darkness settled over the militant-controlled city of Gao, Mali, like a suffocating hand. The air was still and smelled like burnt trash. A dog yelped in the night. Sharia law was in full force. No man or woman left home after dark without a compelling reason. Women went out in daylight, never at night, and only if covered from head to foot. Children were still children but grew up fast in the spare and brutal city.

Desperate cries for help went unanswered constantly. People minded their own business—or died. Gunfire echoed throughout the mountain valley hourly. The "Moral Police" dragged lawbreakers to the public square and punished them daily. Fear ruled Gao. Hopelessness ruled Gao.

Jack cringed in his hiding spot outside Salwa's compound, hearing a woman's shrill cry for help in the night. He didn't speak their language, but her scream spoke for itself. He knew it was not Nina's, but it went against the core of who he was to just sit by and do nothing.

The Zuya raised Jack to be the protector of his people, like his ancestors. He thought of himself more as the protector of all people who were unable to protect themselves, not just Native Americans. Not only were the fighting skills of a Nakota warrior drilled into him, but the wisdom and teachings of their holy man, Sitting Bull, too. After years of being mentored by wrinkled old men from a forgotten world, Jack was the next great Native American fortress to stand against the raging storm of the twenty-first century.

The woman's screams were squelched midscream.

Jack pictured Nina. How many times had she cried out for Jack? How many beatings had she received? It was all his fault. Leaving Barett and Nina alone in their new home. Not having Dewey check in on them when Jack should have known something was wrong. Not having a land line installed instead of using only cell phones to save money. Not putting a bullet in Rolf's head on the Yemeni freighter when he had the chance. Declaring a badal on the El-Hashems. His failures mounted up like the crest of a killer wave before it broke and crushed everything in its path.

He was starting to realize what it felt like to be Travis and what torment PTSD victims went through day and night. If he let the things that had recently gone wrong in his life pile up into a Mount Everest of guilt, a mountain he had to reclimb every day, it would be exhausting just to get out of bed each morning.

In his line of work, Jack knew better than to let that happen. He couldn't remember a time when so many things—big things, bad things—had backfired. But mistakes and miscalculations happened all the time in their high-risk, high-reward business of stalking and eliminating terrorists worldwide. Yesterday's news and the annals of team history bore witness to that with helicopter crashes, IED bombings, 9/11. The list was long.

Jack had to always remind his team that there was no end to the number of terrorists and their creativity for wreaking havoc to accomplish their mission. He and his team had to be just as creative, just as relentless, and just as brutal in their pursuit. Jack saw no other way. Give the terrorists any idea that they were winning, that they had taken control, and things would get ten times worse. Jack would never let that happen. Not while he was still alive.

Jack heard two clicks in his earphone, snapping him back to the mission at hand.

Jack saw Dewey hiding around a dark corner and looked in the direction Dewey was pointing. Several men stepped from a car out front and went inside the building. A Mercedes. Beat up, but still a Mercedes. A big fish car.

Jack looked through his riflescope for a close-up view. As soon as he saw Rami Salwa, his finger went straight to the trigger. But before he pulled, he waited for Nina to get out of the car. She never did. Nina's cry in his head was growing faint. Jack knew he had to follow Salwa to find Nina if he ever wanted to see her again.

"Launch the bird," Jack said.

Jack, Dewey, Dozer, and Snake slid back around the rear of the building.

"Bird's in the air," said Snake, quickly repeating the procedure from earlier.

Dewey took control of their last UAV, his steady hand resting on the toggle. Anything but a direct hit, exactly on target, was unacceptable, or he would kill himself and the rest of the team who were hiding behind the same building he sought to blow up. Everything looked different through the eyes of the infrared camera. Highlights faded. Details were missing. The compounds of Gao all looked the same. He had to be certain.

Jack heard another woman's scream. This time from inside the building. It was followed by men's laughter. The hair on the back of Jack's neck stood up. Jack waved a circling finger at Dewey to hurry up.

Dewey buried his face in the targeting cone. "Fifteen seconds," he whispered.

Jack, Snake, and Dozer quietly chambered rounds, crouched, and put their heads down.

When the drone hit its mark, the Mercedes erupted into a ball of flames, knocking the front door of the building off its hinges. The fireball flashed the night sky and settled in for a slow burn.

Jack and the team jumped to their feet, took up positions, and waited.

Ten seconds later, the same men who arrived in the Mercedes poured back out of the hole where the front door used to be, joined by Salwa and his men. They fanned out, firing their rifles wildly into the night. But with no enemy in sight, they soon focused on watching the twisted car burn, laughing at their good fortune.

"Three, two, one, execute."

Jack and Dewey breached the back door of the building at the same time as Dozer and Snake opened up on the crowd of men out front, Dozer from one side and Snake from the other, cutting them down in a fury of crossfire and frags.

Jack and Dewey quickly entered the back and went room to room, clearing and looking for Nina. They found a woman strapped down to a bed, then another, beaten and battered. But no Nina. They kept moving, working their way toward the front. Looking right, left, forward. Over and over. Enough AK-47s, C-4, ammunition, and shoulder-launching RPGs to start a war. To take control of Gao. Maybe all of Mali.

"Smoked eight," said Dozer. "Two coming back at ya, Jack."

Rami Salwa and another ran through the smoldering front door hole. Salwa yelled something that stopped the man following him in his tracks. The man turned to defend the front door, but Snake drilled him between the eyes with one shot before the man could shoulder his weapon. The man flipped backward onto the still-smoldering door, dead as a doornail.

The whip cracked loud and clear, this time sounding inches from Jack's skull. He ducked.

Jack waited off one side of the only hallway running front to back, and Dewey off the other. He watched a roach spider, the size of a grape, weaving its web in a dark corner. The place reeked from a combination of burned meat, sewage, and rotting flesh. Trash littered the floor.

Salwa sprinted down the hallway toward the rear. Jack timed things perfectly and threw his forearm out, clothes-lining Salwa at the neck. Salwa's feet flew out, his back hit the floor, and Jack jumped on top of him. He pinned Salwa down and blasted him in the face with his right fist several times as Salwa struggled.

Salwa's bodyguard appeared out of nowhere on the other side of the hall and jumped Dewey from behind. Dewey used the bodyguard's momentum and hip-checked him while dropping to one knee and pulling the attacker up and over his shoulder. By the time the bodyguard hit the floor, Dewey pumped two nine-millimeter rounds into his skull, then got right back up to cover Salwa's ass whooping.

With each punch, Jack yelled, "Where is she? Where is she? Where is she?"

Salwa's head flopped from side to side. Not speaking. Not fighting back. Jack stopped.

Salwa opened his swollen eyes, squinted back at Jack, and smiled.

Jack backhanded Salwa again. "What are you laughing at, you son of a bitch?"

Salwa coughed, choking on his own blood, and looked as if he passed out. Jack grabbed his collar in one hand, dragged him back up the hall to the front room, and lifted him into a wooden chair. Tar-black smoke drifted through the front door. The car fire, visible out front, crackled. The shooting had stopped.

"All clear," said Dozer.

Jack threw a bucket of water on Salwa's face, shocking him back to consciousness. Dewey zip-tied Salwa's hands and feet to the chair. He was still wearing his signature black dishdasha and gold pin he wore the night he duped Jack out of 110 million dollars in Palestine, while thousands of miles away, his men were invading Jack's home and kidnapping Nina and Barett.

Jack ripped open Salwa's dishdasha. He pinned Salwa's forehead back with his left hand and pulled out his knife.

Salwa's eyes grew wide for a split second, then he looked up at Jack and smiled again.

"What's so funny, you cocky son of a bitch?"

"Never see the big picture, do you? You didn't get it in Palestine, and you don't get it now. That's why you'll always be taking orders from someone else."

"I got the big picture, asshole. Now where's my wife?"

"Nothing personal, but I don't know what you see in her."

"Save it, you prick. I only want to hear one word out of that hairy, fucking face of yours."

"As you can see, I'm giving the orders now," said Salwa. "I do give you credit, though, for tracking me here, but you're a long way from home. You don't stand a chance."

Jack stretched Salwa's neck back and rested his knife on the crease.

"Where is she?"

"You know, I never had anything against that pretty wife of yours. It was simply business. Badal business," said Salwa. "You should never have come here."

Jack pressed harder with his knife.

"You've looked around. You tell me. Where's your wife?" Salwa started to chuckle. "You can't find her because she isn't here."

Dewey stuck the barrel of his rifle into the side of Salwa's head. Jack took his knife and pointed the tip straight front to back, windpipe to spine.

"Where is she, you piece of shit? This is your last chance."

"If you have half a brain, you would know where she is. Think, you stupid American," said Salwa.

Jack said nothing, but his clenched jaw muscles started straining as if they were going to explode when he pictured Rolf El-Hashem's face.

"Trust me when I say you will never see her again. Not in this world. Not in the next." With that, he laughed hysterically. "Killing me won't—"

Jack sheathed his knife, grabbed Salwa's chin firmly with his right hand, and wrenched his neck to the left until he felt Salwa's spine break and his laugh stop.

"Fuck you and your badal."

Jack grabbed Salwa's gold pin and kicked the chair over. He and Dewey headed for the rear door. Dozer and Snake stuck close behind, as their internal clocks ticked off the seconds before reinforcements arrived. Jack pulled up abruptly at the room full of ammunition. Several dented aluminum suitcases piled in the shadows caught his eye.

"Three minutes, Snake. Do a quick SSE, and don't forget to check the cases."

Snake was a step ahead. The timer was set.

Three minutes later, they jumped the wall, mounted their bikes, and raced out into the desert to the southwest.

Jack did not even look back when the compound erupted in C-4 fireworks. His mind bounced between pictures of Rolf torturing Nina in some Pakistani cave, and the bloody, lifeless bodies of Mack and T-bone.

Between burying teammates, finding the suitcase bombs, and tracking down Rolf, Nina seemed farther away than ever. Her spirit faded like a flickering candle in a windy tomb. Jack twisted the throttle to go faster, but it was already wide open. He strained to see the edge of darkness through his goggles as he flew across the desert sand and rocks. Dewey, Dozer, and Snake following right behind, focused on staying off the main roads to get to a top-secret black-ops airstrip in the middle of the Sahara to catch their flight to a top-secret base on Diego Garcia.

Chapter 20

Unknown Location, Pakistan

"Welcome to Pakistan, Mrs. Gunn."

Rolf gently stroked his face, tugging his beard over and over as he studied Nina through black horn-rimmed glasses. Time in prison had transformed the pudgy plastic surgeon into a hardened jihadist. His gaunt cheeks caved into his bearded face. A gray kaffiyeh was wrapped around his head. There was a sinister edge to every word he said.

Rolf may have gone to prison in Diego Garcia as a baby jihadist, but the leading *emir* of their jihad, the one who called the shots, made sure Rolf came out fully invested in their cause once they discovered that due to photographic memory, Rolf remembered where Mohammed had hidden each of the eleven dirty bombs. For the emir to use so many assets to carry out the kidnapping and dummy suitcase exchange, he had to be convinced with 100 percent certainty that Rolf would follow orders and do whatever he was told when the time came.

Nina sat still and said nothing, duct-taped to a wooden chair. Her head bobbed and bounced off her chest and back up. She tried to look at Rolf El-Hashem, but it was all a blur. She dozed off again.

Rolf stepped closer. "I'm talking to you, bitch. Wake up." He crouched down to study her face. She didn't move or open her eyes. He lifted her chin up and pried open an eye that was bloodshot and whose pupil was constricted to a pinpoint.

He signaled one of his men, who dumped a bucket of cold water over her head. She yelped, and her eyes sprang wide open. Duct tape kept her shoulders pressed against the chair and her hands and feet were shackled together.

"Mrs. Gunn. Or I think I'll call you Nina. It's such a pretty name." Rolf smiled through perfectly straight and dazzling white teeth. "I only have one rule. I'm sure your husband told you."

Nina looked confused. She hurt everywhere. It smelled like burnt tires. She saw tape over the big vein in her left elbow and followed a plastic tube leading from it to a bag of yellow fluid hanging from a coat hanger hooked to the one and only light fixture. She had gone through six rounds of chemotherapy. She knew all about IVs. She went from cloudy unconsciousness to a four-alarm panic in a heartbeat.

"One rule, Nina. When I ask a question, you give me an answer. If you don't give me the answer I want . . ." Rolf nodded once. The cold-water man backhanded Nina across the face. The scab crusting over the corner of her mouth cracked and trickled blood again.

"Who are you? Where am I?" Nina tried to say, but her throat was so dry, nothing came out.

Rolf nodded, and the man gave Nina a drink, spilling most of it down her bloodstained robe they had put on her to replace her nightgown.

She cleared her throat, took another drink, and repeated, "Who are you? Why am I wearing this?"

Her eyes cleared. She saw she was tied to a chair in the middle of a cold, cavernous room with walls of stone, or some sort of gray adobe. The lifeless body of a naked woman hung from chains and shackles anchored to the wall next to her. Shackles dangling from the other three walls were empty. There was one low doorway with a closed, heavy wooden door. No windows. One lightbulb. Her eyes froze on the woman.

"Who do you *think* I am?" asked Rolf.

She shook her head. She started to sweat in the bone-chilling cold. "Some asshole my husband must've pissed off." She turned and wiped the blood from her chin onto her shoulder. "He tends to do that a lot," she said and smiled, even though it caused the crusted corners of her mouth to crack some more.

"You think this is a joke, Nina?" Rolf turned cordial to sinister. "Do you think she thought it was a joke?" He pointed at the dead woman and got in Nina's face. "You should know, I'll do whatever it takes, including killing you."

"You can't kill me, whoever you are." Nina fought every ounce of fear that wanted to cry and beg for mercy.

"I do whatever I want."

"You do whatever you're told to do."

"In your case, Nina, I do whatever I want. You're not that important," Rolf said through clenched teeth and a full beard. His beak nose flared.

"You still don't know who I am?" Rolf stood back up. "We met once, you and I."

"I don't think so. I would remember meeting an asshole like you."

"You've forgotten. How sad. Take a closer look, Nina." He posed under the light, holding his chin up like royalty.

Nina held her head up higher and studied him.

"New York City. Spring of 2000. Ring a bell?" asked Rolf.

Nina said nothing.

"Travis's medical school buddy. Our paths crossed at the World Trade Center."

Nina tried to conceal her shock, but Rolf saw her make the connection and chuckled.

"You were so beautiful, so young and happy." Rolf scowled. "So naïve."

Nina's eyes narrowed, and she stared defiantly back at Rolf.

"You, Travis, your husband—none of you had any idea how screwed up everything was. Even now, you're holding on." He sat tall in a chair facing her and lit up a cigarette. "Travis got his eyes opened, that's for damn sure. He thought we were best friends right up to the point where I had him blown to smithereens. What an idiot. Why would I be friends with an infidel? He was everything I deplored of this world." Rolf exhaled slowly, studying the smoke plume, before inhaling again. "I hated him. I'm glad he's dead."

Nina almost cringed, hearing him talk about her brother-in-law Travis as if he were dead, but she tried to hide her reaction so Rolf would not be suspicious. It was difficult to hear him speak of Travis as public enemy number one. Travis would never escape the nightmares of his captivity and beatings.

Nina did remember meeting Rolf in New York City. He seemed happy. His hair was short, and he was clean shaven. All Travis and Rolf talked about was patients and medical school and girls. Rolf barely resembled the person she remembered.

"Things are underway—big things, things you couldn't possibly understand," said Rolf as he circled Nina, stroking his beard. "Let me dumb this down for you. Your husband has been a royal pain in our ass. He screwed up everything last year. He killed my father. He put me in prison. Need I go on?"

Rolf leaned forward and stopped inches from Nina's nose. "We need your husband dead, or he'll screw up everything again. And what's the best way to catch a bear, I ask? Bait him. Tie the bait, which would be you, Nina," Rolf said, pointing at her, "to a post. And when he comes, which he most certainly will, we'll shoot him in the head," Rolf said with a thrill in his voice.

"I can see your wheels turning, wondering what will happen to you, and I say . . . no matter. After your husband is dead, we won't need the bait anymore. My men will do as they wish, then send you to be with your dead husband, and we go on with our plans. Did you like that story?"

Nina gulped, picturing Barett. Visions of what had happened to her little boy at the hands of Rolf's men replayed in her brain like a horror show. His screams. Him in the van. Him flying overboard, screaming for mommy.

Strangely, things started to glow in the dark room again, as on the ship. A knife under Rolf's dishdasha, a pistol in his hand, a bloody wood club propped up against the wall next to the dead woman. Rolf did not seem to notice the light.

"You're behind all this? You ordered those men to break into my house?"

"So you do understand! Good, Nina." Rolf spoke as though he was praising a dog for rolling over.

"Stop calling me that, you coward."

"It had to start somewhere, Nina." He smiled and flicked the cigarette at her. "Your husband stuck his nose where it didn't belong, and my family paid the price. Our entire security council died because of him. My father died because of him. I won't ever be able to see my wife and children again because of him." He looked her in the eye, "Our grand jihad was postponed because of him."

"But why me? Why my son?"

"Ask your husband and his dead brother. They're the ones who poked the lion."

Nina struggled against her shackles. Again, she tried to hide any trace of a reaction to Rolf saying Travis was dead.

"Enough with the small talk. Let's get down to business." Rolf stood, walked to a small table in the corner, and removed a rolled-up towel from a doctor's bag. He placed the towel on the table and slowly unrolled it to reveal several syringes filled with brown liquid. He picked up the biggest one. "I need you to be a good girl, to do what you're told . . . but I don't think you are."

"What are you going to do?" She struggled frantically as Rolf walked toward her, squirting a stream of liquid into the air from the needle.

"Liars exhaust me." He stuck the needle into the IV tubing in her arm and injected. "Any last words?"

"How about you go fuck yours—"

"Classy. It's about what I would have expected." He checked Nina's eyes. They were glazed over again. "Now Nina, let's stop playing games, shall we? What little secrets are you hiding from me?"

Chapter 21

Children's Hospital, Charleston, SC

"Uncle T. You're here," Barett squealed from his bed, stretching his arms up to Travis.

Overcome with emotion that Barett recognized him after everything he had gone through, Travis was speechless. He simply leaned down and hugged the boy. He flicked a shock of Barett's black bangs out of his eyes. Travis watched every movement, listened to every word. Slowly his nerves calmed as he realized Barett indeed acted tired, but normal.

Barett looked toward the door every time he heard a noise out in the hallway.

"Mommy and Daddy aren't here, honey. They wanted to be, but they were feeling sick, and the doctors don't want sick people coming to the hospital and making you sick. You know what I mean?"

Barett nodded and stopped watching the door, but a deflated look crept into his puppy-dog eyes.

"Mommy and Daddy love you and miss you very much. You know that, right?"

Barett nodded and gave Travis another hug.

Travis unpacked a bag full of Barett's stuffed animals, his favorite blanket, some pictures, some toys, and an iPad Chief Martinez had one of his men gather from Jack's condo, with Detective Porter's permission, and courier down to Charleston.

Barett sat up, his eyes got big, and a smile spread across his sleepy face as he grabbed his blanket and an armful of stuffed animals, which he instinctively arranged in their proper place and order, as if it were common knowledge of who was supposed to sit next to whom. He powered up his iPad and went right to playing his favorite game.

Travis smiled as he watched Barett. He marveled at the healing power of youth, knowing how long it had taken him to recover from his spine surgery. He unpacked a family picture of Jack, Nina, and Barett. Before he set it down on Barett's nightstand, he pondered it for a long time. Where was Jack? Was he okay? Where was Nina? Was she alive? Was her cancer coming back? How long could he keep lying to Barett about where his parents were? His thoughts circled to Jaz and the baby. What kind of a father would he be? What kind of a husband was he when Jaz was the only breadwinner and mother of his child, while all he did was go to rehab and take pills? He started slipping down a very familiar dark and lonely path, one that took only minutes to slide to the depressing bottom of and days to crawl out of.

Travis felt a shift from self-pity to anger as he pictured Rolf's face. How could he have been so stupid to fall into Rolf's trap? Why had he let himself be manipulated by Rolf after Jack had already warned him that Rolf was probably an asshole? His jealousy of Jack—not wanting to admit that Jack was right—had nearly gotten everyone he loved killed.

If he got a second chance, he swore he would kill that bastard Rolf without the slightest bit of remorse. But he knew he would not get a second chance. If anyone did, it would be Jack.

From somewhere deep in his subconscious, the image of Jack and him standing on the bridge over the Konar River back in Afghanistan, facing Rolf and a whole slew of Taliban shooters, came flooding back to him. Travis knew that moment was the turning point of his life. He went from being the victim and blaming everyone else for his problems to being a stand-up guy who called his own shots, come hell or high water. After every terrible thing Rolf and his men had done, Travis was the one who declared a badal on the El-Hashems, not Jack. Even though he and Jack were nearly blown to kingdom come by a five-inch howitzer in the next minute by Rolf El-Hashem, they had survived. Travis had bits of metal shrapnel still imbedded in his body to remind him.

But he was alive, and he was alive for a reason. He started seeing that part of his purpose in life was to help stop terrorists, such as Rolf, who were trying to destroy the world, his world. Terrorists who pretended to be normal members of society until a call came in the middle of the night that transformed them into jihadist monsters. He did not know how an anesthesiologist could help in such a monumental task, but if there was a way he could help Jack's SEALs or Jaz's CIA defeat the enemy, he wanted in.

Barett nudged Uncle T and showed him how he had made it to level five of the game he was playing on his iPad. Travis sat the family picture on the nightstand and congratulated Barett, thinking of what the doctor had said earlier in the day. "Everyone here says he's a miracle child. None of this should ever have happened, but it looks like he's going to be fine. You can stop worrying."

Travis lay down next to Barett in his hospital bed, and they both fell asleep.

Chapter 22

Unknown Location, Pakistan

"Time to bait the bear," said Rolf to no one in particular as he touched the call button on the Skype app of his smartphone. He was enjoying his little bit of trickery.

Jack's face appeared on the screen. "Hello? Who's this?"

Rolf quickly stepped away from the camera, which was clipped to a tripod pointed straight at Nina, before Jack could see Rolf's face.

"Help. Please. Anybody." Nina's whimpers evaporated into the frigid silence of her torture chamber. Her knees buckled as she dangled from shackles around her wrists. The only difference between Nina and the naked woman hanging next to her was that Nina was still breathing. Still pink.

Rolf laughed to himself when he heard Jack gasp and saw shock spread across his slack-jawed face. Rolf stood out of Jack's view but could still see him on-screen, like a stagehand watching a tragic comedy unfold from the wings.

Nina barely looked like Nina. She had lost so much weight. She looked as if she were back on chemotherapy.

"Help. Please. Whoever you are," Nina cried again, in barely a whisper.

"Nina. It's me, Jack." Jack watched the surreal scene play out like a horror movie from his chair in a communications room thousands of miles away to the south, at the CIA Quadrange in Diego Garcia.

Her droopy-eyed head swam around to the voice, like a drunk. "Who are you?" Her voice squeaked like a homeless kitten's. She struggled against her shackles. Her legs swung like wet towels. Blue, swollen, wet towels.

"Mister, please help me." Her head turned to Rolf.

"My name's Rolf, remember? Did you have a nice nap, Nina?" Rolf said gently as he stepped in front of the camera and injected a brownish liquid into her IV. "Here. Let me help you down. Let's get you covered up."

He unlocked the shackles and scooped Nina up in his arms before she collapsed. She locked her arms around his neck, her eyes rolled back, and she laid her head on Rolf's chest as he stood tall, held his nose high, and carried her to a cot. Rolf turned toward the camera and gave Jack a full-screen shot of his face for the first time.

"Isn't that better, my love?" Rolf asked, kissing her on the forehead, making sure Jack saw everything. When her head hit the pillow, she passed out immediately from the heroin.

"I'm coming to get you, baby. Hang in—" Jack said before he was cut off.

Rolf held one finger up to his lips for Jack to be quiet, while he leisurely took a seat at the lone table and turned the camera toward himself. "Time to set the hook on this idiot," he whispered, then unmuted the phone again. "You got what you wanted, Mr. Gunn. As you can see, she is alive. Now it's my turn."

"You listen here, you bastard. You hurt another hair on her head, and—"

"Oh, that ship sailed a long time ago," said Rolf. "The last time I saw you, my father had just died and you were holding a gun to my head." Rolf felt his blood pressure rise and his face turn red as he pointed a finger at his head, thinking of that horrible moment. All he had wanted to do was mourn and honor his father, but even that had been stolen from him by Jack, who had him taken away as a prisoner while his father lay dead. Rolf took a deep breath to steady himself and said, "I've always wondered where you buried him. Or did you just throw him over the side of that ship?"

"I'm going to kill you, just like the rest of your family."

Rolf watched Jack squirm. "That's all you have to say? I guess you've answered my question."

Rolf lit a cigarette and exhaled a blue-gray cloud toward the lone lightbulb hanging from the ceiling of the dungeon-like room. He thought back to the moment when he was told by Mullah Mohammed Abdul that Jack Gunn had killed his father. As it turned out, Jack had only captured Rolf's father, and eventually Rolf did exchange Travis for his father. But deep down, Rolf had loathed Jack Gunn, make that all Gunns, from that moment on.

"I've got your wife. Your son was cast overboard just like you did to my father's body." Rolf inhaled again. "That leaves you. Oh, and the bombs." Rolf forced a laugh for the camera. The sinister, maniacal laugh of a lunatic. "How good of a swimmer is she?"

He held the phone out to give Jack a close-up of Nina. "Say good-bye, Mr. Gunn."

"Nina! Nina!" screamed Jack.

"I'll ask you one time. How far are you willing to take this badal?"

"I want my wife back."

"I want my wife back, *please*," Rolf said and waited. His smoldering cigarette hung from the corner of his mouth. The room swallowed all sound. Nina's raspy breathing came and went eight times a minute. Too slow. Too weak.

"I want my wife back, please," said Jack in a surrendering tone.

"That's a good boy. But I have no idea where your wife is." Rolf brought the camera up close to his face. "The only ones here are me and my newest wife, Rania."

"What?" asked Jack. "What are you talking about?"

"You can't give me back what you stole from me. You can't give me back my wife, my kids, my father, my uncles. They're all gone. You can't give me what I lost." Rolf fell silent. "So, I'm doing the next best thing. I'm taking from you what you took from me. Badal, Mr. Gunn. Rania and I are starting over."

"You can't be serious. You can't just take another man's wife," Jack said.

"Don't be ridiculous. Rania loves me. She says so all the time. Heroin's a funny drug. A funny, funny drug, don't you think? One taste, and she'll do or say anything to get more, if you know what I mean." Rolf pumped his eyebrows up and down for the camera, relishing every second of it.

"You can't do this," Jack said.

"Oh, but I already have," Rolf said. He inhaled slowly, deliberately, then exhaled. "There's another thing I have that you don't."

"What's that?" Jack sounded ready to explode.

"An army," said Rolf. "That's right. You might find me, but it won't matter. You won't get past my army."

"You're a dead man," Jack said. "I found you before. I'll find you again."

"You didn't think the CIA were the *only* ones who used drugs to get what they wanted, did you? I finally figured it out. My father wasn't a traitor. Drugs were the only way you could have gotten him to tell you where our security council was holed up."

"You're nuts. You don't know what you're talking about," said Jack.

"And you can quit pretending," said Rolf. "Rania told me everything. How do you think I got your personal number?"

Jack wiped tears from his eyes and said nothing.

"Oh, I'm sorry. Am I upsetting you?" said Rolf. "Well, let me share some good news. Rania tells me that Travis is still alive and kicking after all," said Rolf. "I may have underestimated that little brother of yours, but you . . . I knew you were an asshole, just like Travis always said."

"You think you know me?" asked Jack. "You don't know shit. But go ahead and keep digging your own grave, you stupid bastard."

"I'm going to give you a little hint of what's coming next," said Rolf.

"Save it, asshole. I don't need your help," said Jack. "I was born to track down losers like you. What's coming next is straight out of your Al-Qaeda cookbook."

"You're a funny man, Mr. Gunn. Simple, but funny."

Rolf pointed his camera back at Nina. "Take a good last look. You'll never see her again. But don't worry. Rania will never want for anything, now that she has a *good* man."

"If it's the last thing I do—"

"But you've got bigger problems now that the clock is ticking, brother," Rolf interrupted. He smirked as he turned the camera back on himself. "You don't mind me calling you that, do you, now that we're family and all?"

Rolf saw Jack grinding his teeth, but Jack said nothing.

"A brother should help a brother. That's what my father always told me." Rolf smiled. "So brother, the time has finally come. The Age of the Crescent is upon us. My suitcases and their martyrs are in place, and my people have sworn to follow me to the top or die trying."

Rolf sat up, back straight, chin out, as if waiting for a signal from over the horizon. He dipped his chin, checked his wrist-watch, and said, "The clock is ticking."

"Think of your wife and kids. We can work out a deal. We can put your family back together. Put your life back together. Don't do this," pleaded Jack.

"I have a new wife. I have a new mission. America's time for suffering has come."

"You can't do this," said Jack.

"Don't bother looking for me," said Rolf, smiling again. "I won't be hard to find even for an idiot like you, but I'll be impossible to stop. See me soon. *Allahu Akbar.*"

The screen went blank.

Chapter 23

Little Creek, VA

"Friday is one of their holy days. It's a big day for jihadists on the fast track to paradise. The insurgents pick crowded civilian targets, like cafés, markets, and mosques to suicide bomb." Lt. Commander Winfield studied the CTF team sitting around the table. "If the clock's ticking like El-Hashem said, next Friday looks like a good bet.

"Mossad intercepted a communication between two Al-Qaeda chiefs following a drone attack in the northern Sinai Peninsula. Looks like Rolf El-Hashem isn't bluffing. They have eleven dirty bombs and intend to use them soon." Winfield's gaze fell on Hector Martinez and then Jack's deadpan face on the computer screen, but he said nothing. All Winfield's criticism of Jack and Martinez had taken place an hour earlier, in his office. Praise in public, criticize in private. Jack was still stinging from that conversation.

Jack, Dewey, Snake, and Dozer had flown from Mali to the CIA's "black site" on Diego Garcia, a small atoll in the middle of the Indian Ocean. Diego Garcia was the most important facility the US had in the region, for a lot of reasons. It sat at the southernmost tip of a fifteen-hundred-mile-long underwater volcanic ridge connecting the northern and central Indian Oceans, which submarines of all nationalities used to hide their movements. The tiny island housed a huge American naval support facility for ships and subs, a large airbase, communications and space-tracking facilities, and a substantial contingency of prepositioned supplies and weaponry for the rapid-response teams supporting regional operations and emergencies.

Jack's team visited the island on occasion when they needed to lock up and question a prisoner terrorist in a place where there were no rules of what could and could not be done to another human being to make them talk. Most of the people at the tip of the spear firmly believed there were people in this world whom everyone was better off not knowing who they were, where they were, or what they had done. Jack and his team fit into that category. In her position with the CIA, Jaz was a believer too. They knew that without places such as their black facilities in Diego Garcia, Romania, and Guam, the world was screwed. Terrorists simply could not be treated humanely and then be expected to cough up vital information. The terrorists knew it. The special forces teams knew it. It was the raw and nasty side of fighting terror.

Jack needed a friendly place, halfway to Pakistan, where he and his team could gear up and gather more intel before he went after Nina. Diego Garcia was the perfect place. Nobody but US military, other off-the-books types, and seagulls were within a thousand miles.

"You guys are slipping, Jack. Slipping badly. How in the hell did you lose eleven bombs and over fifty-five million dollars?" Winfield asked Jack, who was face-timing from a computer screen in Diego Garcia, and Martinez, who was sitting across the desk from Winfield in Little Creek. "You got promoted to the head of CTF because you were the best, Jack. Maybe I made a mistake."

"I know it looks bad, sir," Jack said as convincingly as he could. "Okay, I admit it's bad. As of an hour ago, Nina was a prisoner of Rolf El-Hashem in Pakistan, who also claims to have the eleven dirty bombs and is ready to use them. My team is piecing together different scenarios now. We'll have something within the hour."

Jack was on the defensive, a place he typically avoided by being prepared, judicious, and, occasionally, lucky. He preferred to be, and usually was, three steps ahead of everyone, not playing catch-up. Second-guessed by his superiors, embarrassment filled in the gaps usually occupied by confidence and determination.

"My team didn't discover that the suitcases were dummies until it was too late. These guys are good," said Martinez.

"Better than you?" Winfield said and let it burn while he stared back and forth between Martinez's and Jack's faces on the computer. "And how does a fucking Mali truck driver get the jump on two of your best guys?" He stared some more.

Jack shook his head, bit his cheek, and pictured the driver he wanted to strangle. No time now, but maybe later. *Priorities*, he reminded himself and added the two Malian drivers' names to his long to-do list.

"This is out of my hands now. Way out," said Winfield, sounding exhausted. "The joint chiefs, the national security advisor, and God knows who else will be meeting with SecDef to come up with a plan, and then brief the president on how to get through the next seventy-two hours with his balls intact. As for rescuing

Nina, well, I'm afraid she's not very high on their priority list right now. I don't know what to say, Jack, except I'm sorry."

Jack realized at that very moment that Nina was dead unless he did something about it.

"The list of likely targets is growing," said Winfield, continuing his assessment meeting with the CTF team an hour later with an office full of sections chiefs and Martinez, and Jack back on his computer. "Intel points at the obvious ones: Washington, DC; New York; London; Tel Aviv; Paris. Other soft targets include Disneyland, the Mall of America, the list goes on. We assume they made the radiation undetectable with lead shielding to get this far, necessitating boots and eyes on the ground to find and neutralize the threat."

A suicide mission. That's what it sounded like for the squads assigned to stopping the bombers at the various ground zeroes around the world. One detonation would wipe out an entire squad. Everyone around the table knew what Winfield meant. Casualties of war. Cannon fodder.

"We've got one shot. Fail and thousands of good people die." Winfield looked around the table one last time. "You'll get your orders. Meeting adjourned."

As everyone got up to leave, Lt. Commander Winfield said, "Martinez, I'd like to have a few words with you and Jack in private."

Once the door closed, Winfield sat back down and said matter-of-factly to Martinez and Jack, who was still on the video screen, "I'm pulling you and your teams off."

"What? Sir! You . . . you can't do this! We gotta stop these bastards," said Jack through the video connection.

"You're right, Jack. We gotta stop these bastards, but not you and Martinez. The president was very specific about that," Winfield said.

Jack swallowed hard. It was the first time he could remember ever being substituted. He started every game in every sport he had ever played. A natural athlete. Make that a supernatural athlete. Teams won with him in the game. He still held state records in Montana in the four-hundred-meter run and shot put. He was undefeated throughout four years of wrestling as a heavyweight and had numerous Division I scholarship offers, but stuck with joining the SEALs. He wanted to make a difference and use what the Zuya had taught him.

Tracking and killing terrorists was what he was born and bred to do. There was no one better. *Period.* He slumped in his chair halfway around the world, dumbfounded.

"I can't just sit here in the middle of the Indian Ocean and do nothing. I just can't . . . I won't," said Jack.

"The president knows the sacrifice, the price you and your family have paid. Thankfully, your son is recovering nicely. Your wife . . ." Winfield fell silent, then choked up as he said, "Nina . . ."

All Jack thought about was Nina, now that Barett was doing so well. Nina being all doped up on heroin, the captive wife of the most insane man on the face of the earth. The same insane man who was preparing to light off eleven dirty bombs.

Jack took a breath and said a notch quieter, "Think of me what you will, but if you look at my record compared to anyone else's, I think you'll agree I'm still the man to command the CTF. Plus, I know this guy. He thinks he's baiting me, but I know how this prick thinks. Do you think I *want* to die?

"He took my wife and son. He's holding her in Pakistan, sir. If you were me, what would you do?" Jack threw his hands up in the air and said, "Every bone, every muscle, every fiber of my being tells me this son of a bitch is playing us. I can't prove it. Not yet. But I need your permission to hunt down this crazy bastard before he starts World War III."

Winfield took a deep breath, then another. Leaned back in his chair and scrutinized Jack for a moment as if he could see inside of him. He nodded. "If we do this, it's a tight circle. I don't want CNN or anyone else getting wind of this."

Jack took a big breath himself and relaxed back into his chair, nodding.

"Pakistan's a mess. They've got hundreds of nukes and thousands of nutcases. This Rolf El-Hashem was smart enough to use a phone the NSA couldn't trace," said Winfield. "It took ten years to find bin Laden. We don't expect you to do this alone."

"Thank you, sir. I figure with Martinez back there and my CTF and the CIA, we'll pick up his trail. It's not like we're new to the neighborhood."

There was a knock at Winfield's door and an ensign stepped in. "Sir. Turn the TV to CNN. El-Hashem is claiming to be the new leader of the People's Party of Pakistan. And they've made him an *imam*."

Chapter 24

Unknown Location, Pakistan

Nina floundered in her own delirium like a dead-drunk fighting off a pack of wild dogs.

She kicked. She flailed. Her head flopped from side to side. She screamed for help, but the only sounds that came out were muffled squeals. If anyone had been guarding the sleeping quarters of Imam Rolf El-Hashem, they would have followed orders to shoot her up with another dose of heroin when she came to. But Nina was alone.

Her first conscious thoughts were, *my hands are free*. Her legs were too.

She stopped her head from thrashing and steadied herself on the down pillow. She studied her hands as if she were examining two newly discovered artifacts. As everything came into focus, she was confused by her freshly painted fingernails and ornate jewelry. She rubbed her eyes and looked again. Her hands had never looked better. The jewels looked real, but what did she know? Other than turquoise, silver, and her wedding ring, she had little need for jewelry or makeup. And quite honestly, she needed neither to look beautiful. With vibrant green eyes and an infectious laugh, she had always been someone both men and women gave a second look.

The gag-scabs at the corners of her mouth were healed. Her skin felt smooth. The ruby-red lipstick surprised her even more. A scarf or hat—or something—snuggly covered her head. She wasn't sure. But she smelled clean. Better than she felt.

Everything was spinning. A sudden wave of nausea hit. She leaned over the side of the bed and threw up. She saw it wasn't the first time. A pool of mandarin-orange vomit, possibly blood, stained a white Persian rug. She lay back on her pillow and pleaded for the room to stand still.

Something tugged on her left arm. She was no longer in the robe, but had been dressed in an aqua-blue *abaya* and *hijab*, covering her from head to foot. She dug her left arm out from under the blue waves of cloth to find an IV tube piercing the fat vein at her elbow.

I'm sick. I'm dead. Oh my God, my cancer's back.

Nothing made sense. She suffered a wave of nausea, followed by cold sweats. She was dying of thirst.

She slowly propped herself up and hung her legs off the other side of the bed. A pitcher of water sat a few feet away on a small table, beneath a sheer-curtained window. She struggled to her feet and shuffled several wobbly steps until she managed to steady herself with a hand on the edge of the table.

As she drank a few shaky sips of water, men's voices erupted in a boisterous cheer from the doorway just beyond the table. Loud voices. Close voices.

Nina startled and stood rigidly, still bracing herself on the table like a drunk. She inched closer to the doorway and leaned against the wall. Exhausted, out of breath, and sweating profusely, she slowed her breathing and listened.

"The time has come for the people of Pakistan to stand up and be heard. We're tired of being treated like puppets, servants to the infidel Americans, the English, the French, and the Jews."

Rolf's bodyguards in the other room cheered their new leader's first televised speech. The experts on TV claimed that Rolf El-Hashem was the anointed one, the long-awaited *Mahdi*. The crowd on the TV cheered wildly.

"I've been asked a thousand times, am I the Mahdi? I can't answer that. Only Allah can answer that. But Allah has spoken to me in a clear and holy voice. If you elect me as your next president, I, Imam Dr. Rolf El-Hashem, will lead Pakistan to its rightful place . . ."

That name. That voice sounded vaguely familiar to Nina. She ever-so quietly peeked around the corner. Three men dressed in military-style uniforms sat with their backs to Nina, watching a big-screen TV, each with a rifle propped against his thigh.

While the architecture was adobe and austere, the furnishing spoke otherwise. *Where am I?* Nina wondered.

The face Nina saw on the screen sent shivers through her already twitching and tormented body. Across the bottom of the screen scrolled, "Will an El-Hashem finally control Pakistan's nuclear arsenal?"

Nina ducked back into her bedroom, staggering awkwardly toward the bed with a hand over her mouth, suppressing the urge to scream or vomit.

"The clock is ticking on the United States of America. My high-level informants from deep inside the CIA verify that at this very moment, they're planning to attack us and take over all our nuclear weapons. Believe me, my people of Pakistan, when I say, the clock is ticking for the US and Pakistan. Elect me to throw off the reins of slavery and lead you . . ."

Nina started hallucinating or dreaming, she wasn't sure. Objects in her room started glowing in different colors. Sweat poured from every pore. Adrenaline fueled her sense of panic.

Out of the corner of her eye, she spotted a glowing cell phone. She grabbed it, punched in a series of numbers from her foggy consciousness, and hit enter.

"This is Jack."

"Jack. It's Nina," Nina said as quietly as she could. Like trying to whisper a shout.

"Nina! Where are you?" yelled Jack.

"Jack. Barett?" said Nina.

"Barett is okay. We got him. Where are you?"

"Jack."

"Nina, where are you? Describe what you see, sweetie."

"Jack. Where are you? I want to come home."

"I'm coming to get you. Tell me what you see. Hurry."

"I see him. The man on TV. I don't feel good. I got to go."

"No, Nina. Stop. Don't go," Jack said. "Nina. *Nina.*"

The men next door cheered again as Nina put the phone down. She collapsed on the edge of the bed, a little too noisily. She opened a drawer on the nightstand. Everything glowed as if she had hit the mother lode of weapons. A pistol. A knife. What more could she ask for?

A voice, seemingly her father's, was chattering away in her head. She paid no attention.

Nina felt clammy. She hyperventilated. Her heart felt as if it would burst into a million pieces. She frantically moved down to the next drawer and kept searching. She didn't know what she was looking for until she found it.

"Jackpot," she whispered. Nina was already addicted to Rolf's endless supply of heroin. Pakistani euphoria. Liquid salve for her terminal misery. She felt hopelessly lost in an alien world. Her memory of who she was and how she got there was fading by the hour, so she did the only thing that made sense in her condition, short of sticking a gun in her mouth and pulling the trigger.

The men's chairs next door scraped across the floor. Applause and cheering continued from the TV, but the speech was over.

Nina steadied her hand, stuck the needle into her IV port, and pushed the plunger all the way down. The brown liquid heroin mixed briefly with the clear saline, then raced up the IV tubing into her bloodstream. She felt its warmth move up her arm and, seconds later, flood her brain.

Her sweats stopped, her breathing returned to normal, and her sense of panic evaporated. In her last conscious effort, she tossed the syringe back into the drawer and lay back on her pillow.

Peace again. Six hours of peace until the cycle started all over again. A smile spread across her face. Feeling like a well-fed baby, she closed her eyes.

CHAPTER 25

CIA Quadrangle, Diego Garcia

"No trace again! You gotta be kidding!" screamed Jack as he slammed down the phone in the cradle. He was still sitting in the same Diego Garcia intel office he had been in for the last two hours, talking with Winfield, Martinez, and the rest of his CTF and CIA teams back in Virginia, trying to figure out what to do next. The longer he sat there and the more coffee he drank, the worse he felt.

He took a short walk to the next room where Dewey, Snake, and Dozer were inventorying their gear and resupplying.

It was another in a long line of gray concrete cubes the Diego Garcia architects seemed to have fallen in love with. Two metal doors, no windows, no pictures, bright fluorescent lights, and piped-in air. It had all the personality of a stick of butter. The guys had appropriated a couple fold-up banquet tables and chairs from somewhere. Jack did not bother asking where they got the stuff, because there were two things SEALs were good at: being resourceful (i.e., stealing) and lying. He did not care, anyway. He would have done the same.

They all looked on edge. The lack of a good night's sleep combined with several back-breaking days of bouncing around the wadis of Mali in trucks and on motorcycles, and, worst of all, losing two teammates left the guys inconsolable. Jack felt worse still, since he had just heard Nina's feeble call for help.

Nobody wanted to be consoled. They were not looking for a shoulder to cry on. No SEAL on Jack's teams were big talkers, especially about their feelings. At that moment, if they had revealed their true feelings, it would have sounded brutal. What they wanted to do to the assholes that killed their buddies and kidnapped Nina and Barett would come across the wrong way to most people.

Most people had never put two bullets through someone else's head. Most people did not know what it felt like to twist someone's head until his spine snapped. Most people had never seen what a terrorist could do to another person with a piano wire. But that was just the way SEALs were. Day and night, they prepared in both mind and spirit to do what they were best at . . . killing. They let their actions do their talking, and right then, all four of them were ready for action.

"What's up?" asked Dewey. "You look a little crazy."

"I'm feeling a little crazy. Nina just called on my cell."

"What? What'd she say?"

"She's still all doped up. She didn't make any sense at all and had to hang up before we got a trace," said Jack. "But we know El-Hashem is keeping her close. Winfield is trying to nail down his exact location, but it'll be somewhere in Islamabad, Pakistan."

"Sweet," said Dewey. "We'll be good to go. Just give us the word."

A mission into Mali versus a mission into Pakistan called for different battle plans, different weaponry, and different electronics. Jack, Dewey, and Ghost Team had spent years operating in Afghanistan and Pakistan, so detecting IEDs, defending against RPGs, and not trusting anyone to not shoot them in the back were skills they never lost. The big difference in moving from Mali into Pakistan was they could anticipate military support from the Army and Air Force in neighboring Afghanistan. Helicopters, fighter jets, medical evacuation—everything they could not get in Mali.

Once again Jack's thoughts went to Dozer and T-bone. The hole in his heart hemorrhaged pain and sorrow for his two good buddies and their families. He still could not believe they were gone. He did not want to believe it but knew it was true, that the two Mali drivers he and his team had ridden with from Bamako to Timbuktu—and had joked and shared meals with—had been working for Al-Qaeda. They had killed two of his best men and best friends.

Jack glanced at the tattooed list of his fallen teammates on the inside of his left arm. Good guys and good friends. He pictured their faces. He pictured the missions where they went down. He pictured their funerals. Tears welled up in his eyes as he visually added two new names to his list.

He grimaced, rubbed his eyes, and shook it off. There would be plenty of time to mourn later. He had work to do. He went back inside the EMP-reinforced bunker to his desk and the ongoing video call with Winfield and Martinez back in Virginia.

Nina's voice on the phone had been like a jolt of adrenaline to Jack. A new burst of energy came with that all-important proof-of-life label the military was so focused on having before they committed American troops to a rescue attempt.

"It sounded like El-Hashem still has her on the juice," Jack said to Winfield and Martinez, who were sitting in front of a computer screen on the other side of the world. "Didn't sound like herself at all, but she was trying to tell us where she was. What did she say again?"

"I see him. The man on TV," Martinez said from the monitor.

"That was at the same time we were watching El-Hashem on TV," said Winfield. "It shouldn't be too hard to track down his whereabouts now that he's come out of the closet."

"So he's using her as bait to lure me in," said Jack in a dark and sinister tone. "What kind of lowlife piece of scum would do that?" All expression drained from his face except for one, his death stare. Put El-Hashem in front of him at that moment, and he would not even blink as he put two bullets through his head.

Jack wadded up a map of the Middle East he had snatched off the intel desk and bounced it off the concrete wall as if he were throwing a fastball. He grabbed ahold of the TV, but thought better of it.

"This is getting worse by the second," said Winfield.

"You're telling me! It's a freaking nightmare," said Jack. He wrung his hands, fidgeted in his chair, scrubbed the piles of skin furrowed over his leathery brow as if he were rubbing a genie's bottle, hoping the genie would grant his wish.

There was no magic genie. No magic answer. No answers, period. Only questions. Jack's mind spiraled out of control, caught in a riptide of panic and doubt.

How can I save Nina? Where are the bombs? How can I stop Rolf?

Around and around and around he went.

"He said the clock's ticking. How much time do we have?" Winfield asked.

"What?"

"How much time do we have, Jack? What's this maniac thinking?" asked Winfield.

Jack shrugged his shoulders. His stomach jolted this way and that, as if it were the severed end of a downed power line, chaotically dancing sparks across the ground. His heart pounded loud and fast in his ears. His mind ricocheted back and forth between Nina, Barett, and Rolf. Guilt and failure overwhelmed him as he thought.

What's he thinking? What's he thinking? How the hell do I know what he's thinking? All he could think of was, at that very minute somewhere in Pakistan, Rolf had shot Nina up with heroin, she was passed out, and Rolf was making grand claims to being their savior. It was unbelievable. He had never seen anything like it or imagined it could happen, at least not in the twenty-first century.

Rolf was a raging lunatic by all accounts. Jack had read the CIA reports. How Rolf went from being a world-famous plastic surgeon to a jihadist was something they had never seen before. Rolf was burning with the fire of jihad and was probably the only person alive who knew the locations of all eleven of Mohammed's dirty bombs, which was a disastrous combination.

Jack had thought he was doing the right thing by showing some mercy to Rolf on that Yemeni freighter and sending him to prison, but Rolf had duped him just as he had Travis.

After Jack rescued Travis a year earlier, they had talked about how hard-wired Jack was after years of killing terrorists. How Jack now could not turn off his hyperawareness when he went back home, as he had been able to do in the early years. Travis encouraged Jack that he needed to fight to save his soul before it was too late. To regain hope, Jack needed to have mercy on himself and the little guys who needed defending from bullies.

As it turned out, Rolf was a great actor. He played himself to be a victim of the Taliban too and that he loved Travis like a brother. Jack had felt sorry for him and bought into his little act when he should have done what he was trained to do: put a bullet through his head and move on. For the thousandth time, he castigated himself for his lapse in judgment.

Someone had gotten ahold of him down there and lit the fire of jihad. That much was obvious. He was not wasting a second of his newfound freedom either. He was going straight for the top. The presidency of Pakistan.

Jack cleared his voice as if he had something to say. "He's got a handful of dirty bombs, thanks to me." Jack shook his head, then grabbed a phone, and started waving it at Winfield on-screen. "But he won't stop there. You heard him."

Winfield whistled as he leaned back in his chair. "Pakistan hasn't allowed IAEA inspections in years, but we estimate they have two to three hundred operational nuclear warheads."

"The Taliban and all the other extremist groups are in the minority, but they're a very vocal and violent minority that scares the hell out of everyone," said Jack.

"Pakistanis would never vote him in."

"They would if they had a gun at their head," said Jack.

Winfield stood and walked to the second-story window overlooking the piers on the Chesapeake Bay. The midday sun reflected off the deep-blue water. Seagulls lounged atop wooden pilings, seemingly napping in the Gulf Stream breeze. A couple of shirtless SEALs strolled his way, luminous and laughing after lifting weights. The thick muscles, the confidence, the invincibility of baby SEALs always made him smile.

"So he's going for the jugular. I wonder who's jerking his chain," said Winfield as he sat back down in front of the computer screen.

"He's got some serious backing coming from somewhere," said Jack.

"And what's with this CIA source bullshit? And a US invasion?" asked Winfield.

"He's so full of shit, it's unbelievable," said Jack. "Somewhere along the way, he's picked up the game of international politics. Get everyone watching us, and then start a war when no one's looking."

"The media's taking it hook, line, and sinker," said Winfield.

"Nobody's ever even heard of him or this People's Party of Pakistan, and boom—he's running for president of a nuclear power." Jack hammered his fist on the desk. "And he's not even hiding. He's running around Islamabad holding press conferences. We should pay a local to put a bullet through his skull the next time."

"What about Nina? What about the bombs?" asked Winfield.

Jack suffered such anxiety, knowing that one way or another, either Rolf or a cancer relapse would kill Nina. With all the stress and everything else she was going through, the cancer was probably eating its way through every organ of her body at that very moment. He needed a breakthrough.

"You know, I may have underestimated this prick. He's a lot savvier coming out of prison than when he went in," said Jack.

"Let's find out who he spent time with and wring them out the old-fashioned way," Winfield said to Jack. "Somewhere along the way, he went over the edge."

Winfield's phone rang, and he grabbed it. "Yes, sir, I saw it." He listened. "He's sitting in Diego Garcia." He listened. "The White House! When?" He listened. "Shit." He listened. "I'll be on the next plane," Winfield said and hung up.

"Well, that answers a few questions," Winfield said before he made a quick call to arrange the flight to DC. He stood. "We can worry about him taking over Pakistan later. We've got credible evidence that the clock is definitely ticking. There's been a huge pop in Internet traffic as terrorist cells across the globe are being activated. And those are only the ones we know about. God knows how many sleepers are getting the same green light."

"So do we know where?" asked Jack.

"Take your pick. We've got until midnight *tonight* to figure that out and defuse this thing before an international catastrophe literally blows up in our faces." Winfield studied Jack's stubbled and exhausted face. "The president needs answers. I'll call you as soon as I'm airborne."

"I'll get over to the cell block and see what we can find out," promised Jack.

Winfield stopped before he disappeared out the door, turning back to scowl at Martinez. "And listen you two, no more fuckups. You get me answers, and you get 'em fast. I don't care how, but you get 'em."

"You can count on me, skipper," Martinez said with a nod, seemingly embarrassed that Winfield had lost so much confidence in him to call him and Jack fuckups. Martinez saluted, and Winfield hustled out of his office, leaving Martinez looking at Jack on the computer.

"I picked you to lead Ghost Team for a reason, Martinez," said Jack. "You're a good man. You know what to do."

"I'm on it," said Martinez. "And if I don't hear from you again before the shit hits the fan, well, good luck to you and the guys."

CHAPTER 26

Islamabad, Pakistan

"*Hello* . . . Is anyone in there?"

Someone knocked on the top of Nina's head with his knuckles, then pried her eyes open with a pair of rough fingers.

She winced, swatted the hand away, and rolled over on the bed, buried under layers of exotic blue polyester. With her face covered by a sheer veil, she cracked her eyes open and lay perfectly still, not sure if she was dead or alive. Not sure which she preferred.

The light grew more bearable each time she drifted back to consciousness. The room smelled of burning wood and roses. She tasted bile when she wetted her lips. Out of the corner of her eyes, she saw two men dressed in similar uniforms, rifles at their sides, standing in the doorway, at attention. A television droned on in a foreign language from the adjacent room.

Rolf had his back to Nina, standing on the far side of the bedroom in front of a window, his head down, talking on his smartphone. He started pacing back and forth, from window to bed, seemingly unaware of the machine guns lighting up the volatile Islamabad night sky outside.

"Switch to English. I have visitors," Rolf said into his phone as he leaned over Nina and pulled back the veil. He studied her lifeless face for a second and flipped the veil back over it.

"If anything happens to my family, and I mean anything, you'll be the first to die," Rolf said quietly but menacingly into the receiver. "After you, I'll kill your family. Is that easy enough to understand?" Rolf said as he walked back to the window.

Rolf's family had been secretly sequestered and hidden once his emir got word that Rolf had been sent to prison. His little white lie to Jack that his family was dead was all in good fun.

The fact that he would make Nina his wife was for appearance purposes only. He needed to keep her close to make sure that when Jack made his attempt to rescue her, nothing went wrong. First him and then her. That's how the emir wanted it, that's how it would be.

In the meantime, Rolf had been in prison for a year. He had a lot of pent-up frustration. He justified his actions by proclaiming to his guards, "What harm could there be in my having a little fun with her? She will be dead soon enough."

Nina didn't move a muscle and did her best to play dead.

"I've lost everything. My parents, my life as a world-famous surgeon. Knowing they're safe is all that matters," said Rolf angrily into the phone as he kept pacing.

He dropped into an upholstered Queen Anne chair and waved for one of the guards to open the window by the chair while he rested his head back and listened. The silky sheers filled with a soft breath of fresh air laced with the scent of gunpowder.

"I wanted to die with my father. I held him in my arms as he died from the American poison. It was the worst day of my life . . ." Rolf said quietly into the phone.

Nina watched Rolf through her veil and saw his hands shaking. He wiped his face and stroked his fist-length beard.

He pulled himself together, straightened the tails of his turban, and said, "But it was also the best day of my life. Muhammad took my father home to paradise, and the location of the dirty bombs were revealed to me by Mullah Mohammed Abdul before he was murdered by the American. Allah trusted me to carry on his fight." Rolf seemed overwhelmed. He put the phone down.

He quickly threw his prayer rug on the floor and collapsed to his knees, pressing his forehead to the floor, praying in a Middle Eastern language. The only thing Nina recognized was, "*Allahu Akbar*," which she knew meant, "God is great."

Whatever he said, he said it fervently, over and over. The guards followed suit, at his beckoning. Rolf pounded the floor. He pounded his head. He pounded his chest.

Finally, he stood and picked up the phone. "Is everything as I ordered?" He listened impatiently for three seconds and broke off the response. "Stop talking! I said, is everything as I ordered? Yes or no? I know it's different from my father's grand jihad, you idiot. Do you question me? Is that what you're doing? Who do you think you are?"

Nina felt queasy, the tremors started again, but she lay wide awake under her veil, trying to will her tremors to stop.

The guards were back up, standing at their post. More gunfire and tracers laced the city sky.

"My father sacrificed his life so you could live, you miserable scum. I watched him defy the Americans and win. Muhammed and the rest of the security council sacrificed their lives for Allah, and you disrespect them by questioning me! I should have you shot." Suddenly, he screamed, "Quiet!"

Nina flinched.

Rolf noticed, got up, walked straight across the room to her, and pulled the veil off her face.

She kept her eyes closed and lay motionless.

"Just do exactly as you're told. Screw up, and you die. Clear?" He slammed the phone down on the bedside table on the side away from the pukey carpet.

He leaned over Nina. "It's candy time, my sweet."

Nina tried to play dead, but a glass of cold water in the face ruined that act and shocked her to life.

"I said, it's candy time." Rolf towered over Nina and waved the guards away, who immediately turned and disappeared into the other room.

Nina shook her head, pleading, "No. No. No."

But Rolf seemed to hear, "Yes. Yes. Yes." He pulled up the front of his dishdasha covering his pants.

Pain and anguish, mixed with sorrow, wept from every pore of Nina's body. She wanted to die.

"Well, you're no good to me dead. Not yet, anyway. You might as well make yourself useful, don't you think? On your knees!" Rolf screamed in a tone that left no room for misinterpretation.

She heard a zipper go down on the suit pants he wore under the robe.

"I'm so tense, I'm ready to explode." He grabbed a handful of her hair with his left hand.

A folded piece of paper fell from his pocket and bounced off Nina's hand as his pants slid down to his knees. She forced her eyes open, looked, and flicked it under the bed with a finger.

A cold, hard gun barrel pressed against her skull, right above her ear.

Part of her wanted to reach up and pull the trigger herself and get it over with. But something stronger, deeper, told her to hang on. She wanted to kill the son of a bitch more than anything, but she also wanted to survive. She wanted to see her son again. She wanted to see Jack.

Her sunken eyes shined up at Rolf as she hunkered at his feet, sweating, trembling.

"You want your candy? Do your duty," said Rolf. He clicked the hammer back. "Your choice. Plenty of other women would love to be where you are right now."

Then the best thing possible happened: she threw up all over Rolf's pants and shoes.

"What the hell—" Rolf screamed, jumping back as Nina continued to vomit.

Nina collapsed in a heap when Rolf let go, then looked up into the glaring light. Tears streamed down her splotchy red face. Her eyes begged, pleaded with Rolf to keep his end of the bargain.

"Please!" she said in a pathetic whimper.

"You're worthless, you know that?" yelled Rolf, waving his gun and looking down at the gross mess. "Get me some clean clothes!" he yelled to the guards and stomped from the bedroom.

Nina snatched the piece of paper from under the bed and fumbled to unfold it where she crouched. Her hands felt numb and her brain was fried. In the darkness where the floor and bed met, she read, in English, the names of eleven cities—American, European, and Israeli. Something that seemed so random and out of the blue snapped her back from the miserable spiral she had been trapped in. She fought off the urge to vomit again and tried to focus.

She heard them praying next door. She knew the routine. She had a couple of minutes, at best.

Nina slogged across the bed on her hands and knees as quietly as she could. She pulled open the top drawer of the nightstand, snatched the same cell phone she had used earlier, closed the drawer, and crawled back across the bed. After she powered it up with it buried under a pillow to muffle the start-up sounds, she snapped a picture of the list. Using the only finger that seemed to do what she wanted it to, she punched the number keys and sent the photo in a text message to the phone number she had called earlier: Jack's number.

Rolf and his prayer group stirred next door. Boots scraped on the stone floor. Panicking that she might be discovered with the phone, Nina quickly shut it off and slid it under the bed.

All the focus and moving around had made her feel horribly sick.

"What the hell are you up to?" demanded Rolf.

Nina slid off the pukey side of the bed, onto her knees. "I want my candy," she said as sweetly as she could. She let the folded paper fall from her hand and kneed it back under the bed.

Rolf walked over and grabbed her face with his left hand and wrenched it up toward his. He glared into her glassing-over eyes. "Candy time?"

Nina nodded.

"And have you puke on me again? No thanks. I've got more important matters to attend to right now." Rolf looked at his bodyguards. "Put her down."

Out came the syringe.

Nina got her wish. She had survived another day. She was trying to follow a motto she had heard Jack beat into the heads of new SEAL pups many times.

The only easy day was yesterday. You do what you have to do, but you NEVER, EVER QUIT!

She had to believe it could not end like this. Jack would get her message. He would come. He had to come.

In her rapidly advancing drug-induced delirium, before she passed out for another round of hallucinations, she committed again, in the deepest part of her being, to doing whatever she had to do to make it through one more day.

Chapter 27

Prisoner Block, Diego Garcia

"Rolf El-Hashem was a Section 4 detainee, Warrant Officer Gunn. Camp 4 is where we keep—"

"Save it, Master Sargent. I know all about Section 4. You let the man preparing to blow the lid off the free world roam around, hobnobbing with all the other model-citizen detainees, getting three squares and a flat screen," Jack said as sarcastically as he could. "Hell, I'd sign up if I wasn't so damn busy rounding up these bastards in the first place."

"These men are stuck here until we find someone willing to take them. They are detainees, Mr. Gunn," said Master Sargent.

"Yeah, well, maybe instead of your soldiers worrying about doing suicide checks every three minutes, syncing the prayer clocks, or handing out Qur'ans, they could do something useful."

"Look, Gunn. We don't make the rules, we just enforce them."

"We could go round and round, but I got no time to waste. I think you already know that," said Jack.

Jack looked around the inside of the concrete room three floors below and a half mile away from the intel office he and his team had occupied for the last couple days. The American flag hung limply from a pole in the corner. A framed picture of the president hung on the wall behind the desk. The computer and phone sat on top of a desk covered in some sort of rubberized nonskid. It was typical Army, all the way.

"Where is he?" asked Jack.

"The reservation room, as you so kindly requested," said Master Sargent.

"Reservation room? I need a reservation to talk to a murderer?"

"They're called reservations now, not interrogations," said Master Sargent. "He's over at Section 7—what you types call Camp No."

"My types?" Jack growled. "What type is that?"

"The types that don't obey the Geneva Convention rules. Like I said, your types love Section 7. It's outside my jurisdiction, you son of a bitch," said Master Sargent.

They stood toe to toe. Army versus Navy. Master Sargent had kept up his PT. Jack too. They were both thick with muscle from front to back, side to side.

Jack gave him the slightest hint of a smile and an uptick of his lip. "At ease, Master. I'm just jerking your chain a little. You keep up the good work here, and I'll keep making reservations."

"Ain't got much time for you CIA types, but you got connections, I'll give you that. When SecDef calls me personally to grease the skids, well, who am I to question the president?" He squared up. "Ride's waiting on deck, sir. Good luck."

They shook and saluted.

Jack kicked himself for the thousandth time for sending Rolf to prison instead of paradise. Talking to Master Sargent, knowing how sick the mass murderers and religious fanatics were who occupied the cells, and knowing how naïve the American public was about everything jihad, Jack recognized a time bomb waiting to explode.

Those detainees saw life in an entirely different way than most of the world's citizens. Their cause, their way was all that mattered. If they died promoting their cause, they were rewarded with eternity in paradise. If the infidels died, God willed it. They could not lose. They could not be defeated. That's what scared Jack.

He would probably die trying, but in the end, Jack knew the enemy would win because they had already won in their own minds. It was just a matter of time for it all to play out.

He imagined that was how his ancestors had felt when the white man moved in. The Sioux had lived a nomadic life on the upper Midwest plains for generations. They lived in unison with Mother Earth, needing only what she supplied. They worshiped the sun and moon and stars they lived under. They shared the land with the animals. They honored both and owned neither.

The *Wasichu* saw things differently. They believed in owning land, dominating the animals, and worshiping their god. They also believed in taking the Indian lands so they could mine the gold, lay down tracks, and civilize the blood-thirsty savages. Oh, and the heathens needed to be rounded up and put on reservations so they could be taken care of by the government.

Jack's relatives eventually knew Wasichu would win. There were too many of them. They kept coming and coming and coming. But more importantly, Wasichu knew, sooner or later, they would win. It was just a matter of time.

Jack could see the same ending happening again. The Islamic fundamentalist would win. But all he cared about at that moment was finding Nina, going home to Barett, and hanging on to the two of them for dear life.

Camp No looked nothing like the others. While they spared no concrete and steel in constructing the "black site," it had a more ominous feel. Solid walls. No windows. No guard posts, and miles of concertina wire strung everywhere. It sat apart from the other low-slung, less intimidating concrete bunkers, protected by a thirty-yard kill zone. Even if everyone on the island had top-secret clearances and had been vetted, nothing could be left to chance when it came to the most dangerous terrorists on earth.

Jack's spider clawed into the back of his neck the instant he stepped out of the black Suburban that had spared him the half-mile run across base. Minutes mattered, and that ride had saved him four. He glanced nonchalantly this way and that, and was essentially unconcerned by who might be aiming a gun at him or watching on a computer screen back in the States. The way he saw it, the government had a lot more to lose than he did if word ever got out about what went on at Camp No.

Once inside, Jack felt right at home. He always did inside CIA outposts such as Camp No and the Catacombs in Afghanistan, a secret facility under the runway at Bagram Airfield. An Army specialist led him directly to the reservation room where Hakeem Al-Kabul lay shackled to the cold, concrete floor, naked, and curled up in the fetal position. His prisoner khaki trousers and long white shirt lay crumpled in a corner of the otherwise empty room.

Jack squinted through the one-way glass. "I think I've met that son of a bitch before," he said as he rested a hand on the window. "No time for small talk, though. What do we know, Willy?"

"Tell me about it. I've got everyone from the president on down to my wife crawling up my ass wanting answers," said Special Agent William Clay, pointing at a full new e-mail folder on his computer. Willy looked half Asian, half Native American. He stood five-foot-six, had thin black hair split down the middle, and wore a Fu Manchu mustache. Smoking for thirty years had taken its toll, but he was still one of the best interrogation specialists in the agency.

"He's in for orchestrating the suicide bombings at the resort in Bali. He and your guy spent a lot of time together. No actionable intelligence yet, but we just got started. You only called two hours ago."

"And I need answers now, as in two hours ago. We're gonna have to do this the old-fashioned way. Kill the video," said Jack.

Jack peeled clothes off down to his camouflage T-shirt and pants.

His shirts always looked too small. With a big skin-head planted atop broad, sloping shoulders, it was hard to tell where one started and the other ended. The sleeve tattoo now showing on his right arm resembled an American montage that included a bald eagle, rippling flag, and guns. A list of names ran down the inside of his left bicep, names of his fallen teammates. Whenever he questioned why he did what he did, he looked no further than his tats to be reminded of those who had made the ultimate sacrifice. Nina's and Barett's names were inked over his heart. He had plans for more.

"Knock on the window every five minutes," he said to Willy.

He cracked his neck, cracked his knuckles, chambered a round in his pistol, and opened the door.

Hakeem kept reciting some mantra or prayer as he rolled over to see who had walked in. When they made eye contact, Hakeem started shaking as if he had seen a ghost, and he flailed against his shackles.

"Hello, nightmare. It's been awhile," Jack said with a twisted laugh.

Hakeem tried to slide away, but Jack's boot on his chest stopped that. "Where do you think you're going, shit-for-brains? So much to talk about. So little time."

He flashed his pistol, flipped the safety off for Hakeem to see, and pointed it straight between his eyes from three feet away.

The prisoner stopped everything. "You can't do this. I am a detainee. I have rights."

"You got rights in Camps 1 through 6. But in case you hadn't noticed, you're in Camp No. As in *no* rights, asshole." Jack gave him his best kill stare. "There's only one way you get through the next five minutes alive. And that's by doing everything I say. Waste my time, get cute, and I'll put a bullet through your skull so fast, you won't know what hit you."

There was a knock on the glass.

"That's my signal. You got five minutes to tell me everything you and Rolf El-Hashem talked about. The next time I hear that knock, I put a bullet in your head and move on to the next room."

"I'll tell you everything. First, we talked about paradise and what it will be like in—"

"Shut the hell up, jerkwad. You've got four minutes," said Jack. "What about people, high-up people who have the money and the desire to finance the Taliban or something he called the grand jihad?"

"I . . . I . . . I don't know who you're talking about. Like I said, we talked about—"

"Three minutes." Jack got down on a knee and stuck his gun in Hakeem's nose. "You better know I will pull this fucking trigger. Now, where will the suitcase bombs go off? Name the cities. NOW!"

Hakeem stuttered again but said nothing. With giant, panicky lemur eyes, he looked back and forth between the gun and Jack. "I don't know what you want. Please, I don't know what you want."

"You're a lying son of a bitch. You know it, and I know it. You made your choice," said Jack. "Ten, nine, eight . . ."

"You said I had three minutes."

"I lied. Sue me. Seven, six . . ." Jack's cell phone vibrated in his pocket, annoying the hell out of him, but it might have been Winfield, so he pulled it out.

His jaw dropped as he read the list of eleven cities in the text message from Nina. He stood up and read it again in disbelief. **Hurry Nina** is all it said from the same dead-end phone number Jack recognized from earlier.

"It's your lucky day, dipshit. But don't worry. I'll be back." He left the detainee chained to the floor, rushed out into the observation room, and yelled at Willy, "I need a secure line, NOW!"

Jack was beyond flabbergasted. Nina. It was Nina. Had she escaped? Where was she now? After giving Winfield the list of cities, he called his own CTF to have them trace the text message, just in case. His wheels were spinning in high gear—his brain too. He realized he needed more information to locate Nina, so he put his powers that be at the CTF, CIA, and NSA to work on this latest piece of the puzzle.

In the meantime, there were more imminent threats to the country and the world, as the clock wound down to midnight and Rolf El-Hashem's grand jihad attack.

Chapter 28

CIA Quadrangle, Diego Garcia

Nina's list of eleven cities included the exact locations for all eleven synchronized detonations, such as Times Square and Saint Peter's Basilica. Police and military units around the world scrambled in the remaining few minutes before midnight, East Coast time, searching for shiny aluminum suitcases.

Evacuations of a thirty-mile radius around each ground zero were underway. Millions of citizens from New York; London; Paris; Washington, DC; Hong Kong; Tokyo; Sydney; Moscow; Beijing; Los Angeles; and Rome walked, ran, drove, or rode away—at least the ones who heard the warnings and had the wherewithal to leave. As with any evacuation, the very old, very sick, very poor, or very ignorant stayed behind.

Mustafa El-Hashem, Rolf El-Hashem's uncle who died of radiation poisoning, had made each dirty bomb by packaging twenty pounds of stolen highly enriched uranium (HEU) with the plastic explosive Semtex. He then wrapped the contents in lead X-ray aprons to avoid detection and locked them in identical aluminum suitcases. When triggered, the Semtex explosion would widely disperse the radioactive uranium in all directions. While a Semtex blast was enormous, it wasn't like an explosion of a Hiroshima-type nuclear warhead. Damage from a Semtex explosion spread only several hundred feet, like the Oklahoma City bombing or the Marine barracks bombing in Beirut. But the HEU radiation would spread up to twenty miles and last five to ten years.

Abandoning twelve hundred square miles of New York City and its suburbs, or Washington, or any of the other cities for ten years was inconceivable. Chaos would spread across the globe like a virus. Economies would crumble. Governments too. Societies would go back to the Dark Ages. At least, that is what Rolf and his financiers hoped for. World calamity. World rule.

Jack and his team had been ordered to stand down, stranded in the middle of the Indian Ocean on a corner of Diego Garcia with two hundred caged jihadists enjoying their best or worst day, depending on how it ended. The prisoners insisted on a midnight prayer service to usher in one of their most celebrated holy days.

Jack sat at a desk in a starkly decorated Camp No communications room, where his entire team as well as other unnamed and unknown CIA operatives watched Rolf's grand jihad unfold in high definition. Plenty of backbreaking metal chairs, Styrofoam coffee cups, overflowing ashtrays, and rotating table fans. A haze of blue smoke churned through the room—the ventilation system unable to keep up.

As a boy going to powwows and sweat lodge ceremonies, Jack knew the spiritual importance of smoke. Tobacco and sage grew from Mother Earth, and when burned, its smoke rose to the heavens, connecting this world with the next. Mother Earth with the Great Spirit, Wakan Tanka.

Jack bummed a cigarette from an open pack and lit up, invoking the powers of the ancients to intervene. He bowed his head and said a prayer too, for God to protect Nina and Barett. Without anyone noticing, he held the smoldering cigarette down between his legs and leaned forward over it, slowly waving his fingers through the rising smoke. To the north, the east, the south, and west. Then to the ground, the sky, and lastly to him. All seven points. He did not have a smudging feather or sage or his peace pipe as he would have preferred, but he knew it did not matter. The gods had heard his prayers as it burned.

He made sure he did not inhale the smoke, or his prayers would stay with him instead of rise up to them. He had already done all he could, and it still was not enough. If God, the Jesuit black-robe's god, needed Jack to pray to him before saving Nina and Barett, then Jack was all in. Whatever it took.

Kona's cold, wet nose nuzzled Jack's hand from where she lay curled at his side. Jack had the Belgian Malinois flown over from Little Creek as soon as he realized they were headed back to Afghanistan or Pakistan, just in case. She had a unique set of skills that could come in handy. Jack scratched behind her upright ears. "Good girl, Kona." She was the only hint of normalcy in a dungeon full of flat screens, sweat, and aggravation.

Aggravated to be spectators when they normally took the shots nobody else could or would take, Jack's team fidgeted and cussed, watching top-secret video streaming in from everywhere. They were down to the last few minutes before midnight, and people around the world still ran through the various ground-zero scenes like chickens with their heads cut off.

"What are they still doing there? Don't they know they're going to die?" said Dewey, who was sitting next to Jack.

"At this point, it doesn't matter," said Jack, shaking his head. "They're toast."

"Thank God, Suzy and the kids are at home. Virginia Beach is too far from DC to be affected."

"I talked with Travis and filled him in too. Barett came home from the hospital with him yesterday. Jaz is working, like everyone else, trying to stop this thing. Whatever bunker she's in, you can bet she'll be fine," Jack said. "You still got the same 'bug out' plan, right?"

"That's right. I thought about having them go today, before all hell breaks loose, but Suzy didn't want to freak the girls out," said Dewey.

"Roger that. Me too," said Jack. "Travis and I decided we didn't want to stress Barett any more than he already is. But he's ready to go at the drop of a hat, if need be."

"Same here," said Dewey. "I got my fingers crossed."

"Nothing else we can do, except wait . . . and pray," Jack said solemnly as he bowed his head and closed his eyes . . . and smoked. He was not proud or necessarily sure, so he invoked the powers of all gods to intercede on his behalf to keep Nina safe and to protect and encourage the love of his life until he found a way to save her.

Thousands of police and soldiers from China to France to England searched frantically, combing through thinning crowds for anyone carrying an aluminum suitcase. As the countdown grew shorter and shorter, the searchers at ground zero must have known it was life or death for them. Find the bomb and disable it—or die.

On screen, Jack watched Australian citizens and tourists who must have waited until the last minute to start running away from the Sydney Opera House. There was no audio, but he could see they were screaming. Chinese ran from Beijing's Forbidden City. Russians from Moscow's Gorky Park. On and on they ran, but who could run twenty miles in ten minutes, or 120 miles per hour, to get outside the kill radius of the radiation? The easy answer was no one, seeing as the fastest any human had ever been clocked was twenty-eight miles per hour.

Security cameras overlooking Times Square beamed video channeled through Langley to Diego Garcia, amongst other places. The crowds looked to be in an all-out panic mode, fleeing for their lives as the police had started using bullhorns. DC, London, and Paris all looked the same. The end of the world.

In the middle of all the chaos, on an Arab TV news channel playing off to the side of the front wall of the Camp No communications room, something caught Jack's eye and made the hairs on the back of his neck stand up. He elbowed Dewey.

They saw Rolf El-Hashem shaking hands and speaking animatedly, as if he were pleading with the Pakistani public, outside an Islamabad mosque in the bright sun of a new day, nine hours later than Washington, DC. Trickling across the bottom: **Dr. Rolf El-Hashem shares his message from Allah. Attack is imminent. The Americans are coming.**

Jack called Winfield, who was holed up in a bunker under something called *House Number 3*, somewhere in the DC area with the SecDef.

"What's that son of a bitch up to?" Jack said to Winfield.

"What he's up to is, he's turning the world upside down and seeing what sticks," quipped Winfield, obviously stressed. "T-minus five minutes."

"There. There! THERE!" screamed Jack as he jumped up,

pointing at a helmet-cam video streaming in from a SEAL Team Two member at the National Mall in Washington, DC. "There's a case! There's one of the suitcases!"

"Where? What, Jack?" said Winfield. "Oh shit, there's another in Sydney."

Shiny aluminum suitcases, in eleven cities around the world, simultaneously surfaced in the last minutes before T-minus zero.

The helmet-cam man in Washington, DC, sprinted toward the suitcase Jack had spotted a tourist carrying. Warning shots were fired. Even on the muted screen, panicked screams and terrified faces reminded Jack of a silent horror movie. Helmet-cam man caught up with suitcase man. Shoved him to the ground, face-first with a boot on his back.

"T-minus sixty seconds."

Whether the suitcase was booby-trapped seemed irrelevant. They would die now or a minute from now.

"Open the damned thing now. That's an order," yelled Winfield into a handpiece.

Helmet-cam man viciously slammed the suitcase latches with the butt of his rifle, over and over until the lock shattered. He ripped open the suitcase. He found underwear and shirts and toiletries. Handful after handful, he threw clothes to the side till he reached the bottom.

"It's empty, sir. No bomb."

The same scenario played out again and again around the world.

"What the hell? T-minus zero," said Winfield.

Winfield waited. Jack waited. The world waited. No explosions.

T-plus one. T-plus five. T-plus ten minutes.

And then it happened.

Social media erupted with reports of massive explosions, raging fires, and radiation. Nuclear radiation. The CIA's Facebook and Twitter teams pulled up video streaming in from Pakistan. Bombs went off at T-plus ten minutes simultaneously throughout Pakistan's countryside. From their borders with India, Kashmir, and China, to their borders with Tajikistan, Afghanistan, and Iran, they were under attack. Even in Karachi, their biggest port, and in their capital, Islamabad.

Strangely, Rolf El-Hashem was still on screen. Black smoke filled the sky behind him. Sirens wailed. Women screamed. Children cried. He stood tall, grabbed an AK-47 from one of his bodyguards, and fired it into the air until empty.

"I told you the Americans were preparing to attack. I tried to warn Pakistan's puppet leaders, but they're blind and deaf. They don't care about you, my people. I do." He pumped the gun up and down before his bodyguards hustled him to a blacked-out SUV, surrounded by a Pakistani security convoy.

As they sped away, the caption read: **Under attack, Dr. Rolf El-Hashem of the People's Party of Pakistan stands tall.**

Langley's jaws dropped. The president's jaw dropped. Winfield's jaw dropped. Everyone's jaws dropped but Jack's. He didn't waste a second.

When under attack, move, move, move was a motto he lived and died by.

He did not wait for orders. He did not ask for orders. He ordered his team back on board ASAP and took off headed north across the Indian Ocean before the FAA or FBI or CIA grounded all flights. He knew where he needed to go and what he needed to do.

He needed everyone to stay out of his way so he and his team could do what they did best . . . hunt, track, and kill.

CHAPTER 29

Islamabad, Pakistan

"On your feet, sweetheart," Nina heard Rolf say sarcastically at the same time as he flipped the light on and doused her face with cold water.

"What the hell happened here? Where'd all this blood come from?" said Rolf in pissed-off English.

He always spoke in English, except when giving specific directions to the idiots serving him, who only spoke Pashto or Arabic. Rolf was fluent in French and Spanish too, but Nina had overheard him say that English made him appear regal and presidential and superior. Superior to everyone except the emir. Nina laughed to herself every time Rolf's satphone rang and he cowered like a puppy that had been caught peeing in the house. When the emir called, the big man spoke in whatever language he wanted to, and Rolf listened.

Nina pulled the pillow off her face and rolled over in the direction of Rolf's voice—dizzy, nauseated, and sweating again. Blood stains the size of her head splotched the white satin sheets and her blue *abaya*. Something tore at the hair of her left arm. Still disoriented, she pulled up her sleeve to find the IV catheter stuck to her clothes and no longer in her vein. Blood oozed from the tiny hole in her arm.

"I'm tired of fucking babysitting you. Sleep all day. Make a mess of everything. Don't do anything but use up my drugs." Seething, Rolf snatched a pistol from one of his bodyguards, knelt on the edge of the bed to lean over Nina, and jammed it against the side of her skull, pinning her to the bed.

"You're missing all the fun, sweetheart." He pressed harder till half her face disappeared into the soft mattress.

Nina swallowed hard. Her windpipe felt as tight as a drinking straw. She took one long, suffocating breath after another. Her hands, her whole body trembled. "Please don't . . ."

"Shut the fuck up. Don't you say another word, or I swear I'll put a bullet through your stupid fucking brain." He pressed harder. Nina felt him shaking too. A bead of Rolf's sweat dripped on her cheek.

She went limp and silently prayed, *Please God, don't* . . .

He got off her and started laughing hysterically. The guards laughed too.

"We're moving. Well, at least I'm moving," Rolf said, addressing the room like a king addressing his court. He waved the gun around like his magic wand.

He gestured toward his two bodyguards. "You two have been loyal. You two, I think I will not kill," he declared.

They laughed nervously, having no knowledge of English.

He spun around to Nina and said with a smirk, "You . . . I still need. With you as bait, it's only a matter of time before your dumb-as-a-rock husband shows up. Now, I do admit," Rolf said with a knowing smile, "that it would make my job a lot easier if I didn't have to cart you around, but I'm afraid I'll have to put up with you for a couple more glorious days."

He ambled around, scratching his chin as if in deep thought.

"The new president of Pakistan needs a woman. Someone to take care of his needs. Hmm." He walked to the window and watched the sun setting on his first day as president. "What would my father do, I wonder."

Nina sat up in bed and straightened herself as best she could after another day spent hallucinating. She scooted to the side of the bed.

"I didn't tell you to move."

"I need to go to the bathroom."

"I don't give a shit what you need to do. Piss yourself, for all I care. You've done everything else," he said, nodding his head at the vomit-stained rug.

"But, I have—"

Rolf stomped back to the bed and jammed the pistol into Nina's temple. "Things have changed. I don't have time for a petty game of badal with your knuckle-dragging husband. I have a country to defend and a war to run. I don't want you around anymore. You're a pain in my ass."

Rolf stuck the pistol back in the waistband of his black suit pants, under his white button-down dishdasha. He walked across the bedroom and examined his red-and-white-checked kaffiyeh in a mirror. "How do I look?"

"You look . . ." tried Nina.

"Not you. You do not speak unless I tell you to. Is that understood?" said Rolf.

Nina nodded and said nothing. She felt sick.

"Follow me. I want to show you something." He headed for

the door to the TV room, but stopped Nina before she took her first step. "I said, follow me. You stay two steps behind, and one to my left, nearest my dirty hand."

Nina backed up as he said, "They made me president today. I want you to see."

Rolf queued up a scene on the big screen and paused it. The scene showed him pacing in front of four important-appearing Pakistani men with their hands tied behind their backs. "Those traitors were my predecessors. They were the ones who betrayed our people. What should I have done? Let them run and hide in exile, or pay for their sins of disobedience and greed?"

He let the question hang in the chill for a long second, then pointed the remote at the TV and pushed the play button as if he were pulling a trigger.

The TV scene showed him pulling out the same pistol he had pointed at Nina and shooting all four men in the head. The four cracks of Rolf's pistol were followed by a loud chorus of cheers from an adoring crowd. The prime minister and his cabinet members' bodies fell in a random pile. The crowd of fanatics pulled them off the stage and started going nuts, kicking and mutilating them.

Rolf paused the video.

"I will kill you right here, right now, just like those four traitors. No questions asked. Is that what you want, Nina?" Rolf held the pistol up for her to see.

Nina shook her head rapidly.

"Are you sure?"

Nina nodded.

"Watch this."

Rolf pressed play again. The scene was of his news conference outside the mosque, moments after the bombs went off. "Do you know what that is?" he asked, pointing at the smoke and flames.

She shook her head.

"That bomb was compliments of your husband."

Nina looked puzzled. Her ears pounded with another headache. Her bladder was about to explode.

"Your fool husband paid Rami Salwa for fake bombs. In exchange, I was released from prison to find the real bombs"—Rolf pointed out the window at the smoke again—"and use them for our grand jihad—minus the uranium, of course. You don't think I'd be stupid enough to set off a nuke in my own capital, I hope." Rolf looked at her and scoffed.

Nina made sure he saw her shake her head.

"In fact, I only left uranium in a couple of them down by the Indian border. Give those bastards a taste of their own medicine."

Nina nodded and tried to look interested. She started to understand.

"Oh, you have to see this part. I love this part," said Rolf as the scene on the TV changed again. Rolf was speaking from the steps where, moments earlier, he had executed the four men.

"We are under attack by the United States of America. For your own safety, stay home and stay tuned. Sharia law has been unanimously approved by Pakistan's new cabinet, just until we have a better idea of who to trust. Cell phones, the Internet, movies, television—all of it will be discontinued, except for the government channels, of course. And women, remember your modesty. If you absolutely must go out in daylight, I urge you to be completely covered. It's for your own good. *Allahu Akbar.*"

Rolf smiled at Nina. "So you see, this is not America, but the start of a new age." He summoned one of his guards with an open hand and said to Nina, "Come here."

Nina tentatively shuffled up to Rolf, unsure if he meant right up to him or two steps back.

"Come on. Come on," he urged.

When she was standing in front of him, he tipped her chin down to her chest.

"Eyes down. Never look any man in the eyes," Rolf said.

Nina jerked as Rolf took a dog shock collar from his guard and strapped it around her neck. Two ice-cold metal prongs jammed into her voice box like blunt needles. Nina panicked for a suffocating moment when she gulped for air and prongs dug into her voice box. Her eyes locked on Rolf's twitching index finger, which rested on the collar's remote control button. One push of the button, and enough electricity to stop a Great Dane in its tracks would zap through her neck. Would it kill her? Nina feared the worst. His finger drifted off the button, and Nina felt herself ratchet down from 100 percent to 99 percent terrified.

"Just a little reminder, in case you decide to do anything else I don't approve of," Rolf said as he waved the remote above his head. "Handy little invention, don't you think?" he said, slipping the remote into his pants pocket. He threw a wad of dark clothing to her and ordered, "Get dressed."

As he passed the guards, he said, "Duct-tape her mouth shut. Meet me at the car in five minutes. Bring her. Leave everything else."

They finally let Nina go to the bathroom, then left her alone in the bedroom to put her *burka* on. She checked the door and the guards, who were back watching TV. She quietly opened the dresser drawer, grabbed the phone, and powered it up.

The guard's TV went silent. Every noise seemed amplified. Her brain was on fire. Her headache was worse than ever.

But at the same time, her thinking was clearing up as her liver worked overtime to purge the aftereffects of the heroin from her system and detoxify her blood.

She heard boot scuffles coming.

With duct tape over her mouth, Nina's lips felt as if they had been superglued shut, so she squealed in shrill tones anyone would understand to mean, "I'm not ready!"

As she stripped off her bloody clothes and pulled the burka with its net-covered eye slits down over her body, she typed a five-word text message to Jack and pressed send, hoping the cell phone towers had not been shut down yet.

She said a prayer, powered down the flip phone, and stuck it up inside her, between her legs.

Wearing a shock collar around her neck, and a burka from head to floor, Nina felt like a walking ghost. Or an invisible spy. She gave the phone one last shove, then walked out the door as the First Lady of Pakistan, at least until Rolf killed her.

Chapter 30

Diego Garcia to Afghanistan

The FAA did indeed ground all commercial air travel over the United States. Some airlines grounded their planes worldwide. Some governments did too. Either way, Jack's CIA C-17 flew through all stops, in-flight refueling and all, to touch down on the tarmac of Bagram Airfield, outside Kabul, Afghanistan, by 0400 local.

The inside of the plane had contained nonc of the normal frivolities and conveniences of a commercial airliner, like comfortable chairs and WiFi. The Globemaster had been gutted to haul anything from tanks, to boats, to drones, to troops. Its only cargo that night was Jack and his team. Once they transferred to the Chinook at Bagram for the hourlong hop down to Jalalabad, sleeptime was over, and they focused on the problems at hand.

Earlier, while they were in-flight, Jack spoke with Travis and Barett by satphone. "Everyone's doing fine, Jack," said Travis, "although we did have a little bit of a scare."

Jack held his breath.

"Jaz started feeling contractions as they were counting down to midnight for all the bombs to go off. She was still locked down in some secret CIA hole in the ground that she can't tell me about, but everything worked out okay. That was some scary shit to watch on TV."

"You're telling me! How's she doing? Is the baby okay?" asked Jack, concerned, but relieved it was not Barett who gave them the scare.

"After they were sure bombs weren't going to go off in Norfolk, they transferred her to the hospital in an ambulance and monitored the baby and her overnight. Barett and I stayed in the room with her, sleeping on cots and going to look at the cute new babies through the nursery window," said Travis. "They said she was having false contractions, brought on by the stress, which eventually stopped, and they sent us home this morning. Everything is fine, but they told her to take it easy and no long trips anymore. She could go into labor at any time." By the uptick in Travis's voice, Jack could tell he was excited.

"What about Barett? How's he taking it?"

"As well as can be expected," said Travis. "I can tell he really misses you and Nina, especially Nina. You're always gone, but he's used to Nina being there every day."

Jack felt his insides twist. He knew the things Travis said were true, but hearing them stated in such a matter-of-fact way made him feel as if he were doing a horrible job of being Barett's dad.

"I don't know what else to do, Travis," Jack said dejectedly, turning toward the plane's bulkhead so no one would see his tears. He wanted to hug Barett more than anything at that moment.

Travis filled in the silence: "The doctors set up some visits with a specialist here in Virginia Beach who helps kids who have been through any sort of traumatic experience, to help them deal with PTSD. Apparently, he's one of the world's best. How lucky is that? Right here in our own backyard."

"That's great. Yeah, that's really great," said Jack. "Does he remember what happened?" he asked apprehensively.

"He remembers very little right now. Just the stuff from the hospital," said Travis in a quiet voice. "The doctors say he may remember other things as time goes by. That's why they want him to see the specialist. They deal with this kind of thing every day."

"What about Nina? What are you telling him about us and why we're not there?" asked Jack.

"We're just taking it one day at a time, answering the questions he asks, but keeping it pretty generic," said Travis. "Jaz came up with the idea to tell him that Nina went with you on a mission trip to Africa to bring food to starving children. He actually seems happy about that. He spends hours on his iPad looking at pictures of Africa."

"Tell Jaz that was a great idea." Jack breathed a sigh of relief.

They talked a while longer. Jack could hear Barett talking to Jaz in the background. It gave Jack a huge boost to hear his voice. Barett was in good hands.

The eastern sky phased from black to slate to midnight blue as their chopper descended on the CIA outstation in Jalalabad, barricaded behind twenty-foot-high, two-foot-thick mud walls topped with razor wire.

Winfield had briefed Jack during the flight from Diego Garcia about the mass chaos and anger being directed toward the US—

and toward Winfield personally—from the president to the chiefs of staff, the Israelis, even the Russians, Chinese, and everyone on the United Nations Security Council.

The secretary general of the United Nations wanted answers. No one was buying the story the president was floating about how the Pakistanis bombed themselves. Nobody was that naïve.

The attack was a huge success in Pakistan. Nothing topped what Rolf accomplished by gaining control of the presidential palace, but others tried.

A thousand militants set fire to fifty homes and a church in Peshawar, burning seven Christians to death. At a cemetery in Islamabad, while a family of fourteen women and children gathered round the grave of a relative, a bomb buried in the dirt-and-rock grave exploded, killing all fourteen.

The stories went on and on, but the scariest story of all was that an El-Hashem had been elected president. Worse still, Rolf had instituted Sharia law and put the militants in charge of enforcing the law, including swearing in the Taliban and making them the police. The Taliban flocked to the cities from their mountain hideouts, like a swarm of hillbillies, to enthusiastically enforce their kind of law.

Jack's cell phone vibrated in his left chest pocket. He always kept his phone over his heart. Extra protection, he figured.

Prisoner. I have a phone. Jack's jaw dropped as he read Nina's text message.

"Dewey, check this out." Jack handed the phone to his second-in-command.

Jack saw Kona flash by the window, and he checked outside.

Kona had endured the long flight the same as the rest of the team. She yawned, stretched, and trotted around, looking for a good place to do her business. Compound walls and fortified gates limited her choices, but she found a prime spot under the belly of their still-warm Chinook.

"What the hell is going on over there?" said Dewey as he read the text again.

"She's still his prisoner, but she's alive. That's what's going on. See if they can get a trace or location of where that came from."

"She always was a fighter, Jack," said Dewey, nodding. But before Jack got a word out, Dewey corrected himself, "I mean, *is* a fighter," he said with a long, cleansing breath and relieved smile.

"You're damn right she's a fighter," said Jack, puffing out his chest. "And she's our contact on the inside. In fact, she may kill the son of a bitch before we do. Now get the hell outta here and check out that phone trace."

Dewey ran out of their hooch to the intelligence shack.

Jack looked around the thirty-by-thirty hooch—a little slice of trailer-trash Americana-style sitting smack-dab in the middle of the dark side of the moon. It had aluminum walls, a tin roof, air conditioning, forced-air heat, electricity, and a portable bathroom/shower with hot and cold running water—more than what 95 percent of all Afghans lived without.

The two opposing walls were lined with six-by-eight-foot chain-link fence cages, five to a wall. The swinging gate on each cage hung open, and Jack watched the rest of his team make themselves at home, stowing their gear or stretching out on a cot.

Dozer and Snake got into a little pissing match about who was better, the Patriots or the Packers. They never quit talking sports, never. Jack had heard them going at it during compound take-downs and training jumps. And it did not matter what sport, they never agreed on anything.

A fold-up nylon chair and cot sat inside each hooch. It was their little home away from home. Jack took the hooch nearest the front door. First thing after dropping his gear, he pulled four pictures from his breast pocket and clipped them on the outside of his gate.

Pictures of Mack and T-bone with their families at a team picnic, Barett on the first day of second grade, and Nina at the beach. He studied the pictures and lingered on their faces. He realized he might not see any of them again.

Mack and T-bone had been two of his best friends. Their families were like his own. The lonely feeling of not being able to call or e-mail them hit Jack like a two-by-four to the ribs. And if that were not bad enough, not being able to see them, train with them, or go into combat with them was going to be like going to war without his right and left arms.

He wished it had been him. Except, if it had been him, he'd never see Nina or Barett. Guilty again.

Overwhelmed, his chest or heart or stomach started to well up as if he were going to have a heart attack or throw up. He felt weak in the knees and braced himself against his hooch gate, which loudly rattled shut, as wire gates do. One hand on the gate, one clutched over his heart.

"Jack, you okay?" asked Snake as he hustled to back up Jack. "What's going on?"

"I'm fine, Snake. Fine." Jack cleared his voice and wiped his eyes. "New boots."

Snake studied Jack's pictures, slapped Jack on the shoulder, and said, "Don't worry, bro. We'll get her back." Snake touched a fist to Mack and T-bones's pictures, then solemnly walked back to his hooch and resumed loading thirty-round magazines.

The rest of the guys got back to doing the same: loading magazines, cleaning their primaries, checking electronics, refolding chutes. They all wanted sleep, but first things first. Before they slept, ate, or did anything else, they needed to be ready to go on an instant's notice.

Jack headed out across the baked-dirt compound for the intel shack to find out what Dewey had learned. Kona fell in step at his left hip, ears up, head down slightly, sniffing, hunting. Hunting for haji. Searching for explosives. Protecting her "family."

At home, Kona lived in Dewey's house as the family pet. Play ball, let the little kids crawl all over her, even eat canned dog food on occasion. But when they deployed, Kona was on the job 24/7, just like the rest of the team. The smell of lube oil, the sound of gunmetal sliding on gunmetal or a box of ammo being dumped out onto tables and loaded into magazines, meant the same thing to everyone, including Kona. It was time to go to work. The world needed saving again.

"What the hell's that smell?" Jack complained as he barged into the intel shack.

"A rat or something died inside the wall," said Butch Columbo, who was manning the communications center. "Smell reminds me of my ex-wife."

"Butch, you ole son of a bitch, talk to me," said Jack as he gave him a hearty slap on his shoulder. "Anything on that phone number?"

"It's a good number, but Nina's powered it down." Butch

turned and nodded to Jack. "Smart lady. El-Hashem shut down their cell network, along with everything else, except government propaganda TV bullshit. She's probably too far inland for our rovers to pick up her signal if she powered up again, anyway. Hard to say."

"What's that—a hundred miles?" asked Jack.

"Closer to two."

Jack took a seat between Dewey and Butch.

Butch was a big, loud, hairy Italian. He sweated constantly, couldn't sit still, and always said what he thought. He had played offensive tackle for the Hawkeyes, but once he missed the cut to the pros, he went with the CIA, visiting one hellhole after another, going through one wife after another, living the dream.

Jack stared at the muted TV tuned to CNN in front of Dewey. "So what's going on out there?"

"The world's at its finest. Nobody knows who did what. Everybody blames the Americans, of course," said Butch.

He turned his fan on high, then leaned his metal chair back, propping up against the wall. "Nobody believes that we had nothing to do with this. The president's pretty much screwed, so he's pissed. The Russians, Chinese, UN—pretty much everyone—wants to fuck us over while the fucking's good." He plopped his chair back down and slid back to the desk. "Screw you before you screw me."

"What do we know about these bombs?" asked Dewey.

"A couple of them contained uranium. The two by India did, so the Indians are all amped up. They got their finger on the hot button. It looks like he pulled the uranium from the others. At least, we're not getting reports of radiation, except for those two."

Butch pointed at the screen, which displayed a real-time map of Pakistan showing two red and nine yellow splash stars.

"Gonna take time to prove the HEU was Pakistan's, not ours. In the meantime, we're pretty much on our own. The president wants us to stop your crazy fucking badal buddy before he starts a world war. But of course, if you get caught, you'll die a miserable death, and he won't lift a finger to save you."

"So what's fucking new? They never lift a finger, anyway. Nobody wants to admit guys like us exist—until they need someone to save their ass," said Dewey.

"Roger that," said Jack, and they bumped knuckles. "So let me see if I got this straight. Every crazy son of a bitch—"

"Holy shit. Holy shit," Butch said, sitting up straight, pointing at another defense department computer screen that started alarming and flashing.

A white arch rose up out of mountains north of Islamabad, Pakistan, and rapidly started tracking across the radar screen. It was the type of arch created by a tactical missile launch. The type of launch feared by the civilized world, and it was headed west, across the border toward Afghanistan, straight at Kabul, their biggest city.

Jack, Dewey, and Butch froze. It was out of their hands. A minute after the missile crossed into Afghani air space, the Iron Shield missile defense system intercepted it and blew it up before the nuclear missile had a chance to arm. The radar screen suddenly went blank again and the alarms fell silent.

They waited for more launches, but none followed. The phones started ringing off the hook. Everyone from the White House on down would normally have been put on full alert at that point, but they were already at full alert from the bomb explosions in Pakistan a few days earlier.

"The son of a bitch is nuts. We've got less time than we thought," said Jack, wiping sweat beads from his brow like drips from a leaky faucet.

"He's got a couple hundred of those. Sooner or later, he'll get one through the shield. I've got an idea I want to run by you," said Butch. "It's gonna be risky as hell, but it's already gotten the green light from SecDef."

"As long as it includes me saving Nina, killing the fucking president of Pakistan, and Dewey and me not getting killed, I'm in," said Jack.

"Me too," said Dewey.

Butch leaned forward and said in a quieter, more controlled voice, "When Rolf El-Hashem took over, he assassinated the previous leader and his cabinet, but he didn't kill Abdul and Naveen Halabi, our couple on the inside. We need to get you two over there before this crazy bastard starts World War III."

Chapter 31

Islamabad, Pakistan

The Taliban brute squads wasted no time. They rolled down out of their Hindu Kush mountain hideouts and caves like an invading tempest. Spreading from the ungoverned northern tribal regions to the cities in northern Pakistan, going from house to house, village to village, city to city, they enforced Rolf's law.

Sharia law, in its most basic form, was the moral and religious law of Islam applying to every aspect of a Muslim's life, much like the Bible to a Christian or the Torah to a Jew. But fundamentalists and jihadists corrupted the truth of the Qur'an with their own twisted interpretation, bent on inflicting pain and suffering on those accused of breaking rules or laws invented by them. Islam became whatever they said it was. It became a sheer veil for brutality. An excuse to inflict pain on those who saw things differently.

Abdul Halabi and his wife, Naveen, lived off the main road with Abdul's parents, a mile from the presidential palace in Islamabad. For most of Abdul's life, his father had been a trusted advisor and friend to the recently deceased president of Pakistan. Wherever the president went, Abdul's father went. So, Abdul's family traveled frequently with the presidential entourage when Abdul was a boy. Abdul himself attended the University of Maryland to get a master's degree in accounting with a computer science minor. When he graduated, Abdul joined his father on the president's staff, to computerize the presidential affairs and bring them into the twenty-first century.

Abdul loved his family more than anything. He adored the president and everything he was trying to do to modernize Pakistan and keep the fundamentalists from taking over and blowing them all back to the eighth century. Abdul was well spoken, kind-hearted, and dedicated to the president's causes.

With two children under five and a third due in two months, Naveen had her hands full. A tiny woman with endless energy, she also worked at the presidential palace. While she did not grow up in Islamabad, Naveen was also devoted to the president's family. She loved the First Lady, whom Naveen attended to in her daily affairs. It may have sounded glamorous, but cleaning the bathroom of a president and his wife was no different than cleaning her own. It was bigger and nicer, but a bathroom was still a bathroom, Naveen said. She planned to quit work for good once number three arrived. The president's wife insisted.

Abdul's and Naveen's lives were shattered the day Rolf El-Hashem and his People's Party of Pakistan won the emergency election by a landslide vote after the United States attacked. The Taliban extremists wasted no time making themselves felt by taking control of the palace immediately.

Abdul watched his office TV in horror and disbelief as Rolf assassinated both their president and Abdul's father. Abdul heard the shots from his office. Afraid for his life, he locked the door and hid under the desk until nightfall, but the brute squads never came for him.

Naveen heard Rolf put two bullets through the First Lady's head, followed by everyone else in the royal court who was not dressed appropriately according to Sharia law, including her mother-in-law. Naveen hid in the shower in the presidential quarters until nightfall, fearing for her life, but they never came for her either.

Abdul gathered his parents' bodies—or at least what was left of his father's, after the crowd got through stomping and kicking it—and buried them the next day. Consumed by grief, overwhelmed by fear, they barricaded themselves in Abdul's parents' home, now *their* home. They knew it was only a matter of time before President El-Hashem put two and two together and summoned them both to stand before a firing squad.

Sirens, gunshots, screams of pain and agony, jeeps driving by blasting bullhorn warnings of what was and what was not allowed. Every TV in Pakistan played the same channel, which repeated the Sharia warnings and showed video of citizens being persecuted for not obeying the detailed and confusing laws. The punishment, once seen, could never be forgotten. It was one thing to read in the paper of a decapitation or stoning. It was quite another to see someone's head chopped off with a machete or see someone buried up to their waist in a hole in the ground so he could not run, then be stoned to death. All for what seemed like minor offences or crimes.

Naveen was one of the lucky ones. She at least owned a burka. Forty million Pakistani women did not. On TV, they showed a woman receive a beating for not covering her face in public. Another woman received a knife slash on her cheek, so she would never *want* to show her face again.

A thief, or at least a man accused of stealing a loaf of bread, had his right wrist pinned down on the tailgate of a government truck by two hooded men, then sawed off. Not one swift slice, but ten, fifteen chops as they gradually chiseled their way through the bone. That was followed by a scene of a man whirling a human wrist on a rope above his head, like a cowboy lasso, while the thief collapsed to the ground amongst a jeering crowd of believers.

People were left hanging by the neck along the main roads and markets. Twisted, lifeless bodies lay piled three or four high in front of bloody, bullet-pocked firing-squad mud walls.

The scent of death and decay, panic and confusion, law and disorder crept through the cracks and crevices of Islamabad like a cloud of poisonous gas.

There was nothing left in Islamabad, in Pakistan, for Abdul and Naveen. Everyone who meant anything to them was dead. They feared for their lives, even in their own home.

Abdul went out for food when absolutely necessary. But with the Internet down, working from home became impossible and working at the palace was terrifying. All the yelling and cheering and guns and people hanging from high places was too much for Abdul to handle, especially after his parents had just been murdered.

He wondered when his time would come. Would he go bravely, quietly? Or would he cry like a baby? If he were executed, Naveen, his kids, and Abdul would all be reunited in paradise someday. So, *go bravely* it was.

He saw no other options. The United States had nuked them. Rolf El-Hashem declared martial law. Attacked from both the outside and the inside, the border crossings were closed. The Karachi seaports were closed. The airports were closed.

Abdul knew a lunatic now controlled Pakistan's nuclear arsenal. Something the ex-president and Abdul's father gave their lives trying to prevent. It was a bloody nightmare for the rest of the world, but especially India and Israel, the new Pakistan's closest threats—or so the president proclaimed.

Abdul and Naveen were still in a state of shock, his parents barely in the ground a day. One minute they had shared a joy-filled house with Abdul's parents; the next, they were alone. The house was quiet. His parents' room dark.

Abdul was at a loss. Should he pack up his family and try to escape from Pakistan? Should he illegally get some guns and ammunition? Should they leave all the lights off to make it look abandoned? Should he go to work? Should he stay home?

With no father to ask for advice and paralyzed by fear, a wave of sorrow overwhelmed Abdul, and he started weeping again, certain that at any minute, someone would crash through their front door and drag him off to the firing squad, just as they had his father.

Chapter 32

Presidential Palace, Islamabad, Pakistan

Two steps behind and one to the left of Rolf, Nina shuffled like a Halloween shroud, covered in a thick black sheet head to floor. Even her peephole to the world, a two-by-four-inch rectangle in front of her eyes, was covered in dense mesh. Seen but not seen as she followed Rolf from public appearance to TV appearance to tours of the military and nuclear facilities. Listening but not speaking as he took calls from political leaders around the globe who were extending condolences for Pakistan's losses, giving congratulations for being elected, seeking alliances, yielding concessions, offering fortunes for a nuclear warhead.

"What do you mean, they shot it down?" Rolf screamed.

"When it crossed into Afghanistan, they shot it down, Mr. President," said the new man Rolf had placed in charge of Pakistan's defense. "One missile was easy. Many would be impossible to shoot down."

"Let's fire many weapons, then. How many can you fire, General?"

"I don't know, Mr. President. As a fire control analyst, I never had to know that. But I will find out," said the general. "But . . ."

"But what?" Rolf stuck his hand through a slit at the hip of his dishdasha.

Nina heard a click.

"But why Afghanistan, when they're our friends?" the general asked sheepishly, casting his eyes to the ground. "My wife's family is from there. Why Afghanistan and not Israel, Mr. President?"

Nina stood perfectly still like a ghost in the room. She knew what Rolf's eye twitch meant.

"Hmm." Rolf scratched his beard, looking puzzled by the question. He pulled out the loaded gun and shoved it under the general's chin in one swift move. Too fast for the general.

"Who the fuck do you think you are to tell me what to think, what to do?" Rolf yelled as his face turned red. "Maybe you should worry about doing your job." He jammed the gun into the general's throat so hard, his hand trembled. His trigger finger too. Rolf squinched his eyes to slits.

"Please, Mr. President," the general squeaked, then gasped in another breath. "Give me one more chance. I'll do as you wish. I'll fire many—"

Rolf pulled the trigger, and the general's skull exploded. Blood and globs of the general's brain splattered the low ceiling. The general collapsed at Rolf's feet in a pool of blood.

"Fucking traitor." Rolf kicked him aside and headed for the next room, wiping his gun off on his dishdasha. As he passed out of the room and looked back, Nina still stood frozen, staring at the dead general. Rolf stopped and turned.

"Anyone else been doing any thinking on their own?" Rolf asked.

None of the other weapons people said a word. They kept their eyes directed at the floor.

"Good. Let's keep it that way. I'll do the thinking, and you follow orders," he said as he swept his finger around the circle, pointing at each man.

His finger ended up on Nina. "Coming?" he said sarcastically. "Or would you like to go with the general? Save me a hell of a lot of trouble."

Nina said nothing and caught up to two steps behind Rolf as he walked into some sort of military control room. Nina only knew English. The signs were written in something else.

"I need an El-Hashem. Are there any El-Hashems here?" Rolf yelled into the dead quiet room.

They had all seen the general leave the room with Rolf. They had heard the shot. They watched Rolf reenter the room alone, except for his *jariya*, Nina, whom nobody seemed to notice.

Everyone there knew it was not haram to have Nina as a jariya because she was a conquered infidel. But he was the president. He could do whatever he wanted.

Smoke still wafted in through the door where the general had stood, as a reminder.

A chair scraped at the far end of the control room. A young bearded man, tall and ramrod straight, jumped up, stood at attention, and saluted in Rolf's direction.

Rolf motioned for him to come. "What's your name?"

"Osama El-Hashem."

"Osama! Well, well, well," exclaimed Rolf with a hint of a smile. "Do you know who I am, Osama?"

"Yes, Mr. President. Everyone knows who you are."

"Well, Osama, how is it that you are in this place at this time? The will of Allah, do you suppose?"

"Yes, Mr. President. I believe you worked with my uncle, Mullah Mohammed Abdul, before he—"

Rolf held up a hand. "I see him in your eyes. I hear him in your voice. He was like a father to me when the Americans kidnapped my father. He taught me everything I know." Rolf looked back into Osama's eyes. "What's your training? What do you do here?"

"Computer engineering at MIT. I troubleshoot the weapon control systems, both on the ground and airborne."

"Just down the street from where I went to medical school. What year?"

"I graduated 2012."

"And what do you think of my weapon control systems, Osama?"

"They're antiquated, but functional. They'll do the job," Osama said meekly, as if expecting to be beaten.

"Can you do the job, Osama?" Rolf said, ignoring the disrespectful comment.

"What job is that, Mr. President?"

"Fire one of my nukes into the heart of Israel. Right up the asses of the self-righteous Jews."

Everyone in the room perked up. A murmur spread. Heads turned. Smiles grew.

"By my calculations, that's about twenty-one hundred miles. If we modify the XK-51, she may make it, but right now she'll only make fifteen hundred."

"Can you do it? Can you get me there?"

"It'll take time, Mr. President. A month, I think."

"I don't have a month. I have a week. That's all." Rolf grabbed Osama firmly by the shoulders. "For your uncle, for your people, for me . . . Can you build it in a week?"

"I will try, Mr. President. I will try."

"Good. As of now, you are General Osama El-Hashem. Anything you need, you get." Rolf looked around the room as he made the proclamation. "Anyone who says no to this man will be shot. Is that understood?"

Heads nodded throughout the room.

"Good." He looked back at Osama. "Get to work. You have six days, twenty-three hours, and fifty-nine minutes until we launch. Go. Go. Go." He turned Osama's shoulders to push him back toward the control room, then turned himself and walked out, Nina in tow.

Nina's mind raced. She was sweating like a pig under her burka. The heroin cloud that had followed her the first few days as Pakistan's First Lady had cleared up. She paid attention to her spacing, keeping up with Rolf as he started and stopped, went this way and that.

Shooting a nuclear weapon, no matter where, sent shivers up her spine. All she thought of at that moment as she visualized a Hiroshima-type mushroom cloud over Jerusalem was her baby, Barett.

The last time she had seen Barett alive, he was flying over the rail of a trawler into the Atlantic Ocean. From a foggy talk with Jack, her father's spirit, and the young boy who mimed to her that he threw the life vest, Nina knew Barett had somehow survived.

She desperately wanted to hold her little boy. Give him kisses. Smell his freshly shampooed hair. She breathed in deep and pretended to smell.

She wondered what was taking Jack so long. But she also realized that one of the benefits of being the bait was Rolf needed to keep her alive. She would have been riddled full of bullet holes or hung from a crane long ago, if it had not been for that.

But the longer she was there, the more Nina got the feeling that maybe Jack was not coming. Maybe Barett needed Jack more than she did. Maybe Barett was alive, but very sick or worse. And if that were the case, she needed to start thinking of a backup plan, just in case. One way or another, she was not leaving until she knew Rolf was dead.

Before this all began, Nina had never killed anything with a gun or knife or even her bare hands. She never quite understood how Jack and Dewey could take that next step so easily. Wishing someone were dead, as she did Rolf, was a lot different than having to pull the trigger or stick the knife into his heart herself. But things had changed. She had changed. If she had a gun in her hand at that very moment, she would pull the trigger in a heartbeat. But then they would kill her. She knew she needed a better plan. After everything he had done, putting a bullet in Rolf's head would be easy. Staying alive to see Jack and Barett again would be the tricky part.

Rolf had his head turned away, whispering to an aide or someone. She pulled her arms inside her robe and dug her cell phone out of her vagina, without moving in any unnatural way.

Without looking, she powered up the phone under her robe and squeezed it between her palms until she felt it buzz.

She had started texting on flip phones many years before cell phones with keyboards were invented. A much more tedious process of pressing number keys one, two, or three times for each letter. So, as accurately and quickly as she could text without looking, she texted what might have been her last message ever to Jack. Maybe the most important message she ever sent. She knew pressing "send" probably did nothing, seeing as Rolf had shut down all cell networks, but she did it anyway.

As she focused on sticking the phone back up into her secret hiding spot and getting her arms back out of her robe, Rolf was suddenly standing in front of her, his arms wrapped around hers, face to face, hugging or holding her. All Nina knew was, he had her.

"Nina, my love. I must apologize—I've been so busy. I've been ignoring you."

She looked through her peephole, up at his face. Even through the mesh, she smelled alcohol breath and cigarette smoke. She struggled briefly, then relaxed.

"Nina, Nina, Nina," Rolf said as he forced her backward, through a doorway into an office or phone room or something, pulling up on her burka, handful by handful. "That's what's so great about women in robes. You're always ready to take care of me."

Nina struggled again, but Rolf pinned her against the wall.

"No, Rolf. You can't."

He clamped a hand over her mouth before she said another word. He breathed heavily, wrestling with her clothes. "Hold still, bitch. I don't have all day." He pulled up her cotton slip and jerked her pantaloon bloomers down, while squeezing her face with his giant paw, just above her shock collar.

Nina felt the phone slip and shoved one hand down, as if protecting herself from invasion, and gave the phone one last push up as far as it would go.

"Will you fucking hold still!" he shouted.

One of his bodyguards looked in. Rolf said something. The guards came running. They grabbed Nina's wrists while Rolf swept everything off the desk, computer and all, with one swift move and laid Nina out spread eagle. Rolf took his hand off her mouth, while in the other hand he held up the remote for the collar.

"Shh," he said.

"I'm bleeding down there. You can't. I'm unclean," is all Nina could get out before he pressed the button to her shock collar.

Nina contracted violently, as if having a grand mal seizure. One long, sorry moan, like a foghorn, squeezed through her clenched jaw. She spasmed into the fetal position on the desk, choking and frothing at her mouth. Electrical pain beyond comprehension shot down her spine . . . up her spine . . . through her neck.

Rolf released the button. "Order a million of these. One for every family," he said to the guard with a snicker. "Osama can program my computer to control all of these fucking things from my office." Rolf's eyes opened wide. "The entire country will be putty in my hands. Go get Osama!" he yelled at the bodyguard. "And get me someone to fuck," he yelled louder as he turned and spit in Nina's face, which was still foaming, but breathing.

As he walked from the room, an almost imperceptible buzz like a housefly circling a fluorescent light came and went. Came and went.

After several minutes, Nina roused from her seizure and grabbed her collar. She looked around. Alone, thank God.

When the housefly returned, she jumped as if somebody had poked her in the crotch. She struggled to her feet, grabbed her underclothes—or what was left of them—and her burka, pulled them on, and checked the door. She was still alone.

She dug the warm phone out, still buzzing. It slipped and fell. She scooped it up, wiped it off, and checked the door again. "Damn thing will get me killed."

She flipped it open. **One text message.** She gasped and read: **Stay close. Remember the code. Ditch the phone.**

Mission accomplished. She tingled with excitement and wanted to shout for joy, but more than ever, she had to ratchet her emotions back and focus on her role. She rejoined Rolf, who at the time was screwing another woman in the next room. His bodyguard gave her a sideways glare, as if to say, "What are you looking at?" He flashed his finger, resting on the collar remote, and bared his rotten teeth.

Nina fell to her knees at his feet, head to the floor. If anyone ever needed killing, Rolf did, and Nina prayed to God she would be the one brave enough to shove a knife through his cold heart.

Chapter 33

Afghanistan to Pakistan

"Well, I'll be a son of a bitch," Jack said as he read Nina's text message to Dewey and Butch. "The crazy bastard is going to launch nukes at Israel in seven days."

In one text message, Rolf jolted the intelligence world with an even bigger surprise. An intelligence community still reeling from his last dirty bomb attack on his own country, which he accused the United States of orchestrating. Then in the aftermath, and for the good of his own country, Rolf had assumed its presidency and control of its nuclear arsenal. Most of the world believed President El-Hashem and blamed the United States too, whose story sounded preposterous. Who, in their right mind, would detonate dirty bombs in their own country?

Within a minute's time of Jack receiving Nina's text, Langley was notified. A minute after that, the president of the United States.

The intelligence community as Jack knew it went into high gear. The CIA, NSA, FBI, and most importantly, Jack's CTF devised all kinds of contingency plans. Many doubted the credibility of the information, but once it was corroborated by their in-country CIA operative who was in contact with Abdul and Naveen Halabi, all systems were a go.

The clock was ticking.

Jack, Dewey, and Butch watched the Stealth Hawk approach on radar, but heard nothing until it hovered directly overhead, descending into the CIA compound. It rolled and yawed, its computers struggling to keep her level in the chill winds of a low-pressure system moving in. It finally stabilized when they sank behind the twenty-foot-high walls at 2400, local time.

Inside the compound walls, everything swirled. Dirt, dust, and sand. There had been no rain in months, but high up, four feet of fresh snow already blanketed the Hindu Kush to the north and east. Passes were closed, and isolation was setting in for the locals. Some of the roads stayed closed all winter, until the Taliban came back down the passes to kick their annual spring offensive into high gear again. Jack and his team had dealt with that cycle for years. The winter season was like a terrorist timeout.

But with a new regime controlling Pakistan, and all the crazies being called to action, insanity had spread like a creeping tide. A tide that recognized no nations and no borders. Instability and fear infested the surrounding countries like a communicable disease: India, Kashmir, China, Tajikistan, Afghanistan, and Iran. A group of haves and have-nots. Few had nukes; the others desperately wanted them. Beyond that group, the list of have-nots grew exponentially.

A nuke meant power. A nuke meant respect. A nuke meant everything.

A military coup by Rolf El-Hashem, a devious man descended from a long line of extremists sworn to a life of jihad, would have seemed unfathomable to anyone who remembered Rolf from his days as a high-flying, world-famous plastic surgeon in Dubai. No longer famous, but infamous and a lunatic, he controlled several hundred nuclear warheads and had everyone gearing up for the grand jihad. His grand jihad. The crazy son of a bitch with his finger on the hot button didn't seem to care if he died either. They could not be defeated.

"Report just came in. The missile we intercepted last night *was* a nuke. No question," said Butch as he zipped his jacket, flapping in the bitter November wind.

"Crazy fucker," said Dewey. "Everyone's going apeshit at Langley, I'm sure."

"Langley, London, Moscow, Beijing . . . you name it," said Butch. "Let's get out of this weather."

"How's the president doing?" asked Jack as they walked back inside the intel shack, shivering. It still smelled like a dead rat, but at least it was warm.

"How do you think?" said Butch. "He's had a nuke fired on his forces for the first time in US history. The rest of the world believes the president is the one who started all the trouble in the first place, and then lied to them.

"Diplomacy's at an all-time high, but it's just that the United States is out of the loop. And to top it off, he's got six days to stop a maniac from nuking Israel. I'd say he's got his work cut out for him."

"What about the Israelis?" asked Jack. "Their Iron Shield should be able to shoot it down."

"Nothing is a hundred percent. They're still on our side, but taking precautions behind the scenes," said Butch. "Hacker and our cyberwarfare guys came up with this plan." Butch handed a thumb drive to Jack. "Here, take it. They think it'll work."

"Six days till that crazy fucker launches on Israel, and this is what I get?" Jack held the thumb drive up to the light. "This is a joke, right?"

"Actually, it's so new, there's no time to test it."

"You're shitting me. Your hacker promises it'll work?"

"He's a cocky son of a bitch. Smart too," said Butch. "He *knows* it'll work if you don't 'bugger it up,' as he says."

"Those cybergeeks scare the hell out of me. One click of their mouse is more dangerous than a thousand of my SEALs," said Jack. "The world is changing."

"Never putting their own necks on the line either, the little pricks," said Butch.

"So what am I supposed to do with this?" asked Jack.

"Keep it safe for now. Dewey, here's a backup." Butch handed Dewey a similar thumb drive. "But whatever you do, don't stick it in a computer you don't want to fry. Hacker calls it *Olympic Games.* I'm pretty sure it'll kick El-Hashem's ass if you don't bugger it up," Butch said with a devious smile.

"That's all you're gonna tell me? It'll kick his ass? Whoop-de-fucking-do," said Jack. "Dewey and I are flying solo into an Islamabad freak show to stop a nuclear holocaust and save my wife with a fucking thumb drive. I'm sure they'll be quaking in their boots when they see this thing coming."

"It's a worm, Jack. A computer worm. Okay? Satisfied?"

"Oh, that makes me feel a whole lot better."

"Calm down, Gunner. There're a lot of steps to this thing, and every one of them has to go perfectly for it all to work. If and when the time comes, your contact will fill you in," said Butch. "For now, worry about not getting killed in the next twelve hours.

If you and Dewey are lucky, real lucky, you'll get your shot."

"What odds you giving us?" asked Jack.

"I never bet against a SEAL, dipshit. Bad luck."

"What about the president?"

"He and I aren't exactly on a first-name basis. But from what I hear, if this doesn't work, the fallback plan is to shoot down the Pakistani nuke before it detonates in Israel while simultaneously launching an all-out attack on Pakistan. And by all-out, I mean all-fucking-out." Butch squinted, looking Jack and Dewey square in the eye. "Meaning you two, your wife, and every other clean-living son of a bitch over there will fry too." He let it hang there for a second and checked his watch. "So this better fucking work."

"Roger that. When do we shove off?" Jack arched his aching back.

"Stealth Hawk should be refueled and ready to lift off at 0100. They'll hump you a hundred fifty klicks to the landing zone, well outside Islamabad. My guys, and they're good, will be waiting to hustle you to the black house," said Butch. "At least, that's the plan."

"Roger that," said Jack. "What about the rest of my crew and Kona?"

"I hope we don't need 'em." Butch raised an eyebrow. "Where you're going is no place for a dog, anyway. You two get it done, and these guys get the week off. You get yourselves killed, they're in the game. Either way, Nina's out. That's a promise."

"Thanks, bro. You read my mind."

"Hacker's creating a little diversion for that sick fuck," said Butch. "He'll keep Mr. Looney Tunes looking the other direction while you two insert."

"If all this Hacker's stuff works, I might have a job for him at CTF when this blows over."

"If this works, he goes to the highest bidder, Jack. Like winning the lottery," said Butch. "We'll never see him again."

"Whatever," said Jack, rolling his eyes. "Either way, Hacker or no Hacker, I'll be going in to get Nina. It won't be pretty. A lot of assholes are going to die. But I won't go down without a fight."

"I gotcha, Gunner. I gotcha," said Butch. "Did you get some shut-eye? You look like shit."

"Checked in with Travis about my son," said Jack, rubbing his eyes.

"Oh, yeah, I heard about that," said Butch. "How's he doing?"

"Travis, my brother, is taking care of—"

"I know who Travis is, bro," Butch interrupted. "After what he did last year, everybody in the agency knows who Travis Gunn is."

"Thanks, Butch. I'll make sure to tell him next time I see him," said Jack. "My son's doing pretty well. He misses his mom, though. Travis told him Nina and I are on a mission trip to take food to starving children in Africa. The more I think about it, the more I wish we were," Jack said with a doubtful smile as he held up the thumb drive for one more dubious inspection.

"I'm with you on that, Jack. But first things first, old buddy." Dewey squeezed Jack's shoulder. "Let's go get your gal, kill that sick son of a bitch, save the world, and then *all* fly home together to Barett, Travis, Jaz, Suzy, and the kids. In that order."

"Roger that, Dewey. Roger fucking that," growled Jack.

CHAPTER 34

Presidential Palace, Islamabad, Pakistan

As exhausted as Nina was, once Rolf's guards snapped handcuffs and ankle shackles on her, she slept with one eye open or not at all. Her eyelids scratched over her corneas like sandpaper. They were agonizing to hold open, deadly to let close.

Rolf never slept. Maybe he slept somewhere else, but never around Nina. He acted as if the little white pills he took every time he yawned had turned him into Frankenstein. Yelling and screaming at Osama and having violent outbursts in public, flippantly ordering lawbreakers to death.

Nina didn't know how he or she could keep it up for five more days when an hour seemed like an eternity.

Her bedroom lights were off, but the door stood open. Two guards sat outside her door, in the next room. All other lights remained on, with the TV blaring.

She heard him screaming long before he arrived.

"Shut that off! Shut that off!" Gunshots fired, and she heard someone yell, "Lies! Lies! It's all lies!" Then she heard more gunshots and glass breaking.

Nina's ears rang. She sat up the best she could. *Get through this. Do it for Barett.*

"Bring me the minister of communications. Bring him to me! NOW!" yelled Rolf.

Rolf stomped into the bedroom, to the bed. "You! What are you looking at? Did you have something to do with this?" He was still holding a smoking pistol. He looked worse than ever. His eyes looked insane.

Nina shook her head, dumbfounded. She had no idea what he was talking about, but tried to put an innocent look on her face.

"Yeah, you must have. How else could they know?" He got in her face, seething, drooling.

He reminded Nina of a rabid dog she saw go insane when she was a girl. It snarled and drooled and chased anybody who went near. Her dad killed the dog, humanely putting it out of its misery. She wished her dad would miraculously appear and shoot the dog again.

Rolf smelled like a pair of underwear that had never been changed. Sweat and urine all cooked up into a murky stew.

"How could you betray me? My own wife?"

He fidgeted constantly. His breath smelled like feces. He waved his gun.

Nina said nothing, but she got nervous that he talked about her as his wife more and more. Initially, it seemed a joke, but now it seemed as if he actually believed it.

Rolf kneeled over her, wide-eyed staring. He brushed her cheek with the back of his hand, then fingered her dog collar. A distant glaze came over him, like time travel to another place, a happy place. The furrows creasing across his forehead smoothed, momentarily.

Nina froze.

Commotion in the adjoining room startled Rolf and catapulted him off the bed like a startled cat, straight up and landing with both feet on the ground.

"We have the communications minister for you, Mr. President." They shoved a scrawny man with thick glasses and a thicker black mustache into the middle of the room, like a lamb to the slaughter.

"I'm sorry, Mr. President—"

"Silence!" Rolf walked full circle around the minister, toying with his pistol, his finger in and out of the trigger guard.

"I ordered you to shut down all Internet, all TV, all communications. And this is how you repay me." Rolf pointed his gun at the one TV still in one piece and working.

"To the people of Pakistan," they all heard the US Secretary of Defense Donald Springer say on the television, "this man, Rolf El-Hashem, the man who stole your presidency"—they showed video of Rolf executing the past president and his cabinet—"is the one who bombed Pakistan. He bombed you, his own people."

"Why are these lies still on TV?" Rolf screamed.

While Springer continued presenting America's case to the people of Pakistan, the TV ran footage of the destruction from one of El-Hashem's dirty bombs in Lahore, Pakistan, located near their border with India.

Rolf looked as if he were going to explode or have a coronary, he was so incensed.

"Not the United States or Israel or the British or anyone else," Springer continued. "Some of the bombs contained nuclear material stolen from your uranium refinement facility in Kahuta, Pakistan, over a year ago. Nuclear material has a fingerprint, much like people. There is no mistake. Your president annihilated his own people with dirty bombs created from nuclear material stolen from you so he could preside over you, putting terrorists in control of your law and nuclear weapons. Again I say, America is not your enemy; your president is your enemy."

"Get it off! Get it off!" Rolf yelled and kept yelling.

The minister picked up a phone and yelled panicked instructions.

A minute passed. Rolf ranted and raved. The minister kept yelling orders at someone. Another minute, then a blank screen before normal, scheduled propaganda began again.

There was President Rolf El-Hashem visiting a school, holding a baby, surrounded by a crowd of adoring children and mothers, all dressed according to code.

"You have a traitor in your midst. Who is it?" said Rolf, hovering in the minister's face.

Osama walked in on the confrontation and stayed on the fringe, along the wall.

"Everything appeared to be running normally, Mr. President. We didn't touch a thing. It just happened."

"You don't know what you're doing. You're a fool."

"I swear on my mother's grave, Mr. President. Everything flickered, the screen went black for a second, and when it came back on, that video was there. We tried to turn it off, but it wouldn't let us. It was as if it had a mind of its own."

"You're an imbecile and a fool. I should have you . . ." said Rolf.

"It was hacked, Mr. President. The computers were hacked."

"What? Who said that?" Rolf whirled around, gun in hand, contempt scrawled across his face.

"I did, Mr. President," said Osama.

"Osama. What are you doing here? Is my missile ready so soon?" asked Rolf, instantly transformed, hopefulness back in his voice.

Nina stood near the doorway in the adjoining bedroom, hiding, listening. No one noticed her at the moment.

"No, but we're making good progress," said Osama. "I took a quick look. Someone hacked into the TV station's computer. It would not be difficult. Like I said, these antiquated systems will do the job, but they should be upgraded as soon as possible."

"Who? How could they do it? We've entirely isolated ourselves from the outside world."

"There are ways, if you know what you're doing. Believe me, the Americans and Israelis know what they're doing. But I wanted to tell you personally so you could rest assured. It is impossible to hack into my weapon control systems. I took steps."

"Well, don't let it happen again. I don't want any more hacking or interruptions of any kind. And since you seem to be such an expert, I assume you will take care of this matter too, Osama," Rolf said confidently.

"Yes, Mr. President," said Osama.

"At least not for the next five days." Rolf flashed a knowing smile at Osama. "Five days, right?"

"Yes, Mr. President. Five days."

"You are dismissed," said Rolf with a flip of his hand.

Another aide walked in and handed Rolf a satphone. A big, boxy handset with a three-foot-long chrome antenna that looked like an early cell phone. A series of chirps and clicks could be heard throughout the room as the encryption software kicked in.

One second with his ear to the phone, and his entire persona changed from Rolf the Tyrant, Rolf the Maniac, to Rolf the Submissive.

"Yes, sir. No, sir. It's been taken care of, sir. It won't happen again, sir."

Rolf held the phone away from his ear and winced. Even Nina could hear the screaming coming from whoever was on the other end. Rolf walked to a corner of the room, turned away, and mumbled so no one else could hear.

Nina watched him nod and smile, and she read his lips.

"We're right on schedule, sir. Five days, and we—I mean *you*—will control the world. *Assalamu alaykum.*"

CHAPTER 35

Islamabad, Pakistan

Jack swallowed hard to force the bile out of his throat and back down to his stomach, where it belonged.

Their topsy-turvy helo ride, compliments of their SOAR pilots and night-vision capabilities, clung to every mountain ridge and crevice from Jalalabad to an indifferent pitch of rock ten klicks south of Bahria Town, Pakistan. The Stealth Hawk touched down just long enough for Jack and Dewey to off-load themselves and their gear, then it high-tailed back across the border into Afghanistan before the weather got worse.

Jack and Dewey lay on their bellies at the crest of an outcropping, facing north. A bitter desert north wind laced with intermittent sleet and rain gusted from behind. A low ceiling obliterated the stars. No Big Dipper or North Star to guide them.

Jack loved staring at the Big Dipper as a boy in Montana. He still liked it at forty. It connected him with Sitting Bull, Crazy Horse, Red Cloud, and all the rest who fought Wasichu for the right to live their way of life.

The Big Dipper was 139 light-years away. If Jack's math was

right, that twinkle of light he had seen as a boy had started its journey from Ursa Major at the same time as his great-great-great-grandfather Sitting Bull rode on horseback over the plains of North Dakota and Montana, over a hundred years earlier. When Sitting Bull performed in Buffalo Bill's Wild West shows. When he traveled to Washington, DC, to negotiate a settlement for all Indians with President Grover Cleveland. When he was dragged from his hovel of a cabin on a cold winter night and shot in the head by his fellow Indians, afraid of him and his Ghost Dancers. Jack named his team Ghost Team to honor Sitting Bull, the great leader of his people. Whenever he saw the stars, Jack heard the chants, the drums, the bells, the gunshots.

He looked at Dewey, then up briefly. He knew it was up there, but he focused his gun scope on the SUV winding its way directly toward their jagged pile of bedrock.

"Contact at two o'clock," Jack said into his microphone.

"Roger that," said Dewey.

Swim buddies since BUD/S, they operated like two hands connected to the same body. Dewey swept back from his quadrants and trained in on the approaching contact. Through their grainy green-and-white night-vision scope, they watched a lone Land Rover's infrared headlights as it bounced and weaved its way through blowing sand and sleet, around rock piles and fissures. From the Land Rover's side of the ridge, the only visible parts of Jack and Dewey were the black tops of their Kevlar helmets and the business ends of their HK416s. Their breathing was slow, and their pulses were steady. For them, it was like waiting at a bus stop.

The CIA vehicle stopped abruptly at the base of the outcropping and flashed an infrared flashlight three times. Jack and Dewey waited. They zeroed in on the driver's window with their rifles.

Thirty seconds later, three more flashes. Jack flashed back, then they climbed down, threw their packs in the rear, and jumped in.

"Butch sent a message for you two," Jack said to the two men in the front seats, wearing gray dishdashas, their heads wrapped with black and gray kaffiyehs, and NODs strapped over their eyes.

They turned the black Land Rover around and headed back north, toward Islamabad. Their two AK-47s leaned against the console between them.

"Don't screw this up," said Jack.

"The next time you see Butch, tell him thanks for fucking nothing," said Quinton, their big headed, Australian-accented driver, who was the CIA station chief for the Islamabad region. His partner and copilot, Cajun John Durio, otherwise known as Squirrel, twisted around and said, "Getting down here was a bitch, boys. Fucking weather sucks."

Dust and debris mixed with snow blew sideways across the flat ground. Like driving across Montana and North Dakota, Jack thought, picturing vast fields of wheat and sunflowers and sugar beets. The land of perpetual wind was too arid and flat to stop anything, till it reached the fertile soil of Minnesota and its ten thousand lakes.

"What do you mean? This is perfect. A walk in the park," said Jack to break the ice. "Did you boys have any trouble getting outta town?"

"Our black house is secure, but not for long. They're going house to house, executing anyone they find. We blended in with everyone else running for their lives."

Bahria Town, a southern suburb of Islamabad, looked like a Southern Californian gated community, where stucco homes with manicured lawns, swimming pools, and home theaters sold for

$50,000. While it was walled rather than gated, it operated its own garbage trucks, schools, firehouse, mosques, water supply, and police force. Instead of Pakistani or Muslim icons, a miniature Statue of Liberty, Egyptian sphinx, and Eiffel Tower decorated their roundabouts. It was a well-functioning state within a non-functioning country, for people with money.

"So getting back in is a no-go?" asked Dewey.

"Unless you want your nuts handed to you on a silver platter," said Quinton.

"What's the backup?" asked Jack.

"There are burnouts and dead everywhere. The nationals shoot first, especially at night. Everyone's a target," said Quinton. "We'll make our way across country, stay to the back roads."

"Whatever you say, slick. You're the boss," said Jack. "Just as long as we make it to the base house in one piece."

"Well, if I'm the boss, I say we head the other direction and get the hell outta Dodge while we still can."

"I'm with ya, boss, except my wife is being held prisoner by their whack-job president, and we have four days before he starts World War III. There are only bad options, so get us to that safe house, and I'll put a bullet in his brain with your name on it," said Jack.

"Roger that, sir. We'll get you there," Quinton said with no doubt in his voice. "Behind your seats—put those on."

Jack and Dewey pulled the dishdashas over their gear, wrapped the kaffiyehs over their heads, and put their helmets over the kaffiyehs so they could look through their NODs as they bounced through the dark and blowing snow. With the heater on high and back windows down, Jack hung out the driver rear and Dewey the passenger rear, scanning for threats. Nobody spoke.

Jack's mind wandered to Nina. Where was she? How was he ever going to find her and stop Rolf with an army of maniacs protecting him? He felt for the thumb drive and wondered what secrets a small printed circuit board held that would stop Rolf's missiles. It seemed so innocent and nonthreatening. But buried within hid a monster. A virus, a worm, an electronic invader, the destroyer of dreams. Or so Hacker said.

"Contact, two hundred meters at twelve o'clock," said Quinton as he slammed on the brakes.

Jack and Dewey checked forward, then scanned their quadrants again, weapons out the window in the sideways blowing sleet-snow mix. The contact kept coming, slowly zigzagging across the open ground, straight into the wind with its headlights on.

"What the fuck you doing out here?" asked Quinton to no one except the driver of the contact, who was probably searching for Pakistani traitors trying to flee the country in the dark of night.

"I got a second contact, two hundred meters at nine o'clock," said Jack, quietly, tensely.

"I got a third contact, two hundred meters at three o'clock," said Dewey. "Fuck."

"We're sitting ducks. We gotta go," said Jack. "Drive to the right and sneak right behind contact three and in front of contact one, and hope they can't see worth a shit in this crap."

"Contact number one is still coming," said Quinton.

"I've got the driver in my sights. If he so much as twitches . . ." said Jack. "Nice and easy, now, Quinton." Jack really meant, hold your fire, we don't want a shooting war, four against a million. But that went without saying.

Quinton eased the clutch out on their Land Rover, and they slipped through the hole in the line of enemy contacts like water through fingers. The three hostile contacts continued heading south while Jack's group headed north.

Once back on roads, they moved as quickly as they could through Rawalpindi, into Islamabad. The closer they got to the palace, the more traffic they encountered.

Apparently, the odds of being killed by Rolf's Taliban militia were higher than the odds of dying in a car crash. Everyone drove down the streets and through intersections like maniacs. Rolf's Sharia police, many of whom had apparently never driven, raced after the lawbreakers with equal abandon. Lights, no lights. Horns, no horns. Gunfire, explosions, fires. Mass chaos ruled.

With half the city to cross and against the onslaught of most of the people trying to escape Islamabad, Quinton fishtailed onto University Road and joined the mayhem, swimming against the current.

With over four hundred horsepower in their Land Rover, they kicked up a rooster tail of gravel and slush a hundred feet back when he put the pedal to the metal. Quinton's lights were off, and he power-shifted up through the gears—sixty, seventy, eighty miles an hour down the boulevard.

"We got company," yelled Quinton as headlights appeared in his rearview mirror. He waited until the last second, then braked hard, four-wheel sliding into a left-hand turn, heel-toeing it, keeping one foot on the brake and one on the gas, never letting the engine fall below three thousand RPMs and out of the engine's powerband.

At the apex of the turn, he hit the gas, turning the steering wheel back and forth as they slid sideways around the corner, then punched it up through the gears again down Faisal Avenue.

The front end of a black Mercedes pulled up even with the

passenger door. Quinton's Land Rover was no match for the Mercedes's speed or quickness.

"Fire. Fire. Fire," Jack yelled.

Quinton jerked the wheel to the right, plowing into the driver's side of the Mercedes, but never took his foot off the accelerator. The guns sticking out of the Mercedes's back window pulled in as they careened toward the tree-lined curb. They dropped behind momentarily, but quickly got back on Quinton's tail once they regained control, even with Quinton sticking his foot through the floorboard, urging their Land Rover to go faster.

Quinton went into a right-hand turn onto Kashmir Road the same way, hot and hard. The Mercedes bumped Quinton's right rear bumper, causing him to lose traction and slide sideways.

The Mercedes driver buried his front bumper into the passenger side of the Land Rover.

Dewey and Squirrel opened fire on the windshield of the Mercedes, blowing it out and shredding anything or anybody inside the car.

The Mercedes veered sideways, flames shooting from under the bullet-riddled hood, and crashed into an abandoned storefront.

Quinton slammed on the brakes. Before they came to a stop, Jack jumped out and sprinted toward the car. Four of Rolf's goons cooked inside; two in front, two in back. For operational security, Jack put a bullet through the head of each.

Static squawked through a handheld police radio before the sound of a voice became audible. Jack located the radio buried under a pile of bloody broken glass on the front seat. He grabbed it and jumped back in their Land Rover.

Quinton put distance between them and the police, jacking the Land Rover up again, barreling down the middle of Kashmir

Road, balls to the wall. As they approached the final turn, they radioed the safe house. Quinton dodged off onto surrounding residential side streets and slowed to a crawl to make sure they didn't have a tail. Given the all clear by Abdul in the safe house, Quinton pulled up the gravel street, behind the house, and into the garage as daylight just started to brighten the gloomy Islamabad horizon.

After they got inside the safe house and met the rest of the CIA staff, Quinton said to Jack and Dewey, "There's someone I'd like you to meet."

Chapter 36

Halabi House, Islamabad, Pakistan

"I'd like to introduce Abdul Halabi and his wife, Naveen, the owners of this house and our contacts inside the presidential palace," said Quinton.

Abdul and Naveen shuffled into the front room, just inside the curtain, and stopped. Abdul pulled Naveen close, her seven-month belly obvious under her abaya. Their two children stayed out of sight in back. Abdul and Naveen gave a polite smile, then their faces returned to the uncomfortable state of being a cooperating prisoner in their own house.

"Abdul watched Rolf El-Hashem execute his father, along with the past president. You saw the video, Jack."

Jack nodded.

"Naveen witnessed the execution of Abdul's mother along with their First Lady in much the same way," said Quinton.

Abdul pulled Naveen closer still as they shared tears and silent gasps, pressing their foreheads together.

"I'm very sorry for your loss, sir, ma'am," said Jack, extending his hand.

Abdul shook his hand. Naveen did not.

"They both work in the presidential palace. Naveen in the president's private quarters and Abdul in presidential affairs. With everything going crazy since the El-Hashem coup, they fear for their lives both here and, worse, in the palace. They understand that their president, not the United States, detonated bombs on his own people. Abdul has seen firsthand what the new president of Pakistan is capable of and fully believes he will indeed fire a nuclear weapon at Israel in four days. Naveen has been back to work sporadically since the coup. Abdul has seen documents to the effect that the president has been contacted by numerous suitors from other countries and political groups interested in purchasing one of his nuclear weapons. Rolf El-Hashem is entertaining all offers."

Silence filled the room. A clock ticked. One of their kids playing in a back room giggled.

Jack looked at Abdul and Naveen and said, "He can't do anything if he's dead, right? That's why we're here. We're here as representatives of the United States of America to stop this maniac. But we need your help."

They said nothing. Weary, bloodshot eyes stared back.

"Let me tell you what happened to me last night, and maybe you will understand better about what you ask," said Abdul. "There was a bitter chill in the air and it was dark as I walked home from the palace along the side of the road. I wanted to run, but with all the killing going on since the coup, I thought it might draw attention to myself, so I walked fast and kept my head down.

"I came upon a man's body, abandoned in the ditch. I was unsure of what to do. I didn't want to call the police, as they were most likely the ones who left the body there in the first place. I rolled the frozen man over and was shocked to see it was our neighbor, Alfur, who had been like a second father to me.

"Alfur was a big man, far too big for me to carry. I was even more scared than before and decided to get home as quickly as possible, talk with Naveen, and the two of us would decide what to do.

"Just then, a pair of headlights pulled onto the main road from our street and turned toward me. I thought they might be the people who murdered Alfur. I scrambled back up the shale embankment on my hands and knees and started walking fast toward home and the headlights, keeping my eyes down.

"The military assault vehicle stopped when it got even with me and shined its spotlight on me. The man in the gun turret ratcheted back a lever on the big gun and yelled something that I didn't understand. Every step felt like my last.

"I stopped walking and pulled my hands out of my dishdasha and held them up in the air. Someone inside the vehicle asked me why I was out, and I explained that I worked at the palace for the president.

"Those little red dots from their guns painted circles on my chest where they were going to shoot me. I heard more talking in the vehicle, and then suddenly they took off, but not before the man in the turret yelled a warning that if they saw me again, they would kill me. I took off running as fast as I could. I heard them laughing. When I got home, I collapsed. It was the most scared I have ever been."

Naveen had tears in her eyes.

Jack, Dewey, Quinton, and Squirrel all stood in silence for a moment, listening to the sniffles of Abdul and Naveen.

"We have four days. We have someone on the inside," Jack said.

They both looked puzzled. "Who? We know everyone who works at the palace, and most are dead or in hiding."

"My wife," Jack said. "He has my wife. She's been helping us from the inside."

"Your wife? The only one there is *his* wife. There are no others," Abdul said apologetically but firmly.

Jack swallowed hard. Dewey grabbed his shoulder.

"You don't understand. That woman, his wife, she's my wife. He kidnapped her and my little boy from our home in Virginia," Jack said in a broken voice. He held out a picture for them to see. "Have you seen this woman?"

Naveen gasped. "I saw her. Just for a moment, but I saw her. Yes, I saw her. I had been scrubbing down the shower in the presidential suite a few days ago when armed guards barged into the bedroom, shoving a burka-clad woman before them. That lady, your wife, tripped and fell to the floor. The guards ripped her burka off and were frisking her when I accidentally dropped a scrub brush and startled the guards.

"They rushed me with their guns out. I thought I was going to die, I was so scared. I tried to explain who I was, but they didn't seem to care. They dragged me by my arms and threw me from the bedroom and slammed the door. I was thankful that I landed on my side and that my baby did not get hurt. After that, I ran home as fast as a seven-month-pregnant woman could and have not been back since.

"But there is one other thing. That lady, your wife, is never left alone. She always has two guards. Anyone trying to get close to her or talk to her would be shot on sight. Everyone knows she is the president's lady."

Jack did not flinch. He stood facing Naveen with a blank, distant look on his face. It was all too surreal to hear of such horrible things being done to Nina, in the third person. Like seeing Nina in a movie or reading about her in a thriller.

Naveen reached out and squeezed Jack's forearm, the first infidel man she had touched in years. She released him quickly, but said again, "Yes, I saw your woman. She did not look this pretty, but it was her. In her eyes I saw fear, but I also saw strength."

Naveen's expression changed to one of stern determination. "They had her shackled. She was wearing a collar, like an electrical dog collar. She had bruises, but she was not bleeding. Yes, Mr. Soldier, I will help you stop this man from ruining everything Abdul's parents and our president had accomplished."

Abdul added, "Me too. I will help you kill the president."

Jack looked at Nina's picture, kissed it, and stuck it back in his inside chest pocket, over his heart. The vision of Rolf shackling Nina and doing God knows what drove Jack mad. He wanted to snap Rolf's neck, shoot him in the head, throw him off a cliff, kill him over and over and over again for what he had done.

But Jack needed to be smart. As Dewey said, one step at a time. Save Nina. Save the world. Then kill the son of a bitch.

Chapter 37

Presidential Palace, Islamabad, Pakistan

Nina closed her eyes and let the warm water soak into every pore. She stood motionless under the shower for the longest time, maybe even fell asleep standing up, she was so relaxed.

She thought of her sister-in-law, Jaz, for the first time in weeks and wondered if she had the baby yet. Nina had been really excited for Jaz and Travis, getting pregnant so soon after their wedding. Jaz's pregnancy gave Nina something happy to focus on after finishing chemotherapy. On the weekends, Jaz and Nina enjoyed girls' days out to baby shop and talk. Nina loved having another woman in the family.

Steam started forming inside the shower, clearing Nina's mind for the first time in what seemed like weeks. She inhaled deeply.

Visions of Barett, the first in days, washed over her like the morning sunshine.

Barett loved life and loved his mommy. But he wasn't just any boy, he was hers. She rubbed soap over her stomach, reliving the exact moment when he was born, the final contraction, the final push, Barett's first cry and first breath. At that instant, when Nina had heard his cry and knew without a doubt that Barett had survived something her first two babies had not, Nina's sorrow vanished. There were no words to describe the euphoric dome she lived under from that point on. She remembered the doctor saying, "It's a boy," and placing Barett, all slippery and fragile, on her chest.

As the warm water showered her hair, she wrapped her arms across her chest as if she were cradling Barett in the delivery room, smelling him still wet with amniotic fluid.

"Don't cry, Barett. Mommy loves you," she said over and over until he stopped crying. She missed her little man more than anything. Oh, to hear him laugh, one more time.

Nina tipped her head back and let the water massage her face and wash away her tears. Visions of Jack awkwardly holding his son that first time, like not wanting to crack the egg, made her smile.

Full of apprehension, like any new dad, he jumped into the deep end of parenthood, right beside Nina, rather than tiptoeing in from the shallow end or not getting in at all, like a lot of fathers. But what else was she to expect? That was why she loved Jack in the first place. That was how he did everything in life. All in or not at all. He was Nina's swim buddy for life.

While the world knew Jack as a big, tough SEAL, she knew his teddy-bear side. The side that sang out-of-tune lullabies, that gave baby baths and pushed the stroller, that talked baby talk to Barett. Becoming a father brought out a softer side of Jack that Nina had hoped was in him.

And then her swim buddy left for a four-month-long deployment to Afghanistan, and life instantly became one sink-or-swim challenge after another for Nina. Raising a one-year-old, dealing with day care, working full-time because they could not make ends meet without her income, and eventually dealing with breast cancer too.

Jack was 100 percent committed to them when he was home, but as hard as he tried when he was away, Skyping and calling and texting really did not help that much. In fact, a lot of the times it created longer days for Nina because she and Barett had to stop what they were doing just to talk to Jack on the computer. They were doing the best they could. The three of them became one, for better or worse. But it was not the same for Jack or Nina when Jack was deployed. And they both knew it.

Nina no longer felt scabs or scars on her lips from being gagged on that ship. She rubbed her sore wrists where shackles or zip ties restrained her since being abducted. Her broken ribs seemed mostly healed as she stretched her arms above her head without a twinge in the side.

Her hands came to her neck and the collar. Her smile disappeared. She wondered what would happen if Rolf set it off in the shower. She got paranoid and turned the water off. She grabbed the towel draped over the shower door and buried her face in it, as if hiding and hoping no one would find her. When she opened her eyes, her jaw dropped.

Finger-written in the steam on the glass shower door was a message. Puzzled momentarily, Nina dried her face again and got her bearings. It was written in Sioux! *What the?* She was confused. It glowed, highlighted by the vanity light behind it. A message from Jack!

Interpreted, it read: *Be ready. Tomorrow. I love you.*

Nina read it again, smiled, then instantly grew paranoid and erased it with her hand.

Who?

She wiped the inside of the door down with her towel.

How?

She went to full alert and checked outside the bathroom door. Two guards stood their post and glanced in her direction when her head appeared. One flashed the dog collar remote. She shook her head, held up one finger, and gave them the "I'm hurrying" look.

In the thirty seconds it took to get dressed, Nina's mind raced through many possible scenarios. The word Jack used for "be ready" in Sioux meant, "prepare your mind, prepare for war," which excited Nina.

Finally, every awful thing she had endured just to stay alive seemed worth it. But while the time for victory dances and celebrating was a long way off, adrenaline shot through her like a triple espresso. Hair stood up on her arms and legs; they never trusted her with a razor. Her heart pounded. She heard every creak and whisper. Nothing hurt. Potential weapons in the room appeared to sizzle like drops of water in hot grease, as if they could do the killing by themselves. She felt her father in her soul.

With her burka back on, she walked from the bathroom to the bedroom, holding her arms out in front of her so the guards could zip-tie them back together and check her collar. The guards looked different—like ghosts, doomed ghosts. Nina looked through them, around them, out her burka peephole, cataloging everything.

Growing up, she always won the contests rewarding photographic memory, like the childhood game where everyone got thirty seconds to study a bunch of ordinary household items, then went to another room to write down as many as they could remember. Even years later, she still remembered a stranger's face, a room's décor, a friend's comment.

But she rarely found her photographic memory useful in everyday life. In fact, it aggravated her that she could not forget things most people could let go: trailing glances, cloaked sarcasm, and feigned concern.

The guards led Nina back down cold, damp hallways she knew from memory to a room she dreaded. *Tomorrow. Just stay alive one more day.* She heard Rolf screaming well before she saw him.

"You said it was impossible. It could never happen again, Osama. How could you let this happen?"

"I'm sorry, Mr. President. It won't happen—"

"Stop talking," Rolf yelled.

Osama stood at attention as Rolf circled him, waving a pistol, all the blood in his body apparently rushing to his head. His face looked like a ripe tomato about to burst.

The guards stopped Nina at the office door and motioned her off to an invisible spot along the wall she knew so well.

"And here she is now. The woman of the hour," Rolf said, slamming his fist on his desk. Wired and bloodshot, he threw a wine glass into the wall, where it shattered next to Nina. He raced over and acted as if he were going to coldcock her in the side of the head, but pulled back at the last second and blew a lungful of cigarette smoke into her peephole.

She coughed.

He laughed.

Rolf turned back to Osama. "Now what am I supposed to do with you?" he asked but held up a finger, cautioning him to keep quiet. "You said they couldn't hack into the TV station again. They hacked into the TV station. You said they couldn't hack into your weapon control system. What am I supposed to think? Huh?" asked Rolf. "You told me to trust you. I trusted you. And this is how you thank me?"

Rolf circled Osama again, scratching his head with the gun. "Where did they get those pictures of my wife?" Rolf screamed, pointing the gun at Nina.

Nina's jacked-up mind struggled to stay composed as she processed what was happening. There he was talking about her as his wife again, but she did not panic. She did not jump to the worst-case scenario. She just stayed in the moment and kept quiet.

"They're from before. Before you took her," said Osama.

"No fucking shit. You figured that out all by yourself," said Rolf. "You must make your parents real proud."

"Everyone knows it's the Americans, but nobody here or anywhere trusts anything they say right now since they bombed Pakistan, right?" said Osama. "You've seen what's going on. No one except Israel will side with them. Not even the British. They're desperate. They're wasting time hacking into our TV, making ridiculous claims. Nobody believes them. Nobody cares."

Rolf studied Osama's face and nodded as he listened.

"They know that in three days, you will launch a nuclear warhead on Israel that will annihilate the Jews forever, and they can't do a fucking thing about it. I swear to you on my life—"

Rolf quickly held up a hand to stop Osama. "And how is it that the Americans know all of this?" Rolf asked.

Osama looked as if he swallowed his tongue.

"I asked you a question." Rolf circled Osama again. "You have nothing to say?"

Osama shook his head and kept his eyes down.

"Now maybe you will believe me. Spies are everywhere. I can trust no one. Not even you," declared Rolf. "Who am I to trust, Osama? Who am I to trust?"

Osama bowed down to Rolf and held that position.

"I can't decide if you're incredibly stupid . . . or incredibly smart," said Rolf. "Just because you don't want something to happen and don't think it will happen, doesn't mean it won't happen." He looked over at Nina with disgust in his eyes.

"Please forgive me, Mr. President. I am no match for you. I'll do whatever you tell me to do," said Osama, bowing again.

"Are we on schedule? With all these fuckups, at least tell me we're on schedule."

"We're on schedule, Mr. President. The modifications are going more easily than expected," said Osama.

"What are you waiting for? Get back to work," yelled Rolf, waving his arms in grand circles, releasing the room full of scientists and staff.

He grabbed Nina by her zip-tied wrists, jerked her out of the room, and led her down a cold, marble corridor, each staccato step of Rolf's shoes echoing like a death march.

Nina scanned side to side, an arm's length behind and to the left, jogging to keep up.

Rolf glanced at each door but kept moving. They climbed down stairs, then down more stairs until they were far below ground. The air grew musty and cold. It smelled like someplace from Nina's past.

Nina's father had raised cattle and hogs. When one of them died, he hauled it out to the edge of the farm road with their tractor and left it for the rendering truck to take away to the glue factory or dog food factory or wherever they took dead farm animals. She never gave it much thought. She just wanted them to hurry up and collect the dead animals from the end of their driveway so she did not have to see and smell them every time they came or went. But sometimes it took days before the rendering truck made its rounds. In the heat of summer, a bloated cow smelled something awful.

Nina smelled the same rotten smell as Rolf led her down cold, dark corridors strewn with clusters of dead Pakistanis. She breathed hard, hustling to keep up. She wished for any sort of weapon. A lightning bolt, an earthquake, anything. The victims all looked as if they had been executed at point-blank range.

Rolf did not seem to notice, but his pace slowed.

They arrived at a checkpoint. Two guards stepped aside and saluted, handing Rolf a set of keys as he led Nina through the checkpoint. Rolf's bodyguards stayed behind at the checkpoint too. Around a dark corner Rolf stopped. He stuck a key in and turned. The cell door creaked open, and he threw her in.

She tripped and fell hard, hitting her head on the rough-hewn stone floor.

Rolf said, "Your days as the bait will be over soon, my dear. Make your peace or say your prayers or do whatever you infidels do to prepare to die." He slammed and locked the door and walked away proclaiming, "Till death do us part, sweetheart. Till death do us part."

Chapter 38

Halabi House, Islamabad, Pakistan

"She got the message? You're sure?" Jack asked Naveen.

"I think so, but that's the last time anyone saw her. It is very bad. Not safe to ask questions. They kill everyone," said Naveen, crying again. "Please don't make me go back. They'll kill me too."

Abdul wrapped his arms around his wife and pulled her to his chest. Looking at Jack, he shook his head while saying to her, "You're safe now. No one can hurt you anymore."

"They've moved her," said Jack, biting his lip. "I think she's still alive, but that pretty much fucks plan A."

"How often does plan A work, anyway?" asked Dewey. "If we did it the easy way, we'd be fucking Green Berets."

"Everyone's excited. They kept saying, 'three days, three days,'" said Naveen.

"So by morning, we've got two days to get inside. Abdul, you grew up around the palace. Can you remember any secret entrances, anything?" asked Jack.

"Security is tight. The men with guns are everywhere. All the gates and doors are locked. Now with this hacker stuff going on, everyone is paranoid. They have guards guarding the guards," said Abdul.

"Nothing else. No escape tunnels or—" Jack saw a light go on in Abdul's face. "What? Do you remember something?"

"My father showed me a tunnel or secret escape passage left over from the old days when it was dangerous to be the president. I vaguely remember because he only took me there once as a very small boy." Abdul went silent, and his eyes welled with tears. "I'm sorry, but I cannot forget my father."

"I understand, Abdul," said Jack. "I lost my parents as a little boy. I watched them burn in a car fire. As hard as I tried, I couldn't save them. I'll never forget them, and you won't forget yours either. Now, try to remember, Abdul. The tunnel. Do you know where the entrance is?"

"That was a long time ago. Many things have changed, but I think I have an idea where the entrance is."

"Good, good. Can you take me there?"

"The big earthquake last year probably destroyed it. Many homes collapsed." Abdul shook like a scared puppy. He said nothing, but hugged his wife and kids.

"I understand, Abdul. I do." He walked over and rested his hand gently but firmly on Abdul's shoulder. "But we have two days to stop this maniac. If we don't do this, if you don't do this—" Jack squeezed his shoulder. "Your wife, your kids, everyone will die."

Abdul's shoulders slouched momentarily, he whispered something to his family, then straightened, stood tall, slowly turned to Jack, and nodded.

"That a boy. Dewey will get you ready while I check in with Winfield," said Jack.

"Ever shoot one of these?" Dewey asked Abdul, holding his rifle out.

Abdul held up his shaking hands. "I cannot."

Naveen grabbed him by his shoulders and turned him to her. "Those men are animals. They must be stopped. Take the gun." Naveen took the gun and handed it to Abdul. "If you kill one of those animals, Allah will forgive you."

"We must pray first," said Abdul. He and his family went behind the curtain to a bedroom.

"Roger that, sir," Jack said into their satphone. "I'll get back to you later when we know for sure. We're moving to plan B."

Jack signaled Quinton to fire up the hand-held computer to receive intel from a satellite as he gave details for plan B to Winfield.

"It's downloading now, sir," said Jack, watching a variety of maps pop—one over the other—onto the computer screen. Topographical, satellite, utilities, military.

"Check, but you don't have to worry about plan C, sir. Have I ever let you down?" Jack's confident smile faded quickly. "No, sir. Tell the president it won't be necessary," said Jack. "Dewey and I will get it done or die trying. Just promise me you'll make sure my boy is taken care of. Thank you, sir. Operation Olympic Games, out."

"What's up?" asked Dewey.

"Let's just say if we don't get this done, everyone here is pretty much fucked. Since we don't know exactly where Pakistan's nukes are, the president will fry everything to make sure the bombs don't fall into the wrong hands." Jack fumbled with the thumb drive as if it were the cougar totem he normally carried in his pocket, but left on Barett's pillow. He wondered which possessed more power.

The cougar totem carved for Jack by Grandpa Joe reminded Jack of his ancestry. Be brave and cunning. Prowl like a shadow and silently stalk his prey. Cougar medicine embodied the type of warrior Jack strived to be. Cougar medicine, basically cat medicine, kept him alive through many hellacious missions, although he had exhausted his nine lives ages ago. Jack wondered how many more lives he had left.

The thumb drive possessed twenty-first-century power. Power not from the gods, not passed down from generation to generation, but from computer language commands that told a ceramic chip what to do next. A power Jack used to his advantage but had no interest in understanding.

In his heart, he trusted the cougar medicine. The thumb drive made him nervous.

"Then we better get busy," said Dewey.

Quinton and Squirrel snuck out in the dark and took up sniper positions—Quinton on the roof of the house and Squirrel setting up on a small ridge a quarter mile away. They reported military traffic moving up and down Kashmir Road but nothing on the side streets. People took the military-enforced curfew seriously. In fact, most stayed indoors during the daylight too, or they ended up like Abdul's neighbor.

Jack led the way, followed by Abdul wearing their backup pair of NODs, then Dewey, patrolling across rough terrain, heading away from Kashmir Road. All three wore dishdashas and kaffiyehs, just in case, but there could be no mistake—Jack and Dewey meant business.

Under their disguises, they carried everything but the kitchen sink. They had their main rifles and five hundred rounds of ammunition. They both carried nine-millimeter pistols, in case their mains went down, and throwing knives, compliments of Jack training his men in the good old ways.

The video of Jack throwing a hatchet and hitting the middle of Mullah Mohammed Abdul's chest on a sinking trawler a year earlier lived on in Ghost Team lore. Dewey joked that Jack would have them all shooting arrows and throwing spears if it were entirely up to Jack. Little did Dewey know how close he was to the truth.

Their MOLLE vest bulged more than normal with a variety of grenades; breachers; strip charges; Semtex, sometimes called "terrorist's C4" because of its stability; electronic gizmos; bolt cutters; and bulletproof plates, front and back. They kept the multiple pockets on their pants empty, making it easier to move like cats . . . and because it was a good place to stuff intel when doing SSE during a mission.

Compared to the average Pakistani, Jack looked the size of a yeti, the huge apelike abominable snowman who, local legend claimed, lived in the Himalayas just to the north. Except Jack was no yeti. He wielded more than a growl and a large stone.

They patrolled north and east, out of Abdul's immediate neighborhood. The North Star was at Jack's ten o'clock, over his left shoulder. The dusting of snow from two nights earlier had melted under the midday sun. A crunchy crust of frost formed under a cold, clear sky. The eerie green-lit terrain, as seen through their NODs, looked brittle, cold, and gray. Rigor mortis was setting in for the winter.

"I lost you," they heard Quinton say quietly in their ears from his overlook position.

"Copy, I still got you," said Squirrel.

Jack, Dewey, and Abdul stayed low, up against the base of the rocky ridge Squirrel sat atop.

Jack led their threesome through unfamiliar land ruled by terrorists. Terrorists famous for planting booby traps and pressure plates. Terrorists feared and known for IEDs and suicide bombers. Terrorists that Jack, Dewey, and Ghost Team had hunted for years. He moved slow and steady, looking for disturbed rocks or hand-dug trenches and holes. Jack followed his GPS coordinates to the approximate area where Abdul thought the tunnel entrance would be found. They hunkered down behind a rock pile.

"I lost my visual of you," said Squirrel.

"Check," said Jack. The palace wall was clearly visible, no more than five hundred feet away. They looked through their gun scopes. Sentries armed with automatic weapons moved along the top of the wall. Searchlights scanned the tundra below and sky above, crisscrossing the heavens as if advertising for a Hollywood premiere.

"Okay, Abdul. It's showtime," Jack said. "Stay low." He gave him a nudge.

"Nothing looks familiar. I don't remember any of this," said Abdul, staying put. "Maybe I dreamed it."

"You picked a hell of a time to tell me," said Jack. "Did it fucking happen or not?"

"Just let me think, please," said Abdul, poking his head up to look at the palace and study the land between it and him.

"There has to be a marker or something," said Dewey.

"People in this part of the world have been building underground for centuries to escape the heat," whispered Abdul, "and our enemies. We know how to be invisible. The palace itself is full of secret passageways from the old days. Few know they exist, and fewer still know where they are and how to get in."

"And *you* know where these secret passageways are and how to get in?"

"Yes, of course," said Abdul, now suddenly confident.

Clearly annoyed, Jack said, "Look, Abdul. We have a little over two days until your president, the man who lives over there," Jack pointed at the palace, "the man you and your wife work for, starts a nuclear war. This is no time to keep secrets. You need to tell me everything you know about that palace when we get back. In the meantime, it is crucial we find that tunnel, if one exists. And find it soon. We've got a lot of work to do before morning."

Abdul held up a hand to stop Jack's talking and pointed toward a completely nondescript splotch of rock and sand. "There it is, right under our noses."

He led Jack and Dewey to the spot and swept debris from the top of two heavy iron doors with his gloved hand. Jack grabbed a handle and pulled. Nothing happened. He pulled on one door and Dewey on the other. Still nothing happened.

"It must be locked from the inside. Makes sense," said Jack. "Good job, Abdul." Jack slapped him on the back. "Good fucking job. Let's cover this back up and get back to your place on the double. I need to pick your brain before you go to work in the morning."

The proud smile on Abdul's handsome face was replaced with a look of shock. "Work? I can't go to work. They'll kill me!"

"One more time, Abdul. That's all. It'll only take five minutes," said Jack. "One more time, then Dewey and I will take it from there. What do you say?"

Chapter 39

Presidential Palace, Islamabad, Pakistan

After Nina came to, she groped her way around the tiny cell in the pitch black. She was not alone. A corpse, frozen and forgotten in the human meat locker, lay curled up in the corner, eight feet away. Nina felt breasts on the corpse, cold and hard.

Nina's teeth chattered. She leaned into her corner, next to the door, opposite her cellmate, knees to chest, and huddled under her burka. She ached all over.

"I'm gonna kill you, you son of a bitch," she screamed.

She pounded on the door with her fists, then with the dead woman's shoe.

She heard a voice and strained to hear. She put her ear to the cold steel door and heard it again. An almost imperceptible disturbance of her utter silence, like being at the bottom of the ocean.

"Be ready tomorrow. I love you," spun in her head like a carousel.

Instead of using her time to panic about freezing to death, she replayed everything in her memory from the time Salwa kidnapped her, to the heroin delusions, to the present. She searched for clues or angles, anything to help her, once she got out.

The one thing she knew with certainty: Jack would come for her. With every bone and muscle and fiber of her being, she focused her energy on Jack, drawing him to her.

After his ordeal the previous year, Travis had told Nina how he tried to *will* Jack to find him when he was in Rolf's prison. She remembered a similar moment, onboard the ship, after they threw Barett overboard, when she half expected to see Jack racing over the horizon, leading a cavalry charge of SEAL zodiacs. Him painted up like a Sioux warrior, two eagle feathers tucked in a headband, him standing in the bow, one hand shading his eyes, a Winchester in the other. A war club and knife stuck in his belt.

Her hero. The last of a breed.

Nina also remembered her disappointment when, instead of Jack coming to save her, her bodyguard gave her another beating and introduced her to her dog collar. Huddled under her burka tent to keep warm, she grabbed the collar and jerked, then jerked again.

"Fucking thing! Fucking Rolf!" Nina felt for the lock and clawed at it with her fingers. She crawled to the dead woman and ran her hands over her, feeling for anything.

The woman started to glow in the dark, at least a part of her around her waist. Nina grabbed and searched with her fingers.

That's when she felt it. The sharp end of a clasp or piece of jewelry of some sort.

She sat on the corpse to get off the freezing stone floor and used the pin to carefully pick at the collar lock around her neck with trembling hands, until she felt a slight change. Not a click or snap, but a subtle give. She jerked the collar apart with both hands again, and it opened. She was free.

Nina heard voices coming toward her. Male voices grew louder and louder, echoing ahead off cavernous walls.

She quickly took the collar and snapped it around the corpse's neck, scrambled across to her corner, curled up, and waited.

The door opened. Rolf's bodyguard, the one with trench mouth and a sadistic eye, walked in carrying a torch and whip.

"Go," he ordered in English. "GO!" He kicked her. "GO!" He raised the whip. Nina scrambled out the door on hands and knees. But not fast enough.

He whipped, and she screamed in agony for effect, but it didn't cut as much through her robe as it would through bare skin. She scrambled to her feet and back up the corridor in the direction he pointed, toward the only light she saw, bracing herself against the wall as she went.

At the guard post, they checked her zip ties and moved her on with another whipping. Up, up, up the stairs to fresh air, warmth, and light. Like being born again.

They placed her on display in the hallway outside Rolf's office and threatened her to stay put.

Nina's burka looked as if she'd been dragged around behind a horse, all ripped and torn. She let her head hang like the beaten woman she was, but observed everything. She might have stood out on a normal day, but amidst the constant gunfire, the executions, the Taliban hooligans running around taking and doing whatever they wanted, and a psychotic president who got crazier by the minute, nobody noticed. Even her guards seemed oblivious.

Someone grabbed Nina by the arm and jerked her, pulling her back, down the hallway, stumbling away from Rolf's office and the guards.

"Keep quiet," he whispered.

Nina looked back. The guards were still looking the other way.

"Hurry," he said. A heavily shrouded, dark-skinned Pakistani man led Nina around a corner, then into a cavernous fireplace room. It looked like an important room—maybe a library, judging by the books strewn on the floor. He headed straight for the fireplace.

"Your husband sent me," he said as he pushed and twisted ornate woodwork carvings, part of the fireplace surround.

A guard's yell rose above the din. Then more orders were barked from the other direction as they sounded an all-out alert. A round of machine gun fire got everyone's attention.

Abdul Halabi frantically clawed and pried different parts of the woodwork, while pleading with Allah for mercy.

Suddenly, a wisp of warm, dusty air and a crack in the side of the fireplace appeared out of nowhere. He pulled open the small door and shoved Nina in.

The guards ran past the library door, then slid to a stop.

He stuck something in Nina's hand and closed the door behind her.

A stale darkness enveloped Nina. Her back against a wooden beam, her face against another, the thin sandwich of air between the two walls welcomed their first visitor in years.

From the other side of the wall Nina heard yelling. She felt the guards, inches away, and held her breath. Goose bumps tingled. She felt a tickle in her throat and clamped her hands over her mouth.

She heard panic in her savior's voice. Tension crescendoed as the guards screamed the same demand at him, over and over.

Nina stood perfectly still, when her instincts told her to bolt.

The man cried out as they beat him, then yelled something

back, ending with, "*Allahu akbar. Allahu—*"

Machine gun fire ripped holes through his *akbar*. Bullets splintered the wood around Nina. She squelched a scream and caught it in her throat.

The guard's shouting started again, then faded back out of the library. The footsteps faded too. Then it became dead quiet, like most libraries.

Nina shook, sometimes violently; for how long, she had no idea. *What just happened? Where am I?* She remembered the thing in her hand. She held it up to the light filtering through a bullet hole in the wall. She was shocked and confused to see a thumb drive.

She attacked the zip tie around her wrists with a vengeance, chewing like a ravenous wolf. With her hands free and her mind spinning, she slumped to the floor. She peered out of an eye-level hole in the wall. The mysterious man who had helped her lay motionless and bloody. Dead.

Jack sent him—she heard him say it. But who was he? And what made a thumb drive worth dying for? What was she supposed to do with it?

She stood as a free woman for the first time in weeks. Free inside the walls of a lunatic's asylum. Free in a country two days from annihilating Israel or two days from extinction. Nina figured she was about as free as a rat trapped on a sinking ship.

She kept coming back to the thumb drive. The dead man on the other side of the hole knew what to do with it. She'd only stored family photos or documents on the thumb drives she had used in the past. She knew little beyond that, other than—if Jack sent it—it had to be a big deal. A real big deal.

Nina did not know that Abdul had been sent to put the thumb

drive into his own office computer. But when Abdul recognized Nina standing in the hallway and saw the guards preparing for another round of lynchings, he had acted on instincts and changed his plans on the spot.

Nina got up as quietly as possible. She stripped off her bulky burka down to her bloomers to avoid snags and noise. She kept her burka in a wad for later. She inched her way along the eighteen-inch-wide space, sideways. She normally weighed 110 pounds. After a month of captivity, however, she was lucky to weigh 90. She was closer to Barett's size than her own. Either way, she slid through the space with ease.

The king or sheikh responsible for building Pakistan's presidential palace had thought of everything. Just enough light at just the right intervals, combined with pupils dilated to the size of saucers, and Nina confidently navigated her way around wooden beams, pipes, nails, and wire, out of the library, and shuffled back down the interior wall of the palace corridor.

After thirty minutes of creeping, Nina reached the end of the line. She discovered another access door, like the one in the library, that led to Rolf's office. But Rolf had killed the ex-president before he got the presidential tour and found out about the secret passages—or so she hoped.

Rolf's voice gradually grew loud enough to understand through the panels, even when he wasn't screaming. "What do you mean, you lost her? How could you fucking lose a hundred-pound woman when she's handcuffed and dog collared?"

"I—I—I don't know—"

"Don't you fucking say another word." Rolf spit the words out with such venom that the entire room quieted. "Gimme that fucking remote," he shrieked.

He paced the room breathing like an angry bull, pawing the dirt, preparing to charge. He stopped so close to Nina's spot in the wall that she thought he might hear her heart thumping. She heard the slide of his pistol as he chambered a round. The safety was off. His safety was always off.

"Did you try this?" he asked, then threw the remote against the wall—Nina's wall.

She recoiled instinctively, gasped, put her hand over her mouth, and froze.

Nina heard the shuffle of someone, probably Rolf, walking up next to her wall. He rapped on the wall, startling another gasp out of her. He pounded louder in an ever-widening circle, as if he were checking for something. Nina prayed he did not hit the magic button that would open the door to her secret hiding place. She heard some commotion, like a squad of Rolf's soldiers struggling to drag something heavy into his office.

"Now what?" said Rolf. He pounded the wall directly opposite Nina one last time, and she heard him move away.

"Who's this?" asked Rolf, perturbed for being interrupted.

"He helped your wife escape," said the lead guard. "She had outside help." Even the guards were starting to call Nina Rolf's wife. They said anything to appease the president.

Rolf kicked the dead man over on his back. "Who's this traitor?"

"From what's left of him, we think he was the head of your Presidential Affairs office, Abdul Halabi."

"Why did he betray me when we're so close to victory?"

"You executed his parents your first day in office. They both worked for the president. This man and his wife also worked for the president."

"And his wife? What do we know about her?" asked Rolf.

"We know that she didn't show up for work today, Mr. President."

"Well, well, well." Rolf looked around at the room full of soldiers. "What are you waiting for?"

Nina heard the four guards stomp from the room, one of them squawking orders into his radio.

"As for the rest of you morons, turn this place upside down, inside out. Do whatever it takes. But I want her brought to me on a silver platter," said Rolf. "Now get the fuck out of here." It sounded like a herd of wildebeests stampeding from the room.

Rolf must have left too because it got very quiet.

Nina relaxed and took a deep breath. She knew a thumb drive needed a computer, but the palace seemed to be computer-free, from what she had seen.

Move to survive. That's what Jack always said. Move to survive.

She carefully worked her way back out of Rolf's office, through the wall to a place where her secret passage opened up to another section of the palace.

She needed food and water, but there were far too many people running around. She decided to explore and wait until the middle of the night. Then she would take her best shot.

Chapter 40

Halabi House, Islamabad, Pakistan

"We gotta go," Jack yelled with urgency from the front room of the Halabi house. "We gotta go now!" He stuck the enemy's radio he had stolen from the wrecked Mercedes back in his cargo-pants pocket. He had heard them give orders to come find Naveen.

"We could draw a lot of attention," said Quinton, scanning the sky and listening for threats.

"If they find Naveen, they will kill her too. We've got five minutes at best before we're up to our elbows in assholes. Get his wife and kids in the SUV, and get them the hell out of here. NOW!" said Jack. "And don't say anything to Naveen about Abdul. You can tell her later, once you have them secured at the safe house," Jack said quietly so only Quinton could hear.

Quinton and Squirrel rushed through the curtain to the back bedroom. Thirty seconds later, they reappeared with Naveen and her kids, crying and looking terrified but moving quickly. Quinton signaled with one finger over his lips, then disappeared out the door, his assault rifle leading the way into the overcast November afternoon.

Wind crooned through the pine trees. It smelled like rain or snow. Thirty seconds to herd them to the garage and into their sideswiped Land Rover.

"What's the plan, Jack?" yelled Quinton.

"You know as good as I, if Dewey and I get in that car too, everything here is lost—Nina, the attack on Israel, our chance to nail this bastard, and stop World War III," said Jack.

The radio in Jack's pocket started squawking again. Whoever was on the other end seemed confused as to which side street they were supposed to turn onto. Jack heard an engine rev in the distance, closer than a mile.

Dewey tapped Jack on the shoulder twice and pointed out the opposite door. "Let's go."

"Good luck, Jack," said Quinton.

"Go, go, go." Jack tapped his earpiece once, then pounded the front hood of the Land Rover with his gloved hand as it backed out, pushing them to get moving. Ten seconds later, they disappeared around the corner.

Jack saw no faces looking out neighboring house windows. No steam or smoke rising from chimneys. No sign of life anywhere, other than the ice-filled cry of several peacocks penned up behind a house, down the street. They sounded like Jack felt—on edge, full-alert, locked and loaded.

Jack and Dewey simultaneously heard racing engines and sirens approaching. They took off running in the other direction, across open sand and rubble, each humping a backpack full of war toys over a wall, to Abdul's neighbor's house, still smoldering from a visit by Rolf's goon squad two days earlier.

Jack had no idea if anybody still lived there. He didn't care. He and Dewey needed to get out of sight fast.

Jack shoulder-blasted the door open, barely breaking stride. Dewey had rear guard and pushed the door shut as a couple of pickup trucks with roof-mounted fifty-caliber machine guns barreled around the corner at the end of the street and pulled right up on the sandy yard outside Abdul and Naveen's house.

Jack and Dewey quickly cleared all six rooms of the burned-out home, making sure they were alone. It was filled with charred furniture, scalded walls, and the penetrating smell of a morning-after campfire.

After years of combatting terrorists, nothing surprised Jack at how incredibly cruel people were, but he still never got used to it. It looked like after the goon squad executed Abdul's neighbor and tossed his body on the side of the road, they came back and burned his family to death after first roping them together in a bundle, like firewood.

Jack and Dewey stared at the nightmarish mass of melted humanity, until bullhorn-yelling from Rolf's soldiers next door snapped them back to reality. They had to wipe it out of their memory and move on. They took up secure positions where they could see and hear—Jack out the front, Dewey out the back.

Well past midday on a gloomy day, the wind blew from north to south, from the goons to Jack. Two soldiers rushed the front door of Abdul's house while two others ran around back, and the last two stayed on the fifty calibers.

There was lots of yelling and smashing, even gunfire in the house. The same for the garage.

Jack slapped a hand over the confiscated radio in his pants pocket when it made too much noise as the goons reported back their findings to the head of palace security.

Dewey shot Jack a look across the room, like saying, "What

the fuck?" for allowing the noise from the radio to be loud enough to potentially give away their position.

Jack shot Dewey back a look saying, "Fuck you too," and rolled his eyes. He needed to be able to hear what the death squad was saying. At that point, any information, no matter how trivial, was useful.

True to form, before the goons pulled out, they torched Abdul and Naveen's house and garage. When the plastic jug full of gas exploded and flames shot out the windows, they emptied their machine guns into the walls and windows, carving a rough letter *J* for jihad—their signature, their cause. With the trucks gone, embers and black smoke rolled downwind toward Jack and Dewey. The peacocks chimed in too, sounding like screaming babies.

Jack checked through his scope for left-behinds. Dewey checked their perimeter on the backside.

"Seemed in a hurry," said Dewey.

"Needed to get back for late afternoon prayer time. It's a good time for us to move," said Jack.

"Good time to sit tight too," said Dewey. "They've torched everything on this street. Why don't we get a couple hours shut-eye and move after dark?"

"Roger that. Could be a ballbuster these last thirty-six hours." Jack fired up their satphone to get any last-minute updates from Winfield. Knowing what he knew, Jack figured it would be their last.

"Fuckers killed Abdul," said Dewey, shaking his head, waking up from an hour-long nap.

"He was right. He knew Rolf would kill him, and he went anyway," said Jack, who had been on watch while Dewey slept, returning the favor from the hour before. "He was a good man."

"So much for his secret passageways," said Dewey. "Still got the backup thumb drive?"

Jack fished around in his pocket for a second too long before pulling it out. "Guess it's up to us to get the job done."

"Damn thing is going to get us killed," said Dewey. "If Nina weren't in there, I'd say we should just pull out and let them nuke the fucking place."

"Roger that," said Jack. "But she's in there fighting for her life, and I can guaran-fucking-tee she won't give in to that son of a bitch until one of them is dead. And I'm betting on my wife."

"Roger that," said Dewey. "She's a force, no doubt."

"If you had an ounce of Indian blood in you, you'd know her spirit has been getting stronger every day," said Jack.

Jack's repeating vision of Nina had gradually changed. Nina was no longer on the other side of the great divide, but over the middle of it. Every time Jack quieted himself enough to meditate on it, Nina was closer still to his side.

"Well, okay then, Big Chief," Dewey said in a way only Dewey could. "What do you want to do? What's your plan?"

"Tomorrow is the last day of fasting, so everyone will be getting all worked up for the end-of-fast feast and missile launch the day after that. We know where they'll be, and they still won't have any idea we're here," said Jack.

"Do we know enough about Abdul's secret passages?" asked Dewey.

"No idea. Sounded pretty sketchy," said Jack at the same time as he heard the thumping of a Pakistani military helicopter quickly approaching their location from the palace. It took up a position hovering over Abdul and Naveen's burning house.

"So much for shut-eye." Dewey duck-walked across the room to stay low. From the cover of the neighbor's charred house, Dewey peeked out of a blown-out window, flipped the safety off on the grenade launcher attached to the underside of his assault rifle, and zeroed in on the helo.

Four ropes, two to a side, flipped out each helo door and uncoiled as they fell until the tips reached the ground. Before the four fast-roping soldiers got halfway down the rope, Jack squeezed Dewey's shoulder from behind, and Dewey pulled the trigger, shooting a grenade into the belly of the bird.

A massive explosion, followed by even bigger secondary explosions, spectacularly blew the helicopter to pieces thirty feet above the ground. In the midst of the explosion, Jack and Dewey shot the four ropers, sending them to fiery deaths, roasting under a burning inferno of molten helicopter.

Jack remembered a whole team of his comrades who were killed when a Taliban RPG nailed their helicopter a few years earlier in Afghanistan. He felt no remorse, just a small bit of vindication.

His Pakistani radio started squawking again. Neither Jack nor Dewey understood Pashto very well, but were great at reading between the lines.

Jack sprinted out the back door, through oil-black smoke, with Dewey on his heels.

Forget sleeping. Game on!

CHAPTER 41

Presidential Palace, Islamabad, Pakistan

Adrenaline kept Nina wired, tiptoeing about in the dark on her bare feet for hours, oblivious to the bloody trail her feet left from stepping on the sharp pieces of stone and mortar that littered the floor between the walls. Like a mouse, she crept through the palace walls, using her hands and senses to find her way, trying to picture what her skinny passageway between worlds looked like in full light.

She sidestepped through electrical wire criss-crossings with the grace of a long-legged spider. In the tightest spots, where wooden beams supporting opposite walls pressed close, the space shrunk to a foot. Since her head was the biggest part of her starved body, she traversed those kinks with ease. If she moved too fast, sixteen-penny nails sticking through the walls gouged her skin and snagged her bloomers. Move too slow, and she would never find a computer.

But more than anything, Nina dreaded that the shards of mortar covering every inch of the floor would be her death. With every step, she crunched. If she moved slowly like a cat, she barely made a sound. If she tried to hurry and a sharp piece of mortar cut into her already-bleeding feet, the result was noise and pain. Trapped between two walls where every sound was amplified, she felt as if each second, each breath, would be her last.

She grew tired of carrying her burka-bundle early on and stashed it at a wall junction she planned to get back to at some point. She wrapped her feet in torn strips of hijab after she removed the splinters and stone.

Even as the night wore on well past midnight, and she moved farther into the heart of the palace, she constantly heard people moving past her on the other side of the wall . . . talking, not sleeping. Her space grew warmer the farther into the palace she crept. Jumbles of electrical wire became almost impossible to navigate, but she always found a way to keep going.

Up ahead, for the first time, a bit of filtered light shone like a beacon at eye level. She heard voices, lots of male voices, on the other side, calm and businesslike. She slowed, calculating each step. Sweeping the mortar away ever-so quietly with her foot first, then moving ahead. One step at a time. Over another nest of wires. Controlled breathing. Like a prowling cat.

Finally she peeped through a screen into what looked like some kind of military control room. The room was full of desks with someone at every chair, typing on . . . *computers*. Jackpot.

The hair on the back of Nina's neck stood on end. The room looked familiar. She heard a voice she remembered too. Then she saw him, Osama El-Hashem, pacing behind a row of computer controllers, mumbling to himself.

She remembered Rolf executing the general. She also remembered Osama and how he showed no fear when he took control of the situation and calmed Rolf. He carried himself like the alpha, the man in charge. The room looked to be a very important room too, maybe even launch control.

Nina spotted a clock across the smoky room that said two thirty.

She decided to sit tight and watch until four before she made her move. She recollected Jack's "move to survive" mantra and decided to use the ninety minutes to think of what that move should be.

But before a minute elapsed, everything changed again.

Rolf barged into the cavernous room, ranting like a maniac.

Nina controlled her breathing when Rolf passed in front of her hole, no longer shocked or afraid, but primed like a claws-out tiger waiting for the right moment to pounce on its prey. To rip the skin from his bones, the heart from his chest, and the eyes from their sockets. No longer afraid to kill him, she wanted it all.

"Nobody just disappears without a trace!" Rolf said to Osama. "One minute she's there, and the next—poof." He threw his hands in the air, one still holding his trusty pistol. "She's no magician. I don't think so."

"I had every room in the palace searched, then searched again. The only thing we found was her dog collar strapped to the dead woman in her cell." Osama bowed his head slightly. "Nothing else, Mr. President."

Nina smiled and flipped Rolf the finger from the other side of the wall. She saw and heard everything perfectly.

"Then search again. I know she's here somewhere."

"Yes, Mr. President." Osama bowed.

"Now tell me about the launch. How's my missile coming?" asked Rolf.

"Everything is going according to your plans. I expect to be able to launch on your command"—Osama looked at the clock—"in a little over thirty-two hours. An eleven o'clock launch should put the missile in Tel Aviv shortly after noon. The numbers should be staggering," said Osama.

A smile crept across Rolf's face, and his stress lines relaxed for the first time in days. "Go on."

"The missile will launch from your secret facility in Kahuta and reach Mach 2 as it flies over Afghanistan, Iran, Iraq, and Syria before striking." A pained look crept across Rolf's face before Osama quickly interjected, "Of course, none of those countries, none of our brothers, will be notified in advance. This will be your moment of glory, and no one else's."

"Good. Very good," said Rolf. "And after that? What then?"

"Once the world—the Americans, the British, the Russians—realize you have nukes capable of hitting a target two thousand miles away and are not afraid to use them, they will give you anything you want. Anything," said Osama with a confident smile.

Rolf looked as if he slipped into deep thought as he gave Osama a congratulatory slap on the back. He started to walk away when his satphone rang, stopping him in his tracks.

"Yes, sir. Everything is on schedule for the day after tomorrow." Rolf shielded the mouthpiece with his other hand. "Yes, sir. I will wait for your command. What? No. Everything is under control."

Rolf turned back to Osama, his smile gone, and his face turning red. "I will look into it, you can rest assured. I will look into it," he said and hung up. He turned to Osama. "Why are you keeping secrets, Osama? What are you hiding?" challenged Rolf.

Osama's jaw dropped. "I . . . I . . . I don't know what you

mean. I haven't—"

"One of my helicopters was shot down not even a mile from my palace, and you don't tell me? I suppose you have that 'under control' too?"

"I . . . we are investigating. I didn't mean to—"

"You should stick to what you know and leave the thinking to me," said Rolf. He paced around, waving the pistol again, then stopped inches from Osama's face.

"I have many eyes, Osama. Eyes and ears. Believe me when I say it was no accident. That helicopter was shot down. Do you hear me? Shot down! Now who would do that? Who do you think would shoot down one of my helicopters?"

Osama said nothing, just stared at the floor while standing at attention.

"Did you double security?"

"No, sir. I—"

"Did you send out patrols?"

"No, sir," said Osama, each time more sheepishly than the last.

"Did you do anything?"

"We've been looking for her. And we work twenty-four hours a day on your bomb." He sounded exhausted.

"Does the name Jack Gunn mean anything to you?" asked Rolf.

Osama shook his head.

"He's here. It's got to be him," Rolf said "You think I'm bad—wait until you meet him. He'll put a bullet between your stupid fucking El-Hashem eyes before you can blink, just like he did the rest of the family. He's here for my wife and that stupid badal thing. He shot down one of my helicopters, and you just let him go. I should have you shot right now for being a traitor." Rolf looked around at his bodyguards and nodded. They stepped in close, one on either side of Osama.

Osama looked dumbfounded.

"You are hereby relieved of all duties, except . . . to launch my missile. Screw that up, and you will watch your family die. Your mother, your father, your wife, your children. Everyone. Then you will join them. Do I make myself clear?"

Before Osama could respond, Rolf waved him back to his controllers.

Rolf pulled his bodyguards in close and said loudly, "Like cattle to the butcher, he's right on schedule. Double security, send out patrols. And no matter what you do, even if you have to tear this place down, find my fucking wife."

Nina wanted to scream. Scream a blood-curdling scream right before she slammed a knife deep into Rolf's sick skull.

As she pondered ways to kill Rolf from her musty prison, so thirsty that breathing hurt, clarity came like opening the window blinds on a sunny new day.

She headed back down the wall, over the same wires, around the same beams, quietly placing one foot in front of the other, until she reached her burka. Once dressed, she planned to rest and wait. Wait for the feast she had heard them talking about to begin later that evening. Then, she decided, she would step back out into Rolf's world and take her last shot.

The first thing on her mind?

Find a gun.

CHAPTER 42

Presidential Palace, Islamabad, Pakistan

"That should do the trick," said Dewey. He rechecked the switch, wires, and detonator connected to the booby trap on the underside of the steel doors hiding the tunnel's secret entrance.

With their NODs down, the tunnel ahead looked like something out of a Halloween nightmare. Jack figured the tunnel could tell a few stories that would make his skin crawl.

"Poor son of a bitch almost made it," Jack said, looking at a pile of skeleton bones near the doors. "Let's go."

The rock walls near the entrance glistened with ice. Once they moved a hundred feet up the tunnel, the ice had turned to water, weeping from the walls.

Jack and Dewey had spent so much time underground over the years training and operating with the SEALs, Jack did not give it a second thought that they were heading down a tunnel aimed at a nest full of bad guys, thousands of miles from home, with no backup. They pulled up operating plans forged in their memories from earlier, similar missions, and moved out, full steam ahead. A job to do. No time to waste. No questions to ask.

Terrorists loved tunnels. Jack hunted terrorists. So tunnels became as familiar to Jack as swimming out of a submerged submarine, or skydiving at night, or blowing some dirtball's head off with his sniper rifle, or any one of a thousand other scenarios. They all had their time and place.

The Rock of Gibraltar guarded the entrance to the Mediterranean Sea. Armies had battled over its tactical advantage for centuries. Its strategic waters were deep, cold, and clear. Buried under Gibraltar's granite skin were tunnels, lots of tunnels, both manmade and natural. The rock had become a second training home to Jack and his Ghost Team over the years.

On the actual day of 9/11, Jack, Dewey, and their Ghost Team had been training in Gibraltar's tunnels. In less than a week, his team was covertly shuttled across Europe and Asia, while the rest of the world was on lockdown. True to his motto, Jack kept them moving, under orders from the president, to Uzbekistan, and from there, across the border into Afghanistan to link up with the Northern Alliance.

The Hindu Kush of northern Afghanistan had their share of terrorist-infested tunnels, and that was right were Jack and his team went. Into the tunnels to flush out the rats. Firefights in pitch black. Bullets and tracers unpredictably ricocheting off stone walls. The whip crack sound of bullets snapping by his head at supersonic speeds. The bite of granite shards cutting deep. Of blinding light and infinite darkness.

Sound seemed amplified a thousandfold to Jack as he and Dewey crept now. With every step they took farther into the tunnel came the crunch of broken rock. They paused frequently to listen, but heard nothing in return for the first hour. Gradually, a slight disturbance to the silence came from the other end. The palace end. The closer they snuck, the louder it got. Men's jeers. Women's screams, more like whimpers. The crack of a bullwhip. Leather on skin.

Jack and Dewey kept to the shadows. One on the inside, one on the outside of the turn as the cold and damp granite tube angled right.

Like sneaking up on people standing around a bonfire from the dark of night, Jack and Dewey could see perfectly from their pitch-black hiding spots. The four Talis would have night blindness, their pinpoint pupils unable to see past the bright light bulb they whipped their victim underneath. Jack and Dewey's pupils were big and dilated from creeping up the dark tunnel for the last hour. Everything and everybody before them stood out like spotlighted prey. Easy targets. Deserving targets.

Jack held up four fingers to Dewey without taking his eyes off the targets. There was the bastard doing the whipping, two more holding the woman by her arms and stretching her between them, and one just watching the festivities, drunk from a bottle of homebrewed rotgut.

They blocked the tunnel, Jack and Dewey's only way into the palace. A radio lay on the damp ground beside the drinker. The whipper had his hat and shirt off, working up a sweat and a smile. With each crack, they all chanted. Whatever they were saying only made Jack more mad, knowing they were somehow enjoying themselves.

Watching the whipper enjoy torturing the screaming lady was like opening a hate valve on Jack's emotional water main. He could tolerate watching men torture men. In fact, he had done it many times. Sometimes he took action to stop the injustice. Sometimes he had orders to take no action, which went against everything

Jack stood for. But men torturing women or children was grounds for immediate termination in Jack's mind. Immediate, as in, "you just punched your ticket to paradise, asshole."

As he crouched in the shadows twenty feet from the man raising his arm and snapping it down, the whip peeling the skin from the woman's back while the others counted and laughed, Jack made his decision.

The tunnel was barely high enough for Jack and Dewey to stand tall. Jack silently went to one knee, facing the whipper. He took off his helmet, set it on the ground, and picked up a small rock.

He pulled out his double-edged throwing knife and pinched the razor-sharp blade between his right thumb and forefinger. Dewey put a hand on Jack's left shoulder from behind and squeezed, giving him the go-ahead signal.

Jack tossed the rock a few feet toward the whipper. The whipper stopped and held up a hand. All four men stopped laughing. The whipper turned in Jack and Dewey's direction, trying to see into the abyss through impossibly dilated pupils.

The last thing he would have seen was the dull-black flash of Jack's knife after Jack snapped his arm straight down, uncocked his wrist, and released the knife, which took a full turn and struck the whipper center mass, right in his Adam's apple, severing his windpipe and any chance he had for one last "Allahu akbar" before he collapsed in a sorry heap.

From out of the dark into the light, the heads of the other three bad guys stood out like giant watermelon bull's-eyes. Dewey double-tapped the two guys holding the woman with head shots. A mist of blood showered the far rock. The drunk guy wasted his only chance to scream. Dewey put a round through his mouth and out his neck. He flew backward and ricocheted off the stone wall. The woman flopped to the ground like a side of beef, limp and solid. Her head bounced once.

Dewey slapped Jack on the back. "Good shot, Chief." They looked at each other and smiled.

Jack and Dewey quickly approached her position. Jack grabbed his knife out of the guy's throat, wiped the blood off on his pant leg, and stuck it back in its sheath. Dewey put another round through each dead guy's ear hole, then they turned their attention to the unconscious woman lying facedown in a pool of blood.

It seemed to take an hour for Dewey to roll the woman over, but finally Jack said, "Thank God," and exhaled so completely, his body deflated like a punctured lung. "I thought it was Nina." Emotionally exhausted, he sat next to her, stripped one of the dead guys' cloaks off, and wadded it up as a pillow under her head, switching automatically into first aid mode.

Dewey covered her with another cloak to keep her warm while he took her pulse. "Thready, but she has one." He wiped blood off her face.

"See what you can find on these shitbags," said Jack.

Dewey kicked their bullwhip aside. "Fucking assholes." He started going through their pockets.

Jack pulled the sip tube off his shoulder, put it in her mouth, and gave it a squeeze. First nothing, then she choked, coughed, and started screaming again, spitting water and blood.

"Hey, hey, you're safe now. Shh. Shh," Jack said quietly as he clamped one of his paws over her mouth. The soft spot in his battle-hardened heart opened up to her. The protector in him wanted nothing more than to wrap that woman in his security blanket and kill anyone who tried to harm her.

"Their weapons are shit. Radio's done. Looks like low-level douchebags who got what they deserved," said Dewey.

"Either way, somebody will miss 'em, sooner or later," said Jack. "We gotta keep moving."

"Bring her with?" asked Dewey.

"Either that, or put her out of her misery," said Jack. He looked at her long and hard, picturing Nina. "It might slow us down, but you take the lead. I'll bring her till we find a good place to stash her. We can't leave her down here moaning and screaming."

"Roger that," said Dewey. He wasted no time turning up-tunnel and moving out.

Jack checked his watch. "It's 1845. They should be feasting. Just about time, bro." He cradled her in his arms with his rifle resting on top, staying in close contact with Dewey. She could not have weighed more than a hundred pounds. She did not slow Jack down a bit.

"Check," said Dewey.

Their view gradually brightened the closer they got to the palace. Subliminal light and noise tiptoed into their subterranean aquarium like the flash and rumble of a distant thunderstorm. They moved cautiously.

Jack's spider tickled. He searched for a gun aimed his direction, but found none. Every sensor in his body was on full alert, trying to decipher each step, each bend of the stone corridor, and each sound.

"Bring it up," said Dewey. He kept his eyes and gun down range while pointing at a rusty steel door on the right.

Jack put the woman down and opened the door, gun first. "These are some sick bastards," said Jack. "This one's wearing a dog collar." Jack rolled her robed body over, like flipping a piece of wood, stiff and cold. He said nothing except a silent, "Thank God."

"We good to go?" asked Dewey.

"One way in. One way out, Dewey," said Jack. "It's gonna be a shitstorm when this thing starts."

"I'm good to go, Jack," said Dewey, checking his watch. "Lose the package. It's show time."

"Roger that." Jack put the woman down and covered her as best he could. He left two energy bars and some water, while holding a finger over his mouth. "Shh."

She smiled back weakly and nodded.

They studied an electronic schematic of the palace floor plans that had been spliced together from multiple intel sources. Jack fingered the thumb drive in his pocket. Just checking.

Jack feared failure more than death. He had cheated death many times. But if this was to be the night he went to be with his parents, he wanted to die a good death. And he wanted to make sure he killed Rolf first.

In the final minutes before 1900, he fished a small tin the size of a silver dollar out of a pocket, popped the lid, dabbed the tips of his middle fingers in the black tar, and painted broken arrows under each eye, as he did every time he went to war. Even though Dewey wasn't native, he did the same. They looked like a couple of badasses with their face paint and beards and helmets and death stares.

They bumped fists, and Jack growled, "Let's go get some." Then he and Dewey struck out toward the first checkpoint.

They clung to the murky edge of the tunnel shadows between light and dark, surveying the four guards hovering around the checkpoint table, eating food trucked down from the palace above.

After giving thanks for surviving another month of fasting, they stuffed finger food into their big, fat faces, laughing between gulps and swallows. No radio appeared nearby. All weapons stood at ease, propped against the table or wall.

Jack checked the timer on his watch. He counted down with three, two, then one finger. At exactly 1900, he and Dewey pulled their triggers, and silenced rounds broke the sound barrier before striking home, dropping the four Pakistani guards in mid-celebration . . . Jack and Dewey's own version of cracking the whip.

As he and Dewey came out of the shadows, the ground shook once, then a second, and finally a third time. Each time more violently than before. Soot and dust instantly filled the cave. Screams and gunfire filtered down from the palace above.

"Right on schedule," said Jack with a sinister smile. "Move it or lose it," he said, and up the stairs they bound.

Chapter 43

Presidential Palace, Islamabad, Pakistan

The third explosion reminded Nina of the San Diego earthquakes she had lived through as a young bride. Their rented duplex in the community of Imperial Beach, just south of SEAL team headquarters on Coronado, sat three blocks from the breakers. Jack spent most of his time training at the base. Nina spent most of her time walking the beaches, searching for sea glass and solitude—away from Montana for the first time in her life and adapting to Mexican food and the life of a Southern California beach bum.

Earthquakes hit their beach home without warning. Sometimes shakers, other times rollers. The third explosion outside the palace was more of a shaker, rattling everything, including her hiding spot inside the wall.

She must have dozed off, because the explosions woke her with a start. She caught her gasp before it escaped, then covered up and braced herself, just in case something bigger and grander followed.

What followed sounded like mass chaos. On the other side of her escape door, men yelled, women screamed. She sensed fear and confusion in their tones.

The aroma of food, actual food, somehow made its way through the walls too. Nina licked her lips unconsciously. Her long-forgotten stomach growled. She tried to remember her last meal, but came up with a blur. She knew she had twelve hours to live or die. She needed water. Food she could live without.

They must be under attack, she thought. Jack and his team were making their move. She stood, put on her burka, and listened. The floor rumbled over and over, sometimes one on top of the other, which she figured were guns. Big guns or cannons firing back at Jack and his men.

The rustle and panic of people faded with everyone going outside to fight. Her interior wall space grew dead quiet. The library on the other side too. She looked through the old bullet holes in the wall and saw nothing and nobody.

She made her move.

The door creaked slightly as she released the latch and stepped out into Rolf's palace. Blood still smeared the floor where Rolf's men had killed Abdul, her guardian angel, and dragged him from the room.

She rushed to the opposite wall and hid behind the library door to get her bearings and stretch her aching back. She brushed and straightened her burka as best she could and held on tight to the thumb drive.

She heard screams. Women's and children's screams were drawing near again. Through the crack between the door hinge and wall, she watched the hallway as they ran toward her like a herd through the dark. The guards were rushing them below to a safe place—or to the front lines to be human shields.

She was tempted to join them and possibly escape by blending into the crowd, but there was no way she was going anywhere until she knew Rolf El-Hashem was dead.

After they passed, Nina stepped into the hallway and headed in the opposite direction, the direction of the computer room. Even gathering the folds of her gown and holding them thigh high, she still swooshed every time she moved. But move she did. Move or die.

Drawn by the scent, she dodged into an abandoned banquet room. The tables were still full of food and the candles still burned. She blew them out and wasted no time scarfing down two glasses of water and a chunk of bread.

The room felt familiar. More booms and flashes from a large cannon outside the window, and Nina dove for cover, under a table. She foraged around on her hands and knees for a weapon, but came up empty. She really wanted a gun, but settled for two butcher knives instead.

She rested under the table, eating more bread and drinking.

No longer obsessed with finding food and water, her mind drifted back to Barett. And with that, tears instantly formed and trickled down her filthy cheeks. With the gnawing in her stomach gone, her chest ached as if she were having a heart attack. An elephant with its foot on her sternum, squeezing the last breath out of her. Hard to breathe. Hard to swallow.

She wanted to give the world to her little boy. To be able to watch him grow up and get married. To have children of his own. She wanted so much. She wanted to go home.

The big gun outside the window fired again, startling her back to reality.

Jack was close. But where?

Nina tried to think, but could only picture one thing. The man who died stuffing her into a secret hole in the wall. She would never forget the look on Abdul's face as he put the thumb drive into her hand, then turned away to face his own death. She shook her head, wiped her tears, and prayed.

Her father's faint image appeared again, in the darkness under the table. In her mind or an actual image, she wasn't sure. He re-focused her. The knives in her grip glowed. The thumb drive too. She took one last deep breath, crawled out from under the table, and headed back down the hallway.

She ran with one hand on the wall, her secret space on the other side guiding her. Around a corner, she recognized the entrance to the computer room and quickly backed up around the corner before the sentry spotted her.

She heard footsteps rapidly approaching from behind, footsteps in unison, accompanied by Arabic grumblings.

Trapped. Her mind was racing, processing. Her guardian angel gave his life in order to get the thumb drive into her hands. It must have been important. Important enough to die for. Live or die, she knew she needed to get that thumb drive plugged into one of Rolf's computers. No matter what else happened.

Nina raced back around the corner toward the sentry guarding the computer room entrance, screaming at the top of her lungs, running toward him and his gun. The guards racing up behind her yelled in Arabic for her to stop.

She kept running.

A line of machine gun bullets narrowly missed Nina from behind and ricocheted off the stone floor around her running feet as her pursuers tried to stop her from reaching the door to the computer room.

The computer room sentry Nina was running toward acted furious at his own men for nearly shooting him as they chased

Nina. He fired his AK-47 into the ceiling and screamed for her to stop.

Nina slid to a stop, holding two butcher knives high above her head. Someone from behind knocked her to the floor. The knives clattered harmlessly to the side. She thrust the thumb drive across the floor to make sure it slid to the foot of the sentry, whose eyes fell on it immediately.

"What's this?" he said in English, studying the thumb drive.

The trailing guards pulled her back to her feet. They pulled her burka top up, something they would normally do only with one of their wives. When they saw who they had, they said excitedly into a radio, "We've got her. Tell Mr. President we've got her."

"Hold her right there. Don't move," responded the radio.

Seconds later, the door behind the sentry opened and blazing light flooded the hallway outside.

Rolf stepped into the light, pistol in hand. The guard handed him the thumb drive, which he held up to the light.

"Where'd you get this?" he yelled down the hall at Nina. "Stealing my secrets, and then what? You've got nowhere to—"

Before Rolf finished his sentence, the hallway behind Nina erupted in flashes of silenced gunfire.

The guards all around Nina crumpled to the floor. Blood splattered everywhere.

Nina instinctively dropped for cover.

Rolf dodged behind the bulletproof door and slammed it shut while the sentry was abandoned in the hallway and riddled with bullets.

Nina belly-crawled toward the side wall around the bodies and through pools of blood. Before she got there, a heavy hand on the middle of her back stopped her in her tracks.

She froze. Was it Jack? Was it one of Rolf's goons? Visions of Barett and Jack and her dad and their new home spun like a kaleidoscope through her exhausted brain.

But she gave herself credit. She had earned a good death. She never quit, and in the end, even though it made no sense—while she didn't get to kill Rolf or get the thumb drive into a computer—she got it into the computer room. Hopefully the thumb drive could take it from there. The man who had died getting the thumb drive into her hands had not died in vain. She would not die in vain. She had accomplished her mission. She let every muscle relax at once and melted into the floor to accept her destiny.

A whisper said, "Nina?" Did she dream it? Again she heard, "Nina?"

She flipped over on her back as the hand pulled her up. "*Jack*? *Jack*!" Agony and ecstasy simultaneously overwhelmed her senses. Her breath caught in her throat. "Jack."

He ripped up the face flap of her burka. "Nina."

She threw her arms around his neck and held on for dear life. Dehydrated as she was, tears welled up. "I knew you'd come."

He picked her up and stood. "You're as light as a feather, baby. Are you okay?"

"I am now."

"Hi, stranger," said Dewey as he gave her a hug.

"Dewey. Oh my God!" Her astonishment doubled to imagine what it took for both Jack and Dewey to arrive at the last possible instant and save her at the moment of her death.

"I don't mean to spoil the party, but we gotta move," said Dewey.

"I think our little distraction has worn off. We'll have company, and lots of it, in a few," said Jack.

"Two against whatever. We'll never make it out," said Dewey, already turned to provide rear cover.

"Three, Dewey. Give me a gun," said Nina as she picked up her two knives and stuck them under her waistband.

"We haven't accomplished our mission yet," said Jack.

"What was on that thumb drive?" asked Nina.

"What thumb drive?" asked Jack and Dewey.

"The one the man gave me as he shoved me into the secret passageway in these walls," Nina said, pointing at the wall.

"You mean Abdul? Where is he?"

"Dead. The thumb drive. What was on it?" asked Nina quickly, out of breath but trying to speak softly.

"A worm. A computer worm supposed to shut his launch down," said Jack. "Why? Where is it?"

"He has it," Nina said, pointing at the door. "Rolf has it. I allowed myself to get caught to get it in his hands. Time's running out, right?"

"What! Are you trying to get yourself killed?" asked Jack.

"I'm trying to stop a maniac. I stopped worrying about what happens to me weeks ago," said Nina. "What about my little boy?" Nina said, breaking down again, bracing for the worst.

"Barett is fine. He's with Travis and Jaz. You did good, Nina," said Jack, hugging her again.

"Seems like a big place. We need to get outta this kill zone before every trigger-happy moron in Pakistan shows up," said Dewey.

"I know this place like the back of my hand. I've got an idea. Follow me," said Nina, holding out her hand, scars around her wrist clearly visible. "Gun, please," she demanded.

Jack shrugged his shoulders at Dewey. "Unless you have a better idea," he said as he handed Nina his sidearm.

"I'm not leaving until I know that son of a bitch is dead," said Nina as she led them back down the hallway toward the library, not waiting for an answer.

"Me neither," said Jack as he and Dewey fell in behind.

"Ditto," said Dewey.

The booming cannons fell silent. Lights came back on. Gunfire became more sporadic.

"In here," said Nina. "Hurry!"

Dewey guarded the library door while Nina crossed to the fireplace mantle, repeated Abdul's moves, and opened the secret door again.

"You two are too big to move in here, but you'll fit," said Nina.

Jack took a look inside with his flashlight. "Eighteen inches at best. We'll be packed like sardines."

"You'll be out of sight. I have a plan, unless you have a better one."

Jack was already stripping off his pack. Dewey too.

"I'll go first," said Nina. "I've lived in these walls for almost two days. I have a peephole into the computer room. I'll go make sure they put that thumb drive in."

She stripped her burka off, wadded it up, and jumped in, her knives tucked into the waistband of her bloomers. Jack climbed in next, then Dewey, who pulled the door shut with a soft click.

"No lights. They'll see you through the bullet holes in the wall," said Nina.

"Here, take this," said Jack, handing a headset to Nina. "Radio silence unless absolutely necessary. You want the NODs?"

"Don't need them. I've got cat eyes, remember? How do I use this thing, just in case?" she asked, holding her pistol up.

"There's a round in the chamber. Safety on. Safety off. Pull the trigger. Fifteen rounds in the mag. Here's an extra," said Jack.

She stuck the magazine in her bloomer top. "Wish me luck."

"I love you," said Jack.

Then Nina crept down the secret passage between the walls like a praying mantis, a praying mantis starving to eat her lunatic "husband" Rolf.

Chapter 44

Presidential Palace, Islamabad, Pakistan

Rolf's screaming reached Nina's ears long before she slid in front of her screened-over peephole.

"Hurry up. Stick it in," Rolf said to a computer controller.

Nina had a partially obstructed view of his computer screen. Rolf hunched over the screen with his back to her.

"Where is it?" Rolf demanded, shoving the controller's shoulder.

Nina saw no change in the on-screen image. Sweat trickled down the sides of her temples. Her head throbbed. "Nina to Jack," she whispered.

"Go," she heard in her ear.

"Nothing's happening. It's not working," she whispered.

"Don't you know how to use a fucking computer?" Rolf screamed, shoving the controller off his chair and taking his place. He clicked and scrolled frantically, then stopped, frozen in place by what he saw.

"Wait a minute, I think they got it . . . You sent them a porno?" asked Nina.

"I don't know what Hacker put on there. If they plugged it in, it's working. It works in the background," whispered Jack. "Confirm—you saw them plug it in?"

"They can't take their eyes off the screen. Yeah, it's working," said Nina.

"I suppose Hacker wanted to make sure they left the drive in long enough for the worm to download," said Jack.

"Roger that," said Nina.

"Okay, now get back here ASAP," said Jack.

"My mission isn't accomplished yet," said Nina, sounding like a miniature version of Jack.

"Nina, get the hell out of there. Nina! Nina!"

She turned the radio off.

Rolf circled back into view and had his newly appointed chief of security pinned up against the wall directly on the opposite side of the wall from Nina, with his pistol jammed under the choking man's jaw. She slid far enough away to still have a view but not get shot if Rolf pulled the trigger and the bullet went through the wall.

"If you want to live to see tomorrow, get out there and kill my wife, you imbecile!" Rolf shoved the man toward the door. "And those other two! Kill them all!"

"Yes, Mr. President."

"Three against my army. Do you think you can handle that?" Rolf screamed, doubling the man over with a punch to the guts.

The chief of security, a man twice Rolf's age, said, "Yes, Mr. President." He caught his breath and stumbled toward the reinforced door. He gave orders into his radio. Four of his soldiers came to his side and helped him straighten up and stand erect. They racked rounds simultaneously and approached the door, marching out of Nina's line of sight.

"What are you waiting for?" yelled Rolf.

Rolf picked up a phone and dialed. "Osama, is everything ready? Are you sure? Because you know what will happen if it doesn't."

The captain and guards made some commotion off to the side, distracting Rolf.

"What do you mean? I hate surprises!" Rolf said into the phone, a pained look on his face. "Idiots. I'm surrounded by idiots."

Nina heard mechanical locks turn and ratchet. Rolf looked too.

"Six! Are you kidding me? And you kept this from me?" A smile spread across Rolf's bearded face. "Not one, but six missiles? Fantastic! Program them all for the Jews. I'll arrive in Kahuta by morning. Make final launch preparations." Rolf slammed down the phone. "At least somebody is doing their job."

Nina turned her radio back on. "Jack?"

"Nina, what the hell are you doing? Get back here now," said Jack.

"They have six missiles, not one. All for Israel. Does Kahuta mean anything to you?" she whispered.

"Good job, Nina. Now get your ass back here. That's an order."

"They're opening the door," said Nina. "They're coming out."

"Nina, get down. Get down now! The door's booby-trapped."

Nina dropped to the floor of her crawl space and covered her ears as a fireball blasted past her peephole. She felt heat flash through the wall. Cracks appeared in the mortar. Chunks the size of dinner plates crumbled to the floor on her side of the wall. People in the control room screamed in surprise, then agony.

Nina smiled a devilish smile, giving thanks to Dewey's booby trap. She quickly stood. Things on her side of the wall had shifted. Dust, flames, then searing heat radiated into her secret world. The seal into her secret, parallel world had been broken.

Rolf stood up from where he had fallen, speechless, a confused look on his face. He looked to the left, then the right. Everybody was screaming for help. Alarms sounded. Red emergency lights flashed in the burning dark. The body of the controller—who only moments before Rolf had pushed aside so he could stick the thumb drive in the computer and watch a porno—lay bloody and lifeless at Rolf's feet.

Rolf stepped backward, one step at a time, while frantically punching keys on his satphone that was ringing again. His back bumped into the wall, Nina's wall. Not in front of her peephole, but in front of a missing chunk of her wall, thigh high.

Nina did not waste a second. She stuck Jack's pistol through the hole and pulled the trigger.

Rolf collapsed in agony, holding both hands over his crotch. He screamed for help at the top of his lungs, then rolled over and grabbed his nearby pistol.

As he brought it around, Nina pulled the trigger again, this time hitting him center mass, right in the heart. Rolf's pistol dropped back to the ground.

Rolf gurgled with each breath. He struggled to lift his head. Bloody foam rolled from his mouth like a pot of red pasta boiling over. Confusion registered in his fading eyes, until he regained focus, one last time.

Nina stuck her arm out of the hole, made sure he saw her face, pressed the gun against his forehead, and pulled the trigger.

The impact and noise shocked her, blowing his head one way and her arm the other. Tears poured from her bloodshot eyes. She added another shot for Barett. Another for Jack. And another and another until the gun was empty.

Someone's blood-curdling scream snapped her back to reality. She jumped away from Rolf and back into her hole, then scrambled back down the inside of the wall toward Jack and Dewey.

She heard sirens, chaos, the booming of the cannons again, and heat. Lots of heat. Heat that kept her moving forward. Move or die, she said to herself. Move or die.

Gunfire erupted in the room behind her. A line of bullets popped in a line through the wall, straight at her. She dropped to the floor of her catwalk and curled up in a ball. Plaster and splinters showered her from a bullet hole six inches overhead. She stuck her head up and looked through her new peephole.

The room was filling with angry terrorists confused by the sight of their dead leader. Not killed in an explosion, but shot to death. Executed.

Nina understood nothing of what they said, but knew she was running out of time if she ever wanted to see her little boy again. She picked her way through the obstacle course of wires and beams as fast as humanly possible, while letting Jack know the situation. Around a corner, then another, until she reached the library.

"Mission accomplished," said Nina. "He's dead. Take me home, boys."

Jack and Dewey gave each other an astonished look and smile. "What?" asked Jack.

"Let's go. Time's a-wasting," said Nina. She reached between the two sandwiched SEALs and flipped the latch. The door popped slightly, and Dewey eased it open.

They hurried to the far wall and hid behind the hallway door, where Jack and Dewey geared up and Nina pulled her burka back on. Nina wiped Rolf's blood off her face and hands with her burka.

Dewey took back his radio.

"You okay?" Jack asked Nina.

"Good to go. You?" said Nina with a knowing smile.

"Stay behind me. Dewey will bring up the rear. Stay close—and don't shoot me in the ass," said Jack with a knowing smile.

"Then you better get that cute ass of yours moving," said Nina.

"Ready to move out?" Jack said into his headset.

"Check," said Dewey.

Out the door and to the right they ran. The fire raged behind them. Jack shot out any lights still working. Dewey lobbed a grenade around the corner behind them. Jack threw one around a corner in front of them. Nina plastered her back against the wall and waited for the blasts three seconds later, with her hands cupped over her ears and her eyes shut.

Dewey popped smoke and joined them from the rear, moving rapidly through the debris. Their assault rifles were up, scanning right, left, forward, through night scopes. Around one more corner, then Jack led the way downstairs while Dewey tossed another trailing grenade and popped more smoke.

They ran down one, two, three flights of wide stone stairways. The air grew cold and musty—and quiet. Jack led the way back down their infiltrating tunnel. Past the four dead guards whose feast Jack and Dewey had cut short.

The whipped woman lay right where they left her, farther down the tunnel. Her water and energy bars untouched. She smiled at the sight of Jack and Dewey. They gave her a thumbs-up and kept moving.

Nina stumbled to a stop when they reached the cell, her cell. She rested a hand on the door and bowed her head.

"He kept you in here?" asked Jack.

Nina said nothing. She gave thanks to the woman on the other side of the door for taking her collar from her. "Let's get outta here."

They moved as fast as possible till they reached Dewey's booby-trapped steel doors guarding the entrance. He had wired them just in case one of Rolf's men discovered the tunnel from the outside and tried to cut off Jack, Dewey, and Nina's escape. Dewey went to work immediately rewiring the trigger mechanism while Jack arranged a rendezvous with Quinton.

Sound underground seemed amplified, like sound through bone. Stone bones. Earth bones. The slightest noise, human or otherwise, traveled for miles before dying.

The people chasing Jack, Dewey, and Nina through the tunnel made no effort to hide their presence. And they were a lot closer than a mile. More like a hundred yards.

Their voices arrived before the lights on their flashlights. Jack put Nina behind him, shielded by his body armor. Dewey quickly moved back down the tunnel and set a charge before returning.

Just as the lights and bodies became visible rounding the final turn, Dewey counted "Three, two, one," and twisted the firing switch. The tunnel roof collapsed in a deafening explosion, burying the whole terrorist party.

"You okay?" Jack asked Nina, giving her a bear hug.

She gasped.

"What? You hurt?"

"Just my ribs. What's next?"

"You're one tough son of a bitch, Nina," said Dewey.

"Thanks, Dewey. You too," said Nina.

"Quinton's on the way. We got a half mile to make our extraction point. You ready?"

"Roger that," said Dewey.

"Locked and loaded," said Nina.

Jack eased open the steel door covering their hole in the ground, just enough to get his gun out to do a three-sixty survey.

"Clear," he said and opened the door all the way.

After they were all out, Dewey eased it shut without a sound and rewired the booby trap while Jack watched all four quarters through his scope.

They snuck out the way they came. After fifteen minutes, they arrived back at Abdul and Naveen's burned-out garage. Within five minutes, Quinton came up the street, picked up the trio, and made a U-turn.

Looking out the back window, Jack, Nina, and Dewey saw the palace ablaze. Flames shot high into the clear night sky. Smoke poured out of every window and door. Secondary explosions rocked its foundation.

Jack glanced through his side window. There she was, the North Star, guiding him home again. A shooting star fizzled across the abyss between his star and Cassiopeia, the W-shaped constellation opposite the North Star from the Big Dipper. A sign the gods were happy.

"Too late to catch a bird outta here tonight," said Quinton.

"What time is it, anyway?" asked Nina.

"It's just after midnight," said Quinton. "But, hey, look at the bright side. You'll have a great seat for the end of the world fireworks at high noon."

Dewey rode shotgun, checking his quadrants. Jack and Nina sat in back.

Jack reached over, took Nina's hand, and squeezed. Not a hard squeeze, but just enough to let her know.

She looked back and smiled. She'd never seen the warrior side of him. She'd never known that side of herself. She leaned over and gave him a kiss. Not a passionate kiss, but enough for him to know how lucky they were.

Quinton drove.

The palace burned.

They found refuge from the rising sun in a CIA safe house.

The worm crawled from one computer to the next.

Chapter 45

CIA Black House, Islamabad, Pakistan

"Birds in the air. I count one, two, three, four, five, six birds in the air, sir," said US control from a hundred feet underground in an X-Band early-warning radar facility in Kürecik, Turkey. "EMP doors closing now."

"Roger that. *USS Monterey* standing by to intercept," responded someone from the Ticonderoga-class guided-missile cruiser stationed somewhere in the Mediterranean off the Israeli coast.

Jack, Dewey, and Nina ran to the window and pulled back the light-blocking drapes. The crystal blue sky of a high-front sparkled under the midday sun.

"There they are," said Jack, seeing six individual vapor-trails rise in the east and cross to the west directly overhead. The roar of their rocket engines was audible through stone and glass. "We've got visual confirmation. Six ballistic missiles airborne out of Kahuta," said Jack into the satphone.

"Those boys really know how to celebrate," said Dewey. "Nothing like blowing up a million or two friendlies."

"I thought that worm was supposed to prevent this," said Nina. "Why isn't it working?" She had showered for the first time in days since the palace. Her shoulder-length black hair, still wet, smelled of conditioner.

"Hacker confirms it's in. I hope he's right," said Jack. "We'll know in five minutes."

Naveen Halabi's three children jostled in front of Nina to see the rockets, making curious noises and pointing. Nina hugged the youngest like her favorite squishy pillow.

Naveen stepped up quietly next to Nina and pulled the little one back to her. Tears streamed down Naveen's face.

"I'm so sorry. I really am," said Nina, tears running down her cheeks as well, grateful to be sharing the safe house with Naveen and her family—and to maybe find closure. She spoke quietly. "Your husband was a very brave man to do what he did. He saved my life. He saved his country. He saved the world."

Naveen pulled the little one closer still. The other two clutched her legs and started crying too.

"It was you, wasn't it? You wrote the message on the shower door. After you watched everyone you love die, you still risked your life to help me. Why?" Nina asked.

"He was a monster," she said, pointing in the direction of the palace. "He was not Muslim. He was a monster." She bowed her head and closed her eyes. "He killed the president, his own people, Abdul's parents. Abdul knew he would die if he went back, but he went anyway." Her last words barely more than a whisper.

Nina grabbed Naveen and held her tight, overwhelmed with grief and guilt.

"You were a brave woman too. You did not fear death. You killed the monster . . . you killed the monster," said Naveen.

"Stand tall, brave American woman." Naveen gently pushed Nina back and held her by the sleeves. "You have been sad long enough. The monster can hurt you no more." Naveen took Nina's face in her hands and looked deep into her eyes. "The monster can hurt you no more."

In that instant, Nina's eyes fluttered as if she were having a vision triggered by her memory of all the horrible things Rolf El-Hashem had done to her.

Naveen kissed Nina on the forehead and released her. She and her kids went to a back room to pray.

Nina opened her eyes, took a deep breath, and sighed.

"You okay?" Jack asked, coming up behind Nina. He knew it annoyed her, asking over and over if she was okay, but he did not know what else to say. He felt like kicking in a few doors and celebrating having saved Nina, but Naveen had lost her husband, and God knows what Nina had lost . . . or found. Everyone was on edge.

"I'm tired. So tired."

"Why don't you lie down? We're stuck here at least till tonight," said Jack, rubbing her shoulders.

"I'm glad you came," Nina said. "I knew you would." She turned to give Jack a sideways glance and smile. "I would have killed him, you know. Whether you came or not, I would have killed him. He did too much."

Jack said nothing and just kept rubbing. The matter-of-fact tone of Nina's proclamation choked him up too.

"All I could think of was Barett. That's what kept me going. If it hadn't been for him, I would have made him kill me rather than let him keep doing what he did." Nina's head bobbed to her chest. "Oh God," she whispered and started crying again.

Jack came around front, scooped Nina up, and held her like a baby while she sobbed and sobbed. He carried her to a back room, laid her down on a bed, and covered her with a blanket. She curled up in the fetal position, and Jack rubbed her back until she fell fast asleep.

Jack felt as if his heart had been ripped out. His stupid badal challenge, his bullheaded, cavalier handling of Rolf and the dirty bombs and money had almost taken everyone he loved. He always said he wanted an honorable death in the field of battle, but it was his family—Nina, Barett, and Travis—paying the price for his actions.

What had Rolf done to Nina? Jack had seen enough over the years to know the answer to his own question. One thing he knew for sure, Nina would never say. She would take that to the grave.

He looked at her tiny, almost childlike shape curled up under the blanket and was awestruck. He knew sacrifice, both physical and mental. He knew SEALs who died to save their brother SEALs. He remembered special forces and CIA teammates permanently maimed and injured in the line of duty.

But he had never seen anyone like Nina, who endured so much pain, so much torture, so much humiliation, and did it all willingly, to persevere against unfathomable odds. Outmatched in every way, demonstrating incredible resolve and bravery, she had survived and singlehandedly saved the world. And she did what Jack and his entire team couldn't do . . . she killed Rolf El-Hashem.

"They just crossed into Afghanistan air space," Jack heard from the radio in the other room. "Heading almost due west at Mach 2. We estimate a ground strike on Tel Aviv at 1300. The *Monterey* is spinning up interceptors. The Israeli Iron Shield is up and operational," said Kürecik radar control.

"Copy that," said Jack into the radio. "What's Hacker say? When's this thing supposed to kick in?"

"Hacker's probably sweating it out at happy hour in Manhattan or some damn place," Butch sarcastically chimed in from his outstation in Jalalabad.

"Radar's picking up a course correction. All six missiles are coming around," said radar control. "What the hell?"

"I smell a worm," said Jack.

"It wasn't me," said Dewey.

"Missiles' new heading is almost due east," said radar control.

"This is Hacker."

"This is a secure line, Hacker. How the hell—" said Butch.

"Wasn't that hard," said Hacker. "It's like I said, everything's under control. I turned them into homing pigeons, but the terrorists have no idea. Their computers still make it look like the nukes are heading toward Israel. They're about to get a taste of their own medicine."

"That's fine for you, but we're sitting near ground zero. Six nukes . . ." said Jack.

"No worries. My worm's got you covered. It disarmed the nukes, but the missiles will still pack more than enough punch to destroy their entire nuclear complex," said Hacker. "Oh, and thank you for getting into their system. I understand there was some loss."

"You can take your worm and shove it up your ass, you arrogant bastard," barked Jack. "You'll get the headlines and payday, but some good people died here today. Without them, your worm is nothing more than a worthless piece of plastic."

"Sorry, Jack. I didn't mean—" said Hacker.

"Save it. You people wouldn't understand," said Jack. "Just tell your worm to hit the fucking target and get us the hell out of here, if it's not too much to ask." Jack fished the backup thumb drive out of his pocket, snapped it in two, and trashed it.

"Roger that, Jack," chimed in Butch, who had been listening in from Jalalabad. "Just sit tight, and we'll evacuate you tonight. Get some sleep."

"Check," said Jack, suddenly weary.

A half hour later as he lay in bed next to Nina, he felt deep, ground-shaking booms and got up to look out the window. First nothing, then multiple black plumes etched the eastern horizon like camouflaged blades of smoky grass. He watched for a few minutes, then went back to check on Nina.

She hadn't moved. Sleeping like a baby.

He lay back down beside her and drifted into a fitful sleep.

Later in the day, before their evacuation helicopter and the long ride home began, they got confirmation that the missiles had accomplished what Hacker had said they would. The entire nuclear facility at Kahuta had been leveled.

With Rolf El-Hashem's regime dead, the Taliban brute squads fled back into the rugged Hindu Kush. Over time, rule and order would hopefully be reestablished in Pakistan—but for how long?

Chapter 46

Virginia Beach, VA

Three days of travel had taken its toll on Nina. Jack, Dewey, and Nina had flown from Islamabad to Jalalabad to Bagram to Ramstein Air Base in Germany. Then there was a brief layover at Landstuhl Regional Medical Center, the largest American hospital outside the United States, for physicals and a debriefing of the trio by CIA agents before they concluded their travel with a flight directly to Charleston aboard the director's private jet. Nina was lethargic from jet lag.

But all that exhaustion evaporated, all the worry and anxiety vanished the instant Nina and Jack rounded the corner at Norfolk International Airport to find Barett standing right there, waiting for them with his Uncle T. No matter how much Jack had reassured Nina or how many times they Skyped with Barett, Nina would not believe Barett was okay until she held him in her own arms. When Nina swooped Barett up and whirled around, it felt as if her heart would explode. They laughed and cried and hugged, a family resurrected from the dead.

The only time she had ever experienced such a flood of love and emotion was after she gave birth to Barett. His first cries, the birth smells, opening his eyes for the first time, and her joy and wonder over the whole miracle that had just happened. Nine months of anticipation, and out popped her perfect little boy.

Suzy and her girls were there to welcome the trio home too. She and Nina hugged . . . and cried. Two mothers who shared a bond no man or father could ever fathom. They had brought their children into this world, and they had nurtured and loved those children every day of their lives. Theirs to raise and theirs to protect.

They were both military families. Essentially single-parent families half of the time, as their husbands, God love them, deployed for months on end. Jack and Dewey were doing what they were meant to do, what they loved to do. They were Navy SEALs, the elite of the elite when it came to fighting terrorists. But it all came with a steep price back home.

Jack knew it. Dewey knew it. Nina and Suzy definitely knew it. The kids knew it. Everyone knew it, but also accepted it as part of the price to be paid. Every job had its foibles; loneliness was theirs.

Nina would not let the moment end. She brushed Barett's hair back, stared into his eyes, and hugged him again and again.

"Did you feed the starving kids in Africa, Mommy?"

"Yes, honey, we fed the kids," Nina said, disappointed that her first words to her son were a lie. But she let it go. There would be more lies, she thought, because Barett could never know. Nobody could ever know. Some things were better not knowing, of that she was certain.

For the moment, everyone celebrated.

"Aunt Jaz and Uncle T had a baby last night, Mommy," said Barett as Nina still held him.

"What! Travis Gunn! You're a daddy!" squealed Nina with as much joy and excitement as a person could feel. She put Barett down and grabbed Travis.

Travis, grinning ear to ear, leaned over, and Nina draped herself around his neck. "It's a girl!" he said.

"A girl! And?" asked Nina.

"Six pounds, five ounces, born at seven eighteen last night. She was only thirty-seven weeks. Her name . . ." Travis scratched his chin, teasing as if he had forgotten.

"Name? What's her name?" everyone pleaded.

"Lucy Marie," said Travis with the proud smile of a new daddy.

"Lucy. I love it. Little Lucy," Nina cooed.

"Okay, my turn," said Jack as he gave Travis a big hug. "I love that you gave her Mom's name—Marie." Jack had tears in his eyes. Travis did too.

"Jaz really wanted to. She knows how much Mom meant to us," said Travis.

"And Jaz? How's momma doing?" asked Jack with Nina right there waiting for his answer.

"They were both sleeping when Barett and I left. She can't wait to see you," said Travis.

"Well, then, let's go," they said in unison.

Dewey, Suzy, and their girls said their good-byes to the Gunns for the time being and promised to stop by the hospital to see Jaz and Lucy later.

"Jaz! Mommy!" said Nina as her stress lines curled up into smile lines. She leaned over the hospital bed and hugged Jaz. Nina and Jaz both cried, giving the hug that for the last month they did not know if they were ever going to give.

Nina, Jack, and Barett then gawked at Lucy sleeping in her bassinet while Travis shared a hug with Jaz. After a minute, Nina came back over and sat on the side of the bed next to Jaz while Barett kept watching baby Lucy.

"She's beautiful." Nina rested her hand on Jaz's arm and gave her a knowing squeeze. "Good job." What Nina was really saying without so many words was, "Welcome to the sorority of motherhood."

"Nina. Nina, oh my God," said Jaz. "I'm so proud of you," she said before she went speechless, unable to cry and talk at the same time. "You're so thin."

The sight alone of Nina and Jaz reduced Travis to a blubbering brother-in-law. He just wrapped Nina and Jaz up in his arms and squeezed. After a bit, Travis said, "Anyone want a coffee?" He limped toward the door.

"I do," said Jaz with a smile.

"Me too," said Nina. "I can't remember the last good cup of coffee I had."

"Me three," said Jack.

"Come on, buddy," he said to Barett. "I could use some help." Travis turned and gave Jaz a go-ahead smile as the two of them disappeared out the door.

"So, how are you doing?" Jaz asked Nina.

"I'll be a lot better when I know if Barett's okay," said Nina.

"No, I mean how are *you* doing?"

"We're fine." Her eyes drifted to the floor.

"Nina. Jack and I know what animals they are over there. We can't help if you don't talk. *How are you doing*?" Jaz asked, holding Nina's hand and giving it a squeeze.

Jack held Nina's other hand.

Nina went quiet, bowed her head, and sniffled.

The clock on the wall ticked. Lucy made a gurgling noise, but fell back to sleep.

"My mind's going a thousand miles an hour, and it won't stop. I can't sleep. I can't eat. All I think about is what's going through Barett's mind," said Nina. "I'm terrified he'll remember what happened," she ended in a whisper.

"I'm scared too. I think we all are," said Jaz.

Nina's eyes glazed over. Jack held on to Jaz's hand with his other and bowed his head. "Whatever happens, we're going to make it," said Jack. "But deep down, I feel like Barett's going to pull through this, and so are you, sweetheart."

"Don't call me that," said Nina.

"What do you mean? That's what I always call you," said Jack.

"That's what *he* called me." She felt herself slipping below the surface again, back to Rolf's palace.

Jack looked shocked—the furrows on his forehead cut deep and dark. His eyes squeezed shut.

The clock ticked again, although it seemed to Nina that time had stopped a week ago.

Rolf's maniacal laugh cackled in her brain. She heard the heel click of his shoes coming down the stone cavern and felt the dog collar prongs poking into her throat, ready to explode with another jolt. She rubbed her neck.

She started hyperventilating loud enough for everyone to hear.

"What'd the president say?" Jaz broke the silence. "I heard he called you personally."

"What? Oh, he was very nice. Just thanked me for my sacrifice and saving the world. You know . . . he was very nice." Nina stopped.

"He's a nice man. I'm sure he'll want to meet you when things calm down up there," said Jaz. "What'd your doctor say? I heard they really gave you the once-over."

"My cancer's not back, if that's what you're all worried about," said Nina with an edge.

"I didn't mean—" said Jaz.

"Sorry. I'm sorry. I know you all care. I'm just tired. I'm not myself anymore."

"It'll take time. We're just so, so happy you're safe. Finally, the family's back together again," said Jaz. "The therapists are great at helping Barett deal with what happened. They really know what they're doing. Maybe you and Barett can go together."

"That would be nice," said Nina, more to make everybody relax about it than anything. She knew she had to talk about what happened before she could move on, but that was the last thing she wanted to talk about right then.

Travis and Barett had come back with three coffees and two hot chocolates while the three of them talked. Barett went right back to splitting his time between watching Lucy and watching cartoons on the TV.

"Well, I don't mean to point out the elephant in the room, but somebody has to," said Travis quietly enough so Barett would not hear. Before anyone could stop him, he said, "Thank you for putting a bullet in that fucker Rolf's head. There. I said it."

Jack and Jaz gasped and held their breath.

Nina looked at Travis as if she were looking straight through him and nodded. "You're welcome, Travis. After what he did to you and Barett and me, I'd do it again in a heartbeat. No question."

"You got balls, girl. That's all I can say," said Travis with a smile. "Your daddy would have been proud."

Travis pulled a feather out of his pack, and before he handed it to Nina, he ceremonially used it to smudge, without smoke, the seven directions, ending with Nina. He presented the feather to her, honoring her as a Native American warrior for her extreme bravery and cunning.

Nina was speechless as she took the feather, knowing it was the highest honor a Sioux warrior could receive.

"My daddy *is* proud, Travis," Nina said with a smirk, picturing her father, waving her feather, and instantly feeling a little lighter.

"Does it bother you?" asked Jaz. "Killing him?"

"Surprisingly, it's the only thing that doesn't," said Nina. "No more than taking out the trash." Nina sat quietly with her head down for a bit, then continued. "I've been thinking about him a lot," she said. "I don't think he was in it alone. After being that close to him for a month, I don't think he was that smart."

"What do you mean?" questioned Jaz, like the CIA expert she had been.

"He was more insane than anything. He carried a satphone everywhere he went, and I only saw him use it a few times. He didn't dial so much as he answered it. And he wasn't giving orders, he was taking them," said Nina. "One time, I read his lips. He said, '*you* will control the world in five days.' Not 'me,' but 'you.'"

"What do you make of that?" Jack asked Jaz.

"I've heard some chatter. Nothing solid, but I think Nina's right," said Jaz. "This might not be over."

"And the instant I pulled the trigger, that phone started ringing again . . . There's someone else."

"Anything else?" asked Jaz. "Names? Places you might have heard them say?"

"I heard him negotiating with someone—I don't know who,

maybe this mysterious caller—about selling some of Pakistan's nukes," said Nina.

"Do you know—" Jaz started to ask, but Nina was already shaking her head no.

"There is something else, but it's not what you think." She looked at Jack. "I can't go back to our condo again. I'm sorry, Jack. I know you bought it for me and everything, but Barett and I can't ever go back there."

"I know, baby. I know," said Jack, tears welling up in his eyes. "Don't worry about it. We'll find somewhere else. As long as I have you and Barett, nothing else matters."

Nina threw her arms around Jack's bull neck and gave him a squeeze that would have snapped a normal person's neck.

"There's one more thing, guys," Jack said in an ominous tone.

"What one more thing? I don't think I can handle anymore," said Nina.

"Okay, if that's how you want it. I guess I'll just have to tell them no thanks." Jack started dialing his cell phone.

"Who're you calling?" asked Nina.

Jack hit the call button and stuck the phone to his ear.

"Okay, I give," said Nina. "Put it down and tell me."

"I thought you didn't want to know."

"Jack Gunn, you tell me right now or . . ."

"Or what?" He poked Nina in the side.

She hated when he poked her in the side.

"The Israelis are very grateful for everything you did to stop the attack." Jack canceled the call before anyone answered and took Nina's hand again. "Don't worry. It's all classified. Only those at the very highest levels know what really happened. The Israelis decided that your efforts deserved some sort of recognition. Sort of a token of their appreciation, so to speak."

Nina held up her hands, raised her eyebrows. "What?"

"Nina, the Israelis are rewarding you with a million dollars."

Nina's jaw fell open. She had heard Jack, but it didn't sink in. "What?"

"It's true, love. You're a millionaire," said Jack with the biggest smile. "The British, the French, the Saudis, and our president kicked in a million apiece too. Tax-free!" Jack spoke slowly, letting each word settle in before going on to the next. "What do you think about that?"

"Oh, my gosh. Are you serious, Jack?"

"Absolutely! Now you can really have your dream house!" said Jack. "And travel anywhere you want."

"I'll be happy just to have a nice, safe home and a good school for Barett. I don't know what I'll do with so much money, Jack," said Nina.

"There's only one stipulation."

"What's that?" Nina cringed. Her mother always told her, "If it sounds too good to be true, it probably is."

"You can never tell anyone what happened, especially the media,"said Jack.

Nina acted as if she were pondering a difficult decision for a minute, then smiled back at Jack, her stress lines melting like butter in a hot pan. "No book?"

"No book. Especially no book," said Jack. "Now you'll know how the rest of us feel when we can't talk about what we've been doing."

"For five million dollars, I think I can live with that," said Nina, nodding and picturing their new home.

"Can we go see the lions and elephants too, Mommy? While you and Daddy were in Africa feeding the starving children, I learned about going on a safari to see the wild animals."

"I think that sounds like a great birthday present, sweetie. What do you think, Daddy?" Nina smiled at Jack, relieved that Travis and Jaz had managed to keep Barett in the dark about where Jack and Nina had really been.

Nina was overcome by wave after wave of pure joy and exhilaration after never believing a moment like this would have ever happened again in her lifetime. She held onto Barett and hugged his tiny body while her tears soaked the back of his shirt. "I've never been so happy in my life."

Everyone started laughing and talking and crying at the same time. For the next while, Jack and Nina dreamt out loud about where they would live and what cars they would buy, while they passed Barett back and forth between them, hugging and holding him on their laps and smothering him with kisses.

In the meantime, the OB nurse came in to check Lucy and Jaz. The nurse made small talk with Jaz and Travis while she changed Lucy's diaper, swaddled her back up in a white blanket, pulled on her pink knit hat to keep her warm, and handed her back to Jaz to nuzzle, and eat.

Once the nurse left, Travis said, "I've been doing some thinking."

Jack and Nina stopped talking and looked at him, but Travis just kept staring at Lucy. His hands were shaking.

"So what have you been thinking about, little brother?" asked Jack.

"With all the horrible stuff that's been going on, I've had a lot of time to think. Jaz and I have had a lot of time to talk too. I know you're both going to think I'm crazy, like I'm the least qualified person you know to do this, but . . ." Travis looked at Jaz. Tears were welling up in his eyes. She gave him a smile and a nod. "I'm going back to work . . . for the CIA."

Nina started to speak almost before the words were out of his mouth. "Well, that's wonderful—*the CIA*?" She was shocked. She looked at Jack. His mouth was still hanging open. "But how? What?" One-word sentences were all Nina could muster.

Jaz was laughing. "You two crack me up. Didn't I tell you, Travis? That was priceless."

"Jaz was the one who made the connection of finding a way for me to put my anesthesia skills to use, but also recognized that I probably wasn't going to make it back to work at the hospital because of my disability." Travis slapped his bum left leg.

They watched Jaz put Lucy to her breast. Lucy latched on like an old pro.

"She's beautiful," cooed Nina.

"Jaz introduced me to a man named Preacher, who works for the agency," said Travis.

"Hold on! You and Preacher. That's perfect," said Jack.

"What are you two talking about? Who's Preacher? Your pastor or something?" asked Nina.

"Far from it, although *his* daddy was a pastor too," Travis said, looking at Jaz. "Preacher started experimenting a year ago with some of our anesthesia medicines to do CIA interrogations. He's not all that comfortable with the little ins and outs of the drugs, like I am, though. So they hired me to work with Preacher to refine a new way of getting the information we need out of the bad guys without them knowing we got it and without beating them to a pulp." Travis looked at Jack and shrugged his shoulders. "Less work for you, bro."

"Or more, depending on how you look at it," said Jack. "If you two can get the information faster, and it's credible, my guys might have more work to do. Whatever you can do to help us get ahead of these bastards and catch the kingpin is fine with me."

"Pretty crazy, isn't it?" said Travis. "In a couple months, after Jaz's maternity leave is over, we'll all be working for the same team."

"You working for the CIA. I can't believe it," said Jack. "Who could have ever imagined such a thing?"

"I can't tell you how incredibly happy I am to be here with you all to share this moment," said Nina.

One line like that from Nina was all it took to get the tears and smiles flowing again.

Nina's mind bounced back and forth like a ping-pong ball. She was emotionally overwhelmed, thinking of when she had been a prisoner in Pakistan, never believing she would have another moment like this with Barett or Jack again. She couldn't speak, so she hugged Jack and Travis, one in each arm.

Life had never felt as perfect to Nina as it did at that moment. The past was behind her, the future sounded amazing, and at the present, she was immersed in the love of her family, warming and lifting her spirit like the brilliant rays of a new day's sun.

Jack, Nina, Jaz, and Travis huddled close, witnessing the greatest miracles of all.

The miracle of new life in Lucy, the miracle of innocent life in Barett, and the miracle of saved life in Travis, Jaz, Jack, and Nina.

Epilogue

Border of Burkina Faso and Mali

Jack lay perfectly still on top of a kopje, looking through his gun scope. A pack of hyenas patrolled by the base of the rock outcropping, close enough for Jack to hear their stomachs growl. Dewey lay next to Jack, also watching the festivities going on at their target through his scope. Draped in darkness, clothed in black, they blended in with the bramble and scrub of African backcountry like two lions on the prowl.

Five hundred yards to the south, just across the border into Burkina Faso, sat a roadhouse famous for catering to mercenaries. Soldiers for hire with pockets full of cash. As every civilized nation pulled out of Mali, essentially handing over the keys to Al-Qaeda, there was a free-for-all going on. Anything not nailed down had a price.

"The place is hopping tonight," said Jack as he studied the target area through his gun scope.

"Business is good," said Dewey, doing the same.

With the only generator for twenty miles, the bar was lit up and packed. Music blared. Booze flowed. Women did whatever they had to do to get their share of the money.

"I got Victor coming out the front," said Jack. "Fucking prick."

"Looks like the rest of his crew too," said Dewey. "I got the two drivers who ambushed T-bone and Mack. Do you see them?"

"Roger that," said Jack.

Victor stumbled down the steps, toward one of their trucks. His guys gathered around the front, leaning on the hood, sitting on the fender, passing a bottle, lighting up.

Jack and Dewey couldn't hear, but then they didn't need to hear. They could see. That was all they needed.

Victor swayed around, as if he were drunk-dancing, in front of the guys, who seemed to enjoy seeing their boss wasted and having a good time. After a bit of catcalling, he stopped and said something, as if he were offended or pissed, which suddenly seemed to change the tone of their party. Everyone straightened up, chucked their bottles, and headed for the trucks.

Victor followed the two Malian drivers to their truck, jabbering all the way as they got in and fired it up. While Victor kept talking, he pointed off to the north, right at Jack and Dewey, even though there was no way he would have been able to see them even if he were sober.

"That's our sign," said Jack. "I got the driver."

"I got the other," said Dewey.

The two men in the truck killed the lights, pulled out night vision binoculars, and zeroed in on Jack and Dewey's position.

Jack watched every twitch the two men made. Their shit-eating grins. Their smoldering cigarettes hanging from the corners of their mouths. Squinting as only drunks do when they are struggling to come back out of the fog.

Already adjusted for wind, humidity, elevation, and temperature, neither Dewey nor Jack flinched. They just relaxed their muscles, slowed their breathing, and waited.

Victor screamed at the two in the truck, pointing at Jack's hiding spot again. Loud enough for Jack and Dewey to hear. The men acted frantic and searched harder. They scanned the darkness, side to side, front to back, until one stopped, then the other, locked on target. They were both locked on Jack.

Victor stepped back from the truck.

Jack and Dewey watched everything unfold, just how they had planned it.

Jack counted down, "Three, two, one, execute."

The two men in the truck never had a chance to hear the whip crack of the bullets as they blasted through their binocular lens, shattered their eye sockets at over a thousand miles per hour, and exited out gaping holes in the back of their skulls. They never had a chance to know what hit them.

"That's for T-bone and Mack, you sons of bitches," Jack said. He and Dewey watched the drivers crumple on top of each other in the truck. They also kept an eye on Victor.

Victor's men scrambled for their weapons, until Victor yelled something.

Jack could not hear what Victor said, but whatever it was, it stopped them all dead in their tracks.

Victor turned toward Jack, raised his hands, giving two thumbs-up and a friendly smile.

"What do you think?" asked Dewey. "Drop him?"

"Even though he gave those two up, I don't trust that fucking snake," said Jack.

"He had nothing to do with it, isn't that what he said?" said Dewey.

"He knows a hell of a lot more than he admits, that's for damn sure."

"So what do you want to do? I got him in my sights."

"I should have learned my lesson—isn't that what you're thinking? I didn't take care of Rolf when I had the chance, and look what happened," said Jack, not taking his eye off his scope, watching other mercenaries pour out of the shack bar.

"I wasn't even thinking of that, bro. Different situations. Different solutions," said Dewey. "So what do you say? Up or down?" asked Dewey, still locked on target.

"Aw, screw it, Dewey," said Jack. "We got what we came for. Let's go home."

"Roger that," said Dewey.

"Besides, I just got messaged from Jaz a few minutes ago that Travis and Preacher have extracted some high-level intel from a low-level Al-Qaeda dirtbag by using their anesthesia drugs. They didn't want to talk about it over the phone, but it sounds like they uncovered a lead to the kingpin mystery man."

"Time to rock and roll, brother," said Dewey.

"Roger that," said Jack, pumping his fist to the stars. "Let's go home."

Glossary

Badal: Taliban/Pakistani blood feud challenge involving entire families

Bluebug: Cell phone hacker that receives calls intended for the target phone, sends messages, reads phonebooks, and examines calendars

Breacher: Explosives used to blow doors open

BUD/s: Basic Underwater Demolition/SEAL training; twenty-four-week Navy SEAL boot camp

Comms: Communications, the "talk," the radio connection with other military units

CPR: Cardiopulmonary resuscitation

CTF: Counterterrorism Task Force

Dishdasha: Sometimes called a *thawb*, an ankle-length robe or tunic outergarment, usually with long sleeves, commonly worn in Arab countries

Emir: Title of high office throughout the Muslim world for sheikhs and princes

EMP: Electromagnetic pulse weapons; nuclear warheads detonated in space

Frag: Fragmentation grenade

Haji: Slang for "terrorist," or the enemy in Afghanistan, Pakistan, or Iraq

Haram: Arabic term meaning "sinful"

Harmattan: Dry, dusty West African trade wind

HQ: Headquarters

IAEA: International Atomic Energy Agency

ICU: Intensive care unit

Jariya: Sex slave, concubine

Kaffiyeh: Traditional Middle Eastern headdress fashioned from a square scarf, worn by Arab men

Kurta: Traditional loose-fitting, long-sleeved shirt reaching to the knees, worn by Arab men

MOLLE: Modular Lightweight Load-carrying Equipment vest; outerwear with lots of pockets

NIPRNET: Non-classified Internet Protocol Network, for normal Internet connections at military installations around the world; blue wire

NOD: Night observation device; goggles that see in the dark

PTSD: Post-traumatic stress disorder

RAF: Regionally Aligned Forces

RPG: Rocket-propelled grenade

SecDef: Secretary of Defense

Satphone: Satellite phone

SIPRNET: Secret Internet Protocol Router Network, for secure military or government communications worldwide; red wire

SSE: Sight-sensitive exploitation; to grab anything with intelligence value, such as files, computers, or phones

Switchblade: Backpack drone with offensive capabilities

Talis: Taliban men

Therm: Thermobaric grenade

Wasichu: Sioux word for white man; means “greedy person who steals the fat”

Acknowledgments

With warm thanks to Shannon Miller, Kellyann Zuzulo, and Angie Weichmann, for their insightful editorial skills. To Katy Jo Turner at Beaver's Pond Press, for making things happen and bringing this all together. To Laura Drew, for her unique cover design. To good friends Daniel and Chris, for their patience and skills in redesigning my website and bringing me up to speed in the social media world.

To Steve and Isaiah, who advised me on the technical parts of my writing. Thank you for your service. I'm honored to know you.

To Al (Little Bear), my father-in-law, a tireless reader and my Native American adviser. To Bill, for his vigilant monitoring of global current events and his enthusiasm for this genre. To all my followers and supporters, I hope you are entertained.

And most importantly, I give thanks to God for my wife Kim and all of our children, their spouses, and grandchildren; April, Steve, James, Shayla, Missy, Ryan, Aubrey, Kelsey, Julianne, and Caroline. Without your patience, love, and support, none of this would be possible. None of this would matter. My life is blessed. I love you all.